TWILIGHT IN BABYLON

Suzanne Frank

WARNER BOOKS

An AOL Time Warner Company

WARNER BOOKS EDITION

Copyright © 2002 by J. Suzanne Frank

All rights reserved. No part of this book may be reproduced in any form or by any electronic or mechanical means, including information storage and retrieval systems, without permission in writing from the publisher, except by a reviewer who may quote brief passages in a review.

Cover design by Diane Luger
Cover illustration Franco Accornero
Book design by L&G McRee

Warner Books, Inc.
1271 Avenue of the Americas
New York, NY 10020

Visit our Web site at www.twbookmark.com.

 An AOL Time Warner Company

Printed in the United States of America

First Printing: November 2002

10 9 8 7 6 5 4 3 2 1

To Susan

with everlasting gratitude and abiding affection

Before time was a line, it was a circle.
Before history was about war, it was about water.
Before the divine was male, she was female.
Before Babylon, was Ur.

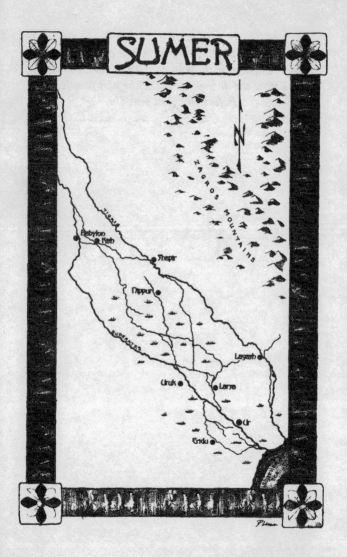

Part One

THE FIRE

$\mathcal{F}$ire! Fire!"

Cheftu could see smoke billowing upward from the city wall. A bad day for a fire; last night's rain would cause the limestone to crack and explode as the heat expanded it. There was no way to avoid that danger; in Jerusalem all the houses were made of limestone.

His house even, was made of limestone.

The plume of smoke was gray against the spring-afternoon sky. It seemed to stab at the breast of heaven from the outer wall of the city. The fire must be on the outer wall.

His home was on the outer wall.

Cheftu hastened his steps. He should anyway; Chloe would be overjoyed they were leaving the city. Cheftu had just been made ambassador to Egypt. He climbed up to the highest point of his walk. From this position, he could see the fields. Everyone was out today, planting the terraced sides of the valley.

He wound around another corner as he walked down to his house.

"Is anyone inside?" the voices of concerned neighbors echoed out to him.

"He works for the king. She's usually here. Just a wife, you know. Barren, poor thing."

He worked for the king; *Chloe* was usually at home. His wife—barren.

Cheftu took the last steps two at a time, up and around another corner, across the courtyard, and up and around again.

The wooden door was black with smoke.

His wooden door was black with smoke.

"Chloe!" he shouted. Cheftu covered his face, then kicked the door open. The heat seared through his sandal. "Bring water," he yelled at the two old women. He ran inside.

He was lost in the gray heat; where was the kitchen? The sleeping platform? "Chloe?" he shouted. "Chloe!" Wind funneled from the back window through the hallway, and fueled the fire. Cheftu dropped to his hands and knees and felt around for her. Limestone popped, and the fire's roar became stronger. Heat singed his skin. He smelled burning hair. "Chloe," he coughed out.

An arm.

A lifeless arm.

He shook her; her skin was rippled and blistered. Black smoke unfurled through the window. Fire crackled behind him. He dragged Chloe's body over his shoulder and back, then ran for the window, hunched over and coughing. He threw her out onto the narrow walkway, then clambered after her.

His neighbors sluiced down their homes.

Cheftu coughed, gasped for air, and spat black phlegm on the white stone. He turned to look at Chloe. His physician's glance was quick and conclusive: burns to 70 percent of her body. A head wound, sticky with blood, staining the stone with red.

He wrapped the remains of his kilt around her head, but it didn't change the facts. She would die, very soon.

Her chest fell in labored breaths. There was no part of her untouched by fire, no inch not black and oozing, burned and bloody.

The first block of limestone exploded, sending shards flying into the air. Cheftu shielded Chloe's body as he pulled her around a ledge. She was beyond his help. Beyond all but the Almighty's assistance. He looked up. A beautiful day; how could this be the day that Chloe would die?

Above him the sun shone golden on the walled city of Jerusalem, this spring equinox, this twenty-third of March. The designated temple grounds with their caverns of—

"There is one thing, *chérie*," he whispered to his unconscious bride. "One way to save you, if God shows His mercy." He gathered her in his arms and ran to the edge of the outer wall, then up the walkway, up the hill, up the plateau, ever leading up. To God.

Fabric walls shielded the space, and a gold-encrusted tabernacle graced the center of the flat-topped hill. Priests must be close by, but Cheftu knew the grounds better than they. A wooden trapdoor concealed an entrance to the tunnels beneath the Temple Mount, but Cheftu found it. Opened it and stepped down inside with Chloe.

It slammed shut above him.

Sealing him inside the catacombs.

Pain stabbed at his body, but he ignored it. Engorged blisters on his arms and legs, what felt like deafness in the cool silence of this cavern, were nothing to him. "It's been so long since we've been here, *chérie*," he said to her. Years since they had chosen to stay in this place, to make Jerusalem home. A mistake, he knew now. Cheftu swallowed painfully. Thank God she still breathed. Raspy, but alive.

He adjusted her head on his shoulder to straighten her neck. Cheftu leaned against a smooth-carved wall, waiting for his eyes to adjust to the night all around him. "I don't remember where the chamber is," he said. He began to discern the shadows of archways and passages. "But we can find it."

For hours he walked, looking into every room, following the warren of walkways, ending back on himself again and again. The wound on her head had scabbed over, but all the other wounds had gotten worse. He'd never felt so helpless, so powerless. It was divine will, what happened next.

She hadn't murmured; it hurt him to speak. Blinded by the sweat of his efforts, he sagged against the wall. *"Bon Dieu,"* he whispered.

When he opened his eyes later, the halls were filled with a faint blue glow. It bounced off the limestone walls until the whole space looked as though it were submerged in tropical, paradisical waters.

Cheftu staggered to his feet and picked up Chloe. Heart pounding, he searched for the source of light. "We found it, *chérie.*"

The archway glowed, a familiar fire. Safe. A healing flame. He laid Chloe's body beneath it. She still inhaled and exhaled, but barely.

"I know it is not the correct time," he whispered to the One he believed listened. "You have set times and appointments in place, and abide by them." He looked into the face of his beloved wife. She must have hit her head, fallen, and somehow started the fire. With her as its fodder. A terrible accident; a slap from the hand of fate.

"I don't ask special compensation because I think I am a good man. I ask because I know you are a good God. You love this woman far more than I, in mortal flesh, can." He looked at her body. Ruined. "She still has so much to give. Let her live, let her find purpose." His voice broke. "Let her know matchless love."

Nothing happened.

"Give her another chance. Give her life."

The blue light of the chamber continued to flicker, glittering along the sides of the true Ark of the Covenant—hidden there to protect the people from its terrifying power—the curved ceilings of limestone, but there was no roar of wind, no mighty thundering voice. Cheftu spun when he heard the scamper of claws. A rat watched him inquisitively, upright on its hind legs, the reflection in its glassy eyes, blue.

Chloe's breath caught.

It stopped.

Cheftu watched her, waited, his hand on her ravaged chest. It didn't move. He closed his eyes, his head bowed. Almost of their own volition, his lips moved. "Thy will be done."

It seemed his heart should stop also, but it plodded on for moments and minutes and quarters and halves and an hour. He remembered the first time he'd seen her, green eyes flashing with excitement and life. Chloe, named for the freshness of a green field. How vibrant she was, springtime every day. Even in the past years when sorrow had licked away at her until he feared there would be nothing left.

No child, no family, no career, no passion.

I'm so sorry, he thought. *I lost focus. Each day your eyes were rimmed with red from weeping was a day I knew I had failed you. I couldn't get you pregnant, I couldn't get you a career, I couldn't get you to be happy. Then I stopped trying. Forgive me. I wasted our days.* Inside him, he felt a crack, a gap inside, and he knew that nothing mattered anymore. Chloe was gone; he would stay here until he was gone, too.

Her chest seemed to sink.

He opened his eyes.

Before him her body was melting into clay.

He reached to close her eyes, but a green fire sprang from them. Cheftu ducked away.

The wax and dust of her flesh and the fire of her soul danced and swirled in the blue light until all that was left of

Chloe Bennett Kingsley Champollion was a scrap of blood-stained wool, a melted wedding band, and a shocked, charred, hopeful husband.

Part Two

THE STAR

Chapter One

*T*he stargazer felt her breath catch in her breast as she watched the flocks in the night sky move. The star of Inana, which burned on the edge of the horizon, bright enough to be seen by day, glowed purple tonight. With trembling hands, the woman consulted the chart she'd been working on for years, now. "This isn't supposed to happen," she muttered to the stillness of the night.

Before her eyes, the moon took on a reddish hue.

She alone stood on this flat rooftop, overlooking the commonwealth of Ur. A few torches burned in their holders in the streets below, lighting the way for those too besotted with drink to see clearly, but it was so late that even the guards snored softly now.

Her chart was simple enough; as Shinar, the plain between the two rivers, was divided into four quadrants, so was the chart. Action in the night sky revealed which section of the plain had need of fear. She craned her neck back, then turned to the chart and counted: Sumer, in the south; Elam in the east; Amurru north; and Akkad, west.

She watched intently as the shadow on the moon passed. If it moved from west to east, it foretold bad luck for Sumer.

As the minutes ticked by, the moon's redness shifted—from west to east.

She covered her mouth, so as not to strengthen the

demons by voicing her thoughts. With a quick prayer to her personal god for fortitude, she turned to the other chart she was composing—a diagram of the flocks in the sky.

This was far more complicated, a division of 360 slivers that comprised the whole of the heavens. Each twelve slivers completed a house, and each of the houses had its champion symbol that rose and fell according to the seasons and the wishes of the gods.

"This isn't usual either," she muttered, peering at the tablet and leaning back to look into the sky.

The Hired Man of spring was visiting the house of the Goatfish of winter. Somehow, for a moment, the skies were pretending it was the season of rains and chill.

Quickly, she consulted the stars for the powers of Ur. The largest star was for the *lugal* and *en*, the leaders of war and commerce. It hung as fat and orange as a fruit, well out of harm's way. The moon was a token of affection from the god Sin to his bride on earth, the *ensi*. It was still red. Not a good sign for the *ensi*.

As she watched, a star streamed down from the heavens in a bold arc that seemed to drop it in the river, just outside of Ur. The fiery blue streak faded in the sky; it had fallen from the north, through the house of the Tails. Rudi shivered from the cool of the evening and shivered again, for she watched the movements of the gods when clay creatures were to be at rest.

She gathered her tablets and charts and slipped down the stairs.

The council would have her head for not predicting the blood moon—so she certainly wasn't going to tell them about the star, though its portents were clear.

Trouble came from the north, trouble that would be water-borne.

And trouble came from the skies.

The marsh girl bobbed in the water and squinted through the darkness to see if anyone else had survived the massive rush of water. She was wary of hitting her head, and afraid to make noise, which would anger the gods. Above her the stars seemed close enough to use as a ladder. One came crashing down. *It's not going to hit me*, she thought. *Stars don't fall on humans.*

But something did hit the marsh girl. She sank, through a black, seemingly endless tunnel. Down through bath-warm water, down through the earth, into the very soil she planted and sowed. *I'm going to Kur*, she thought. *I'll eat dust and live in shadow for eternity. My service to the gods is over.*

The Crone of Ninhursag had predicted that because the marsh girl had been born after two battles of darkness— when the moon hid its face—the marsh girl had two destinies. The marsh girl had twice as much of a task on earth as most people, and twice as much responsibility. "For you," the black-eyed crone had said, "you will live two lives." But now the marsh girl felt blood coursing down the side of her face, and closed her eyes. The Crone of Ninhursag was wrong. She was going to die. Her life had been solitary and counted for nothing.

She missed the fire of blue that surged beneath the water and enveloped her body.

A fire of blue that bore a remarkable likeness to the marsh girl, a DNA match that was exacting, despite the five millennia that separated the two. A fire of blue, born of another eclipse, another birth date, her other destiny.

Two lives that were preordained to meet and intertwine, for they were the same.

Infused with new energy, the marsh girl kicked and fought away from the darkness, away from the earth, up to the day's light. Long grass wrapped around her ankles, but she wrenched free. Her lungs about to burst, she broke through the surface of the water and gasped for air.

She looked, turned around, and looked again.

The whole world was water.

Blue sky mirrored blue water from east to west and north to south. Everything was placid, blue and the same.

"Sacred dung," she whispered to herself.

Propelled by her arms and legs, her head swinging back and forth like a creature in search of prey, she pushed herself farther through the water. Still she saw nothing but more water. Maybe those tufts of green meant something. She started toward them. Things in the water grabbed at her hands and reached for her feet.

A long brown shape slithered by, and she held her breath, aware it meant danger. She continued toward the sprigs of green. The sun reflected off the water's surface to blind her. Gnats and biting flies attacked her face and arms. When she reached up to brush them off her head, she discovered her head was bleeding. "Sacred dung," she said again, though she didn't know why.

Though dung was sacred—it was fuel for cooking and night heat and useful in poultices and medicaments—when she had ever acknowledged this aloud, she didn't know. The sentiment she felt when she said it was more of amazement and a little bit of shock than anything worshipful. As though the meaning were lost in the translation.

What was translation? What did that mean?

Her arms were tired; her legs, too. Somewhere along the way she'd lost her tailed wool kilt and the bangles she'd been given by the Harrapan traders. She reached the green.

They were popular, crowded with birds. She grabbed the fronds and realized they were palms. The crowns of palms.

The waters were at the tops of trees.

Using the last of her strength, she climbed on top of the palms, scaring away birds, stomping the fronds, and perching gingerly on the crown of the tree. All of Shinar was water. No huts, no water buffaloes, no *guf* or *mashuf* boats disturbed the surface.

Where were the other humans? Had her village been so loud the gods drowned the humans again, like they had in the Deluge of generations before? She pressed her lips together, so not to cry out. Her mother used to warn her as she and her siblings played along the marsh to be quiet, or the gods would grow weary of humanity and silence it.

She put a hand to her mouth to hold back the shrieks she felt building inside. *Yet if I'm the only one left, what does it matter if I scream?* The sense of loss was staggering, but she couldn't remember whom she'd lost. A face, indistinct, was in her mind, but it had eyes like she'd never seen before. Eyes like her bangles. Gold eyes.

She clapped a hand over her eyes. Was she thinking of a god? Why would she think of a god? Why would a god come to her? She was no one, with no influence, no power. She peeked through her fingers. No sheep either.

Somehow this seemed a much more serious concern than a god's eyes. And easier to understand. The flock was gone, which meant the goat was, too. And her fields. Her vegetable garden. How she had slaved, carving out the straight irrigation channels, making sure they flowed freely, clean of silt and salt. No leeks and onions, or peas. And forget about barley, about beer.

She suddenly tasted it, heavy with spices and sweetness, rolling over her tongue. She loved beer. It was the best early in the day, when the sun just started across the sky, the air was cool to her skin, and the beer was warming to her belly.

She cradled her stomach for a moment, then looked down at herself. For some reason her body, though healthy and strong, seemed repulsive to her. Hairy. She looked at her legs, lightly furred with black. Hair was good. If she slicked bitumen over it, she was protected from biting bugs. Her womanhood was safe. Her arms, the heat of her armpits, covered. The hair of her head served as a gown at night, to allure and seduce her mate.

Golden eyes.

The pang was back. *Missing.*

Better to think of beer. It was concrete and useful.

She adjusted her position in the tree, sitting on her legs so the spikes of date branches didn't poke her, and looked at the water. It was hard to remember what the village had looked like, where anything had been.

Where were the trees I'm sitting on, she thought. *Which clump were they?* Her mind was blank as a slab of clay. If her village was gone, were the neighboring villages gone also? She craned around, waved away birds who tried to steal her spot, and looked for anything familiar. She'd never been outside her village, only as far as the common grazing grounds. Only the Harrapan traders and the Crone of Ninhursag had come to her village, brought news of a world outside.

Had there been a village on the other side of hers? She tried to visualize the size of her village and fields and grazing grounds, then another village, fields and grazing grounds beside it, and a third village beyond. But she couldn't. She couldn't even remember her own village clearly. Just impressions.

Reed huts, and a warm dung fire. The squishiness of the ground that indicated it was time to put down new matting so the marsh didn't seep up through the floor. The lowing of the water buffalo before they slept. The blackness of the sky, when the gods held meetings. The summer, when the gods had feasts and poured heavenly wine on the fields.

Her head was aching, and she reached up to rub it. Then she remembered the sore and stopped. She didn't even have mud to put on her sore, because there was no ground. That made her angry. She glared at the sky. "This was stupid of them," she told the chamber keeper of the gods. "If we are supposed to serve them, then drowning us means they won't get served. Then they'll have no one to complain to except themselves."

The chamber keeper didn't speak. Of course, she didn't have a sheep to slaughter for its liver, or an exorcist to read the liver, so she would never know if the chamber keeper responded.

"The waters have to go down," she said, liking the sound of her voice against the blue sky and blue water. "A flood can't last long." Birds that usually landed in the marshes would be along in the afternoon. If she could catch one, she could eat. Pigeons, who sought the greening fields, were especially good, and they would be too tired to fly away.

She tore green dates off one of the branches—she couldn't eat them, she'd get sick—then bent the branch back and forth while the sun moved higher in the sky. Finally, it broke off. Careful to spit any of it out, she peeled the edges of the wood back with her teeth and fingernails, sawing the end against the fronds to make it sharp for stabbing and cutting. When she got thirsty, she lapped at the water around her.

Flood water wasn't salty, at least not much.

As the sun lowered, she watched for birds. But the only place for them to stop was her treetop. Reluctantly, she slipped into the warm water with the branch between her teeth and waited for a fat pigeon. When one finally came and plopped down for a rest, she leaped on it. The bird tried to fly away, but she stabbed its neck with her branch. Piece by piece, she plucked its feathers, then stabbed at it to get the blood out. It was the only taboo that couldn't be broken: Never eat anything with blood, and never spill blood unless to eat.

She didn't remember when she'd heard those words, but she knew they were true. It was the only restriction given by the god above gods after the Deluge. She wiped at the bird with palm fronds, sloshed water through it to get it as clean as she could, then tore into it with her teeth.

It would be better cooked, but she didn't have any dung or tinder. Besides, she was hungry. She threw the carcass onto the treetop beside her and watched the bigger birds, the desert birds, tear at it. She watched them through her fingers, to keep her eyes protected so they couldn't blind her, then eat her, too.

As the sky was painted by the gods, and the god Shamash went away, she saw the animal carcasses float by. Onagers and oxen, their legs raised to the heat, their bodies swollen from the day's sun, passed by like rafts on the current of the water. Water tinted with lavender and pink, gold and orange.

Twilight.

This was the assurance of the gods: One day ended and another began. The girl knew if she saw twilight, then after a period of darkness, day would come back. The sun god Shamash, the gods of water and wind and soil, would rise to flog and command their slaves who worked the Plain of Shinar. The twilight was a promise, an assurance. There was comfort, even if she was the only one left. Since she saw twilight, the sun would rise tomorrow. Drawing her hair over her shoulders, she put her head down on her arms and slept.

Three days later, the waters had receded down the trunk of the palm tree. Debris had begun to show up on the face of the waters. Swollen bodies and faces she didn't remember. Bits of huts. And, finally, the skin of a *guf* boat. Without the outer rim, it did her no good to find the bottom, but still she took the skin, wrung it out, and draped it over the newly emerged palms to dry.

On the fifth day, she set off through the waters, looking for useful things. The outlines of islands and levees began to peer through the water. By twilight of the sixth day she had found cloth to tie around her at night, a bone knife to kill birds and fish with, and an oar.

In two more days, the marsh had become a breeding ground for mosquitoes, the water had been poisoned by the rotting remains, and salt had dried on the tree trunks. The water was also shallow enough to walk through, to spy crocodiles before they saw her, and to see the ground on which she trod.

Nothing was left of Shinar; it was wiped clean. She hadn't seen another live animal or person. She'd seen hundreds of corpses. The crocodiles were dining well. If she were the only human left, then she would walk on until she came to the south sea. If she weren't, then maybe there would be people on the south sea. The Harrapan traders said they stayed there, and on the island Dilmun.

In Dilmun, they said, there were tall trees with soft and solid leaves, not like fronds of date palms. They also had orchards, where fruit other than dates grew on the trees. The ground was dry, like Shinar in summertime, but it didn't crack. It had just enough wet and just enough dry to stay green all year. The air smelled good, and the trees were made of incense. The girl would go to Dilmun, see if it existed. Maybe the Harrapan would take her in. She was good with sheep, and she wouldn't drink too much beer.

So she tied the animal skin up into a knot and put it on her head, threw the cloth for a cloak on her back, and clasped her knife in her hand, then set off south. South was the direction that the rivers, when they stayed in their beds, flowed. Marsh birds were plentiful, and fish swam in the shallows. She didn't have fire, but she ate well.

The sun was hot on her body, and eventually she found mud and covered her skin so the mosquitoes wouldn't bite. She watched for crocodiles as she walked, and stopped walking when the sun went to sleep. At night she made noise, to frighten the hungry hyenas away. When she could, she climbed up the rough bark of a palm tree and stayed in the fronds, safe enough to sleep in.

The vision of the god with the golden eyes faded in her mind. She talked to herself, nonsense words, like a child's. These words comforted her, but had no meaning. "Mimi. Home. Love. Chef. Tu. God." Her tongue didn't fit around them easily, and they had no meaning, but they made her feel good. The gods hadn't found her yet; and she was still the only one left.

Baaing woke her in the night; a sheep, as lost as she was. She called to it, then heard another. They ran out of the marshes toward the tree where she stayed. Behind them she saw eyes that glowed with hunger and teeth that were bared. She scampered down the trunk and swung out at the predators with her oar. She made contact, and they ran crying into the night. "It's okay," she told the trembling sheep. "You're safe. You're found." They cuddled next to her, against the palm tree, and she slept warmly for the first time.

When she woke in the day, it was there.

"That must be Dilmun," she said to the sheep. Far to the south, an island rose up. Part of it was red. She gathered her belongings, herded the sheep, and walked faster. All day long the red island hovered on the edge of the world. By night it had grown.

So had her flock. Now she walked with seven sheep, two lambs, and a gamboling goat. No sign of other humans yet, but the sheep were glad for her company. She sang to them and spoke her nonsense words, and they bleated happily as they grazed.

Dilmun got larger.

The river was almost completely in its bed now, and she saw irrigation channels and canals cut through the greening fields. Winter barley; in its second irrigation. For barley to grow as big as the gods allowed, it must have four irrigations. On the last, it would add another tenth of its size. The river hadn't overflowed here; the humans, if there were any left, would not starve.

Her flock continued to grow; she watched over them during the night from her perch in a tree. In the dawn, from her high roost, she saw Dilmun. It must be Dilmun, for nothing else could be so beautiful. Green fields surrounded it, and trees, tall like date palms, but with different leaves, grew in neat rows. As though it were a giant vegetable garden.

The island, with a tall center in blocks of blue and green and red and yellow, rose up into the sky. Little white boxes and blocks clustered around it, like a peafowl with her chicks. The girl crawled down the palm tree, washed the mud off her face and hands, tied the cloth around her womanhood, then folded up the animal skin and balanced it on her head.

With the knife slipped into her waist sash, she walked down to Dilmun, the oar her goad. Common grazing fields stretched out from the gate to the city. The walls were taller than palm trees, and painted blue and yellow. The rest was left the ocher color of clay. She'd never seen anything so impressive, never imagined it. It was no wonder Ziusudra lived here. The gods visited here. After the sheep had fed she looked for a toll taker, for she was sure there would be a charge. Water wasn't free. But she didn't see one. Squaring her shoulders and straightening the parcel on her head, she marched her flock to the open gate set within a deep, shadowy archway.

"Welcome to Ur, welcome, welcome," a man cried from the shade. "You must be a survivor of the flood. Come in, come in. It's dry here, safe."

Chapter Two

She had never seen a man such as he was, in the clothes he wore! His beard was long and white, and his head was covered in a gold basket. White cloth, finer than any felt or wool she'd ever seen, edged with gold, draped over his shoulder and around his chest. His eyes were big and black, his teeth white. When he breathed in her face, it was sweet-smelling—like the breath of the Harrapan. "Welcome to Ur," he said to her. "Welcome, female. You are a wealthy one. How do the gods call you?"

A few other people stepped closer around her, and she crouched, ready to run. The sheep bleated and jostled, the goat nipped at the bearded one's sash, but he pushed him away. "It's safe, female."

"Ningal, she has a sore on her head," someone behind her said.

She put her hand to where the mud and blood had dried on her head, the sore.

"Does it hurt?" the bearded man asked.

"Do you need to sell your sheep?"

"Let's have a look," someone else said, and pulled at her animal skin.

She spun on them with a hiss. The sheep scattered.

"A wild thing."

She called the sheep to her, beckoned the goat away from the arched gate.

"Be at peace. She's obviously from the hills."

"The plain," she said, walking back to them. Her words were the same as theirs.

"You are from the plain? Shinar?"

"Shinar! Yes, in truth. My village."

"Flooded out."

"How did you survive?"

"Were there other survivors?"

"What is your name?"

"Where was your village?"

They surrounded her, with long beards and basket hats. All men, whose words were the same as hers, but whose voices sounded harsh and demanding.

"Dilmun," she said.

They fell silent. "What did you say?" one of them asked. His cloak was white like the others, but where theirs were gold, his was red. He was younger, too, probably not older than . . . than . . . she couldn't remember. None of it made sense.

"Dilmun. I go to Dilmun."

"You aren't Harrapan, girl."

"How do you know Dilmun?"

"She must have some knowledge, if she knows the name of Paradise."

She was dizzy; they were spinning around her like black birds. Cawing and flapping their wings. She couldn't follow their words anymore.

"Step back, gentlemen, she's about to faint." The white-bearded man offered her his hand, and she grabbed it, tried to be still.

"Do you need some water?" he asked. "Does your flock?"

"Yes."

"She was in a flood. I expect she's had plenty of water," someone said with a laugh.

"The dead animals," she said. "They made the water poisoned."

"Kalam, take her flock to the well over there. You, female, come with me."

She turned to look at the man, the one with the red-edged cloak, who stood in the middle of her sheep. Their wondering brown eyes followed her. "It's well," she said to them. "Go drink."

They chased after Kalam into the green grazing grounds, and the bearded man took her arm and led her beneath the arch and into the place he called Ur. "Have a seat," he said, showing her a low stoop. "I'll be back in a minute."

A minute. Sixty seconds make a minute, sixty minutes make an hour, twenty-four hours make a day, but no, here twelve double hours made a day. The girl put her hand to her head, shaky again.

She sat. Nothing here was made of reeds. It was all hard, the ruddy color of mud, but hard. And very tall, buildings reaching up at least as high as trees. People rushed to and fro, as if traders had come to sell their wares. Animals, goats and sheep, dogs and onagers, walked through the streets. Children rode on their backs, played in the alleyways, and dashed everywhere. People rested against the walls, eating their meals and working on their fleeces. Tents were pitched against every building.

The noise. The smell. She fought the desire to run, but it rose in her throat and threatened to choke her. So many people.

"Here you go," the bearded man said, handing her a cup of water. It wasn't a clay cup, nor was it the color of her bangles or the god's eyes. It was a warmer color, like the clay. "It's made of copper," he said. "Drink up."

"Ningal," one of the other men said to him.

"Silence, she can afford it," he said, and brought her another cup. The water was cool, and she drank many cups of it, until her stomach was tight.

"Now how do you feel?" he asked.

"Fine," she said, nodding.

"Do you want something to eat?"

It had been a day or so since her last meal, and she was hungry. She nodded again.

"I tell you what. Wait for me here, can you do that?"

She nodded. "Then what?"

He chuckled. "Then I will come and get you, and we will go eat. I have some people who will be very interested in all you have to say. We haven't seen anyone from the plain since the flood. You may be the only survivor."

"The only one," she said. "I'm alone."

"You're not alone, you're here in Ur. Thirty thousand humans call Ur their home. About ten thousand too many, but that can't be helped. Know you aren't alone. However," he said, "before you can go anywhere, you'll need a bath and some clothes."

People watched them from everywhere. Windows, doorways, market stalls. Not rudely, but in the course of their day. Most were washed, most had clean clothes and looked fed.

She tugged the edge of her cloth skirt down a little.

"But wait here, I'll be back."

"What about my flock?"

He hesitated, then called someone. A man with a bald head, who had green-circled eyes and wore a plucked felt skirt, dodged through the crowd to get to them. "Anything to buy? To sell?" he asked them.

"Do you want to sell your sheep?" the bearded man asked her.

The sheep were her family. Along the way she had named them: Mimi, Moma, Dadi, Kami, Blackie, Franci—silly names, but they made her heart happy. "No. I want to keep them."

"Then perhaps you should consider leasing?" the bald man said.

She looked from the bearded man to the bald man. "Explain please?"

"You leave your sheep at the common grounds," he said, "the commonwealth watches over them, feeds them, and in payment gets a percentage of either the wool or their flesh, depending on what you use them for. All the joys of ownership, none of the pain."

"Should you change your mind and want to sell," the bearded man said, "the commonwealth can be your mediator in that transaction, too."

She looked down at the clay piece before him. "Good. I will lease them."

"Excellent! How many are we talking about?"

She gave him the details, their names, what they liked to eat, how they would try to be sneaky.

With the end of a reed, he made markings for her words. "There is a mark for sheep," he said, pointing to one set of lines. "You have one goat"—he made a mark—"four lambs"—he marked again—"and eight full-grown sheep. Truth?" He drew his marks carefully from the top to the bottom of the slab, moving from right to left. He had to raise the heel of his hand so as not to smear the marks, which made his whole arm stick out like a wing.

"You made only one mark for the lambs and the sheep, and one mark for the goat," she said.

"Good eyes. But these marks," he said, moving the reed

again, adding marks, "these tell me you have eight sheep and four lambs. Because I wrote goat only once, I know it's only one goat."

"I'll be back," the bearded man said, patting her on the shoulder.

"Do you have a seal?" the bald man asked.

An image, a memory? of a wet creature, blue-black and barking, appeared in her head, then vanished. She blinked, confused. "No."

"Can you make a sign for your name?"

She looked at the reed he handed her, then scratched on the damp clay.

"Interesting," the man said, then copied the tally of her animals on a smaller piece of clay and had her sign it again.

"Now what are you doing?" she asked.

He folded a piece of clay over the first piece and covered it completely. He made some scratches on it and had her make her sign a third time. "Today is the sixteenth day of the Hired Man's moon, which I wrote here. You are this sign, I am this sign. This will be filed in the Office of Records. When you want to get your sheep back from the commonwealth, bring your piece of clay. We'll match the two, then go get your sheep."

"How will you know which ones are mine?"

His gaze was sharp. "If the sheep themselves aren't marked, I suggest you find some way to identify them. The commonwealth is not responsible for any loss or damage due to mistaken ownership."

"Thank you," she said. "I will."

The bald man hurried back through the archway, and she looked around. The buildings gave shade to the streets, which were wide and straight. Trees and flowers bloomed everywhere. People with felted skirts moved back and forth, men with important cloaks and basket hats, women with market baskets and swinging hoop earrings, girls with bangles, and boys with blocks of clay. Everyone was going somewhere. And people were leaning against every surface, resting in every shadow and talking. Loud and soft, laughter and shouting, pleading, and threatening. Everyone was making noise, making smells, taking up space.

Thirty thousand. What did it mean? There were more humans here than all the sheep in all the villages she could even think of, or imagine. Were all of these humans together, thirty thousand? Her hand crept to her throat and she felt her blood pounding through her neck. *Think about a million,* she thought. *Now that's a lot of humans. What could be a million?* Her head ached again.

"Make way for the judge. Justice Eli coming through!"

She turned to look. A man carrying a fan of feathers waved at the people walking. Behind him, on an onager, was a long-faced old one, and behind him many clean-faced boys with blocks of clay. The people were pushed out of the way, shouting and crying and protesting, as the man moved through them like water over rocks.

"Coming through! Justice on its way!" His entourage walked a little way farther, then past a large, black stone and beneath another brick arch.

She was still staring after them when the bearded man touched her on the shoulder. "Catching a little of the local color, I see. Well come on, female. We have many things to do today. Kalam," he said to the man who followed them. "Make a list. It will take a while to prepare her to meet the *lugal.* Have the copper tub readied, a hairdresser and makeup artisan waiting, and send someone to the women's atelier."

"The one by the harbor, sir?"

"No, I think the one by the Temple of Sin is much better. Send a collection. And the lapidary? Where is he?"

"Working at the north entrance today."

"Fetch some ear things, whatever they are called."

"Yes, sir."

"What time is my next appointment?"

"After dinner, sir."

"Plenty of time."

He touched the girl on the arm, and she looked at him. "Do you like sweets?"

"Sweet? Dates?"

"Dates are sweet," he said.

"Beer?"

He laughed. "Beer can be sweet. Do you like beer?"

"I like beer a lot!"

He laughed again. "Kalam, have some of the light, sweet beer delivered. Elsa does it best."

"The Scampi Stand?"

"Yes. Send over some scampi, too."

They were walking on a street made of hard clay. Buildings lined both sides of it, and in the buildings people did marvelous things. A thousand scents touched her nose, most of them she didn't know. If this wasn't Dilmun, it was almost as good. It had to be.

Flowers and children and women and laughter and singing and cooking food and shouting . . . she'd never seen so many new things.

But she had seen even more impressive sights.

I must have really *hit my head,* she thought. *That is why I hear this voice, my voice, saying things I don't completely understand. But I know them.*

She felt dizzy again.

"Here we are," the bearded man said.

"I will return shortly," the clean-faced Kalam said, and ran down another street.

"Step inside," the bearded man said to her.

The door opened, and she stepped into a small garden. Empty. Where were the thirty thousand humans?

"Wash your hands," the man said, pouring water from a clay jar into a basin. He rinsed his hands and face, then dumped the dirty water into a plant and poured some more water into the basin. "For you."

She washed her face and hands and dumped the water. It was brown with dirt.

"You can set your things down," he said. "They'll be safe."

She set down the *guf* skin and laid the knife on top of it. The tablet with her sheep she kept in her hand.

"Let's see your sore," he said. "Come into the light."

The house, taller than a palm tree, was like a box with the center cut out, right over the garden. The bearded man sat on a stool and beckoned her to sit on the ground between his knees. She winced as he moved her hair around, and clumps of dried mud fell on her shoulders and breasts. "Does it hurt?"

"Not much."

"How did you get this?"

"I . . . I don't know."

"What do you remember?"

She chewed her lip as images flashed in her mind: white hands, long fingers that were the color of fleece, mixing flour and water and leavening. A fire, the feelings about it were safe, secure. A haven. Then pain in the head. Resignation. "A fire," she said slowly. "Blue light. A black tunnel." She shrugged. "I woke up in the water."

"There were other people?" he said, still touching her head. "A fire? You don't look like you were in a fire. Though something did give you a crack on the head. It's not healing very well."

The fire was such a hazy memory, but it came with her

head hurting. A falling star, trailing blue light. "I don't remember. I—I can't make sense of it."

Ningal patted her on the shoulder. "I think you have the forgetting sickness. Happens often enough with head sores. You'll recall soon enough. Turn around."

She did, and looked up into his face. *"Hello, Sean Connery,"* she said.

He frowned, his pointed eyebrows rising higher. "Speak again?"

She shook her head.

"Were those curses? Are you possessed, female?"

She shook her head. "No, no, I don't know. I'm sorry."

He stared at her. "No matter," he said at last. "It's just that I've never heard those words before. We keep lists of all the words we know, because we are compiling a list of all the lists." He smiled. "This concept is over your muddy head, isn't it?"

She nodded slowly.

"What is your name?"

She stared at him.

"How are you called?"

She continued to stare.

"Did you lose your family? Your husband? Parents?"

"Everyone," she said. "I lost them all. I'm alone, all alone."

"Don't weep," he said. "It's not my intent to upset you, I just need to find out how to classify you, what kind of refugee. Luckily you have sheep. You are wealthy, so you'll be allowed to stay. You can pay for food and water."

"Call me Chloe." Part of her seemed to cry out in protest, but the name she'd never heard before, fit. Chloe. Alive and fresh and green—all good things. A blessing to have such a name. The protests faded away.

"Clo-ee?" he said.

She nodded.

"I wonder what mud god that name is supposed to honor," he mused. "Do you know?"

She shook her head.

"What did you do in your village, Chloe? Besides herding, I mean."

"I took care of the sheep, the goats. I had vegetables. Barley fields. I can make beer."

"Beer making and tavern keeping are always useful skills. Can you spin? Felt? Weave?"

She nodded, but it was a slow, hesitant movement. "I think so."

The door opened and Kalam came in. A half dozen people with parcels followed him. "Go with Kalam," the bearded man said to Chloe. "Do you need anything else?"

"Pomegranates," she said. "Their skins, if nothing else. I know it's spring, but—"

The bearded man looked into Chloe's face. "I'll get them."

She smiled. "Thank you." She followed Kalam out of the garden and into a long, narrow room. Her eyes took a minute to adjust to the darkness.

"This is a copper tub," he said to her. "Get in it, and the slave will wash you."

She didn't know what it was about his tone, but it made her backbone stiffen. He left the room, and she took off her skirt, hid her tablet in its folds, and climbed into the tub. The water was warm, warmer than the Euphrates in the spring, but not as hot as the Euphrates in the summertime.

"The Euphrates!" she said out loud, as if she'd never heard the word before. "Sacred dung!"

"By Sin, what a change! Come, come. Here are your pomegranate husks," the bearded man said.

Chloe walked in, aware that bathing and shaving had given her every advantage. *Men love beautiful women, and men fear smart women, but a beautiful smart woman can have the world in her lily white palms.* It was a voice in her head; an accent she'd never heard and words that weren't like her own. But it was comforting; it made her smile. "Thank you," she said to him.

"Fetch the female some beer," the bearded man said over his shoulder. Two young boys brought in a jar that stood as tall as her waist and set it between her and the bearded man. The boys gave each of them footstools, thrust drinking tubes into the neck of the jar, and gave one to Chloe and one to her host.

"I'm sorry," she said. "I don't believe I know your name?"

"Ningal," he said. "Seventh son of a son from the First Family, but I gather you know little about them, being from the marshes."

"No, I'm afraid I don't."

"Drink up," he said, slurping on the beer. "It's good."

The brew was sweet and heavy, instantly refreshing. "It's delicious," she said. "I don't know these flavors."

"The ale-wife who makes this brew is famous for her mixture of spices. I particularly like this cinnamon and cloves with honey beer. It doesn't go well with food, but it's tasty before or after a meal."

"It is," Chloe agreed.

Ningal leaned back in his chair, and the sunlight fell on his chest and legs. He might be white-bearded, but his body was strong and well-defined, his skin still supple even though it was tanned as dark as leather. "As I told you, I would like you to make a report to the *lugal*. Maybe even more, perhaps to the two houses who rule the commonwealth, just to give them an idea of what kind of damage we're facing."

"What does it matter to you?" she asked, sipping her beer.

"What?" he said, turning his ear toward her.

"Why does it matter to the thirty thousand humans here, what happened on the marsh?" she said, louder.

"We buy our cattle from small villages like yours, we need to know if there is going to be less supply so we can make alternative plans. Also, it's necessary to calculate the taxes on those clients who own property in those fields. The commonwealth gets a percentage. And," he said with a sigh, "we have to figure if the commonwealth will be supporting extra humans who can't support themselves. That has been our lot recently. Too many humans. Mostly, though, we care because that is what humanity is."

She leaned forward, listening.

Ningal smiled at her. "What makes us different here in Ur is not because we know Ziusudra is alive and well, or because we read and write. It's because we are aware we're not the only ones on the Plain of Shinar. Others might need help, care. We are the more affluent, thus it is our responsibility to help our kin." He sat forward, looking at her.

"You know we are all kin, don't you? Even though your eyes are different colors and mine are black, or you are tall and graceful as a willow and I'm shorter and wiry as copper, we are kin. One mother, one father to us all. That is the humanity, that is the spark of the divine in each of us which we must protect." He sipped from his beer. "When a brother thinks he's more divine than his brother, it is the seed of trouble."

Images flashed through her mind, so fast and so saddening she felt as if she'd been hit in the face. Brother against brother, cousin fighting cousin, splits because of gods worshiped or economic policies embraced. Planes, bombs, boats, guns. Blood, everywhere.

"Chloe, are you well, female?" Ningal asked.

She met his gaze.

"You turned as white as river foam. Does your head hurt?"

She turned the drinking tube away from her mouth. "I'm fine. It's just a lot to take in at once." So many things in her head that she didn't know, but she understood. Words with pictures filled her with such emotion, of places and humans she'd never even guessed. But she knew it, knew them. The foreignness was familiar. Chloe turned the tube to her again, and took a small sip to cleanse the bitterness from her mouth.

"Forgive me a justice's ramblings," Ningal said. "You must be hungry, tired, I brought all of those people to groom you, but you know how to do it yourself, obviously—What do you need? Want?"

A Big Mac and an order of fries. She kept her mouth tightly shut. "I need to take care of my sheep," she said, rising with the bag of pomegranate peels.

"Of course, should someone go with you?"

"No, I will be fine," she said. The tablet of her sheep was tied into her skirt, which, though dirty and scratchy, was hers. "I'll be back soon." She slipped out the door into the street. It joined with the other, the big street that led past the multicolored hill, beneath the gate, and out to the grazing grounds. The clumps of people seemed to pay less attention to her this time, and Chloe felt a little more at ease. But there were so many!

Outside the gate a few shepherds watched the sheep, but casually. Chloe saw that animal skins were rigged on posts, making a fence around the territory. She walked up to a reclining shepherd. He was carving something with a small knife and didn't look up. "I'm here to see my sheep," she said.

"Which ones are yours?"

"That one and that one," she said, pointing. "They have only been here a few . . . hours."

He glanced up at her from beneath interwoven eyebrows. "I remember. Eight and four and one. What are you going to do?"

"Mark them."

He grunted and continued his carving. Chloe took her pomegranate peels to the water and opened a small vial of sesame oil for which she'd traded her fish-blade knife. With bleats and baas, she called her flock and chased them down to make her mark on them. It was almost twilight by the time she hurried beneath the archway, down the main street, and into the quiet lane on which Ningal lived. The people had started cooking fires in the streets, eating their meals and entertaining themselves in the open.

They have no homes, she thought. If not for Ningal, she would be one of them, crouched in the filth of the street trying to sleep.

Kalam opened the door for her. His gaze took in the bright yellow of her palms and the mud stains on her knees and chest. "There is water still in the tub," he said.

"Thank you," she said, and walked quickly through the courtyard and into the room.

As she stepped from the tub—again—there was a knock on the door. "Come in. Enter," she said.

"The tradesmen await you," a girl said.

Chloe picked up her skirt, then discarded it in favor of a clean sheet with which to dry her body. She trailed the girl and found herself in a well-lit room. The people who had followed Kalam in were there, waiting.

Cloth and bangles, bottles and brushes, they were all laid out for her to see. The tablet with her sheep was in her hand, but she had nothing left to bargain with. She looked over her shoulder and saw Kalam by the door. He was looking at marks on a tablet, one similar to what she had. The artisans didn't speak, but they watched her look at their things. Finally, she slipped over to Kalam. "Excuse me, but . . . I have no way of paying these people for their goods."

"Don't worry about it," he said, not looking up.

"I have to," she said. "My flock is fine—"

"Unless you are devoted to the *guf* skin you brought, Justice Ningal is willing to buy it from you."

She turned her back to the tradesmen and whispered to Kalam. "I don't know the value of things."

He glanced at the wealth of merchandise spread across the room. "For the *guf* skin, you can buy all of this and five more sheep, pay your taxes, and feast daily for months."

"From the trade of a skin?" But as she said it, she recalled that a *guf* skin was made of the hides of at least four oxen, tanned and weathered, then stitched together and treated with bitumen for waterproofing.

They were invaluable to anyone who wanted to travel the river south, for he would construct a wooden frame, line it with the *guf*, and have a quick means of transportation. Once at his southern destination, he would dismantle and sell the wood, where it was in great demand, then fold up the *guf* for his next journey. *Gufs* were often passed through families as part of funeral goods or wedding gifts. "Of course," she said, as she turned back to the offerings.

Fabric, felted and fleeced, woven and edged; jewelry, including bangles like the Harrapan had; sandals of leather and palm fronds; pots of black for her eyes and red for her lips and bright antimony to shade her lids; oils and fragrances for her hair and body, cloaks and hairpins and earrings. She could have it all?

Kalam walked beside her as she stared. "You might as well get everything," he said. "You aren't going to have much time for shopping in the next weeks, and you'll want to make good impressions. Of course, once you become more aware of the styles, and so forth, you'll want to order more. But you need a start. This is a good one."

She'd never had more than one skirt for the summer and one for the winter. A cloak to sleep in and those few bangles she'd gotten just before the flood. So how did she recognize that the fabric was fine, some of the softest she'd ever touched; the gold was pure; the oils and perfumes expensive blends. It was too much to make a choice. "Then I'll take everything," she said.

The artisans blessed her loudly, praised her personal gods, and offered sacrifices to her personal demons as they scrambled to adorn her.

"The prices Justice Ningal agreed to," Kalam said to them. "Leave your merchandise here, you'll be paid at the door." They thanked Chloe as they left, and Kalam excused himself, too, leaving her with wealth she'd never imagined. Her hands fluttered over the beautiful objects, and she felt like crying.

Why weep now?

"You should dress for dinner," Kalam said, reappearing in the doorway. "Shall I send someone?"

She shook her head, her back to him. "No, thank you."

Chapter Three

*E*zzi, what are you staring at?"

"The stars, Mother. I'm a stargazer. It's what I do."

She sighed as she moved his empty dishes away. "I can't believe I sent you to the Tablet House, scrimped and saved to get you the finest education, and all you do is stare at the stars."

"They are our fortunes, Mother."

She snorted and shuffled away.

He didn't mean to be disdainful, but she was so base. The edge of her skirt dragged in the dirt. The ass slept in the same room as she did. They didn't even own a copper bathing tub. An oversight he meant to rectify just as soon as he got some funds, or at least an advance from a creditor.

First, he needed employment.

If he could have predicted the moon turning to blood, the unexpected flooding, and how devastating the waters would be, then he could have demanded his price and have as many copper tubs as he wanted. But, truth told, he wasn't that good. What he lacked in ability, he compensated for in diligence.

Returning to the Tablet House as a Tablet Father was out of the question. He'd been a lousy student, more concerned with the proper cloak to wear and whom to make a friend of than anything to do with the subjects. No, teaching was not an option.

Out of habit, he recited the stars with names. The year would begin soon, with the Hired Man, then the Bull of Heaven, the Twins, the Crab, the Lion, the Barley Stalk, the Scales, the Scorpion, Dablisag, the Goatfish, the Giant, and the Tails. The stars rose and set in flocks, any fool could see. Each season had its flock, which ruled the night for that whole lunar month.

However, the sky looked different. The New Year was close upon them, so the stars would be changing soon to predict what the year would bring, but the presentation above was even more unusual.

"Ezzi, are you going down to the tavern tonight?" she asked.

He shook his head, not looking at his mother.

"Because if you aren't, then I thought I might."

"Enjoy yourself," he said, staring at the sky.

"Most sons would care if their mothers walked the streets alone at night," she muttered as she tied on a cloak. "Most sons would volunteer to walk their mothers to the tavern and wait patiently until they met and mingled, then walk them home."

"Most sons don't have whores for mothers." He didn't look away from the paths of the stars. The gods hid messages in the heavens; was that a new star he saw?

"I'm not a whore," she said. "Don't class me with those who work at the temple."

"Truth," Ezzi said, finally looking at the woman who had birthed him. "They do it for the goddess. You do it for—"

"Silence yourself, boy," she said. "You have your fancy Tablet House education because of me, because I please men for currency."

"Or you just please the right men," he said. He'd never

forget the chiding at the Tablet House the other boys had given him about his marks being so good because the Elder Brother who reviewed their work was a frequent guest at Ezzi's house on the Crooked Way.

His mother had taken the most prestigious address in Ur and transformed it into a residence of asses and grime.

She adjusted her wig and tightened the sash around her waist, making it look smaller and her breasts look larger. He knew she dabbed a little soot in her cleavage, because by the light of the fires in the tavern, it made the shadows between her breasts even more alluring. The same shadows slimmed years off her jaw. Her secret was never to let any of her customers see her in daylight.

They had to wonder where the soot on their hands or clothes came from, though. Ezzi had always thought about that. "Are you taking a room at the tavern tonight?" The rest of the question didn't need to be voiced: Or are you bringing your customers home. He hated when she did; her cries disturbed his sleep.

Perhaps her career was the true reason he became a stargazer. As a child, he was up all night, every night, with nowhere to escape his mother's business, except the roof. Then there was nothing to do except stare at the lights flickering in front of the temple, or the watchman as he walked the streets. Or the night sky.

"It doesn't matter to me," Ezzi said, standing up and brushing any possible bread crumbs off his Old Boy's robe. "I will be at the temple, discussing the stars with the—"

She snorted. "Be safe on the streets." Then she walked to his side and kissed his head. He flinched; her painted lips had kissed a thousand men, and the thought of being just another man to her made his skin prickle with disgust.

She froze at his movement. She knew his thoughts. Holding herself stiffly, his mother Ulu crossed through the courtyard and slipped out the door, drawing it shut silently behind her.

Ezzi stared at it a moment, toyed with the idea of chasing her down in the street and giving her a hug. They lived in this two-story house, he had the best education and dined on the finest food because—

He couldn't convince himself. The real reason why they lived here was because she was too much of a tramp to keep to one husband, so she had divorced Ezzi's father and supported her son by doing what she loved the most: working on her back.

At the least, he should have a copper tub.

The sky beckoned; was that a new star? Was it his future the gods teased him with? Just in case, Ezzi poured some oil before the statue of his personal god and offered a quick petition.

Then he combed the rest of the oil through his hair, straightened the fringed fabric that wrapped over his shoulder and around his chest, adjusted the basket hat that announced to the residents of Ur that Ezzi was among the best class, wiped his face clean of the peasant's dinner he'd had; and, finally, set off through the dark streets to the staged temple of the Moon God Sin, and his consort, the capricious goddess Inana.

∿

Guli pulled the door shut, debated locking it, then decided against it. If someone broke in and stole all his belongings, he would just file a complaint against the commonwealth for not protecting his property and start over with the credit they'd give him.

Despite those considerations, he still shouldn't make it easy for the criminal element. He tested the handle; it stuck, which was almost as good as a lock, then turned away. The street was dark. It was always dark. "I couldn't have picked a worse location," he muttered. "Too many more weeks of this, and I'll be back in the gardens." As he said this, he walked by a clump of palm trees. He spat at them in the darkness, then looked over his shoulder in case anyone saw him.

Ur was crazy for trees, and bushes and plants of all sorts. Certainly, he understood it kept the city cooler in summer. It was easier to grow vegetable gardens, in the protected shadow of a clump of palms. He wasn't an idiot.

However, he had been one of those poor, unfortunate souls who hauled donkey shit in the early double hours, before the sun even woke, to keep everything that was already green, lush and blooming. He was one of those who dug out irrigation works with his hands until his nails were split and bleeding, who spat and snorted out mud for weeks at a time. His childhood, as a slave to the commonwealth, had been spent shinnying up the curving trunks to get the dates the commonwealth sold, tax-free.

He spat at another group of palms.

According to the cursed *lugal* of Ur, there should be a "spot of greenery" every corner—in every direction.

Guli couldn't prove it, but he was sure the *lugal's* family grew palms and sold them to the commonwealth.

"Those days are behind you," he reminded himself. "Just make a little money, pay off the loans, and stay out of court." He turned onto Tavern Street and inhaled deeply.

Beer. Dark and light, sweet and tart, breakfast beer, lunch beer, beer for the afternoon, and beer for after a good lay. They all served it, and he knew exactly what he wanted, and why.

"Guli!" the ale-wife greeted him. He kissed her lustily, feeling a twinge of craving from the sour taste of mash on her lips. "How does the day greet you?" It was well after twilight, deep into the night.

"Today!" he said, pounding the baked-brick table in front of him. "Today is going to be blessed by the gods!"

"Bribed 'em, have you?" Ge, the old fisherman said.

Guli laughed. "Give me your finest breakfast beer, old girl." He looked at the fisherman. "How is the south sea?"

"The flood confused the fish, yet I got a couple hundred."

Guli clapped the man on his back. "Charge my breakfast to this man!" he said. They all laughed, and Guli cracked the seal on the jar, inserted his drinking tube and settled back for a leisurely sip. *Just stay out of trouble,* he told himself. *No schemes, no plans, and no women.*

No more jail, no more corvées, and no more trouble.

Justice Ningal had told him if he saw Guli in court one more time, it would be the final time. Guli closed his eyes and dedicated himself to enjoying the spices and mash of his fine brew. Beer was the only good thing the gods had ever done for humanity.

That included creation.

He was kissed. "I'd recognize those lips anywhere," he said.

"So would most of Ur," the fisherman said. "Give us a kiss, too."

Guli opened his eyes and saw Ulu straddle the fisherman, her mouth a cubit from his.

His lips pursed out of his bearded face as she drew closer and closer to him. The tension in the tavern rose, until no one was drinking, they all watched, anticipating the kiss and wishing they were the lucky one. Ulu didn't kiss on the mouth often, but it was almost better than when she kissed below the skirt. She was that good a kisser.

And she usually tasted like sweet mash.

Her long, red tongue slid out of her mouth. The old fisherman's mouth opened, almost drooling. His eyes were so popped he looked like one of his fish. Ulu caught the edge of his drinking tube with her tongue and slowly sucked it into her mouth.

Everyone laughed, except the poor fisherman, whose chest moved up and down like a boat on the tide.

"Nice brew," she called to the ale-wife, then turned back to the fisherman. "Are you happy enough to see me, old man? Or do you want your beer instead?"

"Beer or Ulu!" someone cried. "No contest!"

The room laughed again, as she rose off of him and turned to the ale-wife. Her glance at Guli was sideways. "How are you, handsome?"

"The gods are good, Ulu," he said.

"They should be, we bribe them enough," she said.

"What has been the most successful bribe?" Ea, a young lapidary, asked, pushing his way into the conversation. He wasn't even bearded, and he'd cut his lip on the drinking tube.

She looked at him long and hard, then ran her hand down her long neck to one full breast. Ulu lifted it up, like an offering. "Who needs more?"

The boy blushed. Guli turned his back to him and created a close space with Ulu. "Who did your hair?"

She dropped her gaze. Defensive. "I don't know what you mean."

"Your wig is new." He knew it was the beer talking, but he couldn't believe the sense of betrayal he felt. "You told me I was the only one."

"Guli," she said, with a pleading glance. "It's nothing. Really."

"Looks like something to me."

"Just a little frippery."

He wrapped one falsely red curl around his finger and tugged.

She winced and reached for her head, holding the fake hair in place.

"Feels expensive, like asses' tail."

"It's not, I assure you," she said with a false laugh. "You know I would never spend that—"

"I don't know, Ulu. I don't know that I know you anymore at all."

"Guli"—her hand was on his shoulder now—"have another beer. Let's discuss this like friends."

"No, I don't think we have anything left to say." He turned to the ale-wife. "May I pay you on at the week's end?"

"Of course, Guli. God speed you home and have a good day."

"Guli, please, don't leave like this," Ulu pleaded.

He turned and put his face very close to her painted cheek. "Did you get it dyed to match?"

"Guli!"

"Did you?"

She opened her mouth, but nothing came out.

Guilty.

He turned on his heel and walked out. She followed him, called his name, but he ignored her. You think you have friends, you think you really know people; he just couldn't believe it. An asses'-tail wig and dyed to match. What kind of friend would do such a thing?

"And here I am going out of business," he said to the uncaring black night. "Because my so-called friend won't even come down to let me do her hair!"

He kicked open his door and stomped into his cold, dark house. The courtyard smelled like stale fish, and Guli couldn't be bothered to light a fire. He slumped onto the bed and felt the palm fronds sag a little more. "In a week I'll be sleeping on the floor," he muttered. Somewhere in the branches above him, in the cursed palm fronds that were plastered over with mud for a roof, insects scurried.

"I hope you go to Ulu's house and nest in her expensive fake hair," he said to them, then pulled the blanket over his head and turned on his side.

The fronds slipped a little bit more. A revision: He'd be on the floor in three days.

～

The three of them walked in. The girl kept walking, through the courtyard and back into the room where she'd left her belongings. She slammed the door. Kalam and Ningal exchanged glances. "Wine, sir?"

"Yes, I think some of the northern date palm would be nice."

Kalam hurried off to the kitchens to rouse a slave. Ningal sat down in the chair, sighed heavily, and stared up from the courtyard. The stars were sprinkled like precious silver drops on the breast of a Khamite woman. He hadn't seen any Khamite women, not for years, not until today. Chloe, as she called herself, didn't recall anything about her parentage or location, but she was no ordinary marsh girl.

In the last generations, her skin testified, her roots had been with the First Family, albeit the least favored son Kham, and probably—Ningal tugged at the tuft of beard just below his lip—someone fair. A father from the mountains, perhaps? A mother from the desert? At any rate, the girl was extraordinary to look at.

"Your wine, sir," Kalam said, giving Ningal the choice of two hammered gold cups. Ningal selected the one closest to him, showing Kalam he was a trusted aide. Ningal tasted its sweet depths.

"Join me," Ningal invited the man.

Kalam pulled over the chair Chloe had sat in earlier and took a drink of wine. Though Kalam pretended to like it, Ningal had him figured as a sour-mash man.

Wine was sweet, but as Ningal aged and fewer of the things that used to delight him continued to, he enjoyed its sweetness. Sour drinks were for young men with fire in their bellies and burning ambitions. Like his young aide. "What did you think of tonight?" he asked Kalam.

"She made a fool of herself," he said.

Ningal nodded.

"I doubt she will stay through the night. Probably will sneak out before dawn and lie in wait by the grazing grounds for her flock. If they are her flock. Who knows, she could have stolen them. Idiot female."

Ningal tugged at his beard. "What did you think of the council's reactions?"

"I am glad the *ensi* didn't take time from her day to listen. I felt bad enough for wasting the *lugal's* evening."

"How do you think it could have been bettered?" Ningal took another sip of wine. Sweet, sweet. And a little sharpness there. Cloves? He swirled the taste around his mouth.

Kalam snorted, leaned forward so his elbows were braced on his knees. The fringe of his kilt caught the light from the few torches, and Ningal found himself fascinated by the shimmer of gold. "If she had spoken well, it would have helped. If she had taken guidance from an artisan for her makeup or dress, it would have helped. If she had remembered anything, it would have helped."

"What if she hadn't vomited on the *lugal*?"

Kalam glanced over at the kilt the slaves would launder in the morning, and he would return, shamefaced, to the *lugal* by lunchtime. "That was the finishing touch on a disastrous evening. But by then, it was a farce. So it almost fit." Kalam grinned ruefully as he sipped his wine, too caught up in the memory to remember to hide his grimace at its taste. Ningal looked away from the fringe and back at the night sky.

Wind rustled the tops of the palms in the courtyard and whistled around the clay pots set on the roof to catch the seasonal rains. "Can I get you anything else, sir?" Kalam asked.

"No, no. You go on home," Ningal said. "Thank you."

Kalam rose and set his goblet on the tray. "Dawn?"

"No, let's sleep late. What time is my first judgment tomorrow?"

"After lunch."

"And you have to return the cloak. I need to send some letters, hmm, let's say two double hours from dawn."

"Thank you, sir. Good morning."

"Good morning to you, too."

Kalam let himself out, and Ningal forced himself up and over to the door, then he thought better of it. He walked back to the far wall and sat down on the dirt floor. Slowly he stretched to touch his feet. A few more tries, and he laid his nose on his knees. The muscles in his back and arms and legs eased out, long and hard, but it took more time than it used to. He was still bent double when he sensed the movement.

She was dashing across the courtyard, fleet and nearly silent on bare feet. What she'd decided to take, she'd tied up and balanced on her head. A flicker of gold—she was holding the bangles she'd bought tight against her forearm to keep them from jangling.

He stared at her.

She froze, then slipped into a crouch and slowly turned around, peering into the darkest corners of the courtyard.

She felt his gaze. She met it. Chloe looked away, but she didn't turn toward the door. Instead she set down her parcel and let go of her bangles. They rushed down her arm with a melodic ring. She walked toward him, with the long-legged sway of marsh women, shoulders back, breasts and chin thrust out, hips moving to the left, then the right. Her hair covered her like a cloak, falling past her waist. With every step she chimed softly. In one movement she sat, cross-legged, black within the night except for the glitter of her bracelets and the white gleam of her teeth and eyes.

"I don't recall ever feeling that way before," she said to him. "Knowing people were laughing at me, and not because I was taking a stand for something in which they didn't believe, or any other great cause, but because I was foolish. Ignorant. Stupid." She picked at the dirt in front of her. "Well, not stupid, because stupid means I haven't the capacity. There's no truth there. I do have the capacity. I just don't . . . know."

"What don't you know?" he asked softly, also sitting with crossed legs.

"Anything. The words they used, the terms, the concepts. It's like I almost remember it, but it's changed, or it's different, and I can't quite make the connection. When he, the *lugal,* asked how we kept track of fields, I—" She moved her arm to her hair and tucked a black strand behind her ear in a whiff of light perfume. Pomegranates and sesame, he realized. Not perfume, exactly. But seasoning, like the cloves in the wine.

"You didn't know how to count?" he asked.

"It's not like that. If I don't know something, my mind is just blank. But this was so many pictures."

"Pictures like what?"

She drew on the ground, shapes like—3, 4, 5, 6, 7—but she drew with her finger, and made her marks horizontally and backwards. There was no relation to the writing of a reed on clay, when the reed was moved vertically and properly from right to left. What she drew wasn't even pictograms of old, just . . . lines that curved. "What are those pictures of?" he asked.

"These aren't the pictures, not exactly. But they are part of them, like this."

She scooted back, so he could see more of the dirt. With her hand steady, she made more incomprehensible marks. "Speed Limit 55." "Don't mess with Texas." "Must be 18 or older."

"Is this how your village counted, perhaps?"

"Then what are these marks?" She drew again, but these were straight lines crossed at the tops and bottoms, or intersected. I II III IV V. "They aren't irrigation channels or anything. They came to my mind when he said counting." She looked up at him. "I just don't understand."

Ningal looked at the markings she'd made. Her hand had moved without hesitation as she drew them, just like it had moved when she signed her contract for the lease. "How did you sign the lease again?"

"He said just make a mark, so I did."

"Do it for me."

She looked at the dirt, and with confidence and a little flourish she wrote CBK, linking the letters together in a way none of the others had been.

Ningal scratched his head.

"Do you recognize anything?"

"I must confess, I don't."

Dejected, she began to brush the dirt away. "It's why I can't stay."

"Because you have your own marks, and no one else does?"

"I can't be ignorant. I can't *not* know."

Ningal, in the centuries that comprised his life, had been many things. A barber and surgeon, a scribe, an estate manager, a fisherman, a tradesman and a Father of Tablets. In all his time, he had never seen any other markings besides the ones of his people, the Black-Haired Ones, the Sumerians. It set them apart, helped them irrigate fields and promote trade. They could write, they had a language.

He kept a list of all the words he'd ever heard, just so someone would know. In the Tablet House that had been his, on the Blue Street, there were shelves and shelves of his work. Words gleaned from every edge of the Black-Haired Ones' world.

He'd never seen of, nor heard words he didn't recognize as being theirs. And never in a thousand courts of the gods had he seen someone else scribble and call it something.

Did this girl need an exorcist? Or was this a gift from the gods?

"How did you learn," she asked him, pulling him back into the courtyard and away from the dusty memories of the Tablet House. "Who taught you?"

"My father is wealthy. He sent his sons to the Tablet House."

"School?"

Ningal was stunned, but he answered. "Yes, school." How did she know that word? It was new!

"How long were you a student?"

He laughed and was surprised at how loud the sound was at this time of day. "From the day of my ninth birthday, every day from sunup to sundown, until I was twenty."

"No days off?"

"Six days a month. The gods' feasts, you know." But perhaps she didn't.

"And your father was wealthy, so he could spare you from the family business."

"We're shipwrights, and my father wanted us to be more."

"I'll stay here on one condition," she said, her eyes suddenly bright. Greener than they'd looked this afternoon—in fact, he'd thought they were brown. They were luminous. Every muscle of his body was tense with awareness, anticipation. Ningal felt like a fish—strung along and snared at the exact, right moment.

"Which condition?"

"Let me go to the Tablet House." She leaned forward, and the sweetness of pomegranates and sesame washed over him, the clink of her bangles suggested a seductive beat. "I'll be a good student. I'll learn quickly. I won't cause any fuss. I'll make my own lunch. Just let me go."

"Why do you want to learn how to write?" he asked.

"Because, because . . . if you can write, you can read."

"One would hope."

"If you can read, anything is possible. You can go anywhere, be anything. Nothing limits you. Nothing."

"You're a female. An attractive one," he said. The wine must have loosened his tongue, freed him to say what he thought instead of what he should only say. "Crook your finger and any one of a thousand men will give you anything you want, take you anywhere you desire to go, open the world to you."

She sat back, her legs shifted to the side, her arms crossed before her. "I don't want a man's world. I want my own."

"You have no desire for a mate?"

She looked to the side, her profile to him. She wasn't a marsh dweller; her nose was too strong, her neck too long. Neither were the strength of her chin and straightness of her forehead from the molelike people who had tilled the land since Before. Skin like hers hadn't been subject to the unrelenting sun for thirty years. She was an imposter, this marsh girl, but she didn't seem to know it. "I can't answer," she said finally.

Ningal knew he was too old to feel shut out, especially over a creature he'd plucked from the mud, what, yesterday afternoon? He straightened up and tensed his muscles one last time before he stood. He rose to his feet.

"Wait," she said, seated yet. He looked on the top of her head from here. Light shimmered over her hair, caught the glimmer of color still on her eyelids, and focused on her lips. They were bare of paint, and ripe. *I need to get to the temple,* Ningal thought. *I need to bury these feelings in the appropriate vessel for passion and lust, not in this child, who is the age of my great-great-grandchildren.*

"It's not that I won't tell you, it's that I can't. Of course I want a mate, but ... what I want, who I want, is so specific I can't put it into words." She reached a hand up, and he helped her to her feet. They looked eye to eye at each other; he felt her pulse in the hand he held. Her gaze was that of a woman of knowledge. He knew in that instant she was aware of how she made him feel.

He stirred the same feelings in her; in her eyes, he saw she wanted him. He felt it in her touch.

Ningal released her hand, stepped away, and smiled at her. "It's late for me," he said. "Sleep well, female."

"Can I get into school?"

"It's never been done. Female humans don't attend the Tablet House."

"No," she said, her voice firm, her eyes definitely green. "Female humans *haven't* attended the Tablet House."

Ningal smiled, then climbed the stairs to his bed. For this dawn, to be wanted was enough.

Chapter Four

G ood day," Chloe said to Kalam and Ningal, as they sat beneath the shade in the courtyard. "How was everyone's rest?"

A slave offered her some beer and bread, and Ningal gestured for her to join them. Kalam seemed surprised to see her, but he hid it beneath a simpering glance. "I want to attend," she said to Ningal. It was all she had dreamed of: those marks that looked like marsh birds' feet in the mud, making sense! Being able to count, to write, to read! How glorious that could be! "When can I start?"

Kalam turned to Ningal. "What does she mean?" he said in an undertone.

"I want to attend school."

Kalam spewed beer, then inhaled, choked, and coughed until his face was as red as the border of his cloak. "That's a new word," he gasped out at Ningal. "You told her that word?"

"She used it first herself," Ningal said as he slapped his aide on the back. "She knew it already."

Chloe hated that she didn't know what word they were talking about, but she kept quiet while Ningal wiped spewed beer off his bare shoulder and from his beard. "I think I'll be requiring a bath before court," he said to the slave.

"I'm so sorry, sir, but I thought that, well—" Kalam

looked at Chloe, and she looked back. She refused to be intimidated by him. He'd laughed at her last night—she didn't blame him, she'd been ridiculous—but she didn't like that he could do it again.

"She did say it, Kalam," Ningal told him. "Chloe wants to attend the Tablet House."

"Oh. Is that all?" He smiled at her and adjusted his drinking tube again.

"Does that mean I can?"

Kalam's glance was dismissive. "Utterly impossible."

"Kalam is an Old Boy from one of the foremost Tablet Houses in the city," Ningal said.

"It really is an Old Boy network?" Chloe said. She wasn't exactly sure what she meant by it, but the feeling was resignation. "Women aren't allowed, is that what you are telling me?"

"It's not a matter of allowance," Kalam said. "It's that it's impossible."

"Why?"

"It's not done."

"Why not?"

Kalam looked at Ningal, a little bewildered. "Female humans don't attend the Tablet House. Explain to her, sir. It's just not done."

Ningal looked at her, and Chloe knew she'd made a convert. "Chloe pointed out that they haven't, not that they don't."

"But, sir—"

"I'm going to do it," she said.

Kalam snorted. "This isn't worth discussing. Are you ready for your bath, sir? I need to return the skirt to the *lugal*."

"Does the *lugal* decide who attends school?" she asked.

"Tablet Houses," Kalam said, "are private, not commonwealth, institutions. Though the lugal is an Old Boy, he is not a Tablet Father and doesn't make those decisions."

"Although if a female human were to attend," Ningal said, "she would probably have to attain the permission from a *lugal*."

"Sir!"

"If, theoretically, a female human were to attend."

"It's not a theory that . . . can even be theorized!" Kalam said. "It's unheard of!"

"We theorize everything," Ningal said. "If a human is struck, we theorize how much the fine should be. We theorize every single place a human can be struck, we theorize every way a human can be struck, we theorize the most outrageous possibilities because that is what a theory is. Theoretically, a speaking goat could attend the Tablet House, if it was amenable to the Tablet Father, the *lugal*, and the goat," Ningal said.

"A speaking goat would be preferable to a female human in a Tablet House!" Kalam shouted.

"I'm ready for my bath," Ningal said, and followed the slave out.

"I am late for my next appointment due to this, this . . . ludicrous conversation!" Kalam slammed his chair back from his beer jar.

Chloe leaped to her feet. "I'm so sorry I made you late," she said. "I tell you what. I know it's embarrassing for you to return the *lugal's* kilt. I'll do it. Then you don't have to worry about being late, or facing him. I would like to apologize personally anyway."

Kalam glowered at her, then consulted his clay tablet, which presumably carried the day's duties on it. "He will be in the Temple of Sin at noon. When the sun is directly overhead," he explained. "Don't be late. The *lugal* hates lateness. It's a sign of procrastination, and he hates procrastination even more. Justice Ningal and I will be in court all afternoon." He straightened his cloak. "I guess you'll be here by twilight?"

"I guess."

Kalam adjusted his basket hat and nodded at the slave. Chloe followed him to the courtyard gate and closed it behind him. A slave ran out from the kitchens. "Kalam forgot the *lugal's* skirt! He left it, and he won't be back before—"

"It's fine," Chloe said. "I'm going to return it."

"To the *lugal*?" she asked, aghast. "Weren't you the one who threw up on him?"

Chloe felt her face heat. But when you threw up on the leader of the people, word was going to get out, and it was going to be embarrassing. It was just going to be an experience she'd rather forget. "Yes," she said. "I won't be eating before I go visit the *lugal*."

The slave girl shrugged. "The kilt will be dry by then."

"Good. Would it be possible for me to get another bath?"

"Two baths? In two days?" The slave girl's expression showed she thought Chloe was being uppity; in fact, she muttered about living like a justice as she walked to the kitchen to heat the water.

Chloe couldn't explain it, but she felt euphoric. School was a term she felt comfortable with and something inside her resounded with how right the choice was. *You just might have to move heaven and earth to get there,* a voice said inside. *You'd better decide what to wear.*

～

"May I help you?" the scribe said. His head was bald, and his belly bulged. For some unknown reason he wore a kilt rather than a cloak. A cloak would have covered his stomach and looked far more dignified. Of course, it would have shown off his shoulders and arms. Chloe could see he had neither, beyond mere function. She smiled.

"I'm here with a delivery for the *lugal*," she said.

The scribe didn't even look up. "I'm sorry. The *lugal* leaves the office and goes for his afternoon consultation at the Temple of Sin at a few minutes past midday. You missed him by at least fifteen minutes. Good day."

"I know, I got lost." *Never apologize or make excuses when you're late. Just make it up.* The scribe's expression went from polite unconcern to disdain. "But that's not your problem."

"I'm glad you realize that."

"When is he finished at the Temple of Sin? You see, I brought his skirt—"

"Oh. I remember you. The Regurgitating Refugee." He scooted back from Chloe. She fought the desire to show him her middle finger. What use would showing him her middle finger be? He had two middle fingers, and he certainly wouldn't be impressed that she had two, also. "Just leave it here."

"Thank you, but I'd much rather see him. In person."

The scribe leaned forward and beckoned her closer. "You're new to town. I know this. So I'm going to help you. I work for the most powerful man in Ur, consequently, the most powerful man in the known world. He decides if the priests can build another stage for the temple, he decides how many fields will be barley and how many will be emmer. He decides what the rate of exchange is going to be! You, in case you aren't aware, are no one. You can't even keep your peasant stomach to yourself. So leave his skirt, and leave this office." The scribe smiled brightly. "Is that through your stupid little head?"

Chloe just . . . stood.

"And if you think he would be interested in your marshy

Khamite body or sharing his seed with you, know that his afternoon meeting is with the *ensi*, the high priestess of Inana. The incarnation of the goddess of love, you ignorant she-goat. Now get out of here before I throw you out."

Chloe was completely speechless and mostly frozen. He ignored her. She couldn't move; there was no feeling in her body and just the sensation of pins in her face. As if her face had fallen asleep and was just waking up. No words or pictures appeared in her mind. She was too shocked.

The scribe didn't look up, but he spoke. "If your stinking carcass hasn't left this office in a count of five, I'll have your hand cut off for thievery."

She bolted.

"Leave the skirt!" he shouted.

She didn't even turn around, she just dropped the basket containing the skirt on the floor and ran down the steps and into the street. And smack into a wiry, hairy man. They went down in a tangle of legs and arms and long, black hair. Hers and his. "Watch where you're going," he said. "You're so big, you could hurt a person."

"Sorry," she muttered.

"You're the color of dirt; are you ill?" he asked.

Chloe didn't look at him. "I think I'm going to be sick," she whispered, tears starting to sting her eyes. "Oh gods, not again."

"Well, don't do it in the street," he said. "Come with me."

Hot bile filled her mouth, and her body ran cold, then sweaty. Her hands were in fists, and his hand was around her wrist, dragging her behind him. "Excuse me, pardon me, excuse me," he said, as they ran back up the steps into the offices.

"What?" she heard the shout. "You can't—oh, by Nin—"

Chloe's face was thrust into the dirt around a palm tree. She coughed up like a kitten, stomach acid and nerves, a little bit of beer from breakfast. There was nothing except her dress to wipe her face on, to clean her runny nose. It was revolting, but—what choices were there?

"Do you feel better?"

She looked up at the hairy man, and then beyond him.

The scribe, beer-bellied and bald, glared at her over the hairy man's shoulder. Chloe looked around and realized she was at the *lugal's* again, but in the interior office. She looked up at the shelves. The basket she'd just dropped was sitting there, with the freshly washed skirt inside.

"Scribe," the hairy man called, while staring at Chloe. "Clean out this palm plant and repot it, would you? It doesn't smell very good in here. Do you need anything?" he asked Chloe.

The scribe glared at her. She shook her head. The hairy man looked over his shoulder at the scribe. "Get to it." The hairy man held out his hand and picked Chloe up off the ground. The scribe stalked into the *lugal's* office to get the palm.

"Yes. Sir," he ground out through gritted teeth.

~

"A new star?" the stargazer said. "What new star?"

His friend, lover, and confidant waved at the air. "Just a new one, you know I don't understand those sorts of things."

"You should, you're the Tablet Father."

"Exactly why we have experts, like you, to come in and teach those sections," he said, patting the stargazer's arm. He returned both hands and most of his attention to the mutton before him.

"Where did you hear this?"

The Tablet Father couldn't chew and talk at the same time, so he stopped chewing and tucked the piece of mutton in the side of his mouth. "The old babbler at the temple said

some boy came in and claimed he was a stargazer and he'd
seen a new star." The Tablet Father switched the mutton to
the other side of his mouth. "Of course, no one else had,
which caused quite a stir when they stared at the sky."

"They saw a new star?"

"Apparently."

"Where in the sky?"

The Tablet Father swallowed the piece of mutton, mostly
whole. Gods hope he wouldn't choke on it. "Somewhere,
lower. I don't know. It's almost twilight, then you can look.
If it's there, I'm sure you'll see it."

"But I didn't see it first."

"Of course you did. Who is the *ensi* going to believe?
Asa, the official stargazer of Ur, or some plowboy from the
back alley?" *Of course,* the Tablet Father added to himself,
if the ensi *actually knew the stargazer, then she'd undoubt-
edly believe the boy.* But his lover didn't need to know.
They'd been together a long time; they each had secrets best
left buried. "Your wife did an excellent job on this mutton,"
he said, swallowing another huge chunk. "That female
human has the best eye for cuts of meat. Especially sheep."

"Don't talk to me about sheep," the stargazer said.

"What's wrong?" If his lover would start talking, the
Tablet Father could actually eat in peace.

"She's in lust."

"Umm."

"No sooner than I get her one thing she wants, she sees
another. It's exhausting, I tell you. It's probably why I . . .
missed the star, the new one."

"Only by a night or two," the Tablet Father said loyally.
Between bites.

"That female human can nag. A regular goat, that's what
she is. Nagging and nipping. Always what she wants, what
she must have. Why can't we have what the people on

Crooked Way have." The stargazer groaned. "She just doesn't realize that the incomes, combined, of a stargazer and a shepherdess who weaves part-time, don't add up to as much as merchants and traders make."

The Tablet Father would endure a lot of babbling to eat this well. His wife couldn't boil water without setting the house afire. Their relationship was best as it was; she lived on the marshes with the children, and he stayed with whichever protector's son was in his Tablet House, currently Kalam's younger brother. His wife cared nothing for the city, and he was allergic to reeds. The stargazer wasn't eating his meat—he'd pushed his plate away—so the Tablet Father picked the joint off his friend's plate and started to nibble on it.

"They are the fattest, she says, that she's ever seen. With tails like she's never seen."

"Sheep?"

"You think I'm talking about goats?"

The Father closed an ear while he scooped more of the succulent roasted meat onto his bread and into his mouth. This was the reason he didn't have a beard—it was too messy when one enjoyed the table like he did. He swallowed a belch and ripped some more meat off the bone. "Are these a new kind of sheep?"

"What do you mean, a new kind? Sheep are sheep. They're like humans. There is no new kind of human. Some of them just have fat rumps and some skinny. It's not new, it's merely variety."

"So this is a new variety of sheep, the fat-tailed ones your wife likes? Why doesn't she buy one? I know some people who—"

"Not at market, at the grazing fields. The common ones on the north side," the stargazer explained.

The Tablet Father rarely stepped out of the city, and certainly not to the north. He grunted. "Those sheep belong to someone else, then."

"Yes."

"Well," he said, licking his fingers. "I can—" He burped. Ahh, he could almost eat more, but with Asa looking at him disapprovingly, maybe not. "I can make some inquiries for you. Find out who owns them, what they want for them. That sort of thing."

The stargazer's smile showed his broken side tooth. The Tablet Father loved that smile, loved that tooth. "She's out," the stargazer said. "Some felting at the factory, they needed all hands."

The Tablet Father wiped his greasy hands on the edge of his cloak—he'd be out of it in a minute, anyway. "What about the sky?"

"Like you said, it will be there in a few hours. Stars will wait."

He took his hand.

~

"And how was your day, today?" his mother asked Nimrod.

"Fine," Nimrod said.

"Even though there was nothing to kill?" his littlest brother, Roo, smarted off.

"I met a girl," Nimrod said.

"A girl?" his father repeated. "Where did you meet a girl? I didn't realize we had many huntresses in the city."

"I wasn't hunting. There's nothing to hunt here. I miss the mountains." His mother's glance was pleading—not this topic, not during dinner, not again—but Nimrod ignored it. "I'm sorry I ever got married, or came to the city," he said.

Nirg, Nimrod's wife, said nothing, just served him more

food. He would apologize to her later. Lea, his second wife, glared at him. She would throw things at him later.

"You met another female?" Nimrod's father said. "Not hunting?"

"Should you be looking at other females?" Nimrod's mother asked. "I mean, you have two lovely brides now, maybe . . . another onager, or dog?"

"We don't want him to transgress with onagers," his father said. "It wouldn't reflect well on the family or my position." His father was the *lugal*.

Nimrod stabbed his food with a dagger.

"Where'd you meet the female?" his little brother, the brat, asked.

"Father's offices."

"When were you there?" his father asked. "I must have already gone to the temple."

"Why was a female in your father's office?" his mother asked.

Nimrod knew they had an *understanding*. Priestesses, well, it was part of the duty of his father Shem, to spend time and congress with them. But other women, city women, his mother wouldn't have it. It shamed her at council gatherings and meetings of the karums.

"She was returning a skirt, from Justice Ningal," Nimrod said.

"The female who vomited on me?" his father asked, pushing away his plate.

"We're eating," Lea reminded Nimrod.

"Yum!" the brat said.

Nirg dug into her mush. Not much could come between Nirg and food. A hardy mountain female who didn't waste energy on conversation or fancy clothes. Very different from the woman Nimrod had met today. "Your scribe showed his usual charm."

"His task is not to be nice to people but to keep people from taking my daylight. It's valuable!"

"It's voted on by the public," Nimrod said. "Anyway, this female was running out of the building, and we crashed into each other."

"Is she ugly, since she's a female?" the brat said.

Nimrod shrugged. "She's Khamite. Dark, like all the city women." His gaze touched on the fair heads of Nirg and Lea. They were like flax and wheat. "Spoke like she was from somewhere north."

"She's a refugee, a sheepherder. Ningal, out of the goodness of his aged heart, apparently has taken her in, Roo," his father explained.

Nimrod saw the look his mother gave his father. Everyone knew Ningal spent time with priestesses only. There were going to be a lot of unhappy widows, not to mention how his children were going to feel, if the leading justice of Ur took up with a young Khamite girl. A refugee, which was worse.

It was so much simpler in the mountains, Nimrod thought. People meant what they said. If they didn't like you, they killed you. If you didn't like them, you killed them. Animals were honest. Mountain people were honest. Nimrod got tired sometimes, just trying to figure out which smiles were real and which were not.

It was time to meet Kidu, the incoming *en* and Nimrod's friend, for a friendly wrestling match and cool beers. He was straightforward, and a good companion. An honest mountain man.

The girl was like that, today. Honest. No, she couldn't be from the city.

"She was trying to see you," he told his father.

"Why, so she could throw up on something else?"

The brat snickered. Nimrod elbowed him. The little

urchin squealed and fell off his chair. The remonstrations were immediate and expected, and Nimrod helped the brat up and served him some more food. Lea's gaze was laughing now; she hated Roo. Nirg ate on undisturbed.

"Thank the gods I left a few minutes early today," his father said. "I'll do it tomorrow, too, just in case."

The brat snorted a pea up his nose, then made a loud hacking noise and spat it out his mouth onto his dish. Their father turned away. Nimrod looked at his food. He missed the mountain people . . . their honesty, simplicity, the sense it made when you lived in the mountains. You fought to stay alive, you treasured the moments of dawn and twilight, you valued a woman who could feed a fire, and you protected the man who fought at your back.

Everyone had the same goals, to live a good life, to not irritate the gods, to feed the children, the animals, themselves.

But none of them knew how to read or write; for this reason, Nimrod had returned to the city. He was a hunter, and he loved the mountains, but he needed the energy of the city.

He just wished he could start Ur over. Build it up from a slate of blank clay.

Get it right.

~

"See! It's just there!" Ezzi said, pointing at the sky. The men, the venerable priests of the Temple of Sin, stared up at the blackness. "It's new. I think tonight is its fourth night."

They stared long and hard. The exorcist among them held up his clay copy of a sheep's liver and pointed to various spots. They muttered and stared and consulted each other. He could have a cloak like that, Ezzi thought. Then everyone would know he was a stargazer. Dark, like the night, sprinkled with the signs of stars and moon, falling to the ground with the rustle of gold fringe.

"Next week is the New Year," one of them said to Ezzi. "Watch this star every night until then. We'll cast omens and see what secrets the gods hold for us."

"Yes, sirs," he said, bowing his head.

"Keep a good watch on it, boy. We'll talk to the *lugal's* stargazer when he gets here."

"Yes, sirs."

"Let us know if there are any changes in its position, or the time it appears. Anything at all."

Ezzi could barely control his excitement.

"Are you a stargazer professionally?" one of the cloaked men asked.

"Ye-yes, sir."

"Employed by anyone?"

He cleared his throat. "Not yet, I just completed the Tablet House. I'm entertaining some offers from various businessmen around town."

"I see." The man looked back at the sky, and no one else said anything.

Ezzi realized he must have been dismissed. He'd hoped they would offer to pay him or something; he really wanted that tub, but they didn't pay him. Not this time, he reminded himself. Next time they would, for sure. He'd discovered a new star! The *lugal* himself would be thrilled!

He crossed the roof and walked down the stairs. Priests with spears watched the entranceways to each of the floors; they were usually the biggest men and certainly the most handsome. Priests were above all men in Ur, the most physically blessed by the gods.

Would the same could be said for priestesses. Ezzi had seen some servants of the goddess who looked like they guarded the seven gates of Kur instead of danced in the court of the gods. He continued his path around the temple. The night gardeners were out, clearing the small irrigation ditches that lined the walkways and fed the innumerable palm trees that swayed and swooshed in the evening air. Light from the oil lamps illuminated the blue or red or green or yellow on the walls of the staged temple. Ezzi walked down the stairs.

Maybe the *lugal* himself would offer Ezzi employment? Perhaps he would be so impressed and so pleased he would come to Ezzi's house himself. No, Ezzi scoffed. The *lugal* would never visit, but he might send a scribe, or a gentleman. That wouldn't be unheard of. Ezzi's steps quickened. *My mother won't be home tonight; the week before New Year's is one of the busiest at the tavern. This would be a good time for the scribe to come.*

He'd get home and whip those slaves into order to clean the house, get rid of the donkey odor.

When Ezzi heard footsteps behind him, he held his breath. It had happened so quickly! The runner's pace and breath seemed to get faster the closer he got. Ezzi hurried his steps; he wanted to be at home by the time the message arrived. The runner gained on him and Ezzi accelerated. His Old Boy cloak was too formal actually to run in; and it wouldn't be seemly for the *lugal's* newest stargazer to race.

The runner passed him, and Ezzi saw the lapis and pearl shell standard around his neck. It *was* from the *lugal*! Running to his street. The man would just have to wait until Ezzi got home. Aware of his importance, Ezzi slowed his pace and lengthened his steps, like a justice. He lived on the street with Justice Ningal; he'd seen the grave and noteworthy way he walked.

Ezzi turned onto Crooked Way, and the runner ran past him. Going the other direction. "Wait!" Ezzi cried. "I'm not home yet!"

The runner paid him no heed. His hands were empty now.

Ezzi peered down the street and saw one of the doors closing.

Oh. Not for him.

~

"For me?"

"It does say, 'The Female human Chloe.'"

"Good thing there aren't any male human Chloes," she said, stepping up to Kalam. "May I have it?"

"Certainly."

The clay envelope was wrapped around a clay tablet, similar to the one with the record of her sheep. Scribbles and scratches, scribal marks, were all over it. She couldn't read a thing. Not even the part with her name in it. She handed it back to him. "Do you mind?"

He looked at it, then looked at her. Somehow the story of her puking in the potted palm had gotten back to him. Ningal was out tonight, but Kalam was in and had been as irritable as an expectant water buffalo ever since twilight.

Nice analogy, the voice inside her head said. Snidely.

He sighed. "Certainly." With a quick whack, he broke the outer clay envelope and pulled out the letter. He read it quickly. "By the gods," he muttered and tossed it at her.

Chloe dived for it, sliding in the dirt, but she caught it. "You throw like a girl," she said. His expression was confused, on top of angry. She was confused at herself. Did girls throw more than boys? Differently? She shook her head to clear it, and looked at the clay letter.

Marsh bird marks walked across the clay. It was damp. "What does it say?"

"Meet me at the lugal's *office at the double hour before noon. You'll get to meet him."*

"Nimrod!" she exclaimed.

"How do you know the *lugal's* son?"

So the story of the puked-on potted palm hadn't made it to him. "Old friends," she said glibly. "Thank you, Kalam."

"I'm leaving now," he said, slapping his basket hat on and storming through the courtyard. He slammed the door after him.

Chloe looked at the letter; the scratches were familiar somehow. She'd never used them, but she'd seen something similar. In a big room, with lots of light. They were lying on tables, lots of them, with little placards explaining where they'd been found and when.

She walked up to her room, her palm-frond bed. Familiar things.

Sometimes her own mind didn't feel very familiar.

Chapter Five

*G*uli woke to the sound of banging on his door. His palm-frond mattress, which had fallen in less time than he'd expected, left him trapped between the four braces of the bed frame, scrambling like a bug to get on his feet.

His guests didn't wait for him to open the door.

"Perhaps this is why you can't pay us back," his creditor said as he stepped into the room. Two men stood on either side of the tradesman. Unlike him, they were sailors with brawny arms and wide chests. Viza crossed his arms and looked at Guli. "You rest past dawn, as though you were the *en*!"

Guli managed to get up and greet the owner of his shop— by default—if business didn't pick up. "I'm not late," he said to Viza. "Payment isn't due until the first of the year. You swore by Enlil!"

Viza snapped his fingers, and a scribe ran in, with an armful of tablets. "Give Guli a copy of the new agreement," he said.

"I don't read."

"Of course not," Viza said. "Read him a copy of the new rules."

The scribe squinted at the clay.

Guli felt a rush of cold down his back, as if he were wearing his kilt backward during the winter. This was not a good omen.

The scribe cleared his throat and read, in an obnoxious high voice: "I, Guli, who borrowed sixty minae of barley to lease a residence in the fashionable weaving district for my salon, Guli's Karum of Style, will repay the generous and majestic citizen Lord Viza at the prescribed 15 percent. If by the first quarter of the first year I have not made a payment, I will relinquish my residence and submit to being a gardener for Lord Viza."

"I didn't sign that," Guli said. "And I didn't lease a residence in the weaving district. If I had, if would be full of weavers getting their hair done!"

"This is the new agreement, Guli."

"You can't change the conditions after we made a covenant," he said. Guli was a former offender of the commonwealth; he knew his laws.

"I am Lord Viza, you sniveling sifter of shit!"

The two men turned on Guli's house.

"What are you doing? Have you lost your mind?"

"Shut up, or I'll have them work you over," Viza snarled.

One of the sailors upended Guli's palm-frond trunk and spilled his receipts onto the floor. "Wait! You can't touch those!"

With big, bare feet, the sailors stomped on his receipts, smashing them to bits. To pieces. To dust.

Guli watched as the lease of his house, the loan of the furniture, and the purchase of several asses' tails was converted to powder. Lord Viza stepped closer. A small man with a nasty scar on his head, he didn't even wear the cloak of an Old Boy. "Sign the new agreement, Guli."

"No."

"Sign it," the little man said. "I have three witnesses waiting. Sign."

"This is not legal, or ethical."

"Who is going to believe a convict over a freedman?"

Already Guli didn't have the currency; he wasn't going to come up with the rental rate and 15 percent. He didn't do figures, but that would be a lot of earnings. In the months he'd been there, he'd barely made enough to keep in beer and bread. He ripped the seal from his neck, the carved ivory cylinder that proclaimed to one and all that he, Guli, was a worthy client of Ur.

As a symbol for his name, Guli had designed a seal with the goddess Inana seated, and Guli brushing her heavenly hair under the sun of Shamash. He had been so proud to own it, to be free and noble. A client.

His dreams were drowning in the pitiless black eyes of this little, easy-to-break man.

"Sign it," Viza said. "Now."

The two sailors were hunched over Viza's shoulders like vultures. Guli looked at the clay tablet, freshly drawn up. The dust of the past contracts was part of the floor now. If he followed his inclination, he could smash in Viza's face. The two sailors would beat him up. They would all end up in court.

Guli would lose hope of ever owning a seal again.

Biting back the spit he had saved for Viza's face, Guli rolled his seal over the moist clay instead. Viza handed the original to the scribe and gave a copy to Guli. He rolled the image of himself, dressing Inana's hair, across it again. Viza handed that copy to the scribe, for the official files. The last piece he gave Guli was almost dry—it didn't matter. Whenever Viza wanted to change it, he'd just break into Guli's house and grind it to dust.

This was the life of being an honest man. It stunk like the shit in the palms. This reeked worse, because at least that was clean refuse, used for a purpose.

"Keep it," Viza said. The scribe wrapped the other two copies in clay, and Guli sealed them, too. "We'll see you in a few weeks with the first payment?" Viza said. The whole motley crew turned to leave.

Ulu poked her head into the open door. "Guli, are you . . . open?"

Viza smiled at her. "Excuse us, ladies," he said to the three women trailing her; the ale-wife, her daughter, and some pockmarked priestess. Viza looked over his shoulder at Guli. "Glad to see business is doing so well."

He got out of the door before Guli crushed his seal in his hand.

"Should we come back another time?" the ale-wife asked. "We just heard you were open and wanted to be your first customers."

Ulu's form of apology.

His gaze wandered over the broken chairs, the torn-up pots, and the dust of his receipts. "What did you need?" His voice as flat as the Euphrates. The tongs for making curls were broken; the device for smoothing waves was shattered. "All I can do is cut."

"Cut! That's what we wanted!"

"Exactly!"

"Cuts, and can you do a wash?"

One decent pot remained for washing; presumably they hadn't pissed in his well. "Sure," he said. "Cuts and a wash I can do."

"I'll run out and get us some breakfast brews," the ale-wife said.

"Don't—" Guli started; he didn't have the currency to pay.

"There is a competitive tavern around here," the ale-wife said. "I have heard rumors of her mash and want to try it. If you take some, it would help me out."

"Professional opinion and all," the priestess added. He'd seen her at the tavern, too, speaking of professionals.

Ulu's hand on his back was soothing, insistent. "We're your friends," she whispered. "Help us grow in our humanity by helping another human."

Guli looked at the ground of his shop, the house he'd worked so hard to find. "Thank you," he said to the ale-wife. "I'd love a beer."

~

The sheep were wide-awake at dawn, dancing with glee. *The grass is green, the sky is blue, who needs anything else when I have ewe?* The pun wasn't recognizable to the girl, but the intent of it was.

The goat was very interested in her new sash, but she kept his teeth off it as she checked the sheep for any cuts or wounds, any sign they weren't healthy or wouldn't feed well today. The lambs had grown so much, in just a few days. "I'll come back more often," she promised them. They were, after all, her family.

A quick flash of her receipt at the shepherd and she was out of the grazing area and walking back into the city.

A noise reverberated through her, across the bricks of the archway and down into the ground. *Thunder. A train. A 747.* As soon as it started, it stopped. People continued to walk around, though many were touching their ears. Chloe walked five more steps, and it began again.

An earthquake? The fury of the gods? She looked at the sky, which was cloudless and clear. It stopped again.

"No fear," a man shouted, "it's the drums, practicing up for the New Year."

No sooner did he say that, than the drums started again.

The noise got in her breastbone, made her teeth ache. Chloe hurried down the main street, and turned on Crooked Way.

The noise was muffled by the door to Ningal's house, and even quieter after she closed the door to her bedroom. The basin water was a little warm yet, so she washed her face with a cloth, then washed her hands clean of sheep smell. She wanted to curl up in the bed, beneath the new, pretty blankets, and dream of the god with the golden eyes.

Cheftu.

In her dreams he talked to her, he touched her, his kisses were like fire to her deepest core. In her dreams there were no words she didn't know, no expression was closed to her. Or to him.

In her dreams, she was his perfect consort. Moon to his sun, night to his day. He was the god of healing, she the goddess of war; he was the teacher of understanding, she the promoter of information; he made words from pictures, she made pictures for words.

In her dreams.

Instead, she smoothed oil over her head, straightened the sash of her dress, put on her bangles, and went back out. She had a *lugal* to corner.

Nimrod met up with her by the steps that led to the commonwealth's offices. "I can't thank you enough," she said. "I was so surprised—"

"Just don't throw up on him. Or pay attention when he shouts."

"Is he going to shout?"

Nimrod scratched his untamed, shaggy beard. "When he realizes he's in this trap, he's going to shout a lot."

Chloe stepped into the office first.

"You little she-dog—" the scribe muttered.

Nimrod stepped in behind her and stood there like a

hairy, panting bear, cutting the scribe off. "My father, the *lugal*, is in?"

"His door is closed," the scribe choked out. "Sir."

"Good," Nimrod said, taking Chloe's arm and striding past the man. He knocked once, then opened the door.

"What is this? *En*—"

"Father, I believe you've met Chloe."

Oh yeah, he'd met her. He began to enumerate how and why and when. Loudly.

She tuned him out; it was obvious Nimrod did, too. When finally the *lugal* had stopped shouting and had reseated himself, Nimrod reintroduced her. The *lugal's* expression toward his son wasn't pleasant, but Nimrod didn't seem to care. "You wanted to corner the animal in his den," Nimrod said to her. "You have fifteen minutes. I'll be outside."

Minutes. The word translated exactly to fifteen sixty-second intervals, or a quarter of an hour, an eighth of a double hour. *These people know minutes,* part of her mind marveled. *Who are they? Who am I? Where the hell is this?*

The *lugal* was a big man, handsome and meticulous in a way Nimrod was exactly not. He adjusted his Old Boy cloak. "What is it you want, female? Why does my own son catch me in my office?"

"I want to attend the Tablet House."

He blinked.

"Female humans don't go, I've been told," she said. "But it doesn't mean they can't. Or rather I can't. I want to learn how to read and write. I'm a human, it's my choice to learn, but you have to grant permission. At least according to what Justice Ningal said."

The *lugal* drummed his table. "This isn't a good time for a request."

"I've thrown up on you—for which, by the way, I apologize. I guess those oysters from the Scampi Stand were bad—so there is really not a good time for me to ask something of you, regardless of my request. Truth?"

He opened his mouth, then closed it. Pursed his lips and drummed his fingers some more. "Theoretically—"

"Yes?"

"Why go the Tablet House? Shouldn't you have mewling brats or something? A husband or a job? What did your mother do? There are some nice opportunities at the new weaving factory. I could speak to the forewoman on your behalf."

"I want to learn to read."

"Why?"

"Because I want to know."

"What do you need to know?"

She picked up a tablet from his desk. "What does this say?"

"It's a proposal from the silversmiths' karum, about trade."

"I want to know that."

"You do, I just told you."

"You could have told me anything. *I* don't know."

"I'm the *lugal*. I'm elected by the people and held to the standard of Enki, Enlil, Inana, and the council of the gods. I find it offensive you would even consider I'd tell a falsehood." His brown eyes were snapping mad.

"It's not that I don't trust you. It's that I trust myself more. I should be self-sufficient. Everyone should be able to read."

"First a female human should read, and now all of humanity? Who would work the fields? Geld the bulls? Sail the ships!" He sat forward and stacked his tablets. "Get out of my way, girl. You speak nonsense."

"The Tablet House session starts week after New Year's. I want to learn."

"Seduce some Tablet Father and have him teach you. There is no need to waste the time of a host of young and impressionable future clients and gentlemen."

She hadn't expected to win today—not right off the bat. What does that expression mean, she wondered at herself. But she'd made an impression. This was going to be a war of attrition. She wanted to go to school more than he didn't want her to go. It was just a question of patience. Who had more.

"Thank you for your time, *lugal*."

She opened the door, ignored the scribe, and smiled at Nimrod as she walked out. The drums didn't even bother her on the way home. One piece of advice had been useful—she could get someone to start teaching her.

Two someones came to mind, immediately.

The Festival of the New Year began for everyone in Ur at the same moment: The black-leather kettledrums that had been practicing for three days struck in earnest and in concert. Every temple had at least two; the larger and more prestigious the temple and its gods, the more kettledrums they had.

Ur vibrated.

Outside the city, the animals cried in alarm.

Outside the commonwealth, others looked toward the horizon, expecting angry gray clouds and the continued fury of the gods. Inside the other cities, the citizens couldn't hear the kettledrums, because they had their own.

At breakfast, Ningal, Kalam, and Chloe sipped beers and tried to enjoy the relative calm in between the striking of the drums.

"This is why," Ningal finally shouted, "it is best to get drunk on New Year's and stay that way for the whole week."

"Sounds like a plan," Chloe shouted back.

Kalam made notes on his tablets and drank his beer without comment.

Nirg and Nimrod were in their marital bed. The solemn intonation of the drum was too slow for Nimrod, and the rhythm of it was wrong for Nirg. In the end she went to the kitchens and brought back curds and honey. Even when there was no sex, or bad sex, with Nirg there was always food.

Lea, in her own bed, with nothing except a statue of Pazuzu for company, poured a beer libation to the king of demons and asked for either a pregnancy or a lover. It didn't matter which, but she was bored. As the wife of the *lugal's* son, her mother-in-law didn't want her working in the factory. Lea didn't know anything except weaving, and missed the women she used to work with—before Nimrod saw her and carried her into his rooms, seduced her through honey-soaked days until she couldn't refuse him. Then his father found out her father had no money, and the feud began. Since Nimrod had already taken her as a bride, however, not much could be done.

The man had a weakness for fair hair; thank Pazuzu there weren't that many blondes in the city, or she would be praying for a wealth of lovers or a litter of children. Lea drank the rest of Pazuzu's libation offering and hid her head under the pillow. She hated New Year's.

Ezzi had just taken to his bed when the drums began. The stars had gone for the night, and he had finished his last, careful notations. Nothing had changed with the new star. It seemed to be alone, unconcerned with the motion of the other flocks in the sky. Ezzi could be the one to name the twenty-sixth star. He could think of nothing else except the glory of that day.

The drums banged on; he guessed that glory probably wouldn't come this day.

~

Downstairs, Ulu let herself in the front door. Too much beer and three different suitors had made her day fantastic, if half-forgotten. The drums wouldn't be too joyful in a few hours. For gods who turned the whole world to a slab of clay because it was too noisy, it made no sense they would demand noise on New Year's, but who was she to ask. As Ezzi delighted in reminding her, she was a whore.

A prostitute. A well-paid, well-endowed, talented female companion.

She belched.

A whore who wanted her chamber pot and a few hours of quiet in which to sleep. "Though I might have to go to the marsh to get any quiet," she groused as she walked through the courtyard and up the steps to her apartments. Ezzi's door was shut; no light shone through the cracks. She scanned the roof for her son's silhouette, but he wasn't there.

Of course, it was just past dawn, so he would be finished with the stars by now.

Ulu belched again, then opened the door to her apartments and shut it behind her.

Guli was already on his first two clients of the day. Thanks to Ulu's word and a few extra minae of barley, he was back in business. Prostitutes from four corners of the city were in early. Today would be the busiest for them, before the population got completely soused and before the temple priestesses—whores, these women called them—were "released" on duty.

This was a prostitute's golden day.

One was getting her hair straightened; one wanted a cut; one was getting her body waxed—no hair at all? The last girl wanted to be a redhead with ... matching equipment. Guli mixed the dye and hoped to Inana he had enough, for she was a broad woman. He pitied the man who didn't bring enough to pay her; she could break him with her hands.

~

"Most majestic one," they greeted him. Shama bowed his head and accepted the dual-horned crown of the *ensi*. The drums tolled in his stomach as he knocked on the copper-plated doors.

"She who is fair as Inana, strong as Sin, and beloved of the court," they sang. "Wake and greet the New Year, given to thee as a gift for a bride."

Puabi opened the door, naked and painted with gold. Shama bent at the knee and offered her the crown that was hers. For Puabi, a granddaughter of Ziusudra and the most highly cherished woman in Ur, was *ensi*, the elected leader of the temple.

Inana in the flesh, she was the spiritual consort of the commercial leader, who was the *lugal*—another elected position. Puabi appointed the *en*, the high priest who guaranteed fertility within the city of Ur.

Puabi put the crown on her head and smiled greetings at Shama. Because it was the New Year, she was sequestered until the stargazers proclaimed the New Year had actually arrived. Shama didn't keep track, he was only her chamber keeper, but it felt like the New Year came late this year. Usually it happened on the spring equinox, but that had been almost a month ago. Easy to remember, because that was when the moon turned red and the Euphrates had drowned the northern villages and marshes.

The floodwaters had sent rats by the thousands down the riverbed. Some detoured into Ur and were roasted on sticks and sold to those with undiscriminating palates, but most ran headlong into the southern sea. He guessed they either swam their way to Dilmun, or drowned.

Of all things Shama hated, rats were the most despised.

Puabi turned her back to them all, and they prostrated themselves again until her door was shut.

The drums didn't bother Shama; he was deaf to them because he'd lived in the temple since the Deluge. The beat of the kettledrums traveled up through his feet though, until he had to check that bugs weren't on him. Shama hated bugs, too, especially the big black beetles that fell onto his bed in the night, and squished when he rolled over on them.

Shama led the priests and acolytes, those perfect boys and men, into the depths of the temple. The statues were there, the graven images of Ninhursag and Enlil, Inana and Pazuzu, Shamash, Sin, and a half dozen others whose names he couldn't remember. The only one who wasn't represented was the leader of them all.

The god of gods was too mighty for clay or gold. He drew his finger in the sky, he didn't need priests and temples, he spoke to men directly. He didn't confide in the silly gods of the storm, and the clouds, and the sun; they were merely his courtiers, his employees, and thus beneath him.

Humans didn't even know the god of gods' name.

Shama pointed out the newly woven clothes for each of the statues, the jewels they would wear, the tapers and votives that would accompany the statues as they were walked from their temples to Sin's. Then he showed the priests their clothes.

New Year's, as far as Shama could tell, was just about noise and clothes. Everyone got new clothes. It was a conspiracy of the weavers' karum, but he couldn't prove it. And no one listened to an old man who remembered the Deluge.

If he could remember the Deluge and talk about it, he probably would have pleased his parents and become a lawyer. Then people would listen to him, most assuredly. But the same curse that was laid on the crow for its greed had been laid on Shama's speech: He stammered. He sounded like a stuck door. Consequently, other than the ritual words muttered once a year, he hadn't spoken for decades.

Perfect for maintaining the secrets of the temple.

Even if he thought the gods were whining brats who needed discipline.

Shama watched the young priests get to work. The big blond Kidu was Puabi's personal project, brought in from the mountains, trained by her own hands. His was an insatiable appetite for food and procreation; already the females of Ur lined up for his services. The man's mind was disproportionately small for his body, which made him a perfect, malleable vessel within the temple hierarchy. Kidu would be high priest, the *en*, next.

Shama picked up his new fringed skirt and walked up the stairs. If he calculated right, he could take a long nap before he was required again.

The population of Ur danced in the streets below them. Ezzi didn't hear their cries of joy or ecstasy. The blood had drained from his face, and he felt like he might be ill. "Bad?" he repeated. "It's a bad star?"

"Evil," the stargazer said, his eyes closed. Was he speaking from the gods themselves? "The Tablets of Destiny proclaim blood must atone."

"Atone for what?" Ezzi asked.

Another stargazer slapped the back of Ezzi's head and knocked his basket hat askew. "Atone for anything. The gods don't have to give you a reason," he hissed.

Ezzi, trembling, nodded and looked back at the great stargazer. "Who, whose . . . blood?"

The great stargazer bowed his head. Like all priests and servers of the gods, he was a perfectly shaped male human. Ezzi knew that the stargazer's hearing, sight, taste, and touch were to be without flaw. The gods declared who would serve them most closely by making them the most appealing of humans.

Ezzi, as a boy, had been declared unfit because his left ear was a thumb's width higher than his right ear. Across from him sat a worthy man, whose ears were perfectly symmetrical, whose eyes were almond-shaped and long-lashed. His eyebrows curved over his eyes and met in the exact center of his forehead, then progressed down his nose to stop exactly even with his eyes.

Ezzi wasn't worthy to even breathe in his presence.

"I had hoped I was wrong, for I foretold many years ago this star would appear," the stargazer said. Even his voice was perfect. Comforting and strong.

"You, you, knew the star would appear?"

The other stargazer slapped Ezzi's head again. "He is the great stargazer, boy. Did you think you would see something he hadn't?"

Minute by minute, Ezzi felt more miserable. Hopes of a copper tub had faded; now he just hoped he wouldn't be assigned corvée duty for daring to speak to the stargazer.

The man shook his head, the curls of his beard black, glossy, and perfectly even. "It is a sad day for the Black-

Haired Ones between the rivers. What we have done, what humanity has brought upon themselves, what the gods have chosen to take offense over, I cannot imagine."

"Will the earth be as blank clay again?" Ezzi asked. Had the flooding to the north been foreshadowing? Had that been the proclamation of the reddened moon?

"The Tablets of Destiny do not say, boy," the stargazer said. He opened his eyes, as brown as the mud of the city, and fixed them on Ezzi. He fought to keep the great one's gaze. "It touches you personally."

"Me?" Ezzi's voice was a squeak like he hadn't made since his first years at the Tablet House.

The great stargazer nodded. "You must seek out your personal gods and demons and see what service you can offer so the gods will spare you."

Ezzi didn't speak to his personal god very often. He had an altar in his room with a Watcher statue, he poured libations, but more from force of habit; he didn't even remember the name of his personal demon. Maybe that was the problem. Neglect. He wasn't aware the big gods even cared about the little, personal gods.

There were a lot of gods, if each person had his or her own god, his or her personal demon, add in the pantheon of demigods—about five hundred of them, and the court of big gods, which was at least another fifty. Maybe families shared personal gods or demons? He would have to ask his mother who were her personal gods and demons. But if offending any one of them could bring down the wrath of any other one of them . . .

It was a wonder humanity hadn't been destroyed more times than it had.

Thirty thousand times two, plus five hundred, plus fifty . . . 60,550 gods could be offended.

Ezzi needed to relieve himself. And he thought he should probably pray. A lot.

"Come back to me in three days' time, at the end of the festival," the great one said. "I will intercede for you, see what can be done. Go."

Ezzi fled, raced down the stairs, jostled by people and desperate for his chamber pot. He probably shouldn't relieve himself on the temple; one of those 60,550 gods might get offended. He paused by a palm tree—did palm trees have personal gods? Demons? Something could climb up his—he raced on, just in case.

The streets were clogged with dancers and gymnasts, fire breathers and diviners. People were packed together like fish for sale.

It was dark, it was crowded.

He couldn't help himself. He moved his cloak open and stood tight against the person in front of him. The relief he felt was almost spiritual. All the beer from the day, fermented with excitement, date-palm wine and holy water from the Euphrates, rushed through his body and out against the cloak of the person in front of him. He dried off, straightened his robe, and moved across the crowd, content to watch the street show.

Chapter Six

Chloe looked at the scratches on the clay in front of her. Morning light shadowed the deep marks in the clay, so they looked like wedges. "So you're telling me the sign of the man's head, means man."

"It could mean male human," Kalam said patiently.

"Or it could mean head—"

"Or mouth or eyes or face," he said.

"Or, the phonetic rendering of *lu*."

"Truth."

"Or the determinative, to let me know someone's—a male human's, in this case—name is coming up."

"Yes."

She looked at the complicated symbol—five marks to make one word? And he had to write with his elbow sticking out so he wouldn't ruin the symbols he'd made already. "How many signs are there?"

Kalam scribbled something on the clay.

"What's that?"

"The number showing how many—it's approximately seven hundred."

"Each one has all those different meanings, so you need to remember thirty-five hundred different things to be competent."

"Yes."

"Is eleven years, from dawn till twilight, enough time?"

Kalam looked at her, suspicious of ridicule. "The wine clouds your head yet," he said slowly. "Either that or the urine," he said as he elbowed her.

"I only hope I can get that dress clean!" she said. One of last night's revelers had relieved himself on her. *A Mardi Gras ancestor,* the voice in her head said.

"Are you ready to try?" he asked, holding the handle of the reed stylus toward her.

This isn't going to be the way it was before, she thought. *More like memorizing art than learning an alphabet. Those are just syllables and pictures. Writing in this place and time is a rebus.*

"What's wrong?" he asked; Chloe had torn at her head, her hair, rubbed her ears fiercely. "Are you ill?"

Don't tell him you hear voices. Even in this day and age—whenever it is—that's a bad sign.

"Just . . . my head aching," she said.

"Do you need some nourishment?"

"No, no thank you."

"You are becoming quite pale, I mean, for a Khamite." He stood up. "I am going to the tavern to wait for Ningal. You should rest."

She nodded. "I should."

He's being awfully pleasant, the voice said. *What's up with that?* Chloe smiled weakly at Kalam, then hurried off to her apartments.

"Chloe?" he called.

She turned back. "Yes?"

"Who is your personal demon?"

"Pazuzu."

"Ah, good choice. And your personal god?"

Music, unlike a song she'd ever heard before, beat in her

head. A man sang in a rough voice. *"Your own, personal—"*

"Jesus," she called.

"Just one? Well, do you need an altar for him? her? I'm sorry, I don't recognize the name. A god of the marshes?"

"Of shepherds."

"Ahh, I see. Do you have a votary? A statue? A watcher?"

The song continued to play in the background of her mind, words she didn't know, but understood conceptually. The marsh girl knew that votives, statues, and watchers, substitutes for the devoted one, with enormous eyes and fervent expressions, were used to feed the gods' need for attention. Humans were merely slaves before divine owners. "A votive would be nice," she said. "I never thought about it."

"It will be my New Year's gift to you," Kalam said, then waved.

"Kalam," she said, turning to him. "Instead of writing so awkwardly straight down the clay, and right to left, why not write across it, left to right, so you don't smudge the marks as you go?"

Kalam stared at her. Speechless.

"Anyway," she said. "Tell Ningal hello from me." She left him standing in the doorway as she climbed the steps to her apartment. The pounding of the kettledrums was past, but the noise in her head had grown a thousand times louder. Voices, thoughts, and pictures. Her mind ached just being awake. Chloe went to her room, took off her clothes, and crawled into her palm-frond bed.

"Jesus," she said softly to her personal shepherd god, "I think I'm losing my reason. Help me be good, to do the right thing. And please make my head stop aching."

She closed her eyes and willed the voice to sleep, too.

⌒

Shama peered through the darkness, to the tangle of bodies. The smell of opium was thick in the room. He held up his taper and looked at the mass of barely conscious worshipers. Kidu, the mountain man–cum–high priest in training, was flat on his back, with three women curled around him. He was snoring; they were bleary-eyed and drugged.

He shook Kidu's leg.

"Sleep," one woman said. "He's useless."

Another woman demonstrated his uselessness. "Opium," she slurred out. "We took it, too, since he did."

Of course, if the high priest of fertility were unable to perform, why should his followers be frustrated. Shama sighed in disgust. With the flat of his blade, he swatted Kidu's thigh.

Kidu attacked him. Shama had no defense. In a second he was in darkness, his throat constricted. Growling, shouting, pleading tones—Shama couldn't hear clearly. But Shama felt Kidu's hands around his throat.

To live so long and end up killed by a barbarian. Shama's head was hot; perhaps his brains were going to explode from his ears.

"Let him go," he finally heard someone say to Kidu. "You're going to kill Shama, then the *ensi* will kill you."

Kidu dropped him, and Shama fell to the floor, landing on some soft woman. Everything went black. When he awoke, the three women were fanning him, perfuming his wrists, and praying. Fervently.

Kidu stared at him balefully. Shama had met oxen with far more wit. The drugs had melted his brains like beeswax. This wild man had embraced the worst civilization had to offer—and Shama was almost sorry for him. As long as he pleased Puabi, though, he was free to do and be anything he desired. If he didn't, then like so many of his predecessors, he would be removed.

"It's the *ensi's* chamber keeper," one of the women told Kidu, massaging her words into Shama's skin. "Puabi must be requesting you."

"Puabi?" Kidu repeated. "Puabi wants me? Now? Now?"

Shama nodded, and Kidu stood up on the bed, repeating his sentence. *Puabi wants me? Now? Now?* He dragged Shama up. The old man winced as he felt his bones rub together.

"Be careful," one of the women said. The other two proceeded to wish the mountain man a long, fond farewell.

Shama watched Kidu with the women and as his head cleared he realized the barbarian was aroused again. At least Puabi wouldn't be disappointed. As for Shama, he was going to order a long, hot bath in a copper tub. With mint beer.

～

Kalam sat back from his beer tube. In his right hand he held the parcel of Chloe's gift, her votive. Before him was a clay tablet, with the symbols written as she suggested although it was easier to make them sideways from the changed angle. Writing them had been more comfortable, and Kalam was amazed at how quickly he'd been able to write when he didn't have to hold his arm up, away from the clay.

A female human, an ignorant Khamite, couldn't have thought of this. Where did she get it? Who else had she told? He tried to not think of how honored he would be if he made the suggestion to his former Tablet Father.

Kalam rubbed the clay smooth as Ningal took a seat, kissed his greeting to the ale-wife, and ordered wine instead of beer, much to her dismay. After a swat on the bottom and promise of double payment, the two men were left in relative privacy.

"How is Chloe today?" Ningal asked. He'd been visiting today, exchanging New Year's blessings with friends and cousins.

"Complaining of headaches."

"How did your first lesson go?"

Kalam's gaze met his employer's. "You were correct; she was nonplussed when I explained how the signs worked. She was astounded when she learned how many different ways they could be read and interpreted."

"Sometimes with female humans, it is best to give them what they think they want. Or, in this case, a sample of it."

Kalam sipped some beer. "I have never heard you doubt a female before, Justice."

He shrugged. "A lawmaker learns about people. You'll see someday."

Kalam's gaze froze over Ningal's shoulder. "You won't believe who just walked in," he said. "An old acquaintance of yours. Don't turn."

Guli halted when he saw Kalam; Kalam watched his gaze fix on and recognize the justice who had put him in the canals. Guli braced his wide shoulders, waved to the alewife, and came over to their table. "Greetings of the New Year to you, Justice, and you, Kalam."

"Guli!" the justice said. "I assume you are staying out of trouble, since I haven't seen you in court."

Kalam looked at the man's waist; still no seal. Some people never did anything with the chances they were given.

"I have my own shop," he said.

Kalam exchanged a dubious look with Ningal.

"I am a hairdresser."

"Greetings, Guli," a red-haired, voluptuous beauty said,

her long fingers trailing across his shoulders. "Greetings, gentlemen." Her gaze was frankly admiring of Kalam and the justice. Ningal ignored her, not to the point of rudeness, but because he had no use for women other than priestesses . . . and Chloe. Kalam smiled at the woman, but his thoughts were arrested. Chloe? Was the justice keeping the Khamite woman as a concubine?

"That gorgeous creature is one of my clients," Guli said. "You are well, Justice?"

"The gods are good, Guli."

"Glad to hear it, Justice. Well, gentlemen, if you will excuse me. A quick beer before I pick up my seal at the inscribers today."

They bid him a good New Year and he walked off. Kalam couldn't look at his employer. Would he congress with a Khamite woman?

"It's a good omen to see a man taking opportunities," the justice said. "His own shop and a girlfriend, besides. She lives on my street, I believe."

Kalam looked at the justice in shock. "I thought you only, uh, congressed, with priestesses."

The justice's gaze was amused over his clay goblet of wine. "I know where the female lives because I've seen the deed to the house." He held Kalam's glance. "Is something bothering you, young man?"

"Do you think Chloe is pretty?"

"No."

Kalam sighed almost audibly.

"No, not pretty. I think she is the most attractive woman I've ever known. She's radiant, quiet, complicated, and by moonlight . . . not even Inana, in all her glory, can compare."

Kalam was shattered. In his effort to be nonchalant, he accidentally stuffed the drinking tube up his nostril. He jerked back from the reed, cut his lip and nose in the process, and upset the jar so it nearly toppled over.

After the ale-wife straightened the jar, gave Kalam a salve for his nose and lip, and a flax cloth to pat the little bit of blood, then cut him a new reed and buffed the edge to a less than lethal blade, Kalam met the justice's bemused stare.

For all his life, Kalam had known Ningal; no man was more admired for his eloquence, his fairness, and his humanity. He'd turned down the responsibility of *lugal*, had even declined to be *en*, in favor of practicing justice without bias. His children were well established in nearby Lagash, his son served as the *lugal* there. His grandchildren were wealthy shipwrights in Eridu, on the shore of the southern sea. Great-grandchildren of his were scattered through apprenticeships and Tablet Houses across the land of the Black-Haired Ones. Ningal was above reproach in every way.

His concubine was a marsh dweller who kept sheep?

"I need to go to my office," Ningal said. "I have tablets to oversee."

"Shall I come, sir?" Officially, it was Kalam's last day off, before work began in the new year.

"Enjoy today," Ningal said. "I'll see you at dawn tomorrow."

"Thank you," Kalam said, rising as the older man got to his feet and paid the ale-wife."

"One thing," Ningal said, laying a heavy hand on Kalam's shoulder. "Chloe may be taken aback by your first lesson. It won't stop her from pushing to attend school. She'll master all you teach her and be that much further ahead whenever she does get her way." He clapped the aide on the shoulder, a friendly gesture. "Just bear that in mind when you have to tell your old tablet master, or Asa the stargazer, or the *lugal*, or whoever put you up to tutoring her so she'd be scared, that it didn't work. She'll make fools of them all."

Kalam's face was hot. "I, I see sir."

"You don't see dung, but you're young. You can't." Ningal almost laughed, then turned away and left the tavern. Kalam sat back slowly and stared at the drinking tube. Chloe's votive, the one he'd bought her this afternoon, sat on the edge of the table. Chloe, the Khamite concubine of his master. Chloe, who wanted to learn in the Tablet House and upset all of the balance in Ur. Chloe, the shepherdess. Chloe, the wealthy woman. Chloe, the female human. Chloe, who revolutionized how to write, without knowing it. Chloe, who plagued him.

Kalam kneed the table.

The votive crashed to the floor.

⌐

"I can scarcely walk," Ulu announced, plopped down in her chair, legs akimbo. Ezzi didn't even look at her. "Where is all the food?" she asked.

"I, I was hungry," he said. In truth, he was less than hungry. He had walked up and down the Crooked Way leaving beer and bread and morsels of meat for each of the hundred gods and goddesses who had votive alcoves set in the walls along the street.

Ulu's expression was sly. "Making your own heat during New Year's, boy? Tell me, I'll find out her name, and we can work something so you get it at a discount."

His ears burned. "Not a . . . a female human," he said. "I have spent many hours with the stars."

"By Sin," she groaned. "There is nothing to eat after I spent a week getting us gold because you had to watch the sky? When has the sky changed? Even when Ziusudra sailed the sea, it remained the same." She dropped one leg to the ground.

He should offer to get her food, or send for food. The slaves were doing laundry by the river. "The sky changes every twenty-eight days," he said.

"Good," she snapped. "So does my woman's blood."

Ezzi stood there and stared at her. She turned her face to his, and he saw that one eye was bruised shut.

"Don't worry," she said to him. "I enjoyed it."

He wrapped his cloak tighter. "I'll be back in a few minutes," he said.

"Be careful, that's not starlight in the alleyway. It's called daylight, and people who work for a living—"

He shut the courtyard door, then remembered he didn't have anything to barter with. He stepped inside. "There is no—"

She got up and limped to the clothes she'd just stepped out of on her way to the table. She extracted three, four, five bags of jewelry and barley. Ezzi stared in wonder; she made this by having sex?

"Don't look so astounded. I may not know about the stars, but I can tell you how to make a man—"

Ezzi grabbed a bag and ran for the door, closing it on her laughter. So much currency! He looked into it again, just in case he hadn't seen clearly. Had she always been paid this much? All these years, she'd been hoarding this away from him? He could order a copper tub; he could order five copper tubs!

He tied the bag and tucked it inside his cloak. Who did the banking for his mother, that was what he wanted to know. Sleep, gods, and goddesses were forgotten. Even hunger, his and Ulu's.

How did one go about learning about bankers?

~

"Why do you want to learn?" Nimrod asked, tossing a rock at the water. Kami, a fat-tailed, black-spotted sheep, ran after it.

"I've never seen a sheep that plays fetch," Chloe said, watching the sheep look in the swiftly running stream for the rock. And of course, being sheep, the others followed. Mimi, the goat, was too busy nibbling along the edge of the fields. Chloe absently swatted the goat and led it toward the stream, the sheep. "It's a compulsion," she said, as they crossed the narrow black furrows that would sprout lentils, onions, and cucumbers in a few days. "A possession."

He chuckled. "Don't use that word with anyone but me, or you'll be in the exorcist's chair faster than you can say, 'but I only have credit.'"

She chuckled, and they spent a few minutes getting the sheep and goat, then all the sheep, across the stream and onto the northeastern grazing grounds. "What's that?" she said, looking across the plain. A standing stone marred the horizon line.

"A boundary marker for the city of Lagash."

"Is it nicer than Ur?"

Nimrod shrugged. "If you like cities, Ur is a good example. If you like a quieter, simpler place and people, Lagash is fine. They don't have a wall, so it doesn't feel as . . . tight, as Ur can." He scratched his beard. "Even then, neither of them is as impressive or useful as a city could be."

"Is it safe?" Chloe said, turning her attention to the sheep. "I mean, with no wall."

"No one to fear, at least right now."

"Are we really the only people, besides the Harrapan or Dilmuni?"

"In this whole world?" he asked, looking around him.

She looked, too. Green fields, black dirt, and muddy water filled her vision. To the northwest, the direction her village had been, was only water and palm trees. No other survivors had shown up at the gates of Ur. Nimrod said the *lugal* had surmised other survivors went to Nippur or Kish, farther north. Nimrod guessed they took what remained of their flocks and headed farther west. Away from the water, toward the land of Kham. "Why do you ask?" he said.

The sheep were contentedly feeding; even the goat was quiet. Chloe sat down on the soft earth and stretched out her legs. She was in her felted skirt and bare feet, like a sheepherder should be. Nimrod wore a loincloth, but his body hair was so profuse he looked like he wore a black pelt. The sun was warm, pleasant, and a breeze moved across the fields and the water, making it cool and perfumed with the sweetness of growing things.

"Well, you think I'm crazy already, so it doesn't hurt to tell you, I guess," Chloe said, opening the basket she'd brought. With careful motions she untied the parcel within and handed one of the round items to Nimrod.

"What is it?"

"It's good. Try it."

He ate one, gobbled two, then three. Nimrod crossed his arms behind his head and squinted into the sun. "You can tell me anything now. You can't shock me."

"How's that?"

"I just learned you can cook."

She swatted him with the flax cloth. "It surprised me, too."

"You didn't know?"

"That, my friend, is the problem," she said, staring at his upturned face. "I'm two people inside."

He opened an eye and gazed at her for a moment. "Split evenly, or fighting for power?"

"Neither."

"What's the other person like? Which one of you is the cook?" Nimrod sat up. "Are there any more of those round things to eat?"

"One more," she said, handing it to him. "I think I'm the cook. But she's like me, almost exactly."

"Then why do you say two people?" He looked confused.

"Because it's another mind, other memories and knowledge."

"Fighting for control over you?"

"No, not usually. Usually commenting on what I do, but what I do is exactly what she would do. If she were me."

Nimrod lay back down and closed his eyes. Chloe watched the sheep. "Don't go too far," she called to one who was starting to wander. "I'm talking to you."

I'm talking to ewe. Eweee that's baaaad.

Dadi, the sheep, looked up, gave a sheep's pouting huff, and moved back into the flock.

"You're telling me, well . . . let me understand. Here's you," Nimrod said, holding up one hand. "Just you."

"Truth."

"Then this other person, the other mind." He held up his other hand.

"Truth."

"But it's not trying to invade you."

"No, she's there already."

"Not trying to hurt you."

"No."

"Doesn't do anything."

"Chatters a lot, in ways I don't understand."

"Words you don't know?" he said, sitting up on one elbow.

"I understand what she's saying, I just don't comprehend exactly how she's saying it."

He stretched, his hair-tufted fingers playing in the grass. "You have a personal demon, I guess."

Chloe sighed. "I wish. It doesn't do things for me."

"Doesn't carry out curses, huh?"

"Do you think the scribe in your father's office would still be able to walk upright if I could cast curses?" she asked.

Nimrod laughed. "That scribe must have a very powerful exorcist in his employ. No one likes that man."

"That's not the worst part, though."

"It doesn't sound so bad. A friend inside your head. At least it's a friend, not an enemy. Not trying to throw you off a roof, or make you dance naked before your flocks, or something."

She laughed at Nimrod, then shouted at the sheep.

"What's the worst part?" he asked.

"This other person, personality, is in love."

Nimrod sat up and looked at her with great interest. "With whom?"

"I don't know."

"You don't know him? Have you seen him?"

"Only in her dreams. At first I thought he was a god, he had very unusual eyes. Now—I don't know. I don't know how she got in my head or what she's doing there."

"Have you asked her?"

The glance she gave him was withering. "Only madmen and priests talk to themselves. I can barely tell you about this—and you're my closest friend."

He patted her hand. "I am glad you can. What are you going to do?"

"Maybe an exorcism wouldn't be a bad idea."

"I know a good diviner," he said. "And then there's the exorcist my mother used on my father."

"The *lugal* was possessed?"

"I don't think so, but it forced him to be more discreet. That was all she cared about." He tore at the ground a little longer. "Is this other person, is she the compulsion to go to the Tablet House?"

"That is where we are too closely woven to tell apart. The Harrapan have a statue, Pasupati, with several heads and many arms. This is like one body with two heads. Our hearts and desires are the same, but our minds are separate."

"Not in conflict, though?"

"No. Not yet anyway." Dadi was starting to wander again. Chloe got up and herded him back, with a reminding swat on his fat-tailed rump not to do it again. "She might be the reason I don't remember anything before, about my village."

"I thought that was because you hit your head."

She shrugged. "I don't know. I know nothing."

"What is her name?"

"Chloe."

Nimrod frowned. "What's yours then?"

She lifted her hands and shoulders, baffled. "I have no idea."

⟶

"We don't need a new *ensi*!" Rudi the stargazer said.

"Asa said we do; he said it is what the star says," Gem argued.

"Asa hasn't been able to see the stars for six summers," Rudi scoffed. "How can he interpret an omen for a star he can't see?"

Gem adjusted his basket hat and leaned back. "The *ensi* must leave. Asa said that is the message the gods send."

Rudi sat down opposite and looked at the replica sheep's liver—an exorcist's tool. Her charts of the stars were scattered across the table, beside it. "A new star has appeared, there is no doubt of that."

"So Asa says."

"But it has only been a few weeks! How can he know what it means? We haven't had time to study it at all!" Rudi gestured to the materials in front of him. "Generations it took to gauge when and where these known twenty-five stars appeared. Generations before we could recognize the shifting flocks in the sky. Where is Asa's sense of judgment, of intellectual intercourse."

Gem sighed and stared at Rudi. "The lands are at stake. The gods are displeased. The *ensi* must step down in order to protect them. That is what Asa said. He was almost in tears when he told us. A man doesn't cry for no reason."

"Asa cries in hope it will clear his vision."

"You better be careful, Rudi. You are the least favorite at the council, and if anyone overhears what you say, slander, about Asa—"

"They could take me to court, and we would test Asa's vision and everyone would know. He's a stargazer who barely recognizes when it's night!"

"Bitterness is not an attractive cloak, Rudi. Especially not on you."

Rudi looked at the table. "The *ensi* isn't going to surrender her position willingly. Puabi is too cunning for that."

"If she realizes she is doing it for the sake of the lands, she will."

"It won't hold up before the council's scrutiny."

"The *lugal* already believes it."

"A month of probation, and I miss a lot, don't I?"

"You did it to yourself, Rudi. You completely missed the bloodmoon—"

"It was not my—"

"—then you refuse to take responsibility. You're lucky I'm willing to risk—"

"I am, Gem. I apologize for my wretched behavior."

"Since Puabi is your sister, though, I thought you should know."

Rudi looked at the table again. "Thank you." She sighed. "Did Asa have a time line for when the *ensi* had to leave?"

"If he did, he didn't mention it. It wasn't a full cabinet meeting, Rudi, just a few stargazers and the *lugal*."

"Who really discovered the star, Gem? We both know it wasn't Asa."

Gem looked at Rudi. "A young man, barely an Old Boy."

"Whose Tablet House?"

He shook his head. "I don't know, but his name is Ezzi."

"Ezzi. A stargazer." Rudi looked out the window over Gem's shoulder. "I will place a curse on Ezzi. The brat."

~

Outside the window, flattened against the wall, the self-same Ezzi dared not breathe. Overhearing this conversation hadn't been his intent; he'd gotten lost coming back from seeing Asa stargazer. How was he to know that Rudi, the most outspoken and least favored of the stargazers, would be right there?

It was an omen from the gods, that must be it!

A good omen, or bad, a diviner would have to tell him. The stairway behind him, the pathway out of the mass of temples and storehouses and palaces, was somewhere below that. He had to cross the section of light that streamed from the window. The window where Rudi the stargazer had almost seen him.

Inside, they weren't speaking. Ezzi looked over his shoulder; he could walk the circumference of this level of the ziggurat and get to the stairs that way. A much better plan. Keeping to the shadows, he walked away from the staircase to arrive at it.

He prayed at the shrines of all the gods and demons along the way.

Chapter Seven

"Good day, *lugal*," Chloe said, poking her head into his office. The scribe was gone—maybe he was hanging himself. One could hope.

The *lugal* groaned and sat back. "How have you come to cast a bane on me today?"

"Time to break your fast," she said, striding into his office and setting a basket on his desk. "I brought you food."

"Ah, a curse in every bite?"

"Just try one, see what you think." She unwrapped flax cloth from some round items and handed one to him. "Don't be so suspicious. I haven't murdered anyone yet."

He sniffed it, a wary eye on her. Chloe sighed and bit one herself. "See?" she said through the food. "It won't kill you."

The *lugal* bit, chewed, and a beatific expression crossed his face. "This must be an offering for the gods! What is this?"

"It's my specialty. If," she said, leaning over to the rapidly chewing man, "if only I could write, I could make you a recipe."

He rolled his eyes, but kept eating.

"If your wife could read, she could take my recipe and make these for you every day."

He grabbed another one, moaning like a man in love.

"Or if I wanted to, and I could write, I would make them, and write the recipe for them. Then I could open a shop, with other people who could read and write. They could make them and sell them to tradesmen and visitors from other cities."

The *lugal* chewed a little more slowly now.

"Those people, in other cities, if they could read and write, could make the food and sell it. Because it was my recipe that I wrote, and they read, they would pay me a percentage of what they made. Because I would be a citizen of the great, noble, literate city of Ur, that would be taxed."

Chloe sat down and wrapped up the last remaining piece. "If . . . I could write."

The *lugal* swallowed his bite, wiped his mouth, and his eyes followed Chloe's movements as she put the last piece away. "I can't let you attend a Tablet House," he said. "It would be too upsetting to the commonwealth. How are your lessons going?"

She smiled and picked up his reed stylus and a fresh slab of clay. Biting her lip in concentration she wrote out a message, laid it in front of him, smiled, picked up her basket, and walked out.

"You can't call me an idiot!" he shouted at her back after reading the message. "I'm the *lugal*."

"Whore dog," the scribe whispered as he passed her.

"Festering rodent," she whispered back.

Chloe stepped into the sunshine of the street and handed Nimrod the last piece. "Phase one is under way."

He grinned. "Nirg will love you forever for giving her food."

She laughed as she walked home.

"It's all the time," one of the women complained. "Kidu is insatiable."

"Poor Puabi, no wonder no one has seen her for days."

"I've heard on opium, he's more intense."

"Ah, but you can't take drugged seed," another woman said. "It would make a drugged infant."

"Then someone needs to take the opium away, or none of us will fulfill our duties."

The priestesses continued to discuss the newest *en*, Kidu, and the *ensi*. Shama squinted at the necklace he was rebeading and listened to them. He never ceased to wonder at women's capacity to make excuses for worthless male humans. The priests and acolytes had only to smile, and they were fawned upon. Their beauty was legendary, and none more than the *en*. The soon-to-be-*en*, Shama corrected himself. If Puabi continued to be pleased, today she would set the boat of his appointment to sail, and none could reclaim it. Today she would recommend Kidu to the council, formally.

En Kidu. It had a ring, Shama had to admit.

"He looks like the sun god should," one of the women said, leaning back. "Bronze and gold."

"And he's so hot, his very skin is like touching the sun," someone else said.

"Did he do—" they bent their heads together. Shama couldn't hear; he was disappointed. His wasn't prurient interest, he just wanted to be certain Puabi was receiving the best the mountain man had to give.

The women shrieked with laughter, then sighed and groaned and began to discuss who would visit him next.

Shama tied off the end of the necklace and stood. He could have eliminated Kidu's chances by telling Puabi of their confrontation, Kidu's attempt to kill him. However, Shama knew Puabi had worked so hard to get the *en*, to bring him to the temple. For the first time in her life, she had invested herself in someone, given something, embraced her humanity. Shama was pleased with that. If Kidu were the reason why Puabi had a lightness in her step or brightness in her smile, then Shama would help Kidu become *en*.

After the ratification, he would inform Kidu there was an outstanding debt.

Not because Shama cared about payback, but because after centuries of working in the temple, he knew that was how power was brokered here. It was tradition.

～

The next day, Chloe was back. The *lugal* had a group of people in his office. She smiled as she walked in, set a tablet on his desk, smiled at the men again, and left.

Nimrod sat in the shade of a palm with the goat, whittling.

"What is that?" she asked, sitting down beside him. She batted Mimi's inquisitive teeth away.

"A seal," he said.

"Whose?"

"An entrepreneur I know." He pursed his lips as he carved. "Nirg loved those edible things. What do you call them?"

She smiled at him. "It's my secret. I have to know how to write before I can name them."

"Then I hope my father gives in soon," he said. "They were delicious. Nirg hit me when I didn't have more." They watched the clients of Ur come and go from the administrative offices. The sun was getting high, and as it was getting closer to summer, it was getting hotter. "I have business down at the waterfront," he said. "Did you want to visit a diviner?"

"Today?"

He nodded.

"Now?"

He nodded again.

Chloe patted her hair, braided and hanging over her shoulders like rope. "Sure. Why not?" Why was she nervous? *Because if I knew the future, I'd be even more scared?* The sore on her head throbbed, as though the weight of her thoughts irritated it.

"Are you well?" Nimrod asked. "Um, both of you?"

Chloe nodded. "Lead on."

They left the wide streets by the commonwealth offices and joined the crush that passed through the narrow lanes leading to the waterfront. Chloe had a sense of great familiarity, though she'd never left the marsh.

Artisans and craftsmen did their work by open windows; butchers skinned and sliced while blood ran in the streets; storytellers, dancers, and acrobats performed for small groups, passing a basket hat for their day's beer; women and men hawked their wares of herbs and elixirs, fruits and vegetables; the air was dense with the honks of asses, the squawks of geese, and the smell of sheep dung.

The smells of urine, cardamom, and sweat swirled like fabric around them. The press of bodies was tight. Tents sheltered sleeping infants or working children. Women fed their babies, youths relieved themselves, and, everywhere, people talked.

Chloe understood every word used on the street. This struck her as odd; an experience she'd never had. She averted her eyes from those unfortunates who waited in the shade of the walls, legless, eyeless, tongueless, handless, hoping for the mercy of strangers.

Nimrod's hand on her back was firm, assuring. Though he wasn't tall, he projected a great sense of charisma, and humans naturally made way for him. They reached out to touch

Chloe's hair, her skin. They murmured it had been a long time since a Khamite woman had passed their way.

She knew everything they were saying. All the calls, the cries, the conversations. Nothing was cloaked in mystery. Chloe was dizzy again.

"Here," Nimrod said, pushing her toward a dark alley. "The diviner's house."

The houses were ramshackle, stacked on top of each other like collapsing cereal boxes. *What were those?* Children and goats wandered the streets. Trash was piled in the streets, for these people had no courtyard to compost it. Flies and dogs fought for the rotting remains. Underneath the stench of garbage, Chloe smelled the tang of salt. The port.

"The sign for diviner," Nimrod said, pointing to a scratched emblem on the mudbrick wall. "Ninhursag, the goddess of the earth. Her crone is here."

Chloe felt the hair on her neck stiffen. She halted.

"Go in," Nimrod said. "Since I'm a male human, I'm not welcome."

"I just . . . go in? No appointment, no gift?"

"Give her some of those round things. She trades in food."

Chloe was extremely reluctant. "I'm out."

"She won't hurt you, though she is enormous. I'm going to the wharf, I'll be back to walk you home." He smiled, a stretch of white in the mass of his black beard. "Are you fearful? The gods just pass judgments, but that doesn't mean they have baked the future in clay. You have nothing to fear."

"My future is negotiable?"

Nimrod smiled. "This is Ur; everything is negotiable."

She nodded. Opened the door. Stepped inside.

"Ah, Chloe," a chilling voice said. "We meet again."

Chapter Eight

Chloe peered through the darkness in the room; it was almost tar, compared to the sunlight outside. "Have we met?"

The voice laughed, not kindly. "Still adjusting, I gather?"

"To? Adjusting to what?"

The creature, Chloe could see it—her—now, was seated against one wall of the room. She took up the entire space, shaped like an ancient statue of the earth goddess, all pendulous breasts and hips, with gaudy bright lips and black-circled eyes.

Those eyes looked through her.

"Ohmigod," Chloe said. It all rushed back.

The first time Chloe had seen this woman, she'd been a child in Cairo with her sister. The woman had given Chloe a necklace that had been her destiny. The second time had been in ancient Atlantis. She'd given Chloe a ring. And a third time in a marketplace in Jerusalem. "You," Chloe said.

All the pieces fit together in that instant. Chloe had time-traveled and taken over the body of a marsh girl. How and why, she didn't know. But this woman knew everything, Chloe was certain. "Cheftu?" she asked.

"Greetings to you too, Chloe. You're yet such an American, rushing, always in a hurry. Can't even be courteous and inquire about my health. Mimi would be horrified, she taught you better."

Chloe locked her knees; she was afraid she was going to fall over. The woman spoke *English*. "How am I here? Why?"

"I have a message for you," the woman said. "As I seem to be your personal oracle—"

"The Crone of Ninhursag!" The marsh girl had met this woman also. Two destinies. *She always knew I would come?* Chloe touched her head, the wound that hadn't healed, even now.

"It's gratifying that you have some useful memory. Do you want your message or not?"

Chloe nodded.

"You may not feel that way after I tell you, but that's none of my affair. Here it is: You will not find him. You are not ready."

Cheftu? It must be. "How do I get ready?" she asked.

The crone closed her eyes. "You have your message. Leave me now."

"No, one question, please, please—"

She opened one eye. "What?"

"How am I here? Why?"

"The mercy of God," the crone said. Then she began snoring, and her eyes rolled up like window shades.

Mercy?

Chloe stumbled out of the incense-choking room and into the street.

Nimrod touched Chloe's arm, and she almost jumped out of her skin. *I have jumped out of my skin*, she thought. *Into whose?* "A mirror, I need a mirror. Please."

Nimrod searched her face. "Of course, anything I can do to help. But Chloe, only the *ensi* has a mirror."

"Water, then. So I can see my reflection."

They walked with indecorous speed to the city gate, then farther out to the edges of the irrigation channels. Barley climbed into the air, and watchers kept an eye on the ears, wary of rust—*samana*. The first sign would send the city into a panic of prevention.

Chloe didn't care about any of it. She had to see what she looked like.

"This is as clear as you will find," Nimrod said, stopping a few feet in front of her at the edge of an irrigation ditch. "Come look."

Kingsleys don't quit, Chloe said to herself. *That statement has gotten me into a shitload of trouble these past couple of years. Oh God*—Nimrod's hand on her arm steadied her, and Chloe knelt, braced her hands against the moist, warm levee, and opened her eyes.

She stared at the face that looked back her. Minutes ticked by as she watched it. When she spoke, her voice was soft and slow. "My Mimi warned me of this one night when she'd dipped too many times into the fruitcake after Christmas. She said my family had been plantation owners for quite a while. Blood had gotten a little confused, what with sassy young slaves and rascally old slave owners. She said that blood was somewhere in my veins, and I wouldn't know when it was going to show up.

"She had *no* idea."

Nimrod looked into the river with her, and Chloe looked at his face, really looked at it, with her twentieth-century eyes. He seemed to be East Indian, with silky black hair and liquid eyes, delicate features that were well proportioned. And she, she . . .

"I'm black. Dark, anyway. Cheftu is never going to find me. Even if he came here, he'd never recognize me. This is too much of a change."

"You're not dark. One of your parents was dark-skinned, but the other was fair," Nimrod said. "Look at your hair."

She looked at it, dark, thick, heavy, but not kinky curled.

She leaned into the water, looked closely at her eyes. Green, startlingly so in such dark skin. But Nimrod was right, she wasn't black. A mulatto, with skin no darker than mocha, and features that . . . well, were hers. What had the marsh girl's face looked like? There seemed to be nothing new in Chloe's features, no trace of the other girl at all.

Chloe was still tall, still slim, and still had big feet. She sat down on her haunches and looked across the stream at the flat line of the sky. Or the land. It didn't matter, they were both flat. One was green and brown, the other blue. Both with the topography of a pancake.

Nimrod sat next to her. "You're the other one now, aren't you?"

She nodded. "I'm Chloe."

"She was Chloe, too."

She looked at him. "Yes, I guess she was."

He looked into her eyes. "You look changed, more scared. And your eyes are a different color."

"A different color?" Her eyes had always been green— regardless of circumstances.

He moved his head, looking at her with detached observation. "Usually one is green and one is brown, but at this moment, both are green."

"I've had mismatched eyes?" Chloe asked. What did it mean? What—

"Very pretty actually. Striking," Nimrod said. "But now they are both green. And . . . But what is wrong? Didn't you know what you looked like?"

Not really. Chloe rubbed her eyes and face, while she tried to get a grasp of her situation. *I'm mulatto, my eyes are changeable—how did it happen?*

Every time I've traveled through time, it's been because I initiated it. It happened on the twenty-third of December. I was pulled through an archway. There was blue light, rush-

*ing wind. I had to do it. Every single time. Now, I go to bed
as a red-haired, fair-skinned woman in Jerusalem and wake
up where I don't know, as someone I don't know, and when I
don't know? What's with that? I thought I knew the rules.
Why did they change? Why am I here? How did I get here?*

*Cheftu . . . was he snatched out of our bed too, or is he in
Jerusalem yet, wondering what the hell happened to me?
And what did that woman say, I wouldn't find him because I
wasn't ready?* Chloe touched the wound on her head; how
did it fit in with anything? Smoke. For just a second she
thought she smelled smoke. *What happened to my life?*

"Chloe, are you well?"

"I, I just didn't think God was capricious. Why else
would I be here?"

"Of course the gods are capricious! The rains come or
they don't; there is too much water or not enough. The rivers
rise, they fall, they do whatever they want. No amount of
sacrifices or pleading makes any difference. We build temples and offer bribes but . . . we are their playthings. Their
slaves. The gods are nothing *but* capricious. That's why you
have personal gods and demons. They intercede for you."

She looked up at the cloudless blue sky. "Are you saying
there is no reason for things?"

"Of course there is a reason," he said. "That is why you
have diviners and search for omens and read the stars and
the sheep's liver and interpret the birth of spotted lambs.
There's a reason, we just don't know it."

"I hate that attitude."

"Hate it, love it. It's truth."

"Wherever this is, this is definitely the Middle East," she
muttered. "I'd know that kind of fatalism anywhere." She
put a hand on Nimrod's silky arm. "Who is the king?"

But the word didn't come out in . . . whatever language
this was. Which means there is no such term in this lan-

guage, that much I've learned in these years. "Draw me a picture of the land, would you?"

Nimrod shrugged, then drew it: rivers, south sea, mountains, and desert.

"Do you know what the edge of the water looks like over here?" she said, pointing to the land to the west.

"It's the desert, there is no water's edge besides that one. And it is like this, approximately."

She saw curves, straight lines, nothing recognizable. "What about the other side of the sea, the other bank? How wide is it there?"

"A great, long distance. Wider than the whole of Shinar."

A huge, wide sea. Indians someplace close. No mountains, no hills, nothing but flat, flat alluvial plain with two rivers twisting through. Two rivers and a plain. The cradle of civilization.

"Ohmigod. The Tigris and Euphrates."

"Yes, yes. The rivers."

She stared at the map. "Babylonia. Ziggurats." She spoke in English, whispering what she hoped were notes of sanity to herself. "They're not stepped pyramids, they're temples built high so they don't get flooded. I've time-traveled to . . . Iraq. When? Why? It's not the right time of year . . . I didn't choose this . . . I—"

"Are you well, Chloe?" he asked.

"No, I'm not."

"Can I do anything?"

"Turn back time?" she said with a grimace. "Not really, Nimrod." She sighed. "I'll be fine, I have to be. Thank you. Please, please swear to me that you will never tell anyone of this conversation?"

Nimrod looked at her with cocker-spaniel eyes, long-lashed and trustworthy. "If it is that important to you, I swear I will never tell, no matter what the bribe. I will go to my grave with your secret. Both of you?" he asked with a smile.

Chloe looked away. "Thank you." Neither of them spoke, the sounds of the birds and the flowing water filled in the space.

"I need to get back to the city," he said at last. "You shouldn't stay out here alone. You could get lost at twilight."

I'm lost in history, she thought. *Alone. What's twilight matter?* "I'll be behind you directly. I just need . . . a little time to think."

He stared at her a few more minutes, but Chloe couldn't . . . couldn't do anything except hold on to the reins of her racing mind and hope.

"Be safe," he said, and left.

She stared at the water, at the face that was and wasn't hers, the eyes that were green now, but apparently changed frequently. "Just when you think you know the rules, they change."

～

Rudi looked at the sketch she'd made of the night sky, then consulted her charts.

The new star was firmly in the quadrant of Ur. The records were scarce, for observing the stars began only after the Deluge. The language of that time had been sparse, but she could understand that it was, indeed, a new star.

Gem came in, without knocking. "You're working in daylight?"

"I couldn't sleep."

"I could help you get to sleep."

She didn't even look at him. Gem offered himself to everyone, anyone. His talent was accounting. By his reasoning, if he always offered, then for some percentage of the time, his offer would be accepted. Gem, she noted, rarely slept alone. He also usually sported some kind of mark on his face from those who did refuse.

"Asa said the new star is a new *ensi*?" she asked.

"No."

She turned to him now. "You told me that, just weeks ago."

"I said Asa said the new star means we should have a new *ensi*."

Rudi turned back to her charts. "Does Asa know anything about the new *ensi*? What sign the human was born under, what gender? We must give the council some options, at least." And Puabi would have to spend some time training the person before she stepped down. "It seems a bad decision to let go of the *ensi*, just as the crops are coming in."

Gem slit open the seal on a jar of beer. "Do you want any?"

"Whose?"

He squinted at the writing. "It's a sour mash, from the tavern by the northeastern gate."

She nodded. "I have some salted fish and cucumbers in that basket over there to go with it."

Gem bounded toward it. "If only you could cook, Rudi, you would be the perfect female human and I would take you to my house."

"That would be kidnapping and slavery, Gem. I don't cook, and I don't like you."

"Oh. Well," he said, opening the basket.

There was nothing new in their conversations, she could carry on her part half-asleep. "Did you see the falling star the night of the equinox?"

"I wasn't on duty."

"I wasn't either," she said. "Which is why it's so unfair I got punished—"

"Don't start, Rudi. I'm not going to hear Asa criticized again."

She sighed and drank some of the beer. It complemented the fish well. The fish . . . Rudi pulled out her chart of the houses of the sky and compared it to the new star. "The Goatfish," she said. "I think that is the sign of the new *ensi*. Look at this."

Gem leaned over her shoulder. "Could be," he said. "What are the traits of the Goatfish?"

"A traveler. Wise. Hates bureaucracy. Adaptable."

"Then I pity her, to become the *ensi*. Nothing but meetings and sex."

Rudi gave her partner a scolding look. "It is not sex; it is communication and supplication of Inana."

Gem shrugged. Paying for the favors of a priestess was something he bragged he'd never had to do.

"Or," Rudi said, turning her head a little, "by the snake of the tree, it's not a human of the Goatfish. It's . . . exactly what Puabi is."

"Extraordinary to look at, but a demon to bed?"

Rudi didn't like her sister, but she wasn't going to listen to her being belittled. "No, a human born in the moon of the Scales. Loves luxury, peace, calm, and doesn't see evil."

"Perfect for the job," Gem said.

Rudi knew she was going to have to check her hypothesis against the actual night sky, but, "It looks like a human born on the exact same day as Puabi! The third of the moon of the Scales!" She looked at Gem. "What is the likelihood of finding another human born on the third of Scales to be *ensi*?"

Gem bent over a scrap of clay.

That matter of accounting, Rudi thought, should keep him quiet for a while.

~

Ezzi's cloak was too big now. He'd given all of his food away since New Year's, hoping to placate the gods, the goddesses, the demigods, the demons, and his personal god. Ulu scoffed at him for offering incense at all hours, standing outside the temple to be sprayed with the blood of the twice-daily sacrifices.

She didn't understand. Rudi had cast a curse on him.

Ezzi just didn't know what kind of curse.

Was it on his body? He ate almost nothing for fear of consuming evil, and drank beer only when pressed, or when his belly cramped from hunger. Every spot on his skin was cause for double hours of investigation to see if it had grown or changed in the hours since he'd looked at it last.

Was it his manhood? Ezzi checked daily for spots or withering, but it seemed as ordinary as ever. He didn't understand other men's obsession with this stick of flesh, but it seemed to be unchanged.

Had she cursed his mind? Every day he woke up and reviewed the conversations he'd had the day before. As he walked down the street, he recited the lists from the Tablet House, prayers from the temple, and formulas for the fields. Before he washed, he would recall the flocks of the sky, the names of the gods, the days of each month. When he went back to bed, he would repeat every word he'd heard that day.

She must have cursed his career. Ezzi was still unemployed. He went to the stargazers' house every twilight and offered his knowledge and wisdom, but no one had paid him yet. He cast charts and drew the quadrants, but no one wanted his future foretold.

Yes, Ezzi thought, Rudi stargazer had cursed his career. He needed to make money another way, so he could be a stargazer at leisure. His words would be more trusted if they were free. His mother, the wealthy she-dog, wasn't going to share. How could he get more currency?

That was his prayer as he burned his evening meal before the statue of his personal god. *Send me funds! Give me a chance, an opportunity, and I will take it. I will do anything!*

So Ezzi pleaded.

∼

Shama fanned the congressing *ensi*; his mind was lost in the game of draughts he was playing against the gatekeeper. He couldn't believe he'd lost his last match.

Puabi shouted Kidu's name; they must be approaching the apex. Any moment now she would want her bath drawn and her sweet beer. Kidu would request opium and meat. If the young man weren't careful, he would kill himself with carelessness.

Shama switched his angle of fanning, so the air would cool between their sweated bodies. Puabi continued to cry out to her mountain man, who continued to ram into her as though she were a sheep.

Shama had gotten his fill of mating while sailing through the Deluge. Men and women mating from fear, which was better than men and animals mating—part of the reason the god of gods had destroyed the creatures when he wiped the earth clean. Destruction had been decreed when the human females of earth had mated with the males from the heavens. Their progeny had destroyed the plain, by cutting down trees, setting afire the black lakes, using their superior intelligence to bait and maim and ruin life for everything else.

Then they'd started in on the animals, tainted them.

Shama shook his head. There had been such noise inside and outside the great boat, for sixty-one days, that he'd been almost deafened. All of those animals, their never-ending racket. Now, he was glad. He glanced over; Puabi was done, but the mountain man was not.

Perhaps Kidu was a remnant of the antediluvian world. So dumb and innocent that he'd never erred, so he hadn't needed to be destroyed.

"Beer!" his mistress called.

"Opium," Kidu requested. He climbed from her bed and excused himself to the chamber pot. She'd educated him in that, at least.

Shama broke the seal of Puabi's beer jar and inserted a drinking tube, then set the jar beside her bed. He selected some pods and started the apparatus to enable Kidu to enjoy his drug. Then Shama bowed.

She waved him away. "Go have a bath, or something," she said. "We'll want food in a while."

Shama excused himself down the secret steps and into the main hall. He confirmed his earlier order to the kitchens, then set off to the gatekeeper's. It was time for a rematch in draughts; Shama planned his strategy.

∼

Guli didn't have a chance to pay his debts, they came looking for him—Lord Viza and the sailors he'd hired as strongmen for the day. Though business had been good, Guli hadn't made enough. Pleading, begging, promising—the only thing he could do was offer to pay 25 percent next time. Compounding interest. Viza signed a new contract, crushed the last one into dust.

By the time Guli had cleaned up the mess of his house, he had a customer.

For a moment he stood in the doorway, looking out at the palm trees that swayed in the ever-increasing heat. It seemed they would be his destiny unless he got the gods on his side.

~

The first day of school was blistering hot. The slave girl woke Chloe in the dark. She ate barley mash and took the parcel that contained her lunch, then set off through the streets. Chloe watched the ground, avoiding offal, averting her eyes when she saw the remains of wild dogs' meals.

The Tablet House was four streets over. She paused as she watched the students go inside. All ages learned in the same room. She would be the only girl.

A gawky boy stood in the doorway. "Are you here for someone?" he asked coolly.

"I'm a student," she said. But the words came out, "I am a Little Brother of the Tablet House."

"Get in then," he said. "You are late already."

She took a seat in the back. The room was filled with benches for the boys, space for their lunches beneath them, and clay and stylus in their hands. The Tablet Father didn't acknowledge her. The boy she sat next to looked at her in horror. He nudged his friend. "A female," he pointed out.

This boy looked around and sat back. "An old one."

"Gentlemen," the Tablet Father said, "would you like to share with the classroom?"

"Sir, Father, uh, there's an old female sitting beside me."

"Excellent observation, Brother Haki." The other students turned around to look. Chloe was extremely grateful she'd worn a capelet and skirt. She was covered from curious eyes, even though she might die beneath the wool.

"We have a new student today. As there is no other way to refer to her, she is Brother Chloe," the Tablet Father said.

They giggled.

"No doubt you have heard the rumors the *lugal* was going to allow coeducation."

One boy raised his hand.

"Yes, Brother Miga?"

"Does this mean my sister is going to come here?"

The classroom erupted in exaggerated revulsion of "Females!" "Sisters!" and the like. Chloe hid her grin. Ages and civilizations didn't matter. Boys would be boys.

The Tablet Father banged his gavel. "It does not. As you can see, Brother Chloe is older than most of you."

"She's as old as Ziusudra!" someone offered.

The Tablet Father looked down at the miscreant. Though the Father was a short, stocky man, he moved as though he owned the world. His gaze could be oppressive. "Perhaps you should write out the story of the Deluge, as practice, Brother. I will expect to see it by dusk."

The other students shaped up quickly as the victim immersed his piece of clay in water, mashed it blank, and began to scratch the legend, syllable by syllable, into its surface.

"The rest of you, unless you wish to join your brother, will resume with your lists. Chloe, have you the skills to write lists?"

The boys looked at her, sixty black, brown, green, hazel, and blue gazes on her.

"No."

The Tablet Father motioned to an Elder Brother. "Teach her the basics, sir."

The room fell silent, except for the sounds of scratching on clay and the pigeons in their corner keep.

The Elder Brother, whose name was Roi, took Chloe outside beneath the awning. There he started with *lu,* man, and proceeded to give her a list of titles for humans. By lunch Chloe had copied the list four times.

The staff disappeared and left her with thirty curious boys from ages nine to nineteen for a quarter of a double hour.

Somewhere in the background, she thought she heard the tune of *"Frère Jacques."* The boys weren't hesitant.

"Are you really a female?"

"Why aren't you married?"

"Why do you come to the Tablet House? Yuck!"

"Do you have children?"

"You're very pretty."

"You must be stupid, if you can't write lists."

"Are you a Khamite?"

She barely had time to chew and swallow her lunch between answers. They ran and jumped and played ball, but there was always a group hanging around, asking questions. And always someone singing that tune, or close to it.

"My brother knows you," one of them said. "You're his girlfriend."

"No I'm not."

"You don't even know who I'm talking about," the boy said.

"It's an easy answer," she said. "I don't have a boyfriend at all."

The other boys laughed at the questioner. "You thought you knew something, Roo." "Stupid Roo." "Roo, you can't even write *boyfriend*."

"But your brother is my dear friend," she said to him, trying to help the little guy save face. It didn't work. Roo glared at her and walked off alone.

The Tablet Father returned, and class resumed.

It was a constant battle to stay awake after noon. The Elder Brothers roamed the room, looking for those unfortunates who had nodded off. If a boy fell asleep, they rubbed his tablet on his face—ruining his work and branding him for the rest of the day.

Chloe's hand was cramped, because they wrote everything in a column, then lined the columns from right to left.

She had to hold her arm awkwardly so as not to smear her writing. Left-handed boys would have it made.

She looked at her list: man, woman, male child, female child, family. Aunt, uncle, grandfather, grandmother, cousin. Unlike most languages she knew, this was based on additions. The basic term for human was amended to be aunt—human sibling of my father/mother, or grandfather—human male who sired my father/mother. All the syllables were attached, producing a long, unwieldy title. The symbol was so intricate it was unidentifiable as anything concrete. All conceptual.

Chloe wiped sweat off her forehead. Her back ached from sitting so straight, and being so concentrated, for so long. *I won't fall asleep,* she told herself. When she felt the urge, she stabbed her inner wrist with the stylus. It wasn't sharp enough to make a cut in her skin, but it left an impression.

When will this day be over?

And when she got home, she still had to bake some of those round things for the *lugal.* It was part of their "deal."

～

Shama delivered their food and resumed his fanning. Kidu was nibbling on Puabi's breast, and smoke hung like another curtain in the room.

"You are so beautiful, Aiza," he muttered against Puabi's skin.

His mistress, who wasn't intoxicated with opium, shouted and shoved him away. "Who is Aiza?"

"You are," the mountain man slurred. His pupils were swollen, so that his hazel eyes looked soulless and black.

"I am not, you sodden louse! Who is Aiza? Shama," she said, and turned to him. "Bring me the scribe who keeps the list of the women who have visited the *en.*" She pushed Kidu away, and he slid down in the pillows. "You aren't supposed to visit any one female more than once a month," she said to him. "Who is Aiza? Does *she* have your heart?"

Shama watched silently. Puabi was known for her jealousies. It was one of the reasons the commonwealth had had so many *ens*. She couldn't abide a man whose first devotion wasn't to her even though the *en's* job was to impregnate the women of Ur in season. Shama knew the next words that would fall from her lips; she was nothing if not consistent.

"I can make you *en*," she told the slumbering golden giant. "I have the power to unmake you, also. Forget this not. Do you hear me?"

Kidu snored, and Puabi rounded on Shama. "Stop that! Stop fanning! You're making my head ache."

Shama dropped his fan and bowed his head.

Puabi stood silent for a moment, then drew a long, shuddering sigh. "Watch Kidu for me, Shama. He's no more trustworthy than his predecessors."

Shama dug in his waist pouch for the herb that would ease Puabi's head. He dumped it into her beer and stirred, then handed the cup to her. "Why do the gods not smile on me?" she asked. "Why saddle me with weak men who are no more worthy of this role than oxen?

"I brought this man from the barbarous hills, I fed him and clothed him with my own hands, I endured his animalistic urges until I could train him how to congress with a woman—" Puabi threw her hands in the air. "I taught him how to speak beyond grunts, how to read." She shook her head in disgust as Kidu's snoring grew heavier and louder.

"Remove him from my sight," she said to Shama. "And get me a bath." Shama turned to summon the acolytes who could carry Kidu. "If this continues, Shama, these drugs, this insolent behavior, then Kidu must go," she said. "He is on the last of my patience."

The afternoon was divided up into disciplines. Mathematics, for calculating field areas; geometry, for figuring canals and irrigation schemes; medical science, to know how to care for one's livestock; and accounting, to keep one's taxes straight and correct. Each session was taught by a different "Father." Afterward, the Tablet Father motioned for Chloe to come with him. They sat on the side of the building—the awning's shade was too narrow for his bulk. He looked over her feeble attempts to write.

"Do you know why you make the list? It's the first of many you will make. Do you know why?"

"I'll use these words the most?"

He sighed and leaned back. "I was less than enthusiastic about your coming to the Tablet House," he said. "You saw why, at the start of the day. Now . . ." He shook his head. "You don't even know the most basic concepts."

"That's why I'm here," she said. "To learn those most basic concepts."

He glanced at her sharply. "Doctrine of the name. It's the foundation of the commonwealths between the two rivers. It's the reason we have writing. No one else does."

No one else in the world? Or no one else in Iraq? Chloe waited quietly. Sooner or later he would tell her. Until then, sweat would just continue to pool beneath her.

"When you name something, you bring it into being; it becomes self-aware. When you know its name, you control it. To make these lists and identify these things is to take mastery over the world in which you live."

Chloe nodded.

"The First Father called the names of the creatures, and thus he reigned over them as *lugal*.

"Now when you write something," he said, "you make its

life longer, permanent. As you wrote it, it will exist for as long as the writing lasts. It is the call of the scribe. To summon into being and identification and submission, all that is."

"A large task for a mere human."

"It is our job to organize for the gods, to administer their estates—this world."

She swallowed a yawn, but nothing got by his eagle glance. "Your work is awful. Knead it blank and write it again." He got up, and she made to follow suit. "Stay here," he said. "I'll trust you not to fall asleep."

He went back inside, and Chloe yawned so widely she was afraid her jaws would come unhinged. It was hot still and hours before twilight. *Why did I think I wanted to do this,* she wondered. *Was I drunk? School, in any time, any place, is hard. That's why so few go and even less survive. Wasn't primary school, secondary school, junior high, high school, and college—fifteen years of formal education—enough?*

She looked at her hesitant marks in the clay and quickly transferred the information to the dust beside her. She dunked the clay into water and kneaded it until it was soft and pliant. Then she picked up the stylus and started again.

"Human, male."

⌐

Ezzi was trembling, trying desperately hard to stop. Asa stargazer stood behind him, and the throng of stargazers, exorcists, diviners, and *asu,* stood behind him. The *ensi* looked like the goddess Inana, though Ezzi wondered if the goddess was cross often. The *ensi* certainly was.

"What is the meaning of this?" she asked.

The *lugal* stepped forward. "I mentioned there was a sign in the heavens," he said. "The stargazer is here to discuss it."

"Where is Kidu? Where is *en* Kidu? Shama, go find him."

"*Ensi,*" the *lugal* said.

She cut him off. "Nothing, until the *en* arrives."

Ezzi looked around the room while they waited. It was enormous, with colorful cone-studded walls and light, colorful carpets. The furniture was gold; he'd never seen such a thing before. Was it made of solid gold or was it just gilded?

A man came in, blond and big. His eyes were half-open. The *ensi* beckoned him to sit, then she sat on his lap. "Now you can talk."

The *en* nodded off against her chest. She couldn't wake him.

The *lugal* spoke again. "The stars proclaim something dire for our commonwealth," he said. "Asa will tell you."

Asa stepped forward. "The gods require you, ma'am."

She sat up straight, jolted the *en* awake. "What do you mean?"

"Three signs, *ensi*. The first was the blood moon."

"We beat the drums; the demons fled."

He nodded. "The second sign was the flooding of the northern marshes."

"Every season there is a flood."

"Ma'am, Ur lost almost all of its seasonal slave labor. In addition to countless head of cattle, buffalo, and taxpayers. I believe there was one survivor."

"What's your third sign?"

"The sky is going to turn to night, in the middle of the day. The gods are not happy with us."

Puabi looked at the *lugal*. "What does this mean?"

"Ma'am," Asa answered, "the gods are finished with you."

Part Three

THE TABLET HOUSE

Chapter One

*C*heftu's fingers glided down the form next to him. She murmured in her sleep and shifted closer, her bare flesh against his. After months of living in the Jerusalem caverns, waiting, hoping, he was here; he was with Chloe.

He looked around the room, hazy in predawn.

Where were they?

It didn't matter; they were safe. He'd found her, *le bon Dieu* be praised.

He kissed her shoulder as he prepared himself for any changes he might see. Though Cheftu's love for Chloe never ceased, it was always disconcerting when they changed times, and her appearance became that of another woman. He never changed, thank *le bon Dieu*. The woman beside him rolled onto her back and pulled him close. He braced himself while he waited for her to open her brilliant green eyes.

"Wake up, *ma chérie*," he whispered in his native French, one of the many languages they shared. "We are safe."

Her eyes opened. The gaze that met his was black and blank.

"What did you say, *en*?" she asked.

In Cheftu's mind, the words—words he'd never heard before—were communicated by pictures. *My personal logograms,* he realized. He stared at the woman, noticed she was fair-skinned, with a cap of black hair, and grotesquely overgrown eyebrows.

A series of images assaulted him; this woman, covered in mud and weeping in his arms; blood and stink, and his own torn shouting; a sense of loss that was searing and a sense of belonging that was wrenching. He knew this woman; he owed her his very life.

Her gaze was sharp. "Were you waking me with song, my love?" she asked. Her touch moved from his shoulder to his buttocks. "Or were you calling another woman's name again?"

"Chloe?" he said, just in case, if the chance existed, she was somewhere in that body. "Chloe?"

"Are you a bird this morning, my love? Last night you were . . ." She whispered in his ear, and Cheftu blushed at her words. She reclined, her smile sated. "I am pleased with you again."

What had happened? Was he in the wrong time? Had all the prayers and supplications been for naught? The woman kissed his chest, as she hummed *Chloe* beneath her breath.

He couldn't believe there wasn't reason behind his being here, in this specific place. The woman wrapped strong legs around his waist—perhaps not this exact *specific* place. Bon Dieu, *I do not know where I am, or what manner of man, but please don't let me sin,* Cheftu prayed. He tried to sit up, but she tightened her grip.

"Where are you going, *en*? The dawn is for loving. It's a double hour before our obligations."

Oh God, I don't want to be unfaithful to my wife. And Cheftu's body, for all that his mind wrestled with, knew it was morning and she was willing. Moreover, the affection he felt for this woman was almost overwhelming. She meant a great deal to him, but she wasn't his wife.

Thank God.

But no other clue to his identity was within sight. "Forgive me," he said cautiously. He pictured the emotion and hoped it translated to her strange tongue. "I must intercede with the gods."

Cheftu rose from the bed to remove himself from error or temptation. The woman turned onto her side and propped her head on her bent elbow. Her skin was like polished marble, contrasted with black eyes, eyebrows, and eyelashes, and a substantial display of body hair. Egyptians had a preference for a smooth body, and Cheftu shared that feeling.

"Of course you must intercede," she said. "But with me. Everyone else can wait," she said with a smile, leaning back, running her hand down the curves of her breast, waist, and hip. She was exquisite, and she knew it. "I'm the one. Now come kneel between my feet and *intercede*."

He fought the desire to do just that, to lose himself in her. "First, I must—" What was the word? "Relieve myself."

She lay flat and waved toward him. "I'm starting without you then," she said, touching her own body with purpose. "Don't tarry."

Escape.

He went out the door of the bedroom and found himself in a waiting room. Though his need hadn't been real when he spoke, now it was. There didn't appear to be any curtained area, a chamber pot, or a marble seat. Just a lot of potted palms.

For the first time, Cheftu glanced at his own skin.

He was golden brown above the waist and below his thighs, but elsewhere he was ivory. Paler than he'd ever been in his life. What was he? Who did she think he was? Where was this place? He wanted to leave, but was this his home? How did he get here? Where were his clothes? When she addressed him the first time, what had she called him?

En.

Was that his name, or a title? He stared at the dirt in the potted palm, and concentrated. In his mind he rifled through all the records of languages he knew. There was no definition for *en*. He could be the gardener; he could be the king.

"Kidu," she called. "Oh, Kidu."

His feet propelled him toward her, and Cheftu halted at the doorway. His head almost touched it. A low doorway. His "lover" was quite enraptured with herself, calling the name again and again. Perhaps he was Kidu?

He had to get out of there, despite the protests of his mind and body.

Then the realization stabbed him: he was not himself. He wasn't Cheftu the Egyptian scribe, physician, courtier and lord: He wasn't François, his birth name in Napoleon's France, a child of humble origins born with a gift for languages. He wasn't any of the men he'd masqueraded as in these past years: mage, diplomat, alchemist, slave. He had stepped into someone else's body and life.

And Chloe was just . . . gone.

He turned away from the woman, his body fully aroused, his mind fully shocked.

A face appeared before him.

Cheftu started.

It was a man, bent with age and wiry with muscle. His gaze moved from the woman in the throes of passion to Cheftu, completely aroused and standing in the next room. The man didn't say anything, but he peered intently up at Cheftu's face.

Instinctively, Cheftu brushed at his chin. *I have a beard.* Bon Dieu. The woman was growing louder, becoming a nuisance to Cheftu's thoughts, which already careened around madly like a dog with a foaming mouth, acting as a further goad to the part of him who longed to share in her ecstasy. "Clothes," he said to the old man. He didn't care about appearances or anything else. He had to think, to . . . reason out what had happened.

To get away from that woman.

The old man handed him a kilt—that itself was recognizable, though the pattern, cloth, and design were not. Cheftu felt heat in his cheeks as he fought to make it lie flat, especially under the old man's amused, questioning gaze. When Cheftu's fair skin was covered completely, he hurried to the door.

The next room smelled like smoke, and he saw the implements of opium; then he recognized that his head ached, and why his mouth was bitter with bile. Cheftu closed the door behind him, shut away her loud cries, and opened the door to questions.

Three men, in similar kilts, also with beards, scrambled to stand upright and formal in the passageway. They were obviously confused by his presence, considering the woman's cries, but they bowed to him and mumbled greetings. He nodded acknowledgement and walked down the hall. It was dark, with oil torches affixed to the walls. He had no idea where he was going, or where he'd been. He was astounded at how much effort it took to move his body away—he literally pulled with every step.

"*En* Kidu, *en* Kidu," a man called. Cheftu halted and turned on his heel. The man smiled and pulled out a slab of clay. "Good day, sir. Would you like to go over the day's activities?"

The faces of the other men were turned in his direction. Curious.

"Of course," Cheftu said. "Walk with me." *I* must be Enkidu. *En* Kidu?

"Certainly, sir," the man said. "Where are you going?"

"I need some fresh air."

"Then perhaps . . . outside?"

"Excellent choice," Cheftu said. "Lead on."

The scribe, if that's what he was, turned around and walked down the hall, then turned again. Cheftu's first sight of his new world was blue sky and palm trees. And a breeze that hinted at a scorching afternoon.

They walked in silence to the threshold, and Cheftu took in the view.

Sunlight poured on the city, and Cheftu was blinded by ribbons of reflection. Water. Rivers? No, they were irrigation channels. Two-story buildings cast shadows across straight, gridlike streets lined with green palms. An impressive wall enclosed the structure where he was, and directly below him were gardens with flowers, trees, and fountains, just touched by the sunrise. It was a sophisticated town.

He saw no people.

He looked to the south and saw a bay, shimmering silver, in dawn's light. More irrigation channels branched off a broader river that ran through the western part of the city. The smell of garbage, ash, and incense burned his nostrils as he stood. This place was completely foreign.

Steps led down from this platform, and steps led up. Cheftu turned to look behind him, and gaped at the building he'd just left; colorful stages with ramps, steps, and archways, leading from one color and level to another. A manmade mountain. From this perspective, he couldn't see the top. He knew, somehow, that it was a blue temple dedicated to a sky deity.

A sky deity in an unknown land with a language he had never heard. He'd never even heard its like—it bore no similarity to the Semitic tongues of Hebrew, Arabic, Aramaic, Akkadian, Babylonian, and Persian. Nor was this India, for he knew Prakrit and its written derivative, Sanskrit. To his left, the bay stretched away to become a sea. The organization of this city looked almost Greek. But they spoke nothing like Greek or Latin, or any of its offspring tongues: French, Italian, Portuguese, Russian, or the other Indo-European languages he knew, like German or English.

The people were not Chinese, nor was their language— at least none of the six dialects of Chinese that Cheftu knew. The land was flat, the people unfamiliar, the place unrecognizable. He felt a ball of fear and fury rise up in his chest; *why have you brought me here.* The rage was incoherent and apart from him. Fierce, nevertheless.

It was Kidu's emotion, but Cheftu shared it.

This world was not one he knew or had known.

"So tell me," he said to the scribe in this language that was borrowed from the other part of his mind, formed by the strange combination of gluing syllables together. "What does my day hold?"

～

Chloe yawned through the first few hours of class. This was only her second day, and she was exhausted! *We'd get so much further with coffee.* She wondered if there were any coffee beans around. *Or leaves—wasn't that how the first Arabs discovered coffee? Their sheep ate the leaves?* It didn't matter, her sheep weren't that useful.

The heat, the droning, the smoky air, the flies—her head felt as though it were on a string not a neck. It took massive effort to face forward with open eyes.

None of the nine- to nineteen-year-olds seemed to have this problem.

She looked at her attempted homework.

"Prepare your tablets. We're going to have an examination," the Elder Brother, said. The Tablet Father was away on business, so the rumor went. His superior skills were being used to figure the new, postflood, taxes.

The boys got in line, dunked their damp clay, and mashed it smooth. Chloe dodged the splash fights. Five of the boys were disciplined, and the rest of them tittered as the clay dried on the miscreants' faces.

"We begin," the Elder Brother said. "Example one: human, male parent of male parent."

The translation was fairly easy for grandparents, for it was a prefix in English, too. Take a parent, removed once from your immediate family, and they became grand. In . . . whatever these sideways pricking marks were, the answer was the sign for human, a determinative, then male parent twice. Easy enough. Thank God she'd slaved over her homework.

"Slave."

Chloe drew the determinative, then bit her lip. Slave, what was the sign? A human owned by another human? No. A human in debt? A human from someplace else? She skipped to the next question.

"Tablet Father."

Human male determinative, with the symbol of the Tablet House. Whew. Two out of three.

"Administrator," he said.

I didn't learn this one, Chloe thought. *It wasn't on my list.*

"Accountant."

Damn. I can't believe I studied the wrong thing. She scrawled the determinative . . . what was the symbol for numbers?

"En."

"Merchant."

"Sailor."

Chloe sat through the rest of the test, all male humans, all words she didn't know. The Elder Brother smiled at them, "Any questions?"

Chloe raised her hand. "How come there were no females on this list?"

～

Shama felt sorry for Puabi—not because she hadn't enjoyed herself thoroughly, but because afterward when she realized Kidu hadn't returned, she had been lonely.

He knew what it was like to be lonely. She suffered a different kind of loneliness than he did, but in truth it felt the same. He was particularly gentle with her hair, massaged oil into her skin, and fed her the choicest figs.

"I cannot believe he just walked out," she finally said. "Is it another woman?"

Shama shook his head; the *en* had been stringently observing the rules Puabi had laid out for him: only one visit at a time for a woman. If she didn't get pregnant then, she wasn't going to. Puabi seemed to care very little about the consequences. And soon the season would change, and there would be no congressing with the *en*, except with Puabi.

Babies were to be born in the season of cold and rest, not in the heat of harvesttime.

"Watch him for me, Shama," she said. "Last night, I think he got very sick. In fact, I think he almost died. His breath left, and it didn't come back for a long time. I fell asleep waiting. Apparently it did return."

He hung golden hoops through her ears.

"Even if he is *en*, he can't leave me . . . in the middle!" Her breath, blown in Shama's face from frustration, was acidic. Onions and opium had fermented into a bitter brew. He would stir cinnamon into her breakfast mint drink and add a dollop of crushed dates to sweeten her tongue. "Although . . . as long as I've known of Kidu, I can't imagine him walking away from any willing woman. Even were he sick." She shook her head, and Shama had to reset her diadem so it would sit evenly on her braided and coiled wig.

A knock. She grabbed his hand. "If it's him, I'm not available. But he better give you an excuse, a good one for this morning. But why should I care," she asked, sitting back. "I'm the *ensi*, anyone I want is mine."

The knock was firmer. "It's Rudi," the person called.

Puabi sagged in her chair. "Oh. Her."

The sisters greeted each other, and Shama was astonished, as ever, at the variety of physical forms that humans, even sisters, came in. Where Puabi was dark, Rudi was light. Where Rudi was stocky, Puabi was lithe. Though they had the same features, the same day of birth, they were opposites.

Until one learned Puabi's father was green-eyed and her mother was black-eyed; which made sense of the sisters.

"Go check on him," Puabi said to Shama. "Send in some wine."

He bid an acolyte fetch the *ensi* wine, and her sister beer. Rudi liked a beer for breakfast, she'd told him so. Puabi paid no attention to other humans' likes or dislikes; as the *ensi* her thoughts were on greater things.

Shama walked slowly; his hip had been stiff since he'd fallen at Kidu's hand. Or it could have been New Year's, going up and down all the stairs. The lower vaults where the statues' clothes were kept were farther than he walked in a week, and he'd walked it five times in one day. Oh, for the days of his great-grandfather, when men didn't ache so early and had congress with women until the day they died.

Alas, the water of vitality was gone; the Deluge had accomplished that.

Shama went to Kidu's quarters. His female slaves were in various stages of undress as they cleaned his linens and crushed the herbs for his incense. He wasn't in his audience chamber, and the line of women outside was long and growing irritable. The sun was well into the sky; the *en* should be there to fulfill his duties. Where was he?

Shama wandered the offices of the temple complex. The pace of summer was beginning, so people moved more slowly, angered more quickly. And the grass beneath the palms was flattened by the commonwealth's citizens' rear ends since they rested more frequently.

Shama crossed over the Euphrates bridge to the temple factories and storerooms. Occasionally Kidu wandered through there, looking for new conquests, though usually they came to him.

The *en* wasn't with the tanners, or the storehouse that kept leather goods for the temple and its thousands of employees. Nor with the dyers, the weavers, or spinners. Not in their warehouse, now empty since everyone got new clothes at the New Year. The brickmakers hadn't seen him; the coppersmiths and silver workers shook their heads. Shama's hip ached.

He sat down in the common courtyard where the emmer, barley, legumes, and seeds were kept in sealed jars, in the event the crops failed and needed reseeding. The fields were full of workers, as the summer barley was in its next irrigation. No Kidu, and no one to ask if they'd seen him.

Sweat stuck the felt of his skirt to his waist. Shama spied a soft patch of green beneath a clump of palms. No one was about, so he tottered over and lay down. The grass was cool and the earth still soft. Shama fell asleep in minutes.

His last thought was strange, for he couldn't tell some colors apart. Yet it seemed Kidu's eyes had been a different shade of amber this dawn.

I'm an old man, he told himself. *Everything is deteriorating, and now my vision is going, too.*

~

"You want to know why there were no human females on the list?" The Elder Brother looked at his copy. "Can anyone illumine Brother Chloe's mind on this matter?"

There was some rustling as the students looked around at each other. Finally, one little boy raised his hand.

"Brother Roo?"

"Several of these occupations could be filled by women."

"You don't even have mother on this list. Goddess?" Chloe looked at the boys, who were watching her. "Wife? Not to mention priestess, felter, seamstress, cook, ale—"

"Accountant could be answered as female," one boy said.

"Can *lugal*, or sailor or Tablet Father?" she asked.

"Of course not," the Elder Brother said.

Chloe set down her stylus. "Then I'm afraid I have to protest this exam."

"On what grounds?"

"I wasn't properly prepared because I wasn't told the exam would be exclusively about males."

"This is what happens when you let a girl in school," some boy said.

Chloe turned and looked at him, a big, burly boy of almost sixteen. "Yes, what happens is you can't forget half the population is female. That's what happens." She looked around the classroom. "I bet, if you all asked your parents who should be on the list of humans, the answers they'd give would be at least half-female." She looked from one face to another. "I dare you to ask your mothers and fathers."

"You are heard!" the Elder Brother said. "Tomorrow, we'll examine again."

Much loud protesting.

"—and at least half the answers will be female occupations. Though," he said, looking at Chloe, "this is not an excuse on your part. Half will be males."

"Just like the world, truth?"

～

Ulu stepped into the courtyard; this was a house very much like hers. The layout was the same. Nothing else, she had to admit, was similar. A slave appeared, smiled, and guided her to the back room where the banquet was laid out.

None of the guests had yet arrived, and she felt a little uncomfortable kissing her customer in these surroundings. He, however, did not.

When she met him in the tavern, he was always well lubricated with beer, emptied of stories, and aroused from watching her with other men since twilight. Here, it was still light. Guli had done her makeup by daylight, a precaution she was suddenly appreciating.

"Does it feel different, being in my home?" he asked.

"Where are your relatives? You don't live alone, do you?"

He shrugged. "My wife is visiting her family; she took the children and my second wife with her. To Eridu."

"Nice breezes in the springtime."

"You've been?"

Ulu snickered. "No, but I've been with a lot of husbands while their wives have been."

He laughed, then explained the party, how it was going to be served.

Each plate was painted, Ulu saw. The cups were glass—she'd congressed with a glassblower once who said anytime she wanted some glass to come see him. The linens were woven and so soft. His table was wood—very expensive. The chairs were carved, not just pieces of wood nailed together.

Pots of flowers, bowls of incense, and little bowls of water.

"Finger bowls," he said. "It makes touching much more pleasant, without the meal's grease."

She'd never thought of that.

He led her upstairs, where each of the rooms had been swept. Each had rugs on the floors, cloth on the windows, with more flowers, more perfumes. Clothes were stored in trunks. Lamps were used, instead of torches. "My wife hates to clean oil-lamp smudges off the paint," he said.

"From our dalliances at the tavern, I had no idea you had such expensive taste," Ulu said.

"It's why I like you," he said, then kissed her. "You're so delightfully lowlife and seedy."

Ulu looked around the comfortable, elegant home, then looked down at her feet on the even, swept, mudbrick floor. Dirty, scabbed, bare. The edge of her dress was stained with weeks of wearing, and the smell of her body was discernible despite the perfume of flowers and oils. Her nails were black, her wig cheap, and her breath smelled of onions.

For the first time, Ulu saw herself as others did, especially Ezzi. And she knew shame.

～

Cheftu had survived one day; one day in a new place, new language, new customs, and new . . . well, his body definitely wasn't his own. The urges he felt for any female, the fear he felt regarding his position, the fury he felt when thwarted in any little way, were so unlike Cheftu as he knew himself. They were Kidu.

The body Cheftu now inhabited was an unoccupied body, for which Cheftu couldn't find any reason. There were residual feelings and inclinations. Cheftu was going to have to fight against them. The most recurrent was a desire to slide into every woman he saw.

What manner of man was this high priest? In the course of the day, Cheftu had concluded that was his newest career: apprentice high priest to the Moon god Sin. This meant the *ensi*, a woman named Puabi, was his overseer. And already Cheftu was in trouble—he'd left her on her own this morning. Not a diplomatic way to handle anything, he had to admit. A less than auspicious beginning. Especially since Kidu felt so strongly about her.

He had to believe Chloe was here, that his being brought here was because this was where she had gone. In the mass of dark-haired, dark-eyed people, her green eyes and red hair should announce themselves in short order.

Though why should she have the same body? She never had before.

Her eyes, though, always were green. That had never been different.

Why she had come here, he didn't know. His prayers had been for her to find a necessary task, safety, security, and love. Those things must be here for her.

He toyed with the cylinders that hung from his waist. They were an inch to two inches tall, and carved so that when they were rolled across clay they left an imprint. He knew cylinder seals had been popular in most ancient countries. They were a good alternative to a signature. The intriguing and frankly disheartening thing about these cylinders was—he couldn't read them. The writing was familiar, but he didn't know it.

The same with the architecture—familiar, but only vaguely. Of course, the baked-brick mountains proclaimed he must be in the lands between the two rivers. Where in those lands, and when, he had no idea.

It made no difference. Chloe was here, so it was where he wanted to be.

He couldn't explain how either of them had gotten there. After he'd noticed Chloe had traveled on the eve of a lunar eclipse in Jerusalem, Cheftu had considered whether or not the moon and its phases was a factor in their travel. Every day he'd sneak out of the caverns and listen to the seers' predictions before bartering for some food and returning to the dark. When the city had anticipated a blood moon he'd prayed that he would be drawn to Chloe's side.

It worked. He believed.

Thus, as much as Cheftu could tell, short of the hand of God Almighty plucking him up from that time and place, there was no escape.

No escape from apologizing to the jilted priestess, either. Smooth over that relationship so he could begin his search for Chloe. A randy young priest should be able to find a green-eyed girl in a predominantly dark-eyed city within days. Perhaps hours.

He touched the elaborately braided and coifed hair on his head, straightened the fall of his skirt, and left for Puabi's quarters.

The path he'd taken earlier had been quite different, but he had a sense of the temple grounds now. It was a sprawling complex that employed almost ten thousand people.

Two acolytes played a dice game before Puabi's door. Cheftu tapped, heard nothing, knocked again, and the door opened.

All he saw were a pair of luxuriantly lashed green eyes. *Chloe!*

He kissed her.

Chapter Two

"So this is how it is!" Puabi shouted.

The woman Cheftu kissed, kissed him back, then pushed him away. She glared at him and ran to the priestess's side. "Your lover has lost his reason," she said to Puabi. Then to Cheftu: "What was that for?"

Cheftu was dazzled, confused, but unable to look away from the woman's green eyes. "Chloe," he said. *"Ma chérie,* Chloe."

The redheaded, green-eyed girl glared at him. "I don't know your ruse today, Kidu, but do not put me in peril."

"You're already in peril," Puabi said. "I cannot believe this betrayal!"

"Chloe, *ma chérie?"*

"Stop calling that name," Puabi said to him. "What is wrong with you?"

"I told you opium was too strong, it would smoke his brains," Rudi said.

"He doesn't have brains to smoke," Puabi said. "He's the high priest of fertility, not a justice. His task is what he does with his hips, not his head."

Cheftu's euphoria was fading, and he felt shame and anger at her words—emotions from Kidu. Chloe, if it was Chloe, stared at him with righteous indignation, not recognition. Was she pretending? Puabi, his lover/employer, glared at him with disgust, and Shama, the chamber keeper, peered at him with confusion.

"Who are you?" he asked the redhead directly.

"I've been back for two months, Kidu," she said. "You can't have forgotten I'm Puabi's sister."

Cheftu looked from face to face. Had his error been to wind up in the bed of the wrong sister? Did God make mistakes? "A priestess also?"

Rudi stepped closer and looked up into his face. "Are you lost in drugs? I'm a stargazer. Do you remember nothing?"

"Are you ill?" Puabi asked him. "Your eyes look pale."

Cheftu was beginning to feel ill, for certain. "Pale?" he said.

"Fetch a mirror, Shama."

Cheftu plunked down on a carved, gold-plated armchair, and Rudi slipped a footstool beneath his feet. Puabi handed him a copper mirror, and he looked into it.

By all the gods, he was a blonde.

His eyes were his—Cheftu's—bronze and brown. But his eyelashes were tawny, tipped with gold. And his beard was the color of late honey and elaborately curled. He wore more gold beads than a dancing girl. Chloe would never recognize him; he wouldn't recognize himself. "Do you have tweezers?" he asked the woman. Cheftu's honey-colored brows merged above his nose and crept down it. Hair was everywhere.

"What are tweezers?"

Cheftu glanced at them. They, obviously, did not.

Cheftu looked at himself. His chest was hairy, as were his arms and his shoulders. If he didn't get a good Egyptian waxing soon, he would be crawling with lice and fleas. "I want a barber," he said.

Puabi snatched back the mirror. "Why tell me? I am not

your slave, you have plenty of those. Most of them young and flexible, if I recall."

Cheftu looked at his hands; they looked like his if his were encased in large, furry gloves. He laced his fingers together.

"Why are you here, anyway? Did I send for you?" Puabi asked.

He kept his gaze on his fingers. "I came to apologize for . . . this, uh, dawn."

Puabi stilled. "Rudi, I will speak with you later. Shama, see her out."

When the two had left, Puabi sat down across from him. "It's three days until your first official act. Perhaps you should spend some time in prayer and fasting. Away from opium and women."

Cheftu's ears burned; he was horrified to be in the body of a man who had to be reprimanded for his behavior. Ignoble behavior at that. "I bow to your wisdom," he said.

"The chamber is already prepared, if you want to stay there. I can send Shama to bring you food."

Which chamber? Prepared for what?

It would buy him two days at least. Two days until . . . Cheftu didn't know. He was weary, he was aroused—a state he'd been in all day—and he was ravenous. Appetites Cheftu had always controlled seemed to be controlling him now. "Bring a lot," he said. "I hunger."

"What? Oh," she said. "Of course, you eat like most humans' livestock. Which is why you are the priest of fertility."

The pieces began to fall into place. "How are the, uh, crops doing?" Cheftu asked, daring to look at her.

"The final irrigation is in two days. Have you not been listening?"

"Uh," he said.

"I forget your beauty comes at the price of witlessness," she said as she caressed his arm. "I am the *ensi*, remember? I am responsible for the fertility of the crops."

He nodded. "I am the *en*?"

"You will be appointed by me, to be responsible for the fertility of the population."

Women had been lined up outside his office; the women lined up outside his chambers. Fertility priest. "I . . . I have—"

She sighed and rolled her eyes. "You are to congress with my handmaidens and selected matrons from town. They are selected by their generosity to the temple and the gods," she said in the tone of one speaking to an idiot.

Mon Dieu, *I am in trouble*, Cheftu thought.

"For the next two weeks, you are to save yourself for me. The ritual."

"Of course," he said. Ritual what? Perhaps he didn't want to know. Irrigating the crops, impregnating the population, and officiating at a ceremony in a select chamber sounded very much like the *hieros gamos*—Sacred Marriage—practice. Usually the male was killed after the consummation with the high priestess, to promote a good yield. Two weeks to save his carcass and find Chloe? Then what?

Puabi moved behind him, and her strong fingers kneaded the muscles of his neck and shoulders. "Are you ill? Last night . . . I thought you had died. You seem so different today, I could believe you did, and a demon lives in your body now, brought by the dark of the moon."

Cheftu didn't react. So that's how he had ended up in this body; the real Kidu's spirit had flown, and it had coincided with a lunar eclipse here. "I haven't felt my best," Cheftu said.

Puabi tapped his shoulders. "I'll send an exorcist and diviner to your rooms. Maybe the stargazer, too, though not the same one who decried me, and certainly not Rudi, but one of them. The commonwealth depends on your strength."

Was this the end of the season, or the beginning? "It seems uncommonly hot," he said. "For it to be the end of year."

She sighed deeply. "Kidu, my brainless beauty, the year is only a quarter gone. These are the winter crops we're bringing in. The summer crops are in the fields, beneath the earth." Her voice grew harder. "Go to your chambers now, *en* Kidu. Shama will take you. No more opium, truth?"

He looked at her. Puabi was worried, this dark-haired beauty. He didn't have to feign confusion and stupidity, he certainly felt it. She seemed to be waiting for a response. "Truth," he said, and left.

Cheftu followed the old man through hallways and corridors, until he entered some large, lofty quarters. Food steamed on a table, and the linens of his bed were already laid and drawn back.

"Leave me," Cheftu said, and they did.

Cheftu sank onto a chair and laid his head on his knees. When was he? Where was Chloe?

What had he done to them?

∼

Guli looked up as Ulu entered. She looked worn, and the roots of her red hair were long and brown. He winked at her as he finished curling his customer's hair. The customer had paid in steamed fish for today and smoked fish he could sell on the morrow. The aroma had been teasing Guli's nose for the past half double hour, but the customer had exceptionally fine hair that required a great amount of patience to get every curl to make and to stay.

The customer's hands were held palm upward—a Harrapan girl on the wharf had painted them, and the dye was drying.

"There—" he said, laying the last curl. "You are beautiful."

He'd already painted her face, elongating her eyes with kohl and attempting to slim down her wide face with a little oil and ash shading. "Have a wonderful time tonight at the feast." The customer's aged sister was finally marrying, which meant it was finally possible that she herself could marry. What better time did the gods provide for her to meet her intended, than at the feast?

"If good fortune strikes me, I'll bring you barley cakes tomorrow," she said, rising up on her toes to kiss his cheek.

"If *really* good fortune strikes you," Guli said, "you won't rise from your bed!"

The customer blushed, Ulu hooted with laughter, and Guli kissed the girl's cheek. "Stay away from the hanging lamps. Stand only by those which are low."

"Low lamps," the customer repeated. "I'm so nervous. Family is coming from everywhere. As far as Nippur."

Guli listened as he nudged her toward the door. She kissed him again, then set off down the street, wobbling in her festival shoes. He closed the door and turned to Ulu.

"It's been forever! How are you?" he asked, as they kissed. "What happened to your hair?"

"So much," she said, unpacking her basket. "I brought you dates—"

"I love dates."

"I know this about you," she said with a sly smile. "Also three days' worth of peas, lentils, and an onion tart."

"Three days for an ordinary man is not three days for me," he said.

Ulu leaned back, squeezing her breasts together by crossing her arms at the waist. "I know well you are a man of extraordinary appetites. You'll find the rations are substantial."

"Business is going well?"

She sighed. "I couldn't be doing better."

"Well sit here and tell me all about it," he said, then tore a piece of bread. "What do you want me to do to you, in exchange for this bounty?"

"Two things."

He finished the piece of bread and mopped mashed lentils up with another piece. "The first?"

"Get rid of these roots. I'm embarrassed to be seen with myself."

He looked at her hair. "Are you red yet?"

"I was considering brown."

"Ah, you want to be a Shemti?"

She chuckled. "Truth be told, I am Shemti."

"Are we matching, below?" he asked, winking at her.

"The gods have seen fit to do that work for you. Like I said, I truly am Shemti."

"I'll need to go to the market, get some palm trunk to make the dye. What is the other thing you wanted?"

"This other thing I'm doing, I want you to come with me."

"I've come with you many times, dear Ulu."

"Don't be a rascal. I've been changing some things."

Guli's eyebrows rose, and he tore off another piece of bread. "Go on."

"A whole new look, a whole new Ulu." She swallowed. "You recognize fine things, I . . . I don't."

Guli looked at the food—estimated its resale value. "Ulu, you know I would love to help you, but I can't afford it."

"Viza again?"

He nodded.

"I'll pay you."

"Ulu—"

"A few days of shopping. Some clothes, some furnishings. Please?"

"I would love to go spend your money with you, but I can't afford it."

"Are you going to have to sell the food I brought you?"

"It's this location," he said. "It's dreadful. I have those few who know where I am, but almost no foot traffic. Crocodiles surround me, I can't find a way out."

"You could move in with me," she said. "Your own rooms and everything."

Guli chewed the last piece of bread. If he were going to trade this food, he should stop eating it. "I can't imagine the clients of Crooked Way would tolerate that," he said. "Besides, I still have the agreement. It doesn't matter what I do. I owe."

"Viza is a criminal," she snapped. "You're a good man!"

"I did what I couldn't afford," he said, wrapping the rest of the food. "I just thought if I could get started—but, no matter."

"How far in debt are you?"

"With that interest rate? I couldn't sell myself into slavery and make it back."

She looked around the house. "Not to slight your surroundings, Guli, but this space is hardly worth half of what you spend."

"Taxes," he said. "They kill you with leasing. Then compounded interest. When I showed the scribe what I had done, he refused to look any further. He claimed he could do nothing."

"You want to stay out of the courts, I imagine."

Guli chuckled without mirth. "Far away. At least here I'm not stamping clay or digging ditches. I work inside now." He touched his seal. "I'm a client of the commonwealth."

Ulu looked down.

"At least for the next few days," he said. "Come back tomorrow, and I'll have your dye."

Ulu stood up. "I will. Guli, don't sell the food. Eat it. You are too thin already."

He nodded, and she left. He closed the door behind her and turned back to the room. If he ate today, then when the other customer brought barley cakes he could take those to the dyer before breakfast and make the trade, be back here in time to open, with the brown dye.

Maybe his destiny would change in the next two days. Maybe he could escape Viza.

Guli opened the lentil paste and scooped up some. It had been made with fresh goat's cheese and spices. Today he would eat; tomorrow . . He glanced at the small altar in the back of his house. The crude figures had been payment in exchange for waxing a potter's back and trimming his wife's toenails. Guli supposed they were his personal god—gods? Doubtful, but desperate, he cracked a jar of beer and walked over to the altar.

Sitting down heavily on his haunches, he poured a little beer before the male and female lumps of clay. "Please bring me currency," he said. "Make Viza forget about me. Let me keep my business."

Their faces were gashes that approximated eyes and nose and mouth. They had no hands and stood stiffly. Guli had the sinking feeling he had just wasted two sips of beer.

~

"When you don't know what to do, keep doing what you're doing. You can make a U-turn if you have momentum, but if you stop, you're doomed." Chloe smiled. "I can't believe I'm giving a pep talk to sheep."

It was early, or late, depending on one's perspective of day and night. "Early, I guess," she said to Kami, who was gnawing on some grass in her sleep. After finishing her homework—listing hundreds of male human occupations—Chloe had had both a headache and a hand cramp. But attending school was good, it kept her from pining away for Cheftu too much.

"Who knows, if I was yanked out of my bed and dumped here, maybe he was, too." Though no one seemed to recognize any nationalities other than Harrapan and the Black-Haired Ones themselves. "Maybe he's in Egypt, and is on his way here." It had happened before. "Of course, we *chose* to travel before. This was completely spontaneous."

If sheep could snore, hers were.

Chloe stretched back on the grass, her arms above her head. "They have big sky in Texas, but nothing like this," she said. In a pancake-flat land, the heavens looked like a diamond-studded dome. *Domes,* she thought. *These people have them already.* In one of her design classes at university she'd been taught that domes were the invention of the Greeks.

She heard some rustling on the other side of the skin-fence. In a practice that her body knew, but her mind didn't, she tensed, her fingers gripping a clump of turf, preparing to throw. A clod of dirt would be confusing to a wild animal, disintegrating as it came toward him. Enough of it would stay solid, so he would also receive a wallop for his efforts. He'd reason it would be easier to eat someone else's sheep.

She listened intently, but didn't hear anything else. After a moment, Chloe relaxed, her hand around the dirt. There was no moon now, and the night before had been a partial lunar eclipse. The students at school were buzzing before the Tablet Father arrived, wondering what that meant. The last sign from the moon had been the night of the flood.

The night I arrived, Chloe thought. *Apparently, I traveled on March 23. Now it is, as close as I can guess, May 25. Two months I've been gone. Does Cheftu wonder where I am? Does he miss me?*

"Shut up," she said, sitting up. "Just don't go there." *Hope for the best,* she thought. *He'll be here. Just keep an eye open for a tawny-eyed, dark-haired, dark-skinned, intelligent man. Egyptian.*

And keep going to school and learning until then.

"Someday my prince will come," she told the sheep. They didn't appreciate the sarcasm in her voice. She left for the city gate.

~

It was an innocent start. A knock at the door. Cheftu opened it. A woman threw herself at him, kissing his face, grabbing at his body. Someone else sucked on his fingers, and more hands than he could count caressed him.

Kidu had no physical self-control.

Cheftu extricated himself and got the door almost shut. Gilded-nail hands flapped in the narrow opening.

"No," he said to the pleading brown eyes attached to the hands. "You must go."

"I told you," another one said, squeezing into view. "He wants me."

"No, I don't."

"Me then."

"No, it's me!"

The mass of them pushed open the door, and he stepped back and raised his hand. They halted.

"Not you either," he said to the last woman.

"Me?"

"Me?"

Cheftu looked around in exasperation. Women crowded the hallway and the outer room of his bedchamber. "No one," he announced. "I want no one tonight." Puabi had declared it. However— "Unless you happen to know a lost, green-eyed girl."

They looked at each other. "Does he mean Jesi?"

"Durat?"

"These are green-eyed women?" His pulse raced; could it be? "They are here?"

"Well, Jesi is. She's one of Tubal-Cain's daughters, but comely anyway."

"Where is she?"

"We could get her to come here," one of the women, sneaky-looking and fair-haired, said.

"The other one you mentioned, Dura?" Cheftu asked.

"Durat. Well, she does have green eyes. Last I heard her travails were upon her."

"Delivered a boy-child," another one said. "His left foot is curved."

"Poor Durat, the gods are envious of beauty."

Could Chloe be hiding in the body of a recently delivered woman? She could be anywhere. "I want to meet them both," he said.

"And what will you do for us?" the sneaky blonde said. "It is against our advantage to bring you someone else."

By the gods— "I have a preference for green-eyed women," he said. "It cannot be helped."

"Since when?"

"I've never heard that?"

"No others allure you?" a brunette who did "allure" Kidu's sensibilities said, slipping her hand over his bared arm. Damn Kidu's responsive body. "When did that change?"

"Are your abilities so great, you can please several women at once?" someone else asked.

An image flashed through Cheftu's mind: intertwined bodies, legs and arms moving in tandem; heat and fierce power filling his body. "Ah yes," he said. "Kidu can do that." It was truth; though it was certainly not Cheftu's memory.

"If we bring you a green-eyed woman, will you please us all?" the blonde said.

"At the same time?"

There would ten women, plus Chloe. Ha! She would kill him first; it wouldn't matter.

If he found Chloe, she could stake her claim and deal with these others. He grinned. She wouldn't be pleased with him, but the means, in this case, justified the end. "Certainly. The more, the merrier." He'd heard that somewhere.

Probably from her.

The flock of them left, and Cheftu closed the door, then dropped the bolt so he was locked safely in. And they were out.

He picked up a goblet of finely carved obsidian, so delicate he could see the shadow of his finger through it. Would she know him, in this odd configuration of flesh and bone?

He had to believe. Believe in the seven years they'd shared together. Believe in the fact they'd found each other through time and history twice before. Believe that they were here for a reason, and that they couldn't accomplish it unless they were together.

Believe.

~

The copper vase bounced off the wall, and the stargazers ducked its ricochet. The *ensi's* attitude toward the heavenly signs hadn't improved. Ezzi felt a tug on his cloak and stood up again.

Puabi wasn't painted gold today, so she looked pretty much like most black-haired women, he thought. She glared so fiercely at Asa, Ezzi couldn't tell the color of her eyes.

"You have no proof!" she said.

"The time is approaching, *ensi*," Asa said. "The stars are shifting in unknown patterns."

"Why would we presume that to be bad?"

"The dikes are clogged, the river is silting up."

"That is because the slaves and overseers aren't doing their jobs. I'm responsible for the *weather* and the *crops*. The *lugal's* responsibility is for the economics and actual workmen. Go depose him."

There was a disturbance at the door. Puabi sat up straighter and looked at the men. "*En* Kidu joins us. As the high priest of fertility, he should be here."

They bowed as the *en* and his retinue of priests, scribes, and acolytes entered. Ezzi was struck by the difference in the man. They stood again, and Ezzi looked at the *en*. He was tall and broad like a hillside tree and golden, without paint. His eyes, which before had been half-closed in a slumbering face, were bright and sharp.

They almost looked a different color.

The *ensi* motioned for him to approach her, then made him sit in her chair and sat on his lap. The *en's* expression was neutral, but he didn't embrace her. His hands rested on the arms of the chair.

Today, he was awake.

"Continue," she said to the stargazers.

"I just came to warn you the time was approaching," Asa said. "I do not threaten you, *ensi*. I am but a gentleman, fulfilling my responsibility to the commonwealth."

"What has the *ensi* done, that the gods require her dismissal?" the *en* asked. His words were precise, his inflection and tone like an Old Boy's. Ezzi marveled at the change in the man. Was this the difference opium made?

Asa lifted his hands to the heavens. "It is not for me to say."

"I haven't done anything!" Puabi said, turning her glare to Kidu.

"With so many deities to please, *en,* who knows what she might have inadvertently done. Whom she offended inadvertently, I do not know," Asa said. "This I can tell you, though. The days approach when stars will fall from the heavens onto Ur. The sun will be obscured by the moon. Darkness and desolation will fill the land."

The *en* looked from Asa to Ezzi to the other diviners, exorcists, and stargazers. "The sun will only be hidden for a while," the *en* said. "Truth?"

Asa bowed his head. "That is why the *ensi* must step down, to assure the return of the sun."

"What confirmation have you received that your assessment is accurate, Asa?" Kidu asked.

"Are you working with me or against me?" Puabi hissed at him. "Don't offend the man!"

The *en* ignored her and stared at Asa.

Ezzi would almost believe in possession, to see the *en* today.

"I—I have no confirmation," the old stargazer said. "I need none. I am the stargazer. What I say is truth. I alone perceive the judgments in the Tablets of Destiny. I bring those judgments to the attention of the *lugal* and the *ensi* and the council. They decide how to bribe or intercede with the gods. As I said, I am just fulfilling my responsibility by informing you a judgment is coming."

Kidu pursed his lips. "Bring me a time schedule for this

judgment, and the past records of your predictions. Leave us."

They bowed out, while the *ensi* was still seated on *en* Kidu's lap.

When the copper doors had shut behind them, Asa burst into a rage. Ezzi listened as the stargazer railed about the dangers of his job and the obstinacy of the temple. "They will bring death on us all," he said. "Who does the *en* think he is to question me? His job is not to reason. Oh, they bring on themselves evil. Desolation and darkness."

"That was a very nice phrase, sir," Ezzi said.

"Thank you, boy. It took me double hours to find the exact words, to convey the message. Now it falls on deaf ears." His fury was almost spent. "I guess the humans didn't listen to Ziusudra either. For 120 years they ignored him." Asa stopped. "Find a sledge, boy. I need to rest."

The other stargazers followed at a distance. Asa had lost favor, and no one wanted to be associated with him. Ezzi hailed a sledge and helped the old man in, gave the driver directions and assured his employer he wouldn't be far behind. He watched them ride off, then turned back to the temple complex, seeking out the Office of Records.

"Gentleman Nimrod, sir."

Cheftu nodded. It didn't matter—he was too angry to think. Was it his fury, or Kidu's? It was of no consequence where it began; it consumed him. He looked up to see a hairy man walk in. The man was dressed as a fisherman, he even smelled like a fisherman, though he wore a seal at his waist and had the manner of a prince.

Scars marred his hands, and the pointed claw of a bear had once grabbed his shoulder. A blade had cut his forehead, narrowly missing his eye, and, when the man bowed, Cheftu saw the white dots of a bite mark on his back. The man's name meant mighty hunter. Obviously, he was lucky.

Nimrod looked at him. "Greetings, brother of the mountain," he said. "How do the gods bless you today?"

Nimrod, Kidu's wrestling partner, the first male human who had befriended Kidu. Would Nimrod know Kidu was gone? How could he? What would he do?

"It is an infuriating day," Cheftu said, unable to hide the passions stirred so easily in Kidu. The man had no self-control.

"Shall we have a match, brother?" Nimrod said with a smile. "Then we can wear away your anger."

Both men stripped to loincloths, fastened heavy leather belts around their waists, and stepped close. Cheftu knew from Kidu's memories that they would embrace, hold their opponent's waist, and fight to topple him. They must keep both hands on the belt at all times, and their heads side by side. Nimrod was slighter than Kidu was, but Nimrod was sinewy and strong.

They strained with each other until they were wet with exertion. The scribe called the quarters of the match, and at the half, Nimrod whispered in his ear. "I hear Puabi has been asked to step down."

Cheftu's frustration would not be bottled any longer. He heaved at Nimrod and strained to pull him off his feet. In one burst of energy, Cheftu did, and both men fell to the floor. They sat up, sweating and panting. The scribe left for beer and Cheftu watched the perspiration drip from his forehead onto the reed matting.

"Kidu, we are friends," Nimrod said.

Cheftu's anger was spent. "How good a friend?"

Nimrod leaned over, his voice low so only Cheftu could hear. "Close enough to know that you are in danger. The stars don't favor Puabi, and when the new *ensi* is elected, that will be the end of you."

Cheftu said nothing, could say nothing, except marvel.

"The *en* isn't a position you retire from, like *lugal*," Nimrod said. "It's one you die to get out of."

The scribe opened the jar of beer and handed both men drinking tubes. When they had finished the jar, Nimrod rose to leave. "When the time comes and it is reasonable for you to flee, I will help you," Nimrod said. "I owe you that debt." He touched the scar on his shoulder. *Kidu had saved Nimrod's life.* An impression of heat, blood, and fear passed through Cheftu.

He mopped sweat from his eyebrows. "Thank you."

Nimrod walked away, then turned and looked over his shoulder, as though he wished to speak. "Your eyes," he said. "They've always been so light?"

Don't lose the one comrade you've made, Cheftu thought. "I didn't know you were the kind of man to notice," Cheftu gibed.

Nimrod paused, then laughed.

Now all Cheftu had to do was find Chloe.

~

"Asa the Stargazer?" the scribe said. "Past Predictions?"

"Yes please."

"For whom do you request these documents? I can't let just anyone break open the envelopes."

"I request them for Asa, who requests them for the *en*."

"Kidu? Do you have proof of this? His seal?"

Ezzi shook his head. "I just came from a conference with him, though. He—"

The scribe shook his head. "No seal, no records." He looked beyond Ezzi. "May I help you?"

Another scribe, with the temple seal around his arm, stepped to Ezzi's side and addressed the record keeper. "Asa, the Stargazer. All his predictions and the following years' crop reports."

The record keeper looked from Ezzi to the scribe. "It will take me days to find them, sir."

The scribe slid a carnelian seal toward the man. "Then start looking. This request is from *en* Kidu."

The record keeper looked at Ezzi. "Do you know each other?"

The scribe turned to Ezzi. "No."

"He asked—"

Ezzi reached out and knocked over the scribe's jar of beer. "I'm sorry!" he cried. "Here, let me wipe that for you."

The record keeper moved the drying clay documents out of the way, then mopped up the beer with his cloak. He glared at Ezzi. Then he looked at the scribe and scooped up the seal. "I'll look for them and when I find them, I'll send for you to bring a scribe and a wheelbarrow."

The scribe thanked him and left.

"You can just follow him out," the record keeper said to Ezzi.

"I feel so bad about spilling your beer," Ezzi said. "Let me help you this afternoon, it will ease my humanity."

The record keeper looked long and hard at him. "Do you know how tablets are filed?"

Ezzi pointed to the border of his cloak. "I'm an Old Boy," he said. "Just guide me in the right direction, and I'll reason it out."

The record keeper sighed and lifted the countertop up to let Ezzi pass. "Come along then. I'll show you what to file, go change my cloak, and be back before you've sorted all the accounts for the first month."

"Or, I could help you find those tablets the *en* wanted,"

Ezzi suggested. "He'd be very pleased if he received them today, I'd wager."

The record keeper nodded. "Truth. That's an excellent idea."

Ezzi followed him into the storeroom. Tens of thousands of tablets were stacked on wooden shelves: twenty deep, three shelves to a row, and four rows across the room. All the information of Ur was here. Births, deaths, and marriages. Divorces, adoptions, and mergers. Registered ships, the annual yields of all the crops, tax records for every freedman, slave, client, and gentlemen, and deeds to all the properties in the commonwealth.

Every document's double was also left here, filed on these shelves in case a justice needed additional proof for a claim.

"There are eighteen more rooms," the record keeper said. "Asa began stargazing . . . hmm . . . It will be back here," the scribe said, walking through the first three rooms. Dust hung in the air, and sunlight poured down from the high windows. "There," he said, waving to a series of eight rows, five shelves per row, fifty documents per stack, eight stacks per shelf. "Are you sure of this? You don't mind helping?"

"My humanity would be appeased," Ezzi said.

"Very well. I'll close up the front and be back before you know it. I keep a jar of beer behind the desk in case you get thirsty."

"I'll be fine," Ezzi said. "Take your time."

He waited until the door's bolt fell, then tied his cloak tighter, to free his arms, and began to flip through the stacks looking for the phonetics of Asa's name and the symbols of star and eye: stargazer.

Chapter Three

*E*n Kidu, come quick!" an acolyte, panting from his run, said.

Cheftu, alerted to something in the boy's expression, followed him out, barefooted. Twilight had fallen, the quick light that precedes night's fall and promises tomorrow will come. The night was lit with a thousand falling stars.

They zoomed overhead in arcs, streamers of red and orange and blue and yellow lighting the sky before they vanished. "Where are the citizens?" Cheftu asked.

"Most are hiding in their homes," the boy said, from his crouched position.

Cheftu could see Venus, the star of Inana; Jupiter, who protected him and the *lugal,* and the first pinpricks of the constellations, all dimmed by the brilliance of the meteor shower. Was it close enough to damage the fields? What did this sign portend to these people? Tomorrow was his first duty as *en.* Was this a sign of disapproval or anger? Puabi declared weather and crops were her responsibility—how did this affect her? Cheftu told the trembling boy not to be afraid. "The gods shower us with gifts."

"They do?" the boy said, arrested by the thought.

"They do. In fact, I want you to go retrieve one of them."

"You do?"

"See how they fall?" Cheftu said, pointing to the tail of a

particularly colorful falling "star." "Go outside of the city, search the fields, and return with a sky stone for me."

"Me, sir?" the boy asked.

Cheftu estimated the boy was just about nine years old. His voice was high, and he was slight, but like all the males of the temple, his face was perfection, his body without flaw. He would be a dazzlingly handsome man someday. His black eyes were curious. "I can just . . . pick it up? Off the ground? It won't . . . hurt me?"

If he was hurt or disfigured, he would lose his position in the temple for life.

"Take a waterskin with you," Cheftu said. "Check the stone's heat by pouring water on it."

"Like rocks beside the cooking fire?" the boy asked.

"Exactly."

The shower continued, but it was less dramatic than before. Just a few shooting stars. The clients, gentlemen, freedman, and slaves would step outside now, and the deliberations of the council would begin. Soon, if the mob got scared enough, they would come for Puabi. "Go now," Cheftu said. "Be quick, be thorough, and be discreet."

The boy bowed and dashed off.

~

Shama pressed the heated brick against the felt and steamed the pleat. Rudi and Puabi sat in chairs, slaves fanned them, and the *en* paced back and forth.

"You're going to wear out the rug, Kidu."

"He's sly, the old fox," the *en* said. "Clever."

"He took the records. What does it matter?" Puabi asked.

Shama looked up to see Rudi roll her eyes. "Better to be worried about the stars falling last night," the stargazer said.

"What matters," Kidu said, "is that with no proof Asa's

predictions have been wrong in the past, the *lugal,* the council, might believe he's right this time."

Shama wondered at the *en*—was it the weight of the official responsibility that brought about this great change, or the lack of women and drugs, or something more sinister. Although possession, in his case, was an improvement.

"Which means the *lugal* can legitimately and legally ask for you to step down," Rudi explained to her sister.

"How did he get the records?" Puabi wailed. "You're the *en*! My consort! My protector! How could you let this happen to me?"

Shama looked back to his felt, moved the skirt around, pinned the next section into place, and reached for the tongs. The brick hissed as he laid it on the water-soaked fabric, and in his head he sang a song. Many years ago, he'd discovered this song was exactly the right length of time to assure a flat pleat. Any longer, and he'd have scorched the felted wool.

"They are public records," the *en* said. "I'm a priest, not a justice."

Puabi plucked at her necklaces and pouted.

Shama was disappointed in his lady's behavior. For years she had availed herself of the benefits of her position. She had enjoyed its bounty, now she would suffer beneath its lash. Nothing came free from the hands of the gods—there was no mercy.

Except, perhaps, from the god of gods. But he would never be involved in this insignificant tussle.

Rudi leaned forward and placed a freckled hand on her sister's wool-covered knee. "I've seen the stars, too," she said. "There was the blood moon, the new star, the lunar eclipse, but it doesn't—"

Puabi jerked away, refused to look at her sister or lover.

Shama picked up the tongs and placed the brick back in

the fire. He blew on the new pleat, brushed away pieces of crumbling clay, then removed the pins.

"Floods happen," Puabi said. "The fields are growing well. Healthy and strong. There is no reason—"

"We have stars falling out of the sky," Rudi said. "Here, look at this."

Shama leaned over to see what she held in her hand. It looked like a large, dark clod of dirt.

"It's dirt."

"It's part of a star," Kidu said.

"It doesn't look like a star," Puabi said.

"Take it," Rudi said.

"It's dirty. Kidu, hold the star."

He glanced at the piece. "It's not a star, it's just a piece of one."

Shama looked at the *en*, then picked up pins and began to form the next pleat. The man was a man; quite a change from the overgrown boy of weeks ago. And the barbarian from years before that.

"Why are little pieces of star falling to the earth?" Puabi asked.

"That is the omen," Rudi said. "Something has happened which caused a star to die, and a new star to rise in its place."

They grew quiet.

"Then it's even worse than Asa thinks?" Puabi asked.

Shama checked the felt to make sure it was wet, then he picked up the tongs and set the brick on the fabric.

"It's been several different signs, all saying the same thing," Rudi said.

Puabi glared at Kidu and Rudi. "I haven't done anything."

Rudi spoke. "It doesn't matter, sister. You are the *ensi*. The gods require your sacrifice."

"I'm not at fault," she insisted.

"That matters not at all," Rudi said. "You are the *ensi*. You are all of us."

"You always did hate me," Puabi said, turning away from her sister.

Shama picked up the tongs, removed the brick, checked the pleat for perfection, then set about folding the next one.

"She's unreasonable," the *en* said to Rudi.

"How dare you!" Puabi shouted.

He sighed, bowed to them both, and left. The scribes and priests who trailed him bumped into each other as they followed.

Shama set his tongs back in the fire. Rudi was right; it was Puabi's responsibility. However, could the signs be good omens?

And what, really, had happened to Kidu?

∼

"I must go," Ningal said. "As a member of the council, it is my duty."

Chloe rubbed salve into her shoulder. This chicken-wing style of writing fourteen hours a day was killing her arm. "What happens tonight?"

"We ratify the *ensi's* choice of *en*."

Chloe looked at her terrible writing.

"Do you wish to go with me?"

"I have homework."

"Ah yes, lists," Ningal said as he adjusted his basket hat. "What did you start with?"

"Derivations of human."

"Quite a long list. Do you have any questions?"

"They mention the four members of the commonwealth:

slaves, freedmen, clients, and gentlemen. Explain the differences?"

"As a council member, I am a gentleman. Which means I own property, I pay taxes, and I house slaves."

"What's a client?"

"He is in the other house of the council. A client is a male, free, who shows up and votes."

"Then what's a freedman?"

"Male, free, but he has no stock in the commonwealth. He can't vote, he doesn't own property. He carries on his business or trade, but he has no voice."

"Which one do you have to be in order to have a seal?"

"Everyone who conducts business has a seal. Only criminals and slaves don't, unless it states what they've done or whose they are."

"What about slaves? Most seem to be, well, the same race as the Black-Haired Ones."

"Slavery." Ningal chuckled. "Slavery comes in several ways. Debt is the most common path. Anyone in debt can sell himself or a family member into slavery. Or any family member can be substituted for the debtor. And a slave can own slaves and property, have a business, a family, he just happens to be owned by someone else.

"Then there are the temple slaves, who aren't actually slaves at all. They were conceived by the high priest of fertility, the *en,* and when the women of the populace give birth, those children are dedicated to a life at the temple."

"They're bred for slavery?"

"Don't be so alarmed. Within the temple come employment opportunities, same as in the commonwealth. Those humans aren't raised by their parents, that's the only difference. Oh, and of course, if they are not perfect, they are adopted by someone in the commonwealth. Only the most beautiful men may serve the goddess."

"What about the most beautiful women?"

Ningal cocked his head, then spoke after a moment. "Inana is a jealous goddess, so she protects her position by stocking the temple with . . . less than appealing females. Nevertheless, they are flawless. No scars, no disfiguring or debilitating marks, perfect senses. They just . . . aren't the loveliest to gaze upon."

Chloe flexed her fingers as she prepared to write. "So then, the council, composed of clients and gentlemen, meets and votes in the *lugal* and *ensi*?"

"True, and then the *ensi* appoints the *en*."

"The freedmen and slaves are just stuck with the decisions."

"True."

"The women, too."

His expression was wry. "Are you trying to win permission to join the council, in addition to being allowed in the Tablet House?"

"Females are in business all over town. What status are they?"

"In Ur, they are freedmen."

"What if they own land, pay taxes, house slaves?"

"Still, they're freedmen."

"That's unjust."

"In truth, they influence the men who vote, so they get their words in, just not formally."

"She who rocks the cradle rocks the vote?"

Ningal frowned. "Excuse me?"

"Nothing. Go to your meeting. If I go, it will just upset everyone. Especially my Tablet Father, who expects me to be able to read and write the forty humans on my list by dawn tomorrow."

She watched him leave, and had a sudden, almost-hysterical desire to go too. Her legs wanted to get up by themselves. *Will I stop at nothing to avoid this homework,* she thought, and crossed her legs firmly. Then she pounded her clay flat, eased her fingers around the stylus and began her list. Determined. "Human. Male. Human. Female."

～

Ulu rinsed her mouth, spat on the matting, weighed the stone against her carved-duck mina-weights, sighed, then stretched.

"Stretch like that again, Ulu, and I'll have to pay you even more," her customer said, undoing the sash he'd just tied. "I'll just be late for council."

Youth had its accommodations, but she'd made enough currency for the day and looked forward to sleeping in her own apartments, her own bed, and completely through the night. Still, this customer paid well. Deliberately she rubbed her mouth. "Tomorrow, my dear. You've exhausted me."

He laughed—he understood and acknowledged the graceful way she'd gotten out of it. Of course, grace and elegance was his way of life—except for needing her in the darkest of rooms in the daringest of ways. "I'll plan on tomorrow."

"I'll be waiting, with your beer."

"The courts are open late tomorrow," he said. "I won't be back before the double hour at midnight."

Ulu's fingers drifted over her breast as she pinned her dress. "As you know, it's a business of supply and demand."

He set another agate on the table. She moved it to the scale, weighed it against the carved duck, and smiled up at him. "A generous down payment. Your beer will be cool."

"As long as you are hot."

She blew a kiss at him as he walked out, then lay back on

the bed after the door fell shut. Another knock almost immediately. "Not tonight," she shouted.

Disappointed noises.

"Go away!"

Footsteps retreated down the corridor.

She knocked a roach off the scale—he weighed almost a half mina—and sat up. Another knock. "I'm finished for tonight!"

Guli poked his head in.

"Honeysweet!" she shrieked, sitting up, and crawling across the bed to him. "What happened to you?"

He stepped inside. "Let's just say, I don't believe in the gods."

Ulu looked up at the mud-daubed palm fronds of the roof. "How can you doubt them?"

"I don't think they care for us, then," he said.

His face was wrecked. Split lip, one eye swollen shut, the other the color of raw meat in the marketplace. A gap in the front of his smile. His big hands were bruised, the skin split at the knuckles.

"No one said they cared for us," she said. "But they're our masters." Guli sat down on the bed with a wince and buried his head in her bosom. "Is this the work of Viza?" she asked as she rubbed his head.

"Oh yes, Viza indeed."

"The shop?"

"Ruined." He sighed, and his hot breath burned her skin through the wool of her dress. "All the things I bought, to replace the ones they broke before. I can't pay you back—"

"Hush," she said, rocking him back and forth. "Do you have a place to stay?"

His arms went around her back and he hugged her. "I don't need one."

"What do you mean? Guli, what are you thinking?" He

didn't answer, so she moved his hair, to be able to see his face. "Don't do something stupid."

"I'll have a home soon," he said.

"No! I thought you said it would do you no good to sell yourself."

"What do I have left?"

"Be a gardener," she said.

He pulled away. "I hate gardening."

"You have such a gift for it."

"I want to be a hairdresser!"

"Apparently it is not what the gods want."

He sat up, his back to her. "Anyway, I was just telling you, in case you went by. Viza has taken the house."

"Guli, wait. There must be something—"

"I could kill him," he said.

"Then you would be back in the courts."

"Ningal would love to see me hanged," he said.

Ulu froze. She didn't know the details about Guli's life before she met him, but she knew he'd had a severe warning from a justice after serving two sentences for violent crimes. One more mistake, and Guli would be executed. "Justice Ningal?" He lived on her street.

"Yes." He stood there, shaking his head like an ox, side to side. "I can't prove anything against Viza; they destroyed the documents."

"What about the public records?"

"I signed copies for them, but now that I know Viza's business practices, I doubt they were ever filed in the Office of Records."

"Do you want to stay with me tonight?" she asked.

He looked around the rented room, and she knew he saw the bugs, the stains of spit, and other splotches on the matting. She hadn't even rinsed. Guli was fastidious, not with Ezzi's superior manner, but in relation to beauty. Guli needed loveliness, craved order. He was repulsed by grime and stench and coarseness. Even though he'd lived in it for a very long time.

His nature was a gentleman's, who was cursed with the temper of a scorpion.

Doubly awful for him to be sold into slavery and live in the marshes, drinking the same water the buffaloes did.

He pressed his lips to her hand. "Thank you, sweet, but no."

She squeezed his hand; he held it for a moment, then let himself out quietly.

Ulu sagged onto the bed and watched the roach crawl across the scale. She didn't even know what god to bribe on Guli's behalf.

Chapter Four

Cheftu left, following the aide back to his rooms. He'd been ratified; now he wanted sleep. He opened the door and moved through his dark apartments, into the bedroom. He shed his clothes, picked up a flagon of wine and his glass, then got into his bed. The small window let in the scents of the city and garden. It was over. He took a sip of wine and leaned back.

Against a naked torso.

The sensation was so warming, so confusing, that it took Cheftu a second before he leaped away—surrounded by women's giggles. He lit a lamp and beheld them—three women, all undressed, all in his bed. Two he recognized.

"Chloe?" he asked the one he'd never seen, an older, rounded woman, and held the lamp higher.

She smiled, revealing blackened teeth.

"*Ma chérie?*"

Her eyes were green, but like the color of the darkest firs, not like emeralds.

"We brought you your green-eyed girl. This is Jesi." The sneaky-looking blonde kissed Jesi and turned to him. "Are you ready, Kidu?"

Cheftu set the oil lamp down and stared back at the three women. They were certainly staring at him. "No."

"No? We had an agreement!"

"I'm sorry, but the situation has changed."

"How is that? This is an infringement on an agreement between two—"

He held up his hand to ward off her words. "There are grave omens," he said. "I am the priest of fertility, and the barley ripens in the field. I can't allow you lovely women," he said, making eye contact with them all, "to deplete my strength. It would be unfair to the people of Ur."

The blonde cursed. The three of them stayed in his bed, and Cheftu crossed his arms and leaned against the wall. "It would be dishonorable not to be concerned for the fields," the blonde said. She spat the words. "Come along," she said to the women. "We can't stay here."

Cheftu ushered them out the door, dodging their questing hands and greedy mouths.

"Our agreement is still in effect," the blonde said before they left. "You are obligated to meet your side. Maybe not now, but as soon as the fields are in."

"Bring me a different green-eyed woman," he said. Then he endured her kiss and shoved her out the door.

His bed was ripe with the smell of the three women. He picked a spare blanket out of the trunk and threw it on the floor. If this was how Casanova lived, he had been beyond insane.

～

"Samana! Samana!"

The cry began at the city gates, and Cheftu's eyes popped open. Rust.

In seconds, there was a pounding at his door. He was up and wrapped in his cloak by the time the acolyte opened his bedroom door. *"En Kidu!* There is rust!"

"Send runners to the *lugal.*"

"He is being informed as we speak."

"Run tell the *ensi.*"

The boy hesitated, then bowed and ran out the door. Cheftu shut his gathering attendants in the outer chamber and took a moment to dig in his borrowed brain for details on rust.

Barley mold, set on the ripening ears. It could ruin the whole crop, if it spread from field to field. Barley was the staple of the people in the plain. If the barley crop failed, or was even reduced by half, it could spell hard times for the plains dwellers.

If it was reduced further, it could mean famine.

Either way, Samana just confirmed that the *ensi*—whose responsibilities were crops and weather—was in disfavor with the gods.

He threw open his door. "Call me a sledge," Cheftu ordered. "We're going to the fields."

~

School was canceled.

Some places had snow days; in Ur, they had rust days. The population spilled from the gates and into the fields. Though the people were shipwrights and merchants, craftsmen and scribes, no one was so far removed from farming that he couldn't spot rust.

Ningal was no exception, and he and Chloe joined the masses of quickly dressed residents picking their way carefully down the narrow ditches between the barley rows. Every ear had to be examined, every field scrutinized. The *lugal* rode the land on a donkey, moving slowly, scribes in his wake to make notes as the clients ran up to tell him which fields were clean and which weren't.

Any sign of rust on a stalk meant the stalk had to be cut

down and burned, so not to infect the others. There was no singing, no joy as the people—mothers with children in slings, great-great-grandfathers with canes, boys and girls whose eyes were wide with fear, and young farmers who had used credit to plant their fields—threaded through the thousands of acres outside Ur.

Gossip was that the great *en* and *ensi* had been to the fields at dawn, seen the damage, and were even now interceding with the gods.

"Samana!" they would hear the call from one side, then *"Samana!"* from another.

"It's this," Ningal said, pointing to the ear. Chloe crouched down and saw the reddish stripe on the leaf of the plant. He knelt and drew on the ground the sign for "poison." "Go tell the *lugal* there is *samana* in this row."

Chloe noted the location, then inched down the narrow path beside the irrigation channel. It was hard to believe on such a beautiful, cloudless day, destruction was sighted. She reached the main path and saw the people standing five deep around the *lugal's* donkey. Scribes took notes and sent priests to mark the rows. A cart from the far end was making its way down, to take away the poisoned stalks.

"Cut it," the scribes told people. "There's too much. Cut it before it passes on." She listened to them tell this several times, then ran back to her row and picked her way down it.

"Ningal," she called softly. He had knelt again, marked the spot. "Ningal!"

He turned, and she hurried to him, staggered at the number of stalks he'd marked. The rust had spread evenly down the row. "We cut them," she said. "There's too many, they said."

"Do you have a blade?"

Chloe produced a delicate bone knife she had bought with the rest of her wardrobe.

"Make certain to get the root," he said. "Don't let it fall into the water and thus spread the rust, or touch the other stalks. Work from here down, I'll work the other way. We'll meet in the middle."

She nodded and knelt at the first symbol of *poison*. Barley had shallow roots, and her knife wasn't as useful as a pronged fork would be, yet it worked. She laid the stalks on the ground, stepped over them and worked at the roots of another one. The sun climbed in the sky. The calls of *"samana"* had become the chorus of a very sad song. To her right, Ningal sweated and chopped. Between the two of them the row was decimated.

Chloe bundled a stack of poisoned stalks together and carried them to the end of the row. Someone had laid sheeting on the ground so the stalks wouldn't touch any dirt. She walked back to bundle some more. No one had stopped moving. There were no breaks for lunch and only the muddy ditch water to splash on her face and arms and wet her tongue as the day got hotter.

"*En* Kidu!" someone called later. "*En* Kidu appears!"

Chloe looked down her row and saw a line of priests, identifiable by their bald heads and fringed skirts. They walked two abreast. The words *en* Kidu raced like mice through the fields.

The oxen that pulled his sledge were white, with golden rings through their noses and traces of red-and-blue leather. Priests in white and gold flanked him. She stood on tiptoe to see the great *en,* the high priest of the staged temple. What would a high priest of fertility look like?

Ohmigod. He's gorgeous.

He was tall, broad, his fair hair was fixed back, and he wore a golden fillet. His beard was full.

People called to him, and women screamed, like groupies at a concert. They prostrated themselves as he passed. Chloe watched as he shook hands with the people, waved at them, smiled and blessed them.

In her ancient travels, most of the priests and aristocracy ignored the people, especially in a procession. Then again, this was a democracy, and though the *en* wasn't elected by the people, he must be aware of their power. The entourage could barely move for all the congestion. Chloe meandered down her row, transfixed by the man.

In the sun, he was slick with sweat, which just made him look like an overdressed athlete, emphasizing the muscle and sinew of his arms and shoulders. She dumped her stalks on the sheet at the end of her row, and he glanced her way. "Bless you, client. We will win against the *samana*." His smile was white-teethed and his voice low.

She didn't see his eyes, but she felt his magnetism. As she turned, he spoke to another person on the edge of another row, but she had the sensation of his eyes on her body, as strong as touch. The thought made her even warmer than the day, and she knelt by the stream to pat water on her face. When she looked up, he had moved a little farther, but glanced back at her. Their gazes met, and Chloe felt electricity zoom through her.

She turned back at the water, willed her body to stop trembling. *You are married,* she told herself. *Though he may be a thousand miles and a thousand years away, you made promises. You're scoping out the high priest of fertility—have you lost your mind?* She heard the jangle of the oxen's bells as the sledge moved away, and breathed a sigh of relief. Back to the barley.

Cheftu watched the girl splash her face again and marveled at the grace with which she moved. Her hips swung with the unhurried sway of those who are used to carrying enormous bundles on their heads. All the women moved similarly, but most didn't have long, lithe legs and high breasts that even a clumsy felt dress couldn't disguise. Her headdress shadowed her eyes so all he could distinguish were full lips, high cheekbones, and skin that glowed with hard work and an African heritage.

A man worked in the row with her, handsome, with a white beard and camel-colored skin. Her father? Her husband? The lust Kidu felt for all females had become almost an accustomed thing. But never before had Cheftu been intrigued by the details. To Kidu's undiscerning palate, being female and having breath seemed to be the requirements for a bedmate. The girl was returning to her row. Cheftu gestured to the driver, and he drove the oxen forward, hiding her from Cheftu's view completely.

As well he should, Cheftu told himself. *You are a married man.* Maybe she had green eyes, he reasoned. But she was Khamite, dark-skinned. She wouldn't have green eyes.

He returned his attention to his duties and eyed the bundles left at the end of every row for burning. The fields were almost cleared. The clients, freedmen, slaves, and gentlemen of the commonwealth sweated under the sun, but it was too late. There would be an investigation into the watchers, how the rust had progressed so quickly and never been spotted. Still, there was nothing to be done now.

Was the water bad? No one knew how *samana* passed from plant to plant. They left that knowledge in the hands of Ur's sadistic gods. Cheftu offered blessings and encouragement automatically to the citizens while his gaze took in the bigger picture. From the height of his sledge, he could see endless empty rows. Fifty percent was the danger mark, and on this side of the city, they had surpassed it.

He gestured to a scribe. "Go to the south gate. See how their fields fare. Bring me word immediately." He gestured to a second scribe. "Tell the *ensi* Ur will be on famine rations and to summon the record keepers of the granary. Go."

A third scribe. "Find the *lugal,* tell him to convene the council." A final message: "Have Asa the stargazer, his attendants, and Rudi the stargazer in my audience chamber in two double hours."

The sledge moved forward and Cheftu grasped hands, smiled into weary, stricken faces, and kissed children while the sun blazed down and the rust spread throughout the fields of barley.

That day, the power had shifted.

~

Shama finished encircling Puabi's eyes with gold paint, and she sighed, as content as a cat when its desire to be petted is met. He draped the cloak of her gown and secured it with a shell-headed pin, then opened the jewel chests. He bowed and waved to the splendid disarray there.

"I don't know what to pick, Shama," she said. "They expect to see Inana incarnate. Why a goddess would set foot in this place is something I don't understand. If I were a goddess, I think I would stay on Dilmun. They don't have to worry about *samana* there. Those shouts woke me this dawn. And you know I don't sleep well since the *en* has taken to supplicating all night. Every night. He hasn't even sneaked in a little rendezvous with a slave. He's been celibate." She sighed again. "Thank the gods that isn't required of *me.*"

His mistress didn't seem worried. Whether that was truth,

or she was portraying an unflappable front for the people to take courage from, Shama didn't know. He had to believe the best. And dress her like the personification of the goddess that she was.

So he settled on all gold and mother-of-pearl. The wreath of shells and gold beads for her head, then a filigree choker, freshwater pearl necklaces, one on top another, gold hoop earrings, bangles and armbands with inlaid shells and gold drops, and another woven wreath for her head. He belted her gown with a strip of leather the width of his hand, adorned with gold, and white paste beads. The ends fell to her hem, and her every movement was accentuated by the chime of tiny golden bells. Her sandals were bleached leather, and he'd gilded the nails on her toes.

A worthy consort for the bronzed *en*, and dazzling for the council members who had never beheld true beauty. Puabi finished cleaning her teeth with a gold toothpick and dropped it into Shama's outstretched hands. He opened the doors, and her attendants, slaves, scribes, and acolytes, all in white-wool skirts with gold chokers, waving fans of iridescent turquoise feathers, bowed. The acolytes began singing, and Shama laid the toothpick on the table and took his place in the procession.

En Kidu met them on the landing, his wool as white, the amount of gold as dazzling. One perfect pearl the size of a robin's egg dangled from his ear. Smaller pearls, pierced, were woven into his beard, and his filigreed diadem almost blended in with his hair. Like Puabi, he wore gold around his eyes and on his lips, and gold dust on every exposed square of flesh. The attendants to the two blended, and the powermongers of the temple moved to meet the decision-makers of the commonwealth.

Cheftu woke in a sheen of sweat, his hands clenched in the bedclothes. He'd dreamed—oh how vividly—of Chloe. Chloe's mind, her laugh, her smile, the wicked ways she had with her tongue. Alas, to his shame, he dreamed of her in the field girl's body, those legs around his waist, those elegant hands clasping him, guiding him—

He threw water on his head, his chest, and lower. It was lukewarm at best.

Cheftu barked for an acolyte, the boy who had retrieved the meteor the other night. "What do I do for exercise?" he asked him.

"Uh, sir, you wrestle sometimes."

"Anything else?"

"Hunt. Run—"

"Do I swim?"

"Yessir. In the lake outside of town, beside the fields."

"I don't remember how to get there."

"I will guide you, sir," the boy said.

Cheftu finished tying his kilt. "Good, let's go."

∼

Chloe met her sheep in the morning. After a week of fighting *samana,* today was a god's birthday—she didn't remember which one—businesses and schools were closed, and the streets were packed. The *en* was going to be riding around today, flaunting his perfect golden body; she must resist the temptation to join the drooling masses.

She needed to get out of the city. "I bet you guys would like to eat out today," she said. "I just hope I remember how to take care of y'all now that I'm really me again."

The shepherd waved at her—she didn't even need to show her receipt anymore.

Mimi snipped after Kami as soon as they were all

grouped again. "How about we walk through the palm groves?" Chloe asked them. "We'll all stay cool, and those new tender shoots should be perfect for lunch."

They baaed, which she took as assent. Instead of heading out toward the fields now bare of barley, she cut around the wall of the city to the palm groves. They spread out, it seemed, forever.

Palms with not just dates, but a dozen different varieties of palm she wasn't familiar with. Slaves, those who had sold themselves to the commonwealth or to a landowner from indebtedness, scampered through the mud. The sheep poked at the tender grass, and the goat ran after the birds and ground creatures.

It was cool in the shade. Chloe sat down and felt the sweetness of the morning steal up on her. The sheep found a pleasing patch of grass, and the goat, too. Chloe sat on the grass and watched them play. For a moment, she was at peace.

Then she looked up.

A man stood a short distance away, watching her from the shadows of a palm. As though he wanted her to see him, he stepped into the sunlight. He was tall, bronzed. Heat rushed through her body. The *en.* The definition of his thighs and stomach and arms glistened with sweat. His long, blond braids fell over his shoulders and down his back.

What was a high priest of fertility doing standing in the grove with sheep and goats?

He walked over to her, in nothing but a small loincloth. Then she realized it wasn't sweat on his body, but water. He'd been swimming. *She should have come out earlier.*

She felt ashamed, instantly.

He stopped a pace away, and she looked up at him. His height, his nearness, the scent of his hot wet skin made her dizzy.

"I am *en* Kidu," he said, in a voice that made her shiver. Too late, she realized she was supposed to be on her face, kneeling at his feet. She bowed her head.

"On your knees, female," a boy, the *en's* attendant, said. Chloe knelt with closed eyes, to shut out the view of the *en's* perfect legs, burnished skin, strong, modeled calves—she squeezed her eyes shut, tried to block out the image.

"Let me see your face, beautiful one," Kidu said. "Is such a one missing the festival today?"

She nodded.

"Raise your head, ma'am," a young boy said. "It is the *en* Kidu's request."

"The *en* should be concerned for the fields and the skies, he should be pleasing the *ensi*, not seeking his pleasures in the fields," Chloe stuttered out. In this day and age, could he just rape her?

Be honest, she said to herself. *With one kiss, it would be completely consensual.* He reminded her of Cheftu, when she first met him and he was a cold, golden Egyptian lord with a chip on his shoulder the size of Baltimore. The way he walked, the lift of his head, his intonation.

Could it be? Did she dare . . . ?

"I believe the luckiest inhabitants of Ur must be these sheep," the *en* said. "They get to frolic with you out in these cool groves."

The man had some lines, that was certain. Chloe stared at Kidu's legs; they were cast in gold, perfectly proportioned and muscled. She looked up, her gaze slid over his flat, muscled stomach, his broad chest, past the gold-beaded ends of his braids to his face.

Amber eyes.

"Does Kidu wish to frolic?" she asked him. Dared him. And hoped she wasn't propositioning the wrong man.

He frowned slightly, and she knew—hoped—he was trying to see past her mismatched eyes, her darker skin, her almost-African hair.

"Not unless you are named . . . Chloe," he said.

The boy watched them both intently.

Cheftu. *Cheftu?* reached down for her hand and drew her up. Standing, she was shorter than he was. That had never happened before. Was she sure this was Cheftu?

"Chérie," he whispered, and squeezed her hand.

"Ohmigod."

He kissed her.

Chloe was dizzy—Cheftu was here. He was the golden high priest. Had he been here this whole time, had . . . ?

He pressed his mouth to her ear; the vibrations of his words made goose bumps break out on her shoulders. "Spies are everywhere. Even in my bedchamber."

Conversation wasn't Chloe's first priority when they got to his bedchamber.

"I've been forbidden by the *ensi* to take the same girl as a lover more than once."

How many lovers *had* he taken?

"We must be very careful, *chérie*. We are both in danger here. Puabi will not hesitate to condemn me—I haven't pleased her at all since I got here. And she will recognize your name because I have used it several times. She's suspicious already."

What was he telling her?

"Tonight, I will sneak away and find you." He finished his embrace. "Enjoy the feast," he said, stepping back to being the *en* again.

Chloe knelt, more because her knees gave way than anything else. The boy and the *en*—Cheftu was blond now?—mounted a small cart and took a straight path out of the groves. She watched them drive away. This was it? The great reunion? She blinked away tears.

Chloe sat down in the shade of some palms and stared at the blue/brown horizon line.

The good news was that Cheftu was here and they had found each other.

The bad news was that it didn't seem to matter: He was the high priest of fertility.

"Shit!" Chloe screamed. What had happened to her life? The extreme silence of the grove penetrated her mind. "My sheep!" she cried, as she spun around. Every last one of them had disappeared. "Fine!" she shouted. "I was a lousy shepherdess anyway!"

She leaned against a palm and let the tears stream down her cheeks. Was she crying from relief? Joy? Gratitude? More like frustration. Slowly, her eyes shut.

~

"See how the gods provided for our amusement," a voice said. "A tasty little Khamite morsel."

Chloe jolted awake. A group of males looked down on her. It was midafternoon; the sun was behind them, so she was blinded.

"Steady there," one of them said, placing his foot on her leg as she attempted to stand up, applying just enough pressure to hold her there. "Don't rush anywhere on our count." That voice. It was the burly guy from school.

"Please," another said. "Go back to sleep, we won't disturb you."

The beer and opium fumes were almost suffocating.

I. Am. In. Deep. Shit.

Chloe jerked her leg away and slid up the palm. They stepped closer to her. But she was tall and, except for the ringleader and his crony, they were all young boys. Not quite into facial hair. Except the leader, whose words were spiked with sexual innuendo. He was trouble.

"She's taller than most Khamites," one said.

"Silence yourself. You've never seen a Khamite woman."

They were her classmates, emboldened by false courage. Curious and suspicious and feeling strong because they were in a gang.

"Khamite women don't usually work in the marshes," one of them said, and took a step closer to her.

"Nor are they usually in school," another said, "instead of where they should be, cooking and cleaning."

Misogyny or racism or a little of both? Was this payback for insisting on a test that gave half female-human answers? She'd been the only one in the school to pass. Her "brothers" had not been pleased.

"Did you boys want something?" she asked. "Are your fathers and Elder Brothers aware you are crawling through the palm groves like vermin?"

A few laughed, a few got angry.

One against seven, she thought. Not the greatest odds.

"Maybe we just want to ingrain some respect for education in ignorant marsh girls," the burly one said. "And I know just how to do it."

She fixed her gaze on him. "If you lay a finger on me, I'll break it." He hesitated; the others listened. "I'll pull the digit out of its socket. Then I'll turn it until the two bones no longer fit, and one has to make room for the other. It will be very painful. Then you'll hear a snap, a crack, like breaking a piece of wood."

The other five backed away, making excuses, urging the two biggest to join them.

"Or," she said, "I could poke out your eyes." Chloe made a Y with her fingers and jabbed at the air.

"She's just trying to scare you!" the burly one said to the boys. "She can't do anything. Look—"

The slap was unexpected. That wasn't fighting—that was abuse, power, a precursor to rape. A bitch-slap. Chloe fought to keep her feet. Her cheek was on fire. Her head spun.

"See?" he said.

Chloe kicked him in the chest. The second kick was in his stomach. He grabbed her leg in the middle of the third kick and jerked her down.

Pain.

Sharp.

Instant.

Chloe couldn't move. Her breath rasped in her ears. She felt warmth ooze into her hair. The boys gathered around her, their voices like the buzzing of bees. *I landed on something*, she thought. It was her last thought as the grove faded away to silent blackness.

~

Nirg said nothing when Nimrod asked how her day was. He kissed her, then asked what was for dinner.

"Did you bring fish?" she asked.

Nimrod smelled like fish, but he hadn't brought any. He shook his head.

"Did the *lugal* have any leftover food balls? Chloe's?"

Nimrod shook his head. The *samana* had kept Chloe from cooking. Instead, she'd helped in the fields.

"She won't tell me what—"

There was a knock at the door, then the brat Roo poked his head in. "Follow," he said to Nimrod, then slammed the door. They heard his footsteps race along the portico, then down the steps and out into the courtyard.

Nirg sighed and continued to fold Nimrod's clothes.

"That boy has been a nuisance to me all afternoon," she said. "Asking when you were coming home."

"Roo never speaks to me," Nimrod said. "It's some new game of his."

She fixed her humorless, almost-transparent, blue eyes on him. "I think not."

"Why?"

"When he came home today, he sneaked in beneath the courtyard door. I saw him because I was sifting the trash. He was covered in mud."

"Probably went out to the groves today, skipped the feast in favor of pretending to be a brickmaker." All the city boys who had no sense did those things. Growing up in the city deadened a human's capacity to hear animals and smell danger. Those ignorant boys who weren't allowed to know danger, or kill for food, sought to fill that space in themselves. They pretended things. Made up things. "Most likely, he drank too much beer."

"Roo is an underling, a brat and a pest," she said. "But his muddy face was streaked. The boy had been crying."

"Perhaps he trespassed, or—"

Nirg turned back to her work and shrugged her shoulders. "As you like."

The very way she said the words implied that the way he "liked" was completely, inherently wrong. She was becoming as impossible to comprehend as any city-born and -bred woman.

Another knock. "Nimrod. Come on!"

Again the brat slammed the door and raced away.

Nimrod rose; he might as well ferret out Roo. Nirg gave him a dismissive glance. He would be sleeping with Lea tonight. Probably just as well—she'd been spending too many nights waiting for the *en* Kidu to make time for her.

It was almost dark by the time Nimrod caught up with his

young idiot half brother. Whether it was from tears or sweat, the boy's face was muddy and streaked. "You better wash before dinner," Nimrod said. "And you best tell me what this is all about." He'd refrain from saying Roo was making Nirg angry; it would just make Roo even more of a handful.

"The Khamite, the friend of yours, she goes to my Tablet House."

"Yes," Nimrod said.

"Some boys, they . . . they saw her today."

When an animal is frightened, don't make any sudden moves. Nimrod remained still and kept his voice even. "Where did they see her?"

Roo shook his head. "The groves—" He looked up at Nimrod. "She made the boys violent."

"What boys? How do you know this?"

"Some boys," he said. "I followed them when they left the feast."

"Where did they go?"

"First they went drinking. It was really boring. Then they went to the palm groves. I was about to go home when I saw the yellow-speckled sheep."

"Go on."

"They did, too, then they found her. She was asleep."

"It's very important you tell me, did they touch her?"

Roo shook his head. "No, she told us what she would do to us if we touched her, but mostly she was talking to—" Roo caught himself before mentioning the name. "He's older and bigger. He really wanted to touch her beneath her skirt, but then—"

Roo handed Nimrod a mud-covered garden tool. "They wrestled and he pu—she fell on this."

Nimrod looked at the three-pronged fork, useful for fluffing mud. A few black hairs were stuck to the metal. It wasn't stained with mud, but blood. "Where is she now?"

"Everyone got scared when they saw the blood."

"Where is she, Roo?"

"We took the fork—"

Nimrod was on his feet. "Where?"

"We left her."

~

Kalam almost fell on the messenger when he arrived. "Justice Ningal requests you immediately," the man said.

Kalam was dressed already, prepared. The boys had found the girl; they'd done their work. He poured the remains of his beer before his personal god's statue. The god had been good to him, vanquished his enemy. When he returned, Kalam would bring the god some food. Something savory, perhaps.

He followed the messenger to the house on Crooked Way.

"You called me, sir?"

Ningal looked composed, which surprised Kalam. "I need you to fetch a few things for me," Ningal said without preamble. *So he is distraught*, Kalam thought. *Otherwise, he would never be so rude.*

"Of—"

Ningal began with his list: wax, a new, sharp blade for his knife, flax strips—about twenty—willow bark, hyssop and citrus branches, a goat and the redheaded prostitute from down the street.

"I . . . I thought you only congressed with—"

"She'll be at the tavern tonight. Pay her anything, promise her anything, but get her here within the hour."

Kalam looked at his list. "A . . . live goat, sir?"

"Live, and young. Never touched. Pure."

Kalam nodded.

"Go."

Kalam closed the door and berated himself for not asking about Chloe. Ah well, he'd do it when he returned.

~

Ningal was finished with his dinner of peas and bread by the time Kalam brought in the redhead. She removed her cloak slowly as she looked around. She sauntered over to his table, and Ningal poured her a cup of wine. He dismissed Kalam and waited until his assistant had closed the courtyard's door.

The woman's cleavage was painfully deep. Ulu smiled at him and ran a sandaled foot up the side of his leg. Ningal stared at her. "You're not here for me."

She made a production of looking over her shoulder. "I don't see anyone else."

"You're here as a duty to the gods."

Her manner changed completely. "What do you mean? I get paid—"

"You will be paid. No doubt of that. The highest fee, be assured. What I need you to do is go into that chamber and keep a watch over the young woman there. If she wakes, call for me."

"A woman is here?"

"She is dear to me."

"A concubine?"

"Not at all. An adopted daughter, if you will."

"She's sick?"

"Not sick . . . wounded."

"Why don't you see to her?"

"I am neither her husband, nor her father, not even her beloved," Ningal said. "It is not seemly for me to be in her chambers."

"A man who wants to be seemly, how unusual," the woman muttered as she stood. She adjusted her dress to less alluring lines, then pointed to Chloe's room. "Up there?"

~

Guli stepped up on the block, the seller's block. The breeze off the southern river was cooler this dawn than the previous day's and the previous week's. A good omen. The wind rustled the trees that lined the wharf, and the trill of birdsong filled the air. Buyers milled around and inspected the merchandise.

"Your attention please!" the auctioneer called. "Greetings of Sin and Inana to you this fine dawn. We have some quite spectacular humans for sale today. Remember the laws—slavery lasts for three years. Should your slave marry a freedman, their human offspring will be born free. All transactions must be filed in duplicate at the Office of Records, and feeding and clothing the slave is the responsibility of the slave owner." He looked over the crowd; very few foreigners, and these laws were well-known to any of the black-haired race.

"Very well. We begin today with Guli. Due to circumstances beyond his control, he is selling himself into slavery to pay a debt to the infamous Lord Viza. Let's help a fellow client out and trade a fine ass, or maybe some gold jewelry, so that in three years, he can rejoin the commonwealth as a barber."

"Hairdresser," Guli corrected.

"Forgive me," the auctioneer said. "He's a hairdresser," he announced. "I'm sure he would also be an excellent *mashuf* rower, a bodyguard or a gardener."

Guli groaned.

The bidding began.

I hate the out of doors, he thought. *Mud and shit and mosquitoes and always-wet feet. Nails that are never truly clean and men who stink like animals. I wish I had just killed Lord Viza when I had a chance. Execution is preferable.*

"Sold!" the auctioneer cried. "For the price of two gold necklaces, a white donkey, and a wheelbarrow of timber." He clapped Guli on the back. "You should be very pleased. You won't owe Viza a thing when you get out."

That, at least, was encouraging. They met with the buyer, a pleasant-faced, bald-headed woman and her Khamite overseer, and made the exchange, Guli paid the auctioneer one gold necklace and agreed to meet with the woman later in the day. First he had to take care of the documentation, the forms and process necessary to clear his debt.

"Come to this house," she said, and told him the address. It was a newer estate, close to the Uruk gate. "Ask for Duda."

Guli walked back through town. Sweat prickled in his armpits and around his waist. He held the cylinder seal he'd worked so hard for, tight in his hand. Maybe he could imprint the design on his palm, so even when it was black with mud it would remind him he would be free. He would dress hair again.

This was just a three-year detour in his plans.

He stepped into the shadow of the scribe's office. Guli was going to do this truthfully; he would eradicate his debt and be ready to start anew.

After he waited in line, he was offered a seat on the ground and a small cup of cool, sweet tea. He explained the situation to the scribe, who assured Guli that he would see Lord Viza received the payment and the documents would be filed. "I just got out of slavery a few years ago," he confided. "It took two weeks for the temple to find my seal. You are leaving yours there, truth?"

Guli nodded.

"The administration is overrun with documentation. So, who bought you?"

Guli sipped his tea. The cup was glazed clay, a pleasing yellow color decorated around the rim with a delicate pattern of marsh birds. "I don't know, it's Number Fifteen, Moonlit Palm Way."

The scribe looked up, shocked. He held out the damp clay tablet. "Why are you paying for me to conduct this to Lord Viza? Just take it to him. He's your owner now."

Guli crushed the cup in his hand.

⌒

Ezzi was sitting at the table when his mother came home. Her makeup was worn away, and in the dawnlight she looked tired. He stifled a pang of sympathy for her; he had his own worries. Last night had seen more starfall. He'd watched every minute of it, waiting for death to come to them all. It hadn't. In fact, only good things had happened to Ezzi recently. If he were honest, he would admit they shouldn't be—if the gods blessed good behavior.

Maybe they blessed bad actions, instead? "The butcher sent a bill," he said to Ulu. "We are behind in our payments?"

"I forgot," she said.

"Not just the butcher, Mother. Everyone. Have you paid even one tradesman?"

She sighed and wiped her forehead. "I've been up all night—"

"You're always up all night."

She walked over to him, and he averted his face. "You smell like a goat!"

"Keep your cloak on," she snapped. "I've been up all

night and all day, with a goat for company. I can't tell you, but I'm trying to help a man reverse a curse."

"I haven't heard that term for it before."

Her eyes snapped at him, and she pulled off her wig. Her hair beneath was straw. She scratched her head, and he thought he saw black spots fly around. No doubt, from the goat.

"Are you making currency?" he asked.

"Yes."

"Well . . . where is it?"

"What does it matter to you? I will pay the tradesmen. Why are you acting like a *lugal*? If you starve, it's because you refuse to eat, not because we lack food!"

The slave girl came in with beer and bread for them both. Ezzi had lost his appetite.

"Why are you up?" Ulu asked, sitting down. "My legs are exhausted. I'm not used to being on my feet so much."

"That is truth, truer than you've ever told."

She glared at her son.

"What does a goat have to do with a curse?" he asked, tearing a corner of the bread. He'd give the gods the remainder. Just in case.

She ripped her half in pieces, then sucked down half her jar of beer through a drinking tube with a loud slurp. "The goat is a replacement, but it hasn't worked because the cursed girl hasn't woken up."

"Why does she have to be awake?"

"The goat is supposed to become her. They share a bed—"

"By Sin!"

"Not in that fashion, but until the goat can be identified as the cursed one instead of the girl. They eat from the same dishes, wear the same clothes, do everything together."

"For how long?"

"Until the goat smells like the girl and the girl smells like the goat."

Ezzi sipped a little of his beer.

"But she hasn't woken up. We feed her beer through the drinking tube, sit her up, change her clothes, but she is lifeless. Like the statues of the gods on New Year's."

"Those gods are not lifeless!" Ezzi said, horrified and scared. "They are very much alive. They can curse you or me in a minute!"

"Calm yourself," she said, then sucked down some more beer. "They *appear* to be lifeless. Does saying it that way make your devout humanity any happier?"

He nodded. Once.

"After the transference takes place, then we'll kill the goat and bury it under Chloe's name."

"Chloe is the girl?"

His mother jumped forward, clutching his hands. "Don't ever say that name. I'm paid well to keep the secret. You're my son, you won't endanger us, truth?"

She was scared, worried. She pleaded with him through her eyes.

Ezzi liked this, feeling her fear. Having the power to change it. Or not. "Of course not," he said, extricating himself with a smile. "I'll never mention it again."

"You swear on the gods?"

"I swear. But Mother, Ulu, where did this magic come from?"

She bit her lip, as though deciding what to tell him. "She has a powerful protector who used to be an *asipu.*"

A medicine man, diviner and exorcist, in one person. No wonder his mother was scared. A man like that could see into the future, ascertain the gods' desires, and get anything he wanted in life. He'd have deep pockets, as well. "He picked you? For what?"

"My hands, the control I have over how much pressure I apply."

Ezzi snorted a laugh. "Does he know what you usually grapple?"

"He's a gentleman."

Ezzi shrugged. "He pays you, to stay with this girl and goat, truth?"

"He pays well. I just lost track of the time. I'll pay the tradesmen."

"You squeeze this girl?"

"Massage her. She has a sore on her head, and the *asipu* is wary of it getting worse. He checks her eyes, and he hits her on the knee, to see if it swings out. He's odd, but very devoted to her."

"Then why doesn't he save himself the funds and take care of her?"

"He's very proper, refuses to touch her or be alone with her. That's why he hired me." She drank some more beer. "How are you?"

"I'm working at Asa stargazer's side." He'd wanted the words to impress her, but since she was keeping company with an *asipu* and his whore, she just muttered that was nice and finished her beer. Ezzi tried to persuade her to let him carry currency to the tradesmen, but she said she didn't have the balance yet, she'd have to get it tonight.

She refused to tell Ezzi the name of her source.

Ulu never let him touch her earnings; she never shared any of it with him. He had to petition her for every little thing. It wasn't right; she was a whore. He was educated, intelligent, gifted. The gods would smile on him, if only he could bribe them better.

If only he had something with which to bribe them.

Cheftu had just sat on his bed. The sun was peeking over the tenemos wall of the temple. Chloe was here. She had money and position. Security. In truth, she had more freedom than he did. He hadn't been able to go to her the previous night, as he had said he would; he knew she'd be angry, but understand eventually. He glanced up at the four acolytes who stood between him and the door. Then he looked at the three females who dozed on the couches. Two guards watched his inner and outer doors. Who knew how many of them reported to Puabi.

He'd kissed his beloved yesterday. Touched her. Remembered her scent. Then he'd spent the day moving through the streets, with women throwing themselves at him, but all he'd seen was her.

So beautiful. Intelligent. He wouldn't have dared to hope Chloe was in that guise of flesh. Yet she'd recognized him, and when he heard her speak—Cheftu groaned. He ached for his wife. Chloe.

He buried his head in his hands and rubbed his temples. How would he get to her? When he did, then what? Walk in and claim her as his bride? The *en* was forbidden marriage; it was a conflict of the commonwealth's interests. Not that Chloe would stomach a continuation of this current career choice.

Marriage aside for the moment, he just wanted Chloe in his bed for a year or two. However, even congressing, at this point, would be unwise. Would the situation be any different if a different *ensi* reigned? How could Cheftu retire from being *en*? It was an appointed position—and dismissal meant death.

So he had to die to get out of this position? Nimrod said he would help Cheftu; the tides of popularity were shifting. For the friendship Nimrod bore Kidu he would aid and abet Cheftu's escape.

Chloe and Cheftu could both escape. Together.

She was here; he could make sense of the rest of it later. Now, he just needed some sleep. *Thank You* le bon Dieu *for answering my prayers.*

~

Ezzi stood in the doorway, summoned by Asa. The old man couldn't see the sky, but his eyes were sharp on Ezzi. "Get your things and go," Asa told him. "You are no longer a stargazer in this administration."

Ezzi couldn't speak. He was too shocked. He rubbed his ear with a finger.

"Your hearing is fine, boy. Get out."

"Wh-wh-why my lord?"

"Should the *en* choose to investigate, he will learn one of my assistants appeared at the Office of Records on the same day no records about me could be found. My humanity is clothed in honor. You have befouled it and my reputation. Get out."

The stargazer's pompous tone made Ezzi burn. The man was as false as Ulu's hair; he pretended perfection yet chided Ezzi for helping him maintain that illusion? As though something or someone else was ordering his actions, Ezzi stepped into the room.

"What are you doing? I told you to leave!"

Fury vanquished Ezzi's smile and his subservient attitude. "Don't speak to me of honor, sir. Your ability to see the stars is gone and has been for years. You lie about every prediction, and you steal information from every source that comes your way."

"This is an outrage!" the older man said, but his perfect voice lacked conviction.

Ezzi's mouth continued to move, words he'd thought but

never dared voice. "If it is, then a simple examination of the night sky, with witnesses, will clear the confusion completely. The justice Ningal lives on my street. I'm sure he would make time to see the honorable Asa stargazer in his court tomorrow." Ezzi's hands trembled as he waited to see what Asa would say. He didn't dare speak.

Asa stared at the artfully mosaicked wall for a long while. "What is it you want?" he asked finally.

Ezzi closed the door carefully. "I want to be a stargazer."

"What else?"

"I have the tablets. The ones from the Office of Records."

"By Sin—"

"They're not with me, though . . ." Ezzi paused. He was astounded at the assurance in his voice, the strength. Asa was negotiating with him!

A few moments ticked by. "You planted them here."

"Your intelligence is not underestimated, but then, how else could you fool the entire council."

"You have no proof of your accusations."

The outrage Ezzi had felt, the shame at discovering a "bad" star, overflowed. His words were sharp and swift as arrows. "It's why you didn't see the new star. And you missed the stars falling for two nights, until I 'observed' them for you. Then you readily agreed. You blamed Rudi for missing the blood moon. It took a while, but then I realized it is easy to hide the truth when you are known for your extreme concentration and deliberate solitude. The council thinks you are on the platform of the gods, sneaking glances at their Tablets of Destiny. I know you couldn't tell it was night unless someone told you."

Asa didn't look at him, or express any emotion.

Ezzi's steps brought him closer to Asa, even though his knees were knocking and hands trembling, still his words shot out with deadly accuracy. "You are in disfavor. The crops are failing. The *ensi* will step down, and you might not be chosen as the succeeding stargazer. If you listen to me, I can save us all."

"You can make the rust go away?"

The stargazer was listening! Ezzi stifled a triumphant chuckle. "Not that, but I can assure that you will remain stargazer, that the gods' need for a new *ensi* will be met, and that the people will be satisfied."

"I am sure you will be compensated, too," Asa said dryly.

Ezzi inclined his head. "My years may be few, but my ambition is limitless." As he said it, he realized it was truth. He would do anything to feel the rush and flow of authority that he rode on at that moment.

"Unlike your humanity and honor," Asa said.

Ezzi slammed his hand down beside Asa's resting arm. "Don't mock me."

"What reasonless idea do you have?"

"I want a scribe, before I speak further," Ezzi said, suddenly aware of what he was doing. How far away from the safety of his established life he was stepping.

"You are correct about my dishonesty regarding my sight," Asa said, "but if I give you my word, then it is a contract between gentlemen I will never break."

Ezzi doubted that, but he needed to speak with Asa now and get his plan in motion before Asa changed his mind. "I will trust your word as a gentleman then," he said hesitantly.

Asa leaned back. "Astound me."

"The crops are failed. Another sign the *ensi* must step down."

Asa didn't nod in agreement.

Ezzi paused.

"Is there something else?" Asa asked. "You might be able to see the night sky, but I can tell you what the signs mean.

The crops are failed. There is no confusion about this omen."

"It foretells what?"

"The *ensi* must die."

Part Four

THE PIT

Chapter One

Kalam had informed him gleefully this morning, when Ningal arrived at the court, that Guli had been arrested.

All day long, Ningal, heart heavy at the waste, had waited to see Guli appear before him again. Now it was past twilight; and he hadn't heard from Guli himself. The neighbor had testified Viza had been walking peaceably in his garden when this giant hurled himself at the gentleman Viza and strangled him with his bare hands.

Ningal clarified that Viza wasn't a gentleman, he wasn't even an established member of the commonwealth. "As evidenced by his foreign title, *lord*," he said. "Where is the accused?"

At long last they brought him in at spearpoint. Guli held himself stiffly; his hands were stained with blood. Ningal noted his blackened eye, the other eye healing, the split knuckles, and the way he breathed in stages—his ribs were most assuredly cracked. Ningal doubted the authenticity of the neighbor's testimony; Guli had obviously been in a fight. Kalam's glance was derogatory, and Ningal's heart gained sorrow.

"Client Guli."

"Slave Guli, sir," the scribe corrected.

"Whose slave?" Ningal asked.

"Lord Viza's. The murder victim."

Killing a man, and killing one's owner, were two different judgments. Guli refused to meet his eyes, and Ningal knew why. One was a debt that could be paid, the other was a debt that only Guli's death could pay.

"How long was his servitude?" Ningal asked.

"He became a slave two days ago, sir. The documents haven't even been filed." Ningal gave him a curious look. "The scribe who was working on them is a friend of mine. We discussed it," the scribe explained.

"I see." He looked at Guli. "Tell me truth. What happened?"

Guli looked into his eyes. "I'm thrice-convicted. It doesn't matter what happened. I killed a man. I'm his slave, and I slayed my owner. We both know the penalty."

I wanted to give you the benefit of a doubt, you young jackass! Ningal raged internally. He gestured with his hand. "Take him away to await judgment."

"Your Honor," Kalam said. "Your judgments, inscribed on the standard outside—"

The stone standards stood before his offices, proclaiming the way Justice Ningal perceived the law. Never had a thrice-convicted criminal escaped with his life. Never had a slave who killed his owner been shown mercy. Fast and sure was the method Ningal believed served the commonwealth. Should mercy be shown even once, then it would be anticipated, and finally expected. Should leniency be applied, it would appear as favoritism and promote division within the populace.

Kalam continued, "According to your—"

Ningal cut him off with a glance. The slaves were lighting torches inside. Guli had left the room. The day was finally cooling. "What is next?"

⌒

"Transfer the curse," Ezzi said to Asa. "Substitute another woman for Puabi. Within the temple, everything stays the same. Outside, the people think the sacrifice has been made, the gods receive their named victim, and life returns to the instability we are accustomed to."

"What do you get from this?"

"I am your assistant, at a substantial salary, until you retire. I'm your eyes—between us. Then I am your inheritor."

"Your ambitions don't extend beyond stargazing?"

Ezzi laughed. It was working! The gods *did* reward those who dared conventions and morality! "If you managed it correctly, stargazer could be a position more important and powerful than the council, the *lugal* and the *ensi* combined." Ezzi ticked off the details on his fingers. "You are the only one who can foresee the gods' judgments of destiny. You decide what you are going to tell the council, the *lugal* and the *ensi*. With that knowledge and power, you can shape the world like a scribe preparing clay."

"This is what you intend?"

This is what the gods have taught me. "Yes."

"Tell me, my corrupt, inhuman client, did you suspect my predictions were based on poor vision before you cast your shadow on my door?" Asa asked.

The voice within him that was confident and brazen, spoke. Lied. "I kept records of predictions and results throughout my years at the Tablet House. You've been wrong for so many seasons, that it is only the goddess of perversity who sustains your position."

Asa sat forward, his eyes burning with anger. "I am agreed. You have your contract. All your terms, except this one."

"Which is?"

"I never want to see you again. Messenger information to me. Leave me notes scrawled on tablets. I can read those yet. When my presence is required in public, walk behind me. I will never address you. I will never acknowledge you. You have manipulated the situation so you are guaranteed to be my eyes. Clever tricks and a wily mind have preserved that title for you. I can't promise your position as inheritor, but I will recommend you if I am asked.

"Never set foot in these chambers again when I am here. You are no friend, no customer, no relation to me. I think more highly of my slaves. But you get what you want." He stood. "Write out the contract, I'll sign it in triplicate." He turned his back to Ezzi and adjusted his robes. "The *en* has requested our attendance on him. Do not let one fringe from your robe intrude on my vision. I'll send you the documents to seal. Now, get out. I have a council meeting to attend."

~

Ulu didn't go to the tavern, for she was too tired from having spent her day at Chloe's side. Her hands ached, her arms did, too, from applying pressure the way the justice had instructed. No wonder it took so much time and effort to become an *asu* or *asipu*. She had learned all sorts of things about the body, so her mind was tired also.

She was ruminating on this when Ezzi walked in. He didn't look up, just trudged across the courtyard to his staircase. "Hello, son," she called.

He jerked as though he'd been struck.

"Don't look so surprised," she said with a smile. "I live here, remember?"

He glanced up at the exposed sky. "Aren't you late for the tavern?"

"I'm taking the night off. Have you eaten?"

He shook his head.

"The kitchen has a wonderful fish; would you like it fried or smoked?"

"I'm not going to eat, Ulu."

"Was your day blessed?"

"The stargazer Asa needed my assistance today. In fact, I should wash and change. We meet with the *en* tonight, at the council meeting."

"He is certainly a great example of a fertility priest," she said. "I bet he's hung like a bull." Ezzi looked at his feet. He was so uncomfortable with the basics of life. *How can he be my child*? she wondered. "With the fields like they are, though, he hasn't pleased the gods."

Ezzi snorted. "You don't know anything. It's the *ensi* the gods are unhappy with. She's responsible for the crops and the weather." He turned around and took a few steps up. "Send some fish to my room. I'll eat while I dress."

"We can have it later, when you get home. I'll wait for you."

"Don't bother," he said, and took the remaining steps two at a time. He slammed the door and left Ulu in silence. *Well*, she thought, *maybe I'll just go to the tavern to say my greetings*. Her dress wasn't fresh though, and she wasn't really in the mood. A nice dinner, with some pleasant conversation, had been her only wish. She could just make out the light flickering through the slits in the wood of Ezzi's closed door.

The house was so nice now, even without Guli's assistance in picking things out. Clean, with fresh sheeting and fronds on the beds, the warm smell of baking bread, new matting, blooming flowers, light incense. Ezzi hadn't even noticed. She'd hoped to please him, but maybe she couldn't. Such a delicate boy, with great sensibilities. What did he think about? What did he want?

How could she have given birth to him? They were as dissimilar as fish and peafowl.

As she watched, the light went out and he came downstairs, his hair wet and his cloak scented with sunshine and soap. He adjusted the pin and his cylinder seals.

"You look wonderful," she said. "If I weren't your mother I'd want you to be my customer."

"You're disgusting," he said.

"I didn't mean it badly," she protested. "You look handsome—"

He slammed the courtyard door shut. Ulu pressed her lips together. She never said the right thing, she never looked appropriate. Her son was ashamed of her.

"Ma'am," the kitchen slave asked. "How do you want the fish?"

Ulu looked at her hands, red and raw from hot water and oils for the girl. It had been a long time since she'd done anything with them other than count earnings and earn the counting. "Just bring me some beer," she said. "Save the fish."

"Would you like it smoked or jellied or pickled, ma'am?"

Ezzi said only peasants ate food that was smoked because they couldn't buy fresh every day. Jellied was too vulgar. "How about a nice stew?"

The slave left and returned with a jar of beer and drinking tube. Ulu dismissed the girl and broke the seal herself. The markings were familiar, but she couldn't read them. It seemed she saw markings everywhere from everyone now. Writing. The world had gotten so fast, she was almost lost. She took her first sip—the beer was bitter. Not her favorite, but she'd opened it already. She looked at the seal. Perhaps it warned her that it was a bitter brew?

No one she knew would know. Guli could figure some math, so he could mix dyes and water and make hair beautiful; most people could figure weights and exchanges, but to just . . . read? What purpose would that serve?

Guli, she thought. He would be delightful company tonight, just a pleasant meal and conversation. Ulu called for the slave and sent her down the street, but not before pulling another jar, whose writing looked different, and checking that the barley cakes were fresh. Ulu washed her face, made sure her robe was clean, and sat back to wait.

The slave returned. Alone. All the anticipation melted away.

"The male Guli hasn't been to the tavern. At his former house he didn't answer my knock."

Ulu looked down. "Thank you," she said. The slave left Ulu alone with her own company.

~

Cheftu couldn't believe what he was seeing, and he couldn't figure out what year, what time period in which he was seeing it, but it appeared that this society had put democracy in motion long before Athens claimed to have created it. The two houses of the commonwealth of Ur stood opposite each other. The *lugal* mediated, and Cheftu and Puabi sat to the side. Hers was the tie-breaking vote, if needed.

Commerce was the topic tonight. The barley crop was blighted. If nothing else went wrong, they would have 30 percent of the normal yield. Scribes were working furiously to recalculate taxes, and thus the commonwealth's budget. Spies had been sent north to learn the cost of grain in the cities along the river above them, before formal inquiries were made about buying grain. The reconnaissance would keep Ur's money-loving northern cousins honest.

Ships were sailing tonight to canvass the known world for a replacement crop. Cheftu had the numbers of the surplus in his hands. They would have almost nothing left if they dispersed the stores, but if they distributed half of them, they could guard against another bad year.

Puabi sat like a statue. He doubted she heard even every other word, and he suspected she didn't care. The stargazers waited in his chambers, and he waited while the long-winded gentlemen of the council debated each other.

Women clustered around the edges of the room, watching their husbands, brothers, and sons as they made choices that would affect them all. Though Cheftu had recognized the older man from the field, Justice Ningal, a much-respected gentleman, he didn't see Chloe. He didn't dare send her a note; for now, she would just have to be secure in the knowledge that they were both in the same time, in the same place. Puabi had more eyes on him than any king had ever assigned to his pretender to the throne.

No decisions would be voted on tonight, it was just information. The *lugal* dismissed them all, and Puabi and Cheftu left first, protected by a phalanx of priests, scribes, and Puabi's multitudes of handmaidens. "Do I have to go?" she asked, as they mounted the sledge.

"Back to the temple?" he asked. The driver goaded the oxen and the vehicle jerked forward.

"No, of course I want to go to the temple. I mean to the meeting, with all the stargazers. They're just going to talk about the rust and how it means I should resign. I don't want to hear it. I have—"she shut up.

"You have what?"

"Other things to do," she said. Her tone was defensive.

"I don't care with whom you congress," he said.

"Obviously."

"We're discussing your life, Puabi. Don't you want to be there?"

"I vote I get to rule!" she said. "There is no more discussion, as far as I am concerned."

Perhaps when they first woke together and Cheftu gauged her gaze to be sharp or intelligent, he was overstating it. Aware, perhaps. Smarter than the oxen, but as self-absorbed as a snake. Yet he also felt a great warmth toward her—Kidu's unexplained emotions. They rode in silence. Night had fallen again, cooling the earth.

He sighed as they pulled into the temple complex.

"Are you angry with me?" Puabi asked, touching his arm.

He looked into her beautiful face. Her eyes were clear, concerned. If he didn't know her better, he would think she cared about her people, her land. He knew better. There was no point in directing anger at her. He'd just have to apologize and endure her pouting. "Of course not," he said, and patted her arm. "I will let you know what happens."

"I want to be *ensi*," she said, squeezing his arm. "There is no one trained to take my place, and I haven't even had a child. I'm young, Kidu. Vital. Don't dismiss me just to satisfy wishes of gods who loathe us and plague us for their amusement. Protect me, please. And I'll protect you." The handmaidens came panting into the courtyard, racing to catch up with Puabi. She kissed his cheek, and Cheftu watched the whole retinue disappear into the maze of buildings.

"Bring me some food," he told an acolyte. "I'll be in my audience chamber." Wondering how to get to Chloe.

~

Ezzi bowed as the *en* swept in on a cloud of smoke and incense. The golden-haired man didn't sit, but crossed his arms and greeted Asa curtly. "I won't discuss the past," he said. "Situations have arisen, of which I'm sure you are aware, that prohibit me knowing the truth about predictions you've made and whether or not they've been accurate." Ezzi waited for Asa to turn and denounce him as the thief in the Office of Records. The moment passed, and the *en* turned away.

"The crop has failed. Officially, Ur anticipates a famine."

He spun on his heel and faced the stargazers. "You claim disaster will be averted by the dismissal of the *ensi*. When is that to be?"

The stargazer stepped closer to the *en*. "Because of the delicacy of this discussion, it would be best if we spoke alone. The two of us." He stared into the *en's* face.

Ezzi coughed lightly into his palm; he wasn't going to be left out of this.

Kidu surveyed the stargazer's face, then dismissed everyone. Ezzi didn't move, and the *en* looked at him with a raised eyebrow. Asa didn't look, but said Ezzi must stay. The *en* didn't offer them seats or refreshment; there was no hospitality, which Ezzi thought extremely rude. Instead, the man crossed his arms, sent cold amber glances over both men, and said he was listening.

"For the sake of the people, the *ensi* must die," Asa said.

The *en* sat down. "This is quite a different story than the one you bore before," he said. "Why the change?"

"Will you believe my words, or do you need verification from the stargazer Rudi?"

The *en* didn't respond to the provocation, just templed his fingers and inclined his head for Asa to speak.

"First there was the blood moon, then stars falling through the house of Puabi's birth, and now the failed crops. The gods are displeased. The blood moon means blood is needed to wipe the clay smooth. So we can be free from curses, and starvation. Such are the ways of the gods."

Kidu spoke calmly. "What of the *lugal* and me?"

"Your star is safe, secure. Just the *ensi*." Asa swallowed audibly. "Just Puabi."

The three fell silent. Ezzi watched the *en's* face, blank, though his eyes seemed to search the air before him for answers. "Who will bear her this news?" Kidu asked.

"Actually," Asa said, "as it will be an official funeral, all her handmaidens, attendants, and the like will go with her, to serve her in Kur."

The *en* blinked. He said nothing.

"Perhaps, we can negotiate with the gods?" Asa said.

Again, the *en* didn't speak. However, he did raise a brow in query. Finally, he said, "Speak at your will."

"The gods need a sacrifice to be named the *ensi*, they don't actually need Puabi—"

"Substitute another for her!" Ezzi interjected.

The *en* looked from one man to the other. "Is this your suggestion, stargazer Asa?"

The stargazer didn't acknowledge Ezzi, but Ezzi felt Asa's ire and his surprise. "The *asu* and *asipu* have used this technique with the ill for quite some time," Asa said. "It is a secret practice among the initiated."

Ezzi felt the *en's* gaze again, this time not quite as dismissive. The *en* assumed Ezzi was among the initiated. The gods rewarded bad behavior, Ezzi was sure of it now. Though perhaps from the gods' point of view, his behavior was good. After all, who knew what those divinities had planned for the slave humans?

"Let us speak directly, Asa," the *en* said dryly. "You enter these chambers, with news that Puabi must die. Now you suggest the gods will be pleased if another woman goes to her death in the guise of Puabi, and the *ensi* actually lives."

Asa shrugged. "The minds of the gods are convoluted. This arrangement would not be offensive to them. A man may assume the debts of a family member and be sold into slavery for him."

"It's the same principle," Ezzi said.

The *en's* smile was thin. "Death and slavery are not the same, sir."

"Truth."

"Do you know any woman who would do this? By being

buried as Puabi, she would lose her own name and face in the . . . afterlife, truth?"

"In Kur, it matters little," Ezzi said.

Silence.

"My . . . assistant speaks the truth," Asa said. "In Kur, the names matter little. As you well know, there is no hierarchy, no luxury, no reward or punishment."

Ezzi thought the *en's* golden eyes flashed for a moment, but perhaps it was his own excitement. "I know a woman—" Ezzi said.

The *en* swung on him. "Boy, if you do not keep silent, you will join the retinue of Puabi in the tomb!"

Ezzi trembled as those cold eyes swept over him. This was not the same man as before; perhaps a demon had taken possession of the *en*. Perhaps *he* should die.

"Do you know anyone who would do this willingly?" Kidu asked Asa.

"Uh, willingly, with no accolades? I, I must confess at this moment, no one comes to mind."

Ezzi bit his lip; he wouldn't waste his idea on the *en*, he would go directly to the *ensi*. She, after all, was the one with power. She made the decision. She was the one they were trying to kill.

"Then perhaps this plan is a little premature," the *en* said, rising. "Come to me when you have a willing victim." He strode from the room, barely giving them time to bow.

⌒

The Tablet Father belched and leaned back. "Your wife can do more with sheep—"

"Sheep!" Asa shouted. "Gods, how I tire of that word."

"I'm sorry," the Tablet Father said. "I didn't mean to remind you. Your wife pines for those sheep yet?"

"The yellow spotted ones, kept at the gate." Asa rubbed his temples. "She has approached the herders repeatedly, but they will tell her nothing except the female Chloe is the one who owns the sheep. Nothing about where to find her, or how much she might charge—"

"Chloe?" the Tablet Father said. He could imagine how the conversation went between Asa's culinary genius of a wife and the sheep-dip-stained shepherd. First, Asa's wife would look down her long, sharp Shemti nose and request to speak to the head sheepherder. It would take producing a seal before she would believe she was speaking to him.

Then she would demand the yellow sheep. The shepherd would tell her they were on loan to the commonwealth. She would demand he tell her the name and address of the owner, to notify him the sheep had been purchased—oh yes, the Tablet Father could see quite easily that Asa's wife would learn nothing except the name.

"I believe," he said, covering Asa's hand, "I know who this Chloe female is."

The stargazer, whose eyes were bloodshot and bleary from attempting to see into the heavens, looked hopeful. "Who is she? I'll pay anything, I swear by Ninhursag I will."

"Chloe is the female little brother in my Tablet House," the Tablet Father said. "I was pressured by the *lugal* to take her but . . . " he pondered. Several of his Boys had come to him, complaining about her presence, threatening to change Tablet Houses. The Tablet Father dreaded the day their fathers came to him and made good the threats. Then there had been rumors of a tussle, but Kalam had handled that situation before it went anywhere. That Old Boy was a tribute to the House.

"A female human has been attending the Tablet House?" the stargazer said. "That could be . . . well, possibly, the reason for the evil omens."

"You mean, instead of the *ensi*?"

"No, no," the stargazer said. "The signs are clear enough for the *ensi's* judgment by the gods, but . . . " Asa's words came to a stop. His gaze was fixed on some distant point, and the Tablet Father had a sense Asa was weighing something of which the Father knew nothing about. "Does she have family who would protest? The sheep, I mean?"

The Tablet Father straightened his cloak. "She is a protégé of Ningal's."

"She's that beautiful?"

The Tablet Father shrugged. "If you care for Khamite females, I guess."

Asa looked interested. "Khamite?"

"She owns the sheep your wife will stop at nothing to get." The Tablet Father spoke of the sheep, but he knew they were discussing something else. "Think of the silence."

Asa looked away, his red-rimmed eyes thoughtful.

"*Ensi* Puabi will need attendants, will she not?"

The stargazer's head jerked back at his lover's words. "She . . . will."

"I will add Chloe's name to the council's list," the Tablet Father said. "I can tell several of my Old Boys to do the same."

"Won't Ningal—"

"He is a just man. Surely, he can see the relation. Floodwaters brought the girl, she's sought to bring chaos to the commonwealth by her demands and ideas, it is right she should pass into Kur on the day of an eclipse." The Tablet Father put his arm around Asa's shoulders and spoke softly. "You are the stargazer, your words to the *lugal* are beyond truth."

Asa reached for the Tablet Father's hand and placed it on his body. They spoke no more.

Chapter Two

 S he woke up with one thought: Cheftu is a big blond now.

Sean Connery was seated by her bed: Ningal. "How are you, Chloe?"

Chloe followed the hand that was holding hers, up a white arm to the painted face of a brown-haired woman. The woman smiled. Chloe smiled back.

"This is Ulu; she helped me while you were sick."

"Thank you," Chloe said through dry, cracked lips. Ulu handed her a drinking tube, and Chloe sucked down some sweet breakfast beer. She immediately felt light-headed. She turned to Ningal, then turned to Ulu. She lifted a hand to her head; it was lighter.

"He had to cut your hair," Ulu said. "The fever."

Her hair was chin- and ear-length. Short. Chopped. "I had a fever?" she asked.

Ningal nodded and proceeded to tell her she'd been in bed for the last four days. Mostly unconscious. "Do you remember what happened?"

Cheftu said he'd come see me that night. Did he? Does he know I was hurt? "Those boys," she said carefully. "I fell—"

"You landed on a gardening fork."

"No wonder it hurt." *Please leave*, Chloe thought. *Let me be alone so I can figure out what to do about Cheftu. Spies everywhere, he'd said*. Puabi would recognize Chloe's name. Simple: She'd use another name, and now with cut hair, she probably looked like someone else, too.

"Would you like some food?" Ningal asked. "More beer?"

"And don't worry about your hair, child. I have a friend Guli, who is a master hairdresser."

Ningal froze, his eyes on the woman.

"I'm sure the justice did a wonderful job, but it wouldn't hurt to have Guli trim it up."

Especially since I want to make a good impression on Cheftu. Not that she doubted his love, or attraction, but when your husband is the high priest of fertility it helps to look one's best. And short hair, in all of Chloe's travels, had never been in vogue. Either it was a sign of shame, of public humiliation, or illness.

I may have to start a whole new trend.

Ningal stood. "Ulu and I must converse, but I'll send you something to eat. And a bath; would you like a bath?"

He didn't have Connery's brogue, but he had everything else, including the pointed eyebrows and broad chest. "Yes, please," Chloe said. She felt a little tired already.

They left the room, and Chloe fell asleep.

~

Ezzi walked down the stairs. The table was clear, the scent of fresh bread filled the air.

"What's wrong?" his mother asked from the courtyard.

She was clean and coifed, her makeup lightly done and her dress fresh. The house even looked better, smelled better.

"What is bothering you? You are in and out, you never mention the copper tub anymore. Something has you worried. Don't insult me with lies."

He halted. His body went hot when he realized the opportunity facing him. He could have everything, if he would just be bold enough. The gods had blessed his bad behavior—what more blessings could they give?

Or perhaps he should seize any blessing he wanted. Ezzi sighed and stared at his feet, his shoulders suddenly slumping. He swallowed and ran a shaky hand across his brow. He blinked, until he felt moisture in his eyes. Then he looked up. "You don't want to be insulted with lies? Very well, I will tell you." He took a deep breath. "The *en* has declared I will be buried as Puabi."

"Buried?" Ulu said. "What babbling is this?"

"Because of discovering the star," he said. "I am committed to die."

"With Puabi?"

"In her place."

"You're a man, the *ensi* is a woman."

"I will be substituted, no one will know."

Ulu's eyes narrowed. "Nonsense," she said. "The *ensi* is supposed to step down, no one has mentioned anything about dying. The gods are heartless, but they are not cruel."

Ezzi shrugged and sat down at the table. "Of course, you know, don't you." He started to pick at a piece of bread. Ulu watched him, silent.

"What do you know?" she asked at long last.

"Asa just revealed that the *ensi* must die. But," he forced a halfhearted chuckle, "we both know that won't happen. I go in her place. I'm nobody, with nothing really to live for."

"Don't say that, Ezzi, you have a fine future ahead of you," Ulu said. "I just cannot believe this is serious."

He looked into his mother's eyes. "It's serious." He looked away.

"This is why you haven't asked about the copper tub?"

"Why ask? It makes no matter to me anymore. I'll be dead." Ezzi got up, straightened his kilt, and walked to the door. When he reached it, she spoke.

"You won't be killed," she said. "I won't allow it."

"Words mean nothing, female." He smiled as he faced the painted wood. "You are just trying to assuage your guilt," he said. "You don't really care."

She rushed at him, hugged him around the waist, spoke against his back. "Ezzi, my son. Don't you know how I love you? I will go to Sin and beg for your life. Don't say—"

Ezzi turned to face her. He was repelled by the press of her breasts against his chest, the fragrance of her in his nostrils. "You won't have to worry about me anymore," he said. "You'll be able to have customers here, you won't even have to be quiet." He tore away from her. "I was always just in the way."

"What? Never! I fought for your life, to give you—"

"I doesn't matter, I'm going to die."

"Stop saying that. You are not going to die. No one has that authority—"

"The stargazer, Puabi, the *en*." He blinked the tears in his eyes, so they fell down his cheeks. "You probably think I deserve it."

"Don't babble. You won't die."

"You can't change their minds."

"No, but I can go in your place. I'm female. I'm old. I'm of your family."

Ezzi buried his face in his mother's neck. "You would do such for me?"

Her voice was choked, but she finally believed him. "I would do anything for you, son."

He'd won.

⌇

Cheftu's door flew open and Puabi stood there, proud of her nudity, red in the face. "I have a substitute!"

He put his head in his hands. He'd known that young stargazer wasn't to be trusted. Puabi marched up to him and pulled his hands away, holding them in hers. "A woman is willing to die as Puabi. Then the *lugal* can assure my win as *ensi* in the next election, under another name of course."

"No one can know, should we choose to use a substitute," Cheftu said. "Not even the *lugal*."

"It's impossible. The *lugal* will know. I see him every afternoon. It's my duty."

Cheftu had forgotten her relationship with the man. "What woman?" he asked. "What woman is willing to die as you? Have you met her?"

"I'll summon her," Puabi said, as she looked at her fingernails. "I am the *ensi*. You'd do best to remember that."

"She agreed to it?" He couldn't keep the surprise from his voice.

"Of course. It's a great honor to her."

He didn't know what to say.

"Now that we have her, the ceremony can take place anytime. I don't care."

"You know it means the death of all your attendants, your maids, your scribes," he said.

"Yes."

"Even Shama."

"Yes."

"Does this woman know her name won't be mentioned? She'll die unknown."

Puabi looked at him. "Of course, but she will have attendants, friends. The stargazer gave me their names. She won't die alone. You think me cruel, but I'm not. I'm just searching for the best situation for the commonwealth. Which is my survival."

"More will die?" Cheftu asked, horrified.

"Have you seen the fields? Many women must die, preferably of childbearing age. The ones you got pregnant will, of course, be spared, but how else are the rest of the people supposed to survive?"

"How many?" he asked. "Which women?"

"Oh, they have to be beautiful. Young. Maybe . . . a hundred, I think?"

Cheftu felt his throat growing tight. "Who?"

"There's a whole list; I don't know specifically, just some females."

"You told them they're going to die?"

"They'll be collected, and informed. It's not inhumane. They'll have wonderful drugs, they won't even be scared."

"Why was this woman picked?"

"Ulu, the woman, well, we were born on the same day."

"How do you know? Have you met her?"

"No, no, the stargazer," she said. "The young one. He came to me because he'd had a dream, and I was the only one who could answer it. I am the goddess Inana, consort of the Moon god Sin," she said as a reminder.

"I've met Ezzi," he said. "How does he know Ulu?"

"I don't know, but he must have told her immediately after your meeting, because he told me last night."

Cheftu was dubious about this woman volunteer and Ezzi's relationship with her.

"So that is settled," Puabi said. "Now, come tell me how happy you are that I'll still be *ensi*, because you know that means you'll still be *en* Kidu," she said as she kissed his chest. "Unless you stay out of my bed and displease me further." She poked his chest with a long fingernail. "Be wary, Kidu, you are becoming a nuisance to me."

"Then get rid of me," he said, exhausted and reeling from her callousness. A hundred women would be put to death, and no one was trying to prevent it? It was some form of population control?

She opened her mouth to speak, but a knock at the door saved him. A scribe opened it, and the *lugal* chose this moment to walk into the room. "Greetings of the dawn to you *en*, and *ensi*. The list is complete."

∼

Shama broke the seal to the deepest passageway and tottered in. The tablets were there—written in the priestly code that required an equality of minds, a divine balance. Lesser male humans, and females, had shunted them in here as nonsense written by their forefathers.

One by one, Shama loaded them into his wheelbarrow.

The *en* might be interested. And Shama had a feeling that this new side of Kidu might be able to attain the balance needed to read, and comprehend them.

∼

Her third night since waking up with short hair and without a concussion, Chloe swore she heard Cheftu calling her name. Either that, or she was hallucinating that the trees were. No other sounds in the house. Probably Ningal was in the courtyard drinking his evening wine. Ulu hadn't been around since Chloe had met her.

She couldn't very well stride through the courtyard and say she had a date with the *en*. She heaved herself up the ladder, a shaky contraption meant for kittens and kids, and poked her head out through the rush roof. The night was, of course, cloudless and blanketed with stars that looked big enough to wear as stones. A palm tree shaded the space and was conveniently planted on the street.

Chloe took the last few steps and crawled onto the roof. The regular night noises of cats, dogs, goats, and sheep filled the air, laughter from a tavern nearby, and the carried sounds of activity in the port. She wet her lips and breathed his name.

"Cheftu."

She didn't see movement in the shadows, or hear any response. Hiking her skirt up and tucking it beneath her belt, she jumped at the palm's trunk.

The marsh girl took over. Chloe wrapped her arms around the trunk and straddled it, her legs bent like a locust. She edged her way down, then dropped to the ground.

The Crooked Way was a wide street, and the houses that lined it were hidden behind high, blank walls. As in the Middle East of the twentieth century, these people didn't believe in advertising the wealth or comfort of their homes. Most of them had extinguished the torches outside their doors. It was late.

Down the street, a door closed, and Chloe stepped into the darkness of the palm's shadow. She saw his shadow first, dancing along, larger than life against the wall, then the man himself.

The *en*.

Cheftu.

He walked down the street, moving with caution and grace. It was so hard to believe.

He was blond. The high priest of the people. The fertility priest!

He stared at Ningal's house, then stepped toward the tree.

"Cheftu?" she choked out. Was she dreaming or was this real?

He halted and stared straight at her, though she knew he couldn't see her. The light fell on his face. It was Cheftu. Her black-haired, dark-skinned, Egyptian husband had been transformed into an Aryan fantasy wearing the body of a halfback. "Is it you, really?" she asked.

The door to the courtyard opened and Chloe froze. Cheftu turned around and faced Ningal.

"Sir," the justice said. "I thought I heard voices." He peered into the night. "Do you have a scribe with you?"

"I . . . just sent him ahead," Cheftu said.

"It's always best to have your work waiting for you," Ningal concurred. "I am enjoying the breeze with a glass of date wine. I would be most honored if you would join me. My houseguest has gone off to bed, already."

He's talking about me, Chloe thought. *And he's lonely. Why didn't I see that before?*

"Uh, thank you, sir," Cheftu—Cheftu? As a blonde? As a beefed-up, brawny blonde? "I am just returning to the temple."

Ningal stepped out and closed the door behind him. "You shouldn't walk alone."

"Really, sir," Cheftu hedged. "I hate to take you away from your wine and peace."

Ningal smiled as he patted Cheftu on the shoulder. "A nice stroll will make the taste of the wine much sweeter." Ningal stopped, and his manner became very formal. "Unless I intrude on your thoughts."

Cheftu gave up. "I welcome the company," he said, and the two men walked on.

This was beginning to take on the elements of a farce—without the humor. Chloe waited until the men were around the corner, then she slipped inside the door, ran across the courtyard, and up to her apartments. She was wet with sweat, and trembling. Weak from her days in bed.

Weak from being in lust with her husband; weak from frustration at not being able to get close to him.

Weak-headed, she thought as she lay down, ready to dream of him again.

⌐

The *en* didn't even look at Ezzi when he caught up with them in the corridor. "How long?" he asked Asa. Kidu's face looked like a mask, and his voice was chilling it was so emotionless. "Don't give me guesses, tell me how many days until this exhibition."

"The stars say—"

The *en* spun on him, taller and wider, looking down into Asa's face. "You read the stars. You tell me the interpretation. I prepare the temple. How many days?"

"Seven days," Asa said. "Give or take a few double hours."

The *en* looked at both of them. "Thank you. You're no longer needed."

Asa and Ezzi halted in shock. The *en* stopped at his door, as the attendant shot to attention. "The *lugal* and the *ensi* are . . . congressing, sir."

The *en* gave the man a look as cold as snow on the Zagros Mountains, and walked into his chambers. He slammed the door shut behind him, and everyone in the corridor jumped.

Ezzi didn't know what to say. The *en* had no manners, no doubt. And he had seven days to orchestrate the sacrifice. Ezzi just hoped his mother would take the initiative soon, before Puabi sent for Ulu and his duplicity was revealed.

Not that it mattered; he was only working for the good of the commonwealth.

Doing what the gods desired.

～

Cheftu was sleeping, finally. He'd talked with Ningal until early morning, learning of Chloe, though Ningal had never named her. It was an interesting position, to watch a man fall in love with one's wife. Cheftu couldn't blame the man, but from time to time he still had the desire to bloody Ningal's nose.

Kidu's notion? No, Cheftu admitted, that was his own impulse.

Ningal was living with Chloe. Cheftu didn't dare write

her a note, or send a word. No way to show her she was in his thoughts. After seven years, she had to trust that.

Unfortunately, she was not in his bed. The fantasy that he would wake up with her was what had finally enabled him to sleep. Now, in his deepest consciousness, he heard a gentle sigh.

In his room.

Chloe, that ever-resourceful woman, had found her way to him. He smiled in his sleep. The hands on him were strong and sure. And extremely adept. Cheftu floated on a sea of feeling remarkably good as the woman ministered to his flesh.

"Anything you ask, *en* Kidu," she whispered. "You are the keeper of life and death. I would please you with the last breath of my body, in any way you wish."

Not Chloe.

He'd never heard her voice before, in fact he'd never heard her accent. And her smell was unlike the heavy perfumes and incenses of those who sought him through the temple's channels.

She wasn't Chloe, though his body and mind cared far less about that than his integrity and soul did. With effort he sat up and pulled away. "Don't touch me," he said, though even to his ears his voice lacked any enthusiasm or conviction. "What do you want?"

"Take me in place of Puabi," she said. "I wish to die as the *ensi.*"

Cheftu blinked, as he summoned alertness from his body. "What do you speak of?" He couldn't see her clearly in the dark, but he could sense her presence. Underneath her confident sexuality lay terror.

"Puabi will not die, I know this. I also know you need someone who wants to, who is willing, to serve in her place. I have come to offer myself." She slid down flat, sinuously slipping to lie beside him. "Anything you want, *en*, I will give. Just take me in her place. Please."

This was the second volunteer for a remarkably awful job. "Did someone put you up to this?"

"No."

Her breath touched the skin of his chest, while the heat of her body pulsed next to him in the bed. Cheftu jumped out of bed. "I will consult with the stargazers," he said in a hurry. "I will let you know. What's your name?"

"Ulu," the woman said, sliding across the bed toward him. "I will stay here while we await the dawn."

"Ulu?" Cheftu said, surprised. "Your offer has already been accepted."

"What?" she said, the sexy tone dropped.

"Puabi has already decided to let you sacrifice for her. Ezzi, I believe, suggested your name."

He didn't hear anything from her for a moment—not even breath. Her body seemed to grow cold.

"Ulu?"

"What do you want?" she asked. Her voice was a hundred years older. Resigned. The tone of a slave who has been beaten into submission.

"Nothing. You may go home. I'm sure the stargazer will send for you soon."

"I have no home," she whispered, then slipped away.

~

Ningal came home late, sated from a visit to the temple after he left the company of the *en*. His old bones felt rejuvenated, his flesh at ease. Now he would be able to think reasonably about his problems, instead of like a fiery youth. The problem was Chloe.

Years had passed since his wife's breath had left and not

returned. Though he had missed the hubbub of activity she had stirred, he had grown used to calm and quiet. The slaves were well mannered and efficient, his forays into court kept him apprised of the goings-on in the community. He'd had his offspring, and theirs and theirs. The earth would not pass away without record of Ningal.

Chloe made him feel alive. He looked forward to the day, just because she would learn something new and be amazed by it. He anticipated her return at twilight, when her leggy shadow was even longer and the mingled scents of sesame and pomegranate would float on the evening air. What would it be like to see her eyes shine with passion, or hear his name on her lips? What joy would it be to wake with her, to gaze at that face, to see those luminous eyes as dawn broke?

His hours at the temple tonight had proved he still could sate her as a man. His wealth was exceptional, even in Ur, and his bloodline impeccable. Should she desire children, he could give them to her. For a second his heart seized at the thought of a tiny girl with Khamite hair and one green eye and one brown, chewing on the end of her finger as she spoke to him, called him father. May the gods wish it, he thought fervently.

He stepped into the courtyard; it was quiet. At the top of the stairs, Chloe's room was dark. She was resting yet. He'd never gone to her portico, the rooms she'd made her own, for he'd never known what he had to offer her, or really what he wanted from her. Now, he did. He put his foot on the first step.

Should I do this when wine yet floats in my blood, he thought. *When another woman's scent clings to my cloak?*

He stepped away. Chloe deserved more. In the morning, he would speak to her and be sure they were going to share the evening meal together. He would be clean and shaved and sober. She deserved as much. Then, perhaps, he would climb these stairs, her hand in his, pulling him along.

Ningal smiled in hope and went to his own bed.

~

"I've graduated to animals?" Chloe asked the Tablet Father. After the week she'd missed, she still remembered all her forty humans.

"Because of this, uh, illness of yours," the Tablet Father said, "I think you should stay at home, close to the care of Justice Ningal. List the animals, then when you are finished, come show them to me."

Chloe nodded, shouldered her basket of clay—since her head was healing, it didn't seem smart to balance things on it—and set off back home. It was early yet, the streets were empty. With the decrease in food had come a decrease in activity. *I did my part,* Chloe thought. *I didn't eat for a few days.*

All of this served to keep her mind off the most pressing question: Where the hell was Cheftu and what was going on?

Most men would love a position where their job was to sleep with other women. Cheftu wasn't like that, never had been. Puabi's jealousies must be fierce, Chloe thought as she cut through the alleyway that led to the back door of the Crooked Way mansions.

Other footsteps didn't disturb her. It was broad daylight; she was ten steps from home. Her mouth was covered before she could scream. All she heard was a whisper in her ear. "You won't make a fool of me again, little Khamite morsel."

~

Puabi was singing, a curious reaction from a woman who was condemned to die. If she didn't at least attempt pretense, no one was going to believe in her substitution. Shama watched her carefully. When did the girl who had been the darling of her venerable grandfather Ziusudra become so self-centered and self-serving? When did she turn her back on the behavior asked by the god of gods.

Kidu entered the room, without knocking. Puabi smiled at him and wrapped her arms around him for a kiss. Shama saw the big blond endured the embrace, but did not enjoy it. He freed himself from her grasp. "The commonwealth is mobilized," Kidu said.

Puabi leaned back against her pillows and stretched. "Good."

"What are you taking?"

"Taking?"

"On your journey to the skies?" he said.

She laughed. "I have a sub—"

"Silence yourself!"

She waved at Shama. "He's nothing, a deaf, mute old man. Besides, he knows."

Shama focused on cleaning her sandals, but his ears burned with embarrassment. Puabi used to love him, protect him, trust him.

"You are shameful," Kidu said, then looked around the room. "Shouldn't you be packing?"

"I have already."

The *en* looked around the room; baskets and bags were strewn haphazardly as Puabi had moved from task to task, never finishing the first one. "Not for your trip to Dilmun, for the tomb."

"The tomb?"

"We have to bury your belongings," he said.

"My clothes?" She sounded more horrified than she had anytime before. Shama was embarrassed for her.

"Let me make this clear because I don't believe you understand," the *en* said. "You are escaping with your life, but it is going to cost you every bauble and bangle you own."

Shama looked up. It seemed light poured down on the *en*;

in that moment, Shama knew Kidu was possessed of a different spirit. One from the god of gods. He turned back to packing Puabi's sandals.

"What? Why?" Puabi said, sitting up straight.

"You want to dupe the people and please the gods? You have to give them as close to the real thing as can be managed."

"I don't care," she said.

"You will care when the sky turns black, the moon battles the sun, and the clients and gentleman you think are so easily manipulated turn on you like wild dogs because you are responsible, and it is with you the gods are displeased."

Shama glanced at the *ensi's* face. She was a shade paler.

"They would . . . hurt me?"

"Have you seen a wild dog fight for its life?" Kidu said. "First it rips the tendons in the legs of the other dog, so it can't fight back. Then it tears at the victim's throat, gives it a mortal wound so it loses its ability to fight back. Then the dog rips at the tenderest parts, the belly, the groin—"

Puabi had drawn her knees up and was staring at him with huge eyes.

"The dogs lick at the blood and devour the insides of the creature as it watches. They—"

"Cease!" she cried, covering her ears. "Take it all, my jewelry, my gowns, everything. But promise me I won't be here. Make the woman, what was her name—"

"Ulu."

"Yes, make her come live here and I'll go visit . . . Dilmun."

"You will not journey to paradise on earth while we are suffering because of your cowardice. You will be here for every moment, until the final walk into the pit."

Shama marveled at the difference in the man. *And none of us has really noticed,* he thought. *Will humans always see only what they expect to see?*

"We'll substitute you at the last moment," the *en* said to

Puabi. "Are your maids aware? Do they know they are going to die?"

"Not yet. They will be the last who are informed, after the others are gathered."

He turned away to leave, then looked at Shama. "Is he going with you, or—"

"I told you. Send him with my substitute."

Shama would willingly die with his mistress, as awful as she had become. However, he refused to die with her substitute. He looked up and met the translucent gaze of the *en*. Somehow, he knew Kidu knew. Shama's hands trembled as he set down one pair of sandals and picked another pair up. Kidu closed the door.

"Kidu's lost all sense of decorum," Puabi said of the *en*. "He doesn't even travel with a retinue anymore. What has become of the dignity of the temple?" She looked at the old man. "Get me some fruit, I'm hungry."

Shama bowed to her, then left.

Puabi had claimed Shama was deaf: so by her own proclamation, he never heard her request. Besides, Shama needed the time. He had to teach the *en* how to read the secret tablets.

Chloe came to in a cell, dark and hot. Her lip was split, her eye swollen shut, the knuckles of her right hand crusted with blood. She'd fought, but the burly boy from school and his adult henchmen had still gotten her here.

Wherever here was.

Ningal would figure out she been taken. Then it was a simple matter of finding out how, by whom. It was a wonder that boy had dared to attack her again. Why would he risk it? Maybe he's an idiot, she reasoned. "Hello?" she called. "Hello, can anyone hear me?"

Ningal would figure it out.

And Cheftu was the most powerful man in the temple. He'd probably come for her last night, and when she didn't show he'd started a search for her. He'd find her in no time.

They were stupid to not have gagged her or something. She would shout the place down.

Unless they knew there was no hope.

What if she was outside of town?

Almost in answer to her thought, she heard the long lowing of a water buffalo. *I'm no longer in Ur,* she thought and bowed her head. *They didn't rape me, or kill me, or torture me, so why did they take me?*

Did Cheftu's jealous girlfriend Puabi find out about me? She's grabbed me and is going to let me rot here?

No, that boy was the same one who had attacked her in the grove. He had to have had help, to cart a long-legged, deadweight female from behind Ningal's house to here. *He was lying in wait for me,* she realized. *He'd planned this.*

How did he know I would be returning from school that way, at that time?

Why, she asked herself again, *why?*

The room wasn't tall enough to stand up in, or long enough to take more than six steps. Memories of television she'd seen, photographs, flashed through her mind. POW camps, the cages captured soldiers were kept in. The stories of how the captives kept in shape, how they stayed sane, ran through her mind.

Who helped that boy?

Ningal had still been in bed when Chloe left. Kalam hadn't arrived yet. The Tablet Father had sent her home—odd. But it could be he really was being considerate.

Chloe lay down on the dirt packed floor and began to test the strength of the brick walls. She'd try each brick, then she would come up with a plan. Along the way she'd figure out who'd set her up.

Chapter Three

Cheftu was washing his face when the panel in his bedroom moved, then slid back. Shama stood there, coughing from the dust. Cheftu moved forward to help the man. Shama pushed a wheelbarrow, filled with even dustier tablets.

He handed one to Cheftu, then took it back and rinsed its face off. He offered it back to Cheftu, who took it, mystified. Cheftu looked at the words, which made no sense. The tablet was obviously ancient, the signs even more complicated then than they were in the present.

Shama touched him on the arm, then gestured from his throat.

"Aloud?" Cheftu asked.

The old man nodded enthusiastically.

"My male human parent's female human parent's tame feline is a mighty catcher of four-legged field rodents." Four lines of this same phrase. What meaning did this have? "My grandmother's cat catches rats well?" Cheftu said, and looked up at Shama.

He just smiled and nodded. Then he indicated Cheftu read it again.

Cheftu frowned, and his hands grew slick with sweat as they gripped the edges of the clay. What was he supposed to understand? He read the sentence; then he read the paragraph that followed. "Again?" Cheftu asked the old man. What purpose did this serve?

Shama nodded, and Cheftu read the first three words. Then Shama slipped his hand in front of Cheftu's face, close to his eyes, just touching his nose. The man's palms smelled of Puabi's perfume and dust. He held his hand there and Cheftu waited. Slowly, he relaxed. His forehead smoothed out, his hands eased their hold, and he stared through the old man's hand.

Shama moved his palm away and Cheftu's eyes didn't react fast enough—he stared through the writing on the tablet. He saw the pattern. The hidden message that concentration could obscure, but relaxation and calm revealed. He blinked, and it vanished.

He looked at the old man, who reached for the tablet, then laid it on the bed. He rinsed a second one for Cheftu. Now, Cheftu knew what to do. He focused his vision through the tablet and saw the pattern immediately: lines that intersected and paralleled each other.

On a hunch, he laid the two tablets side by side. They connected in three places.

He turned to the old man. "A map?"

Shama shook his head. Cheftu took a few more tablets, rinsed them, and placed them next to the first two. "A plan?" he asked, when he had seven of them connected.

The old man nodded.

For the next two hours, Cheftu and Shama rinsed the tablets and built the image. When there were no more, Cheftu looked at the enormous architectural rendering in stone they'd created. "Where is this?"

Shama pointed down.

Then he crooked a finger, and Cheftu leaned over the tablets with him. Shama pointed to a drawing of a stick figure in a box. With his fingers Shama walked through the rooms, then out a narrow passageway. "Substitute." His voice was as worn and dusty as the tablets.

Cheftu looked at the tablets. A very crude crown was drawn on the head of the figure. "This has happened before," Cheftu said.

Shama nodded.

"The substitute . . . escaped?"

Shama nodded. Then he handed Cheftu a goblet, built of clay, with a wide base.

~

Ningal was frantic. Chloe had vanished like a dust storm. The Tablet Father said she hadn't attended school. Kalam, who had informed him of her disappearance, had claimed she hadn't come down to break her fast. "I assumed she was weary and stayed in bed."

The girl had been on fire to get back to school. She'd mastered her words. Ningal had seen her clay—and when she wrote to herself, she wrote sideways. For her homework, she wrote properly. Nevertheless, she'd been fearful she would forget what she'd learned if any more time passed. From the moment she woke up, she'd be practicing her words, expanding her vocabulary past what they'd taught her. She was learning foods and furniture, actions and intentions. And carefully writing everything down.

They had settled into a comfortable routine. She usually was gone before he woke, but in the evening he'd be waiting with cool beer when she returned from school. They'd share the events of their days, then dine. While Ningal worked with Kalam on the list of lists or the next day's schedule, Chloe would do her homework.

Consequently, it had been two days since anyone had seen her. Ningal had thought they were missing each other.

The slaves thought she was eating out. No one had thought to ask anyone else about her.

"She left, Justice," Kalam said. "That is why her rooms are cleared out."

It had been the most damning evidence: an empty room.

"What about her sheep?" The sheep Ningal had personally rounded up after she'd been hurt. They had been left in the care of the commonwealth's head sheepherder with strict orders not to let them out of his sight. Ningal didn't want Chloe to lose her wealth, her independence.

Kalam shrugged. "I don't know. He said a few must have run away."

Sheep didn't flee; they were led. Ningal looked away. He'd tried to ignore the signs, but they were too clear. *Please,* he prayed, *give me an omen if I'm being too suspicious.* His chest ached with betrayal.

"Maybe she hit her head again, you know, opened the wound that garden fork made."

Ningal didn't flinch, but his heart broke. Kalam couldn't have known Chloe's head wound was made with a garden fork unless he'd had something to do with it. Ningal hadn't shared that information with anyone. *I didn't want a sign that I was right,* Ningal complained to the deity. *I wanted to know that I was wrong.*

"I can't believe she left so abruptly," Kalam said. "After you labored to get her into school, it's the height of bad manners to go. I thought she was really committed to her 'franchise' idea." He shook his head. "We can only trust our own kind, in the end."

Kalam was behind this; he knew where Chloe was. How could the man Ningal had loved as a son betray him so? Ningal needed to be as slippery as the first snake and wheedle it from him. *How was I so blind to the nature of this human?* he wondered. *How did the root get so rotten?*

Kalam finished his wine in one swig. "Shall we go to the council meeting?"

"I will meet you."

"Don't worry for her," Kalam said, his voice thick as honey with sentiment. "She will be fine. Best to see if she took your gold, in addition to her own."

Ningal looked into the face of the man who'd been his family, his protégé. Kalam didn't realize he'd betrayed himself; his pride blinded him there, too.

"I will meet you," Ningal said, staring at the table once more. "Go now."

Kalam closed the courtyard door. Ningal called for his slave. "The morning that Chloe went missing, did Kalam come to the house?"

She nodded. "Same as usual. Maybe a bit later. He seemed to be in and out."

Ningal nodded and rose. "Bring me my finest cloak," he said. "And the golden basket hat." Ningal had a meeting to attend.

~

"Clients, freedmen, slaves, and gentlemen," the *lugal* said to the gathered council members. "We are in a grave situation. As you know, the rust has depleted our food source. We have no surplus. Stars are falling from heaven, the moon turned to blood, the stargazers predict worse. The portents for the future are grim."

His eyes shone with tears, and Nimrod watched the corresponding reactions as each man realized a dire judgment loomed.

"We have displeased the gods. As a community or individuals, I do not know. This I do know, the personification of Inana is going to intercede for us with Sin and the court of the skies."

There was rustling, worry, but the men were silent.

"In five days' time, Puabi will go meet her lover Sin in an eternal marriage—"

Cries. Shouts. Declamations.

"—the sun and moon will debate over the issue, with Puabi as a bartering device—"

More shouting. It was almost impossible to hear the *lugal*.

"—and we shall see if Ur will survive."

He waited until the group quieted. Nimrod watched them, men of circumstance and power, stripped free of their control by one thought of heaven.

"I need from you all the accoutrements a goddess requires for a journey to heaven. All that we can offer, to barter with the gods."

"Do they threaten another Deluge?" someone asked.

"The rainbow is their seal!" someone else protested. "They can't break their contract!"

The *lugal* held up his hand. "I do not know their threats. I do know they are displeased, and the skies reveal that displeasure. Go to your homes and businesses, and think of extreme forfeiture. If we don't, there will be nothing to build on in the future. There will be no future."

As the men dispersed, the *lugal* mingled with them, asking this one to donate a sledge and that one to give his finest furniture. Puabi wasn't being buried; she was being outfitted for a journey to an unknown world where the commonwealth hoped the trading system was the same. Nimrod looked up at the sky. It seemed benign, but the *lugal* said five days would bring disaster.

Kalam bumped into Nimrod, his eyes wide with fear. "The *ensi* is going to die?" he asked.

"Puabi is going to intercede for us. It is her duty to the commonwealth." Nimrod repeated what his father had said in all twelve rehearsals he'd made Nimrod endure.

"The gods would listen to a woman?"

Nimrod stepped away. The Old Boy was so ignorant, so vain. "Before your parents' parents walked, women were justices. They were the first. Inana is the queen of heaven because she is an honorable and even-handed ruler."

"What about the Deluge?"

Nimrod sighed. Even Nirg, for all of being a mountain woman, knew these tales. "Some young god, whose bouts of drinking hurt his head, got violent at the noise the humans were making. He appealed to the god of gods, who looked down and saw how far humanity had fallen, how lost it had become. The god of gods decreed the world must be washed clean and begun again. Inana bartered so each man could live at least 120 years." Ningal shrugged. "As her eloquence won him over, and his reasoning occurred to her, it was concluded the earth should be wiped clean, and when begun again, humans would have 120 years."

"What about Ziusudra?"

"His family was the means to sustain life, so the gods didn't have to make humans again."

"A female did this?"

"Which is why a female journeys to heaven to argue for us again."

"If that's the truth, why are there no women justices?" Kalam was trying to play a game with Nimrod; Nimrod was above games.

"Perhaps because male humans' blood runs too hot to listen to the reason of a female. We would rather solve a problem with fists instead of conversation. A spear is the choice, more often than a conciliatory drink. It's easier to fight than to compromise." Nirg had told him this often enough.

But he wondered, what was the cause for the change, for females not to have an equal share in ruling, for men to promote bloodletting? What effect did those differences have on their cumulative humanity.

We need to start again, he thought. *Without 120 years as a guarantee; then maybe we would use our time and energies better.*

∽

Rudi heard footsteps outside her door before she heard the soft tap. She drew a cloak over her shoulders and opened the door. Immediately, she bowed. "Asa, stargazer," she muttered, her voice still groggy with sleep.

"Don your robes," he said. "I have a task for you."

"Of course, sir, but . . . I am on suspension, if you don't recall."

"No longer," he said. "Be quick."

Rudi ran back to her room and threw on her stargazer's robe, a cloak that fell from her neck to the floor, dyed dark with stars emblazoned on it. She'd been forbidden to wear it since the day after the blood moon.

"What has happened?" she asked, as they walked down the torchlit corridor.

"I need you to bring the *en,*" he said.

"Bring him where?"

Asa handed her a small tablet. "The location is written here. Bring him at dawn, if you will."

She bowed her head. Even now he didn't trust her with actual information. She heard his footsteps fade on the stairs, then lifted the tablet to the light and read its directions. Why was she to bring the *en* to the marshes?

Somewhere in the temple, the singers practiced. Soon, it would be dawn. Rudi recalled the location of the *en's* rooms and set off for them. What was she going to say to persuade him?

⌒

Guli rose to his feet as the door opened. Two guards stood there. "You're the hairdresser Guli?" a young stargazer asked.

He nodded.

"Come with us."

He followed them, and climbed up into the sledge. Rather than riding toward the gallows beside the southwestern gate, they drove through the gate in the tenemos walls of the temple grounds and into the back courtyard complex.

Priests, acolytes, guards, stargazers, clients, gentlemen . . . they were all scurrying around in the early dawn, all glancing fearfully at the sky. Guli had been in the total darkness of the cell—but he found himself looking up also. The day seemed as any other—a prophecy of scorching heat. The stargazer said nothing, but his very attitude indicated that merely standing beside Guli was an insult.

Weary of him, of them, of the system that condemned, Guli said nothing. What did it matter what they did, where? He was a dead man.

He just couldn't reason out why the sentence hadn't been carried out, when it happened. Justice had never been slow before.

The sledge halted, and the stargazer dismounted. "These are your things, I am told?" he asked as he pointed to Guli's belongings—the remnants of his little shop, with additions Guli could never afford: a packet of gold dust, a blade with a metal edge, vials and pots he didn't recognize.

"Enter that room and prepare the lady for a great journey," the stargazer said. "She is to be the goddess Inana."

Guli stepped toward the man, and the guards, spears pointed, stepped toward him. The stargazer's expression was hard to read, but he seemed almost frightened. Guli bent slowly and picked up the bags with dyes and blade and curling tongs and backed to the door.

"Open it," the stargazer said.

Guli lifted the bolt and stepped inside. "Hello?" he called. The smell of roasted meat and damp fleece greeted him. He blinked in the contrasting darkness. "Greetings?"

A creature sitting against the wall raised its head. "Guli?"

"Ulu?"

The door slammed shut.

⌒

En Kidu opened the door before Rudi knocked. He was awake, clear-eyed, and dressed formally. To her surprise, he didn't question her insistence and request. Instead, he sent the acolytes to retrieve a cart and onagers for travel.

As the sky turned dark before the light of day, they were on their way out of the gates. Kidu was at the reins, and Rudi hung on to the sides of the vehicle as they bounced along the road at breakneck speed. Sledges were so much steadier, but slower.

"It's here," she said a while later.

In the middle of a palm grove, a foreigner had built a palace.

Asa himself opened the door. "I have our substitute," he said to the *en*. "She awaits you."

Kidu looked puzzled. "A second substitute?" he asked, as they all walked to a shed in the back.

Asa looked a little uncomfortable. "She is truly the one the gods require."

"Is she willing?"

Asa turned to Rudi. "The night you missed the blood moon and were thus suspended, what night was it?"

"The night the flood struck."

"And the skies warned of evil coming from the north, truth?"

Rudi nodded. Kidu watched them both, inscrutable.

"This female came into Ur and demanded things no one ever has before, then *samana* struck. Her requests upset the—"

"Open the door," Kidu said.

"She is the reason for it, the famine and the flooding," Asa explained. "She is the one who deserves to die!"

"Open the door!"

Asa opened it, and Rudi peered into the dark depths of the mud shack. A woman had curled into a fetal position on the ground. Flies clustered around her face and hands. Kidu said nothing, but Rudi felt his fury as though it was the rays of Shamash. Two slaves doused her with water. They dragged her into the dawn.

"She's the reason," Asa said. "The female Chloe."

Kidu inhaled so sharply that he hissed like a snake. "Lift her head," he said.

"Why?" Asa asked.

"Lift her head," Kidu commanded through clenched teeth.

Asa grabbed the girl's head by her hair and turned her face to them. Rudi had never seen her before. Khamite, and beaten. One green eye, glazed from pain, stared at them.

Kidu was entranced. He crouched at her side, and spoke softly. "Who . . . who did this to you?"

"The Old Boys who collected her had a little fun," Asa said.

Kidu moved like lightning, standing toe to toe with the older man, glaring down into his face. "Did they—"

"They took some petty revenge, but they didn't violate her," Asa said. "She's the one who should die, *en* Kidu. She brought this on us."

"Die?" the girl said through her scabbed mouth. "I'm supposed to die?"

"The moon and sun will fight in a few days," Rudi explained. The girl's one-eyed gaze, now intelligent and aware, fixed on her. "They require a death in order to assure us the sun will win."

Kidu's gaze on the girl was intent, almost frightening. Rudi saw the lines around his mouth and eyes had whitened, his breathing was shallow. Did he know her? she wondered.

The girl closed her eyes and bowed her head.

"Are you willing to die for the welfare of the commonwealth of Ur?" Kidu asked her, in a tone gentle as a breeze. "Look at me when you answer."

She turned to him, then was struck motionless for a moment when she looked into his face.

Rudi had seen his extreme beauty cause that reaction before. They stared at each other.

"Answer the question, female," Asa said. "Are you willing to die for the commonwealth of Ur?"

"No! I'm not willing to die for an eclipse! It's not a sign from the gods, it's just . . ." She seemed to be searching for a word. "They happen often. Do people get sacrificed every time there's an eclipse?"

Rudi felt chills. How did this female know what an eclipse was? How did she know they occurred more than once?

The female continued to protest. "I'm not willing. I was kidnapped on my way home. I don't know this has happened to me, I—"

Kidu spun on his heel, looked straight at Asa. "She'll be the substitute."

"What!" she shouted. Rudi saw she turned extremely pale beneath her Khamite skin. "I will not!"

"She, she doesn't seem willing," Rudi pointed out.

"It seems if we are trying to convince the gods that the *ensi* is dying, Puabi should this day leave Ur and go far away until after the danger of this event has passed," Kidu said.

"But there are rituals, there are—" Asa began.

"I'm not going to die!" the girl said, now earnestly fighting against her captors. She had height and skill, but she was exhausted and dehydrated and could barely keep her feet.

"She will," Kidu said. "She will become Puabi this day." He looked at Rudi. "Take the cart, return to your sister, and tell her to set sail immediately." He turned to Asa. "I will bring the girl into Ur tonight."

"What about—"

"You've done your part, Asa. Leave me your slaves. Rudi, send back a sledge and clothes, for me and the new Puabi."

"I will not—" the female raved.

The *en* looked at the woman. "She will be perfect." He turned away from her. "Go now. We are losing time."

"Less than three days," Asa said.

"May the gods give you haste," Kidu said.

"Don't just let this happen to me," the woman said to Rudi. "I . . ." she fell silent at the expression on Rudi's face.

"It is your destiny, female," Rudi said. She just wished they'd had time to converse. This Chloe was the only other female Rudi had met who knew anything of the stars. How did she know, a simple Khamite girl?

Asa bowed, and the two of them left. Kidu stood in the shade of the palms and watched them mount into the carts and ride off. Rudi looked back. The girl was slumped between the two slaves, Kidu standing to her side, his hands on his hips. He wouldn't hurt her, Rudi thought. She shouldn't fight against destiny.

Rudi looked forward, to the walls of Ur.

~

"You're to be Puabi?" Guli asked.

Ulu nodded.

"How did this happen?"

She shrugged. She seemed less alive than he'd ever seen her. Not even a glimmer of the woman he'd known. "What happened to the 'new' Ulu?"

"A waste. That seed wasn't watered, so it withered."

He sat down on the grimy bed and tried not to look around. How much of his life he'd spent in cells. Or in shit. "What is wrong with you?"

She said nothing. Guli settled back, to wait. He couldn't paint someone in this mood. Weeping, screaming, anything was better than this monotone statue. "We don't have much time left, either of us," he said. "So I'll wait. When you want to talk, talk. The only place I have left to go is Kur."

~

"This is a bad plan," Chloe said to Cheftu/Kidu. "Killing me?"

"Release her," he said to the guards.

They let go of her arms, and Chloe fought to stand upright. Cheftu/Kidu towered over her, draped in golden chains and white wool. Chloe could smell her stink and was superaware of how nice he smelled. And she couldn't forget the slaves and guards who stood all around them. Hadn't he said he had spies? Was that the reason for this charade?

But he looked so foreign, so alien. And God, he was huge. Cheftu had never been delicate or small, but this guy—this new body—was a rugby player's.

"What makes you think you can persuade me to die for this woman?" she asked, not quite daring to meet his eyes. The slaves stood there, waiting for orders.

"Go prepare some food," he said to them. "Now."

Both of them left. Two other slaves stood just out of earshot, but within easy distance to see every expression on her face. Cheftu stepped closer to her. Chloe wanted to melt into him, but were they putting on a show? Or was he psycho? "Are you trying to scare me back into the shed?" she asked. Where they could talk.

His golden eyes flashed with heat. Talking wasn't on his mind. "Who did this to you?" he asked. His tone was soft, caring. "Who hit you, who did you have to defend yourself against?"

The wounds on her body, the soreness and dried blood underlined how real this game was. She knew the slaves, or guards, or whoever, were curious. "It doesn't matter. I'm not going to be alive long enough for the wounds to heal, am I?"

He took her wrists in his hand. Both of them fit within the circle of his fingers. He tugged her toward him. "You serve the commonwealth by your sacrifice."

Do I resist? Can I resist? Am I supposed to resist?

"I have promised Asa I will tame you," he said.

She tugged at him.

"For the sake of those who watch, I must be seen to do so," he said quietly.

"That's an interesting line," Chloe said, but her words were breathy, and she trembled. "Does it work often?"

He bent close to her, so close she could see the flecks of brown and amber in his eyes. "I don't want to hurt your mouth, but I must kiss you."

"Part of the show, huh?" she whispered.

When his mouth touched hers, his kiss was soft, gentle, and quick. Chloe acknowledged she wanted it to be endless, to seduce her, to make her so dizzy she would abandon any semblance of control. "Don't stop," she pleaded.

"Make the female a bath!" he shouted over his shoulder. One of the slaves left. One stayed. "Come into the house," he said. "Eat, sleep, wash. We'll return to the temple soon."

"Both of us? Tonight?" she asked.

"Earlier." His voice dropped to a shade of a whisper. "I must be free of these spies before I touch you."

Her knees were wobbly.

He scooped her up in his arms, against the hot gold that decorated his chest. "Just play your part," he said in an undertone. "And know it's killing me to play mine."

Cheftu carried her into the house, set her in the tub, and left her in privacy to bathe. After she ate, a slave ministered to her black eye, another to her cuts and bruises, and a third fanned her while she napped.

~

It must be dark outside now; a trickle of cool air blew through the cramped cell. Guli had been resting, his forehead on his knees.

"What happened?" she asked finally. "I asked you to dinner, but I couldn't find you. Then I heard from Ningal that you had killed a man. Your owner."

Guli smiled. If only Ulu could hear herself—she sounded like a lady. She even sat like a lady now, instead of sprawling for attention.

"It doesn't matter," he said. "I killed Viza. I would do it again, I just wish I had done it sooner." Before Viza had ruined other people's lives. "And you? Talk to me, Ulu."

"I have a son," she began.

By the time she was finished with her tale, Guli wished to kill again. "You don't have to be a substitute," he said. "I won't do the makeup, and they will have to use Puabi."

Ulu sniffed, the first sign of her spirit breaking that he'd heard. "Ezzi was so ashamed of me that he plotted my death. Ezzi was so sure he could get me to offer myself for him that he told Puabi my name even before he lied to me, manipulated me. He cares that little for me—" She didn't say anything else for a long time. Guli reached across the space and took her hot, grimy hand in his.

"If he has worked this hard to have me dead, then dead I shall be," she said.

He took her in his arms.

⁓

"Chloe?" Puabi said. "That was her name?"

"The marsh girl, yes," Rudi said. "Come, the *en* said we must go."

"I imagine he did. No," Puabi said. "I'm not leaving until I see this girl."

Rudi frowned. "What is your reasoning for that? Puabi, your life is at risk. You don't have the time for jealousies now."

"Chloe. He called out that name the morning after I thought he'd died. Do you not remember? He even called you Chloe. Who is this female? How does he know her?"

Rudi groaned. "You should know, you have set enough spies on him."

"I should dismiss them all. No one has ever heard of this Chloe, until I mentioned her to the *lugal*. She's been babbling at him to attend the Tablet House."

"Truth is, Puabi, she's going to be dead in less than three days. You will get a chance to live, to have the *en* all to yourself. Why not allow this woman a little joy before she dies in your stead?"

"Kidu," Puabi said, tightening her sash, "has not congressed with me since that morning. That night, actually. Before I thought he died."

Rudi's head was beginning to ache, a not uncommon feeling around her sister. "What do you want, Puabi?"

"Tonight, at the Sacred Marriage—he'll be expecting his Chloe at the temple. I'll be there instead."

"Is he so great a lover that you'll risk your life?" Rudi asked. "You've lost your reason! You are scoffing at the opportunity you've been given to escape. He might decide to tell the council about the substitution, then you would find yourself reviled, poisoned, and buried."

"Shama!" Puabi shouted, though the old man was sitting almost beside them. "I want to be in the temple tonight. Make sure that Chloe thing isn't there. But she will die for me."

Shama bobbed his head. Rudi buried hers in her hands. Puabi's reason had fled. Obviously.

～

Guli withdrew himself, and they both lay panting, drenched and calm. They'd spent themselves, in all ways. Weeping until they were both weak. Congressing until collapse. Laughing from exhaustion and hunger. Finally, holding each other, savoring every minute left.

Guli took Ulu's hand in his big one and held them up to the dim light of the torch. It was bright outside now, but dark in the room. "You've always had the most beautiful hands," he said. "I used to watch them, at the tavern. You use them when you speak. Sometimes, without even knowing what the conversation was, I could guess your words. From your hands."

He kissed the back of her palm.

His hands were beaten up, scarred, but gentle in her hair and exquisite on her body. Ulu ached for a moment; could they have had this for all the years they'd known each other? This peace? This joy? This calm? Was this sacred world just waiting for them, and only the hands of the gods could force them to enter?

No, she thought. *I would never be content without sampling other men, and he is dear to me, but he wouldn't understand. Still, wouldn't it have been lovely to have been loved in this lifetime.*

Guli leaned over, braced on his arm. "You are supposed to be dark, I hear."

"Sumerian, not Shemti," she said. "Then, covered in gold. In truth, it matters little who goes to the tomb. No one but the *lugal* has really seen Puabi, and when anyone does, she's always in gold paint and formal dress." Ulu laughed. "Anyone could pretend at being the *ensi*. Anyone."

He touched her face with delicacy, smoothed her frown away with his fingertips. "You are of my heart, Ulu." His dark eyes were shiny in the light and he closed them. A tear fell on her bare breast.

Ulu pressed his face against the tear, into her flesh, and held him. The drums began outside. "Take my heart when you take my body, this time," she whispered to him. "Make love with me."

～

"He must see me!" Ningal said. "I have waited all day."

"The *en* has just returned and—"

Ningal drew himself up. "Tell the *en* Justice Ningal is here. He will see me."

A half-hour later, the *en* entered the room. "Greetings, Justice," he said.

Ningal bowed his head. How the *en* had changed, once he'd stopped the opium. Ningal had quite enjoyed their conversation, just days ago. He was certainly more than a wrestler and temple stud. The man had a mind.

Kidu motioned for food and drink as he sat on his chair. "What do you need from me?"

"The female Chloe," Ningal said. "She has disappeared, and I fear for her welfare."

"The female Chloe," Kidu repeated. Her name tripped

easily off his tongue—though his accent was a little different. "Your houseguest, I believe?"

"Yes, sir. Thank you for your kind remembrance. I fear for her safety."

The *en* glanced at the scribe who took notes, the slave who fanned him, the slave who poured his wine, the two girls who lounged in the shadow of the wall, then back to Ningal. "I will see what I can do," he said, and stood.

He didn't have the details yet, Ningal thought. "She was returning to our home—"

The *en* looked at him, and Ningal wondered if he imagined the compassion in the man's eyes. "Do not fear for her, I'm sure she will be well."

"Have you heard something?" Ningal asked.

The *en* hesitated. "I will send you a message after I've made some inquiries."

"There are some boys, from the Tablet House. They've roughed her up before. I think they took her."

The *en's* eyes narrowed, and Ningal was reminded of a giant cat, just before a killing leap. "They will not escape," he said.

"Search for her," Ningal said. "Please. I will pay any cost, do anything within my power, but bring her home to me. That is all I wish for." He looked at the young man, healthy and perfect. "You might not understand, since you are forbidden to marry or limit yourself to one woman, but she is all I want. No one else. Chloe alone."

The *en* stared at him, the warmth in his gaze gone. "Leave me."

Ningal was rushed out the doors and back into the hallway. His cloak was soaked with sweat, and his legs felt as weak as though he'd walked a long distance. Who else would help him? He sensed Chloe would be the last priority for the *en*. Who knew Chloe, appreciated her? Who—Nimrod. Ningal braced his shoulders and left the temple, his direction the *lugal's* house.

～

Nimrod opened the missive from Kidu. It bore only one word.

"Now."

～

While she waited, Chloe watched the old man Cheftu had stashed her with when they returned, silently and in two carts, to the temple. This old guy was someone's servant, for he was gone a lot. When he wasn't, he and Chloe played draughts and ate the leftovers of rich food. His room had no sunlight, but at least it wasn't hot.

After feeding her again, he brought her some clothes. When she stripped, he rubbed frankincense and gold dust into her skin and tucked her hair beneath a wig. *So it begins,* Chloe thought. *This is the first of my impersonations of* ensi *Puabi. What would happen if I just stopped in the middle of the speech or procession or whatever, and shouted that I wasn't Puabi.*

I'd be dead there and then, she realized.

The old man draped a pirate ship's worth of jewelry around her neck, on her arms, and in her hair. With careful strokes he painted around her eyes, mumbling in surprise when she opened the second one and he saw the disparity of color. She couldn't explain why they hadn't both changed to green when she realized she was completely herself—but they hadn't. He continued his work. Finally, he smiled and clapped.

Two slaves entered. Sandwiched between them and trailed by the old man, Chloe was led up some narrow stairs into luxurious apartments, filled with flowers and scattered with the remains of hasty packing. "Oh God, it's real," Chloe whispered.

Here, in this room, she heard the chanting of priests, the clear soprano singing of priestesses. It was dark again. *I've lost so much time,* she thought. *My last days weren't supposed to be like this.*

A huge group of people arrived at the door. The old man draped her face. They left the palace and walked down the avenue to the staged temple. At the foot of the staircase they festooned her with flowers. Shama motioned her up, so Chloe took the first step.

Seven stages: white, black, red, blue, orange, silver, and gold. Sixty steps a stage. It was going to be a long walk.

Chapter Four

Cheftu climbed the stairs slowly. His retainers waited at the bottom, and Chloe waited in the blue temple to heaven, at the top, on the golden stage. He was exhausted; and the day's activities had prevented him getting any meals.

The temple's stores were distributed now. The clients, freedmen, and gentlemen had delivered their bribes all day and night; the precious items piled up against the walls of the temple. Temple slaves and priests had dug out the tunnel to the ancient death pit. Its roof was the new pit's floor, now matted down anticipating its new inhabitants. Other priests had worked on securing the arched brick roof.

Cheftu's responsibilities until the "new" *ensi* took her place, were enormous. He alone would verify the women were dead, that the potent drug they took had worked. His coterie of priests would kill the animals in their tracks, leave the offerings, and fill the passageway with dirt once more.

That was when he would need to save Chloe.

At the top, on the golden stage of the stepped temple, Shama pulled back the silver-cloth curtain that shrouded the doorway. Cheftu was blinded by hammered gold walls that reflected a single candle a dozen dozen times. He stepped inside, and Shama dropped the curtain behind him.

It was a giant's room, a room for gods, not mortals. Everything was shaped from gold; the bed was nine feet long, the chair and table proportionate. The woman, re-splendent in veils and jewels, who stood beside the bed, looked like a fairy creature. Fragile, elegant, and also gold.

She turned to face him.

Puabi.

～

"Chloe," she heard a familiar voice say. "When you go around the next corner, step into the shadows."

Nimrod.

She hesitated.

"Kidu sent me," he said.

Chloe almost stumbled, but gained her footing and turned around the corner. Another woman waited—a tall blonde who looked no more like Chloe than Godzilla. But she was female. Nimrod introduced her as his wife, Nirg, while they threw Chloe's veils and beads on the blonde. Then off she went, continuing up to the little blue room for anyone who might be watching from below. After appearing to enter the room, she would sneak back down to the courtyard, through the shadows.

"Where is Kidu?" Chloe asked.

"At the apex," Nimrod said. "But that's not where we're going."

"Where is that?" she said as she took his hand. He pressed a panel, and the wall opened to reveal a horizontal slab.

"Sit down," he told her as he sat on the stone. "It's a quick drop."

It's a dumbwaiter, Chloe thought as they experienced a controlled fall. *And I'm inside the ziggurat? I thought they were solid.* The landing was rough, but Nimrod didn't apologize or wait; he just pulled her along passage after passage.

"Are we inside the temple still?" she asked.

"Now we are beneath it. Tales from Before say these corridors run under the ground from here to the mountains. These were ancient places where the humans hid when the gods turned against them."

She was almost breathless by the time they stopped at a doorway.

"Ningal waits within."

She felt her eyebrows hit her hairline with surprise.

"Ssh. All the women will be given nepenthe to make them pliable, you especially. Ningal will give you something to combat it. You have to memorize his directions quickly."

"Is nepenthe the poison?"

"No, Kidu has the answer to defeating the poison."

"Ningal's here?"

"He refused to help unless he could see you, make certain you were well."

"When does the sacrifice take place?"

"Twenty-four double hours."

Chloe nodded, and stepped inside.

~

Cheftu looked down from the heights of the golden chamber into the courtyard of the stepped temple. There, men protested the "nomination" of their wives, daughters, sisters, and mothers for the "journey."

Yet, this was the way it was done. The *ensi* was accompanied by the finest women the gods would accept. The most beautiful, skilled, successful—the city was beggaring itself of talent and funds, Cheftu thought. How could he change this tradition? There was no higher authority than the council. The list was published; it was decreed.

The meteor showers had exacerbated the society's fears. The new star that had precipitated this whole series of events burned even brighter. Cheftu needed to ask Chloe what was really going on out there, in space, as she called it. Her nation had landed on the moon, she'd once claimed. Maybe she could offer an explanation. Someday.

"Are you going to say nothing?"

"What should I say, Puabi? You court your death by staying here."

"Surprised to see me, I gather?"

He glanced at her. "Not especially. You seem to be everywhere that I am. This is no different."

"Your Chloe is going to die. I let Ulu go. Some underling brought her to me. She was painted with gold and had the worst dye job. She would never pass as me. She was old, with jowls. I told her she was free."

"How did she react?"

Puabi shrugged. "Strangely, actually. Said something like, 'Of course I walk away. Now that I have nothing to walk to. I guess I'll just keep walking.' I didn't understand. But the question is, do you understand me? Chloe is going to die."

"I heard you the first time."

"Do you not care for her?"

Cheftu shrugged. "She is particularly talented in the bedchamber."

"Better than me?" Puabi asked. "That can't be! I'm the goddess!"

He shrugged again. "What happens after all of this is over?"

"I come back. I become *ensi* again, and we carry on as before."

"How many days before you come back?"

"Rudi insists I be gone a week. To be sure it's safe, and that the gods have accepted my substitute, and so forth."

Cheftu sat down. "Good journey, then."

She put her hands on her hips. "That's it? All you have to say to me? You care so little for your position?"

He bowed his head. Calm. Cool.

"You better reconsider your options, Kidu," she said. "You can be replaced easily."

Good.

Shama opened the curtain again, and Chloe, dressed as Chloe, stepped in. Puabi turned on her with a hiss. Cheftu felt his stomach knot. How had this happened? "You must be Puabi?" Chloe asked the *ensi.*

Puabi stood tall—though she was still considerably shorter than Chloe, and she looked puffy and pale in comparison. His wife's shorn hair sprang from her head in fat curls, and Cheftu had to smile. They were so indicative of her personality. Unfettered and alive.

"Chloe, the Khamite?" Puabi said in her haughtiest tone.

"Chloe, yes."

"Why are you here? Didn't Rudi restrain you?"

"Rudi sent me up to remind you that you have a sledge waiting and a ship that sets sail on the tide."

"You're dying in my place."

"Actually, I'm not," Chloe said.

No, *chérie,* don't tell her! Cheftu almost leaped to his feet, shouting.

"What is your meaning?"

"I mean, it's going to cost you."

Puabi looked at Cheftu. He held his hands out in bewilderment, a feeling that was not feigned.

"I am the *ensi.*"

"Then you're going to die."

"I am not! I'm leaving!"

"On one condition," Chloe said.

"I don't have to listen to this, I can send you into that tomb, and no one will know."

"They will know, because I will tell them. Paint me, sit me down, disguise me however you want, Puabi. You can't hide the fact that I have a scar, right here," Chloe said, and pulled back her hair just above the nape of her neck. Cheftu could see the long, jagged cut, healing nicely. "You don't."

A scar that the *ensi,* who was supposed to be perfect, flawless, and unmarred, could never have.

"Kidu—" Puabi said. "She—"

"This is between us," Chloe said to Puabi. "Human female to human female. I will denounce you and send them after you unless you promise me on your own life, something."

"What? Gold? Jewels? You have the *en!*"

"A school."

"A what?"

"A Tablet House for girls."

"Have you lost your reason?"

"With a female Tablet Father. Mother. Whatever."

"You want a school?"

"Yes. I want it paid for by public funds, and I want any girl who has the capacity to learn to be free to attend. Regardless of her financial status, or family connections."

Puabi couldn't have been more at a loss. She stared at Chloe as though she were a speaking tree. "That's . . . all?"

"Swear to me, Puabi."

"Certainly. I swear."

Chloe pulled out a document, densely written on clay, and Cheftu felt his world shift. Cuneiform! For the first time he recognized the writing of the pre-Babylonians. Was that the present, was that when they were living? The other writing he'd seen, it had used the same marks, but it had been written before the characters were turned on their sides, which is the way the ideograms would be read for the next millennia. The way he'd learned it. When did this turn happen?

"I don't have my seals," Puabi said calmly.

"You don't have to. I do." Chloe smiled. "Remember? I'm Puabi. You've already signed it, I just thought I would

give you your copy. The Justice Ningal is acting on my behalf and will keep my copy. Of course, a third copy is already in the Office of Records and the fourth, well, should
it become necessary to reveal its location, someone will."

Cheftu felt like he was going to burst with joy. His Chloe,
being as Chloe as ever. *Mon Dieu,* how he loved this woman.

Chloe smiled at Puabi. "You can go now."

Puabi glared at Kidu, then took her tablet and walked to
the door. Shama didn't even open the curtain for her; she
had to lift it herself. They heard her steps fade away.

"Is she going to come back with a knife?" Chloe asked.

"That would require climbing the steps again," Cheftu
said. "I doubt she has the breath for it."

They stood, feet apart, looking at each other.

"You are really . . . tall," she said. Her breath was light, a
little ragged.

Kidu's body—Cheftu's body—raged. "*Chérie,*" he said
and opened his arms.

∾

"Why did you nominate me?" Chloe asked softly. He felt
her breath on his chest. She was alert. "You could have told
Asa no, find someone else."

"It's the only way I can have you."

"Dead?"

"You're not going to be dead. I've shown you the plans
to the tomb. You know the way out."

"If I survive the antidote, the nepenthe, and the poison."
She turned the goblet he had given her over. "The bottom is
hollow?"

"Filled with sea sponges. Thus, when you turn it horizontal, the liquid will run through that tiny hole in the bot-

tom and be absorbed by the sponges in the base. You will appear to drink but not actually consume anything."

"Oh good. So all I have to worry about is the nepenthe and the antidote."

"Do you trust Ningal?" He kissed her head.

"Do you?"

His arms tightened around her. "With all my heart."

"Me too, though with all my body." She kissed his stomach. "Speaking of, this new body of yours is quite, uh, nice." Her hands touched him, ran over his skin with strength and purpose.

"As the *en,* I can't marry you. I can't be faithful to you. The only way out of this is for both of us to die," he said.

She sat up and looked at him. One brown eye, one green. It should have been odd, but it seemed completely normal. It was an oft-repeated Egyptian saying, but the eyes were the windows to the soul. These travels had changed her; she was half-ancient, half-modern.

"Both of us?" she said.

"I'll finish my responsibilities here, then appear to die. The populace will take it as a sign from the gods."

"Do these people know about the real god, the big one?"

A change in the light caught Cheftu's eye; he drew Chloe to his side, protectively. "Shama?"

The old man waved through the curtain.

"I must go, *chérie.*"

"Will you come back?" Chloe's tone was calm, but her expression was alarmed.

"They will have sequestered you," he said.

"Will I be here?"

"No, you'll be in the temple complex with the other women."

She handed him his skirt and belt. "Are you in there yet, in that body, Cheftu?"

He froze in the act of putting on his necklace. "I am, but

part of me has become Kidu." He looked at the clasp to catch it. "I can't explain it."

"I understand better than you think."

"You know your way through the pit now, but, *chérie*, you must put a handmaid in your place. She must wear your coronet and jewels." He took a deep breath. "You must be sure she is attended by two women. Do this all before I come into the tomb."

She opened her mouth. "I'm going to have to move corpses? And you wisely waited until now to mention it?"

He continued to speak. "Go to the well, as we discussed. Wait there. It may be for a day, or it may be for several. Make sure the scene is complete. Priests might return. We want no cause for suspicion. Nimrod will come for you at the well."

"And then?"

He kissed her, moving in a fluid instant motion, enveloped in her scents of sesame and pomegranate, his senses filling with heady heat, erotic memory, and passion. "We'll build a life together, some other place. We'll leave here, carefully. Mix in with the many who flee these gods and head for other cities."

She nodded; he could still taste her.

The love that had grown to be the comfort of every day in Jerusalem—waking up together, making love before dawn, holding each other at night and finding each other in the dark—peaceful, rested, calm—now surged like liquid fire that threatened to inundate him. "You are mine. We'll be together."

"Yes," she said, and captured his lips, devoured his mouth until he groaned. Cheftu's hands clenched her bottom, caressed her legs, then he pulled away, set her aside.

"We'll survive. Trust me."

"Don't I always," she muttered, just as the curtain fell behind him.

Four double hours later, the drums rolled. Chloe opened the bottle, the antidote for the nepenthe, that Ningal had given her, said a prayer, and swallowed the stuff. It tasted like she thought petroleum would—thick and bitter—it coated her throat and stomach like milk of magnesia. That's what it felt like, and what she imagined.

Eight hours, now. Four double hours.

She'd committed Ningal's instructions, the blueprint of the tomb, with the placement of the grave offerings, to her memory. Now, the antidote would help her protect that memory. Nepenthe would make dying easy for the women—they wouldn't care what was happening or why. Chloe had to remember what was happening and why, and act accordingly. She licked her lips, sure to get all of her liquid protection.

The very air of Ur was rife with tension. The drums filled the air, assembling the stargazers, warning the people. They would bang again in two double hours.

The antidote's aftertaste was awful, but Chloe didn't dare try to wash it away. *It's your salvation,* she told herself. Salvation, often, was bitter.

～

The citizens of Ur watched the sky in silence. The sun still shone, but beside it they could just discern the shape of the moon. Children clutched at their fathers and sons stood braced, daring the future, challenging the gods. A smothered hiccup or swallowed sob rose occasionally from the crowd, but there was nothing else.

The drums tolled, the enormous kettledrums that needed two drummers, as the procession moved across the temple grounds.

The wealth of Ur, in oxen-drawn carts—golden vessels,

inlaid furniture, bejeweled weapons—the finest the commonwealth had to offer, rolled forward. A last bribe for the gods.

The women followed, the loveliest of Ur's wives and sisters, mothers and daughters, clad in robes of the softest wool, with woven diadems, stone-studded collars, and gold hoop earrings. Beads of carnelian, lapis, agate, and malachite hung from their necks. Beaded belts with fringed ends fell close to their sandaled feet.

Above them all, seated for her final journey, was the *ensi* who gave her life for the people, for the commonwealth. Puabi's diadem was a wreath of gold leaves and flowers with a hundred narrow hoops hanging over her forehead. A spray of lapis blossoms arched over her head, and bobbed with every step.

The handsome priests and attendants wore the finest felted skirts, with gold woven sashes. Seals and cylinders had been left behind, for this was not their funeral; they were merely company. Their sacrifice was for all eternity. Not only leaving the sunshine for the gloom of Kur, but leaving behind their names and identities, to be buried as strangers.

The minutes clicked by as the procession passed.

The moon edged closer to the sun.

The shaft that led into the pit was lined with priests, their spears pointing toward the ground. As she passed into the earth, each woman was given a golden goblet. Rudi heard the rings on the women's headdresses clink against each other.

The eclipse began; the moon nibbled a bite from the sun. The people squinted at the sky, or watched the reflection in huge pools set in the courtyard. The shadows on the ground were crescent-shaped, impressions of the gobbled-up sun.

The procession sped up, the ground swallowing ten, then twenty, then forty—

Then the *ensi*.

Encircling the citizens of Ur, the sky took on an eerie violet color. The people whimpered. The pageant continued, as women progressed into the pit by sixty, then seventy, then five soldiers—

Rudi was astounded; the Khamite had actually done it. Given her life for the people. The stargazer's eyes glassed with tears. May the gods bless the female named Chloe.

Chloe didn't glance around; she didn't dare. Nepenthe meant she was supposed to be blissed-out, unaware, unconcerned. *I just happen to be rigid, too,* she thought. The women who walked beside her moved calmly, evenly. Unlike them, Chloe wasn't calm. But she was trusting. Cheftu was here. She would get out of this. He'd sworn it. Cheftu had never failed her.

"This isn't some English playwright's tragedy," he'd told her in the giant's temple. "No matter what you think has happened, don't fear. You'll be safe, we'll be together, we'll make a new life."

She thought of the thousands of historians who would be thrilled to see this; protoliterate man, in action. But she doubted very seriously that any of them would actually trade places with her at that moment.

The women and soldiers and servants progressed down a long, steep tunnel, dark except for the torches, then down a ramp and into the main chamber. As she had been instructed, each woman paused in the doorway and dipped her cup in the copper caldron, then moved in an orderly fashion, into the room. The lutenists played, no one spoke.

Are you thinking of your family? Chloe wondered about the woman who walked past her. *You think you're doing this to save your children's lives, to give them a chance to live in a better world.* Chloe knew this, she understood even, but she also fought against the modern knowledge that eclipses occurred regularly. Would the people of Ur always send a group to their death at an eclipse?

Puabi's handmaidens, painted in ritual gold, just like Chloe was, walked through the antechamber and climbed down a ladder into the burial chamber. The rest of the women sat down on the mat-covered floor of the main room. The lutenist strummed, and the priests organized the front of the room to make space for the oxen-drawn sledge. Two more women climbed down the ladder. *I'm next,* Chloe realized, and fought not to cry out. She stepped from the sledge, and one of the soldiers helped her descend the ladder. Chloe would lie on the bier, the three maids by her head, feet, and side.

Chloe dipped her fake cup in the poison and walked to the bier. Carefully she stepped up and sat down. She would have to play dead until the priests came back and killed the oxen. After everyone else was deceased, Chloe would be alive.

Chloe watched the three handmaidens embrace. Already their expressions were vacant. *I'm so alone,* Chloe thought. Music flowed, muffling the noises of people sitting down, arranging jewelry and bodies. *Oh God.*

"We are assembled, ma'am," a soldier called to her.

This is my only line, Chloe thought, and took a deep breath. "Drink," she called to them.

The politicians and priests had spun the story so well that the people who were sacrificing themselves thought they were going on a cosmic caravan to the gods, not to death.

How do you do one and not the other? Chloe asked herself. *Has anyone thought it through?*

They drank, in one movement, then they all lay down. As Cheftu had promised, the cup drained away the poison. *Please let this all work,* Chloe prayed. *Please oh please, I'm not ready to die.* Cheftu was out there, praying the same thing, she knew. Ningal had said she would feel some narcotic effects, but she would be able to move, at least for up to a quarter of a double hour. Translated: thirty minutes.

After the eclipse had passed, the oxen would be slaughtered. Then the priests would seal up the tomb, a process that was going to take a few days and, depending on the outcome of the eclipse, possibly include a few more human bribes for the gods. Chloe had to be up and out of here before then. She was on her own until she reached the well beyond the western wall. She had to go through the original death pit, beneath this one, to get there.

The drug was taking effect on the others: One by one, the small sighs and sniffled tears, the whispers and words, then finally the lyre–players died out.

Chloe sat up, her heart pounding, her palms wet. The racket above would drown out any noise she would make. One of the maids was kneeling by the side of the bier. Carefully, Chloe took off her flower-studded crown and set it on the ground. She approached the girl. The female was still breathing, but barely. Her pupils were dilated, and her body was heavy.

Chloe tugged on her arm. Nothing. Chloe knelt and took hold of the girl in a fireman's carry, then staggered the two steps over and laid her down on the platform.

She landed harder than Chloe intended. Now the woman's eyes were closed. Chloe didn't know if it was the drug, death, or unconsciousness.

Oh God, I'm going to be in here with all these dead people.

Chloe put on the handmaiden's wreath, then draped more of her beads on the unconscious woman's body and left Puabi's cylinder seal. She stepped back to gauge the effect, and almost stepped on the girl's cup. Gritting her teeth, she wrapped those stiffening fingers around it.

It took a while to do everything, longer than she'd planned; Chloe was feeling the effects of the drug, the antidote. She collapsed onto her knees, then keeled over. According to Ningal, her body would be paralyzed, but she would be completely awake. To the priests, it would appear her breath had left and not returned. Her eyes wouldn't even react to light.

This really is *shades of* Romeo and Juliet, she thought.

Chloe's body was falling asleep, it prickled the same way, and she couldn't move a muscle anymore. Her bones felt soldered together. She swore her heart was slowing down audibly.

The ground above throbbed with the drumbeats.

They ceased.

Chapter Five

*T*otal blackness encased the land. Bright daylight became pitch midnight. Screams and shouts rose from the multitude as night seemed to hold its own. Birds ceased their song; animals were silent. The air was cool, like the breath of the grave. Then, on the edge of the black sphere, a flash of red, next, a sliver of sunlight. More and more. The cold shadow of judgment rushed away from the commonwealth, back into the sky. The sun was accepting the bribes of the moon. Waves of light moved across the ground and buildings; the net the gods had cast on Ur was lifting.

The gods were appeased.

Ezzi stared at the hole, the one that had swallowed his mother. The one he had put her in. *What is good in one's sight is evil for a god,* he reminded himself of the adage. *What is bad for one's mind is good for his god.* Ezzi had merely acted under direction from his gods, and for the good of his commonwealth. Ulu wanted to do it, to show some sign of nobility in her life. He'd been a sacred vessel—nothing more.

"How do we know it won't happen again?" a soft voice asked. The question fired like thunder in the silence. "What assurance do we have?"

Everyone looked at the *en,* Kidu. He raised his hands, and gave the ritual response.

"Does our house last forever?

Do contracts last forever?

Do brothers stay in business equally forever?

Does division in the land last forever?

Does the river forever rise up and bring floods?

The dragonfly leaves its casing, just for a minute of heat on its face.

Since Before, there has been nothing that lasts.

The dead are the same, whoever they are.

Despite their position, they sleep beside one another in the earth indistinguishable once they have embraced their destiny.

A destiny decreed by the court of gods, by the judge of destinies. Death and life they write in the Tablet, but the days of death they hide from us.

We never know beyond the moment."

The people bowed their heads. Music no longer rose from the shaft. For those journeying below, it was ended. For those above, the journey through days of loss was just beginning. The *en,* together with his coterie, took the *lugal's* golden-hafted blade and walked down into the earth.

As he disappeared from sight, priests with carts of dirt and enormous pots of freshly mixed clay drew up to the hole.

Had Ulu felt any pain? Ezzi wondered. The drug was supposed to be the most pleasant of them all; in fact, Puabi was well-known for her love of it. The new *ensi* would be crowned at the end of the following week after a hasty election. Of course, the new *ensi* would be Puabi under a different name. Life would return to normal. If the gods were mollified. Ezzi looked at the sky. With so many deities to please, had the humans of Ur forgotten someone who would enlist demons to torture them?

I did nothing wrong, he protested. *Nothing. I served my*

commonwealth. The greater good of the people. He'd even served the gods, for his actions had led to saving the *ensi's* life. He was a tool, by merely following his own desires.

Priests brought up the huge copper pot from below. The masses hissed as it was rolled in. Was the poison still there? Would others be asked to give their lives for their families? The priests wheeled the pot past the standing watchers and into the inner court.

An audible sigh.

"What is Kidu doing down there?" Ezzi whispered to Asa.

"Killing them," the stargazer said. "Completing the sacrifice."

~

The smell was everywhere. Offal. The remnants of the human body as its functions ceased. Chloe wanted to retch, but she didn't have the control. Instead, she concentrated on not getting sick—dying in her own vomit, minutes before she was rescued, would be more ironic than she could stand.

They clanged as they walked down the shaft, the priests and Cheftu. The ox bawled, then there was a gurgle, a loud clatter as the ox sagged. Another cry, another dead ox. They crashed to the ground. "I will arrange the women," Cheftu said to the men. "Bring the rest of the donations. You, come with me."

Her eyes were open, but Chloe couldn't focus, just stare into the flickering darkness. She listened as Cheftu and another, who held the lamp for him, moved among the people, sprinkled the bodies with dirt. She heard the whisper of the lyre as they moved it. Clods falling to earth. A brush against wood. Was it the chest or the sledge they had just passed?

Metal, the music of dirt on shields. They must be by the soldiers. A row of women lay opposite them.

"Sir, I think she might still be alive!" the priest whispered.

They couldn't have seen Chloe; the floor of the antechamber was roof level to this room. They were too far on the other side to see down to her.

She heard necklaces grate against each other. They were checking out someone else. "Just the final throes of the poison," Cheftu said. "She is dead."

Chloe smelled the refuse of the oxen. She would have to be careful of so much gross stuff when she moved around. No footprints, an essential detail, just in case someone came back. Though Cheftu's plan was going to make it nearly impossible for a return visit.

They were moving toward her, into the grave of Puabi.

"I'm out of amulets," Cheftu said. "There are some more in the bag."

"Where's the bag?"

"By the sledge. Just pass me the light."

Down the ladder, jewelry clinking, then soft sounds as he walked across the floor.

She felt the heat of the flame, saw light moving.

He touched her, but it felt as though his hands were on heavy wool over her body. He closed her eyes and turned her on her side, arranged her arms at right angles, her legs in the fetal position, her head facing north. "Thank you," he said to the other priest, and she felt small weights laid on her shoulder and leg. Dirt cascaded onto her, not much, but heavily symbolic.

She wanted to jump up and scream, protest that she was alive.

Thank God for the drug, which restrained her.

They moved to the other two servants, then the new Puabi-substitute. Chloe smelled the heat of the dust that rose from the ritual of dirt. The least deserving person,

Puabi, got to live. And she'd get credit for female education. Ironic.

Then the men were gone, climbing out of the pit and walking across the antechamber.

A little more rustling, then the huffs of the priests.

Chloe couldn't distinguish the noises, but she knew there was a ton of gold, a wealth of inlaid furniture, trunks' worth of clothes and foodstuffs, to be moved in, all of it a bribe for the gods. Gods who had to be fed and clothed and who could die and get sick were not her idea of divinity, but to these people, the gods were exactly like them, only with longer life spans.

And more control.

"Is there more, *en*?"

"No, hand me the wine." Cheftu's voice was too low to distinguish the words, but it was reverent, and Chloe wouldn't be surprised if it carried the Last Rites. That would be just like him, to slip in Catholicism over a pagan human sacrifice. Her eyes filled with tears; that was one of the reasons she loved her husband so.

Dirt, falling into the shaft the sacrifices had walked down. Drums above, beating softly. It must be almost night now; the numbness was starting to wear off. Chloe opened her eyes in slits. Darkness, except for the faint light from the shaft that was being filled with clods of dirt. They fell like heavy rain. They were burying her alive.

Thank God her voice was frozen—if not, she might have cried out, instinctively. She was here with dead people, and would be for a long time. Dirt continued falling, but it would take hours to fill the shaft deep enough to ensure her safety.

But she had to move now, get up the rickety ladder while she still could, before even that dim light was gone. Chloe creaked upright, disturbing dirt and amulets. It felt as though a lead weight sat on her chest. The dozens of necklaces around her neck and falling to the floor were heavy ties, chaining her to the earth. She was going to throw up; the bile was in her throat. Chloe swallowed it down again and again.

Her eyes had adjusted to the near darkness, and she wished they hadn't.

The attendants were dead. The sound of earth falling was steady, comforting. Those were live people doing that work. She tucked the cup into her belt.

It seemed to take hours to climb the ladder. Chloe couldn't feel her hands or her feet very well. The stink of released bowels gagged her. Finally, she grabbed the edge of the roof/floor and dragged herself over it. The ladder swayed and would have crashed, but she caught it.

She eased it against the wall, then lay down to catch her breath. She was shaking like a palm in a wind storm. Nauseated still. Chloe sat up and looked around.

The landscape was curves. Mounds of colored wool between her and the shaft. Soon, beneath those cloaks, new life would start to breed.

Twelve hours was the time between death and fullgrown maggots. *God, why do I know that? I wish I didn't.* When her Mimi had first died, Chloe's nightmares had been of the body as it rotted.

Which poet had written "To His Coy Mistress" and discussed the futility of the woman preserving her virginity because she would ultimately be invaded by worms? *I hate him,* Chloe decided. *Which poet was that?*

Who wrote about the fly buzzing as she died? Some New England poet who had been a recluse and an invalid. Never married, always wrote about death? Emily . . . what, what kind of Emily?

Brontë. Talk about a family obsessed with death. Jane

Eyre and fire. Heathcliff with Cathy's ghost banging on his window.

Was there anything in high-school literature that wasn't about death? Old Man and the Sea—*death.* For Whom the Bell Tolls—*a lot of death.* Death in the Afternoon—*no-brainer there.* The Great Gatsby—*who's left standing?* The Jungle—*gory death.*

Are we a nation obsessed?

She heard a deep inhalation and froze.

Ohmigod, someone else is alive.

She curled into fetal position—like the rest of the corpses—and listened hard.

Dirt falling was loud when you were trying to hear a small sound, like the shift of a body on reed matting or the first jangle of jewelry as a human moved.

If someone else is alive—what do I do? We didn't plan on this, Cheftu. Do I take the person with me and make the escape for two, not one? Do I . . . what do I do? I can't kill them. They deserve to live as much as I do.

A clatter of jewelry; so loud that the priests halted shoveling.

"Should we go down there?" one of them asked. He was whispering, but the shaft acted as a megaphone.

Oh please no, Chloe thought. The numbness had mostly worn off—her heartbeat was probably audible, and she had body heat. Plus, her pupils would most likely react. *Pass out, I have to pass out. How can I pass out without hyperventilating? How can I hyperventilate quietly? I'm not in the correct location? I'm out here on my own!*

"Think someone survived?" one of the priests said. "The *en* checked everyone."

"Sounded like they got up, banged into something."

"Ask the *en.*"

"Why have you stopped?" Cheftu's voice was clear, it carried well.

"Something in the pit, sir. It sounded like movement. Clangs and clatters."

"The bodies settling," Cheftu said calmly. "As the corpses stiffen and relax in death, there will be noises. Especially around the sledge, with the oxen and the weight of the gifts. The sacrifice has been made, you needn't worry."

"Of course, sir," one of them said.

"I want this shaft filled to the roof of the pit as soon as possible. We need to offer drink and food offerings in two double hours. We'll have to lay a clay floor first."

"Of course, sir, we'll hurry."

"The gods will bless your diligence. Your work is just as vital as those who gave their lives today."

The dirt started to fall again—double time.

Chloe almost wet herself with relief. Could those sounds just be settling, like he said? Her heartbeat was so loud. *I mustn't be jumpy,* she told herself. *I can't hiss or scream or even make a peep.* Jewelry clanging is one thing—if the shaft is a megaphone down, it might be one going up, too.

Obviously these diligent priests were listening.

Why couldn't Cheftu have found some drunken slackers for this job instead?

She dared to peek. The dirt was falling very slowly. Two double hours—four more hours to lie here. With the dead. Then, to move among them, slide back the chest, and escape into the tomb below.

A sigh.

Chloe held her breath when the priests paused, but then there were four shovelfuls of dirt falling, one on each side. The light trickling down was fainter. Cheftu was going to keep them there all night. *Which is really good, because I think I'm going to lose it if this takes longer.*

Think words. Logograms and phonetic signs and the seven hundred other syllables that were this language. That would occupy her mind, and it was getting easier to manipulate, but Chloe needed to draw the symbols. Which required moving. Moving. She didn't dare move. No one was watching, but still, she was in easy view for someone sticking his head down into the shaft.

Her body prickled with a thousand needle points. Feeling returning.

Where in history is this; that question should keep her busy for hours. The clues were innumerable, but she was an idiot when it came to chronologies and dates, and didn't know where to put them. In all her memories, she couldn't place the cone-shaped mosaics. It was hard to believe the place would become Iraq. The soldiers in the Gulf War had talked about nothing besides sand, sand dunes, dust storms, and the parching sun.

She'd seen the endless green of orchards and fields. Sure, there was lots of sun, but mostly floods and water and rivers and growth. When did the climate change? Or was it altered by man?

A small sob.

Was that sound from Puabi's pit? One of the women against the wall? Or opposite, one of the bodies Cheftu had so graciously turned away from her? Maybe it wasn't a woman, but one of the soldiers or grooms? Chloe could probably get away with adding a woman to the escape, but a soldier or a groom—that made her uneasy.

The dirt was a quarter ways up the shaft.

The cramps started; Ningal had warned her it would be uncomfortable, and worse, because she couldn't move. Sweat beaded her forehead, and she was glad for the last little bit of drug that helped her resist jerking.

This must be like childbirth, she reasoned. Phases of

pain interspersed with moments of rest. She felt a trickle of sweat roll across her forehead and drop onto her gold beech-nut leaf earring. The ping was deafening, and Chloe waited for a response from the darkness.

I left a headdress on the floor. I forgot to pick it up.

But Cheftu and the priest hadn't said anything, so it must be okay.

The cramps fixed on her back, and she had to bite her tongue to keep from reacting audibly. After a while, the pain passed. She opened her eyes and thanked God—the shaft was almost two-thirds filled.

The next and final phase of coming out of the drug was the itching. Ningal had said it was the worst part—a punishment for abusing the drug, according to the *asipu*. A warning from the gods against it. Once you experienced the itching, no part of taking it was appealing, regardless of the high involved.

What high? I guess I was too terrified to experience the high, Chloe thought.

The itching would start on her extremities and work its way in toward her heart, Ningal had explained. She'd feel like the thing was beneath her skin, consuming her. At the end she would vomit, then be fine. They scheduled her vomiting right about when the shaft would be full, the priests deaf to the sound, and she would have the leisure to hide all marks of her presence.

Absence, by that time.

Shit! she thought, *That isn't itching, that's fire inside!* Jellyfish had stung her toes, the soles of her feet, her ankles—that's what it felt like.

I can't handle this, Chloe thought. *If I don't scratch, I'm going to die.*

Don't scratch, Ningal had told her. It spread the poison and infected the skin.

Her fingers were on fire; minute legs crawled underneath her fingernails and through the skin of her palms. Tears flowed down Chloe's face, and her forehead ached from the fierceness of her grimace.

If it would just work faster, she thought. *Just get it over with.* But the itching took its sweet time. Her scalp was ablaze; she could almost feel blisters rising up.

A noise—she'd been too engrossed in her agony to notice what, or from where. The darkness was almost complete, just a fraction left before it reached the roof.

When the drug seized her gut, Chloe buried her cry against the woven matting.

"Death is preferable to surviving," Ningal had said, tears in his eyes at the thought of her pain. Then he had given her a wry smile, "Except for the side effect of death's permanence."

How would she have the strength to move? Chloe curled more tightly around her stomach as the poison raced into her throat and chest. She dug her nails into her arms to resist clawing away at her breasts.

The vomiting was explosive and spontaneous.

When she opened her eyes, the chamber was completely dark.

And she felt fine.

Fear, which had been upstaged by agony, came back with long, fanged teeth.

No sound from above, no sound from within. Had she been wrong about the breathing? The other survivor?

Surreptitiously, she slipped out her dagger and carved out her mess from the matting on the floor, then turned it over and plastered it to the ground. She moved her fingers around the edge to make sure it matched.

The place stank; she might get sick again.

No, she told herself. *Get up and get the hell out of here.*

She slipped the knife back into her beaded belt and slowly sat up. Carnelian and lapis and gold beads clanged together. The bangles she shoved up her arm slid down and clattered. Chloe froze and listened.

"Sss—" she hissed softly. Her whole body trembled; if someone else were alive there, then she wasn't alone. If no one else breathed, she was in a room with seventy-three corpses.

She closed her eyes, tried to shut out the image of skin bubbling with larvae. *Why do I recall how a body decays and I can't remember the name of this ancient land? Because I never knew it.*

"A fly buzzed as I died."

Damn Emily Dickinson.

She got to her feet, dust and gold powder falling off her body, sprinkling the ground. Dizziness assailed her, but from fear, or from the remnants of the poison, she couldn't guess. It didn't matter. She had to get out of there. "Sss—" she hissed again, and waited.

They were all around her, dozens of bodies right here. She couldn't see them, though. She couldn't see anything. You need a tiny bit of light for any kind of glitter or glow. In this silent, sealed tomb, there was nothing.

It was going to take a very long time to get to the chest.

A line of corpses was opposite her, their faces turned away. She got down on her hands and knees and felt for the edges of cloaks. One body on the left, there, one on the right. Holding her hands in place, she put her foot in the blank space, then stood. Hesitantly, she reached for another step. Empty space. In another step she should be past their heads.

The floor of the pit was not even, the matting was slippery with . . . *oh God, don't think about what you might be stepping in,* she told herself. Her toe nudged a lock of hair, and Chloe jumped forward, into empty space.

Past the line of dead women.

There had been no more sounds—and it was deafening, this silence. In two steps, she knew she was approaching the sledge, it was at the foot of the ramp. The smell of blood overrode the smell of refuse here. She couldn't step in it, make any marks. Though how she was supposed to tell in the dark, she didn't know. Chloe leaned forward with her hands extended, feeling for anything.

Another step.

Reaching forward again.

A leather sandal.

But was it the groom closest to the door, or the one closest to the sledge?

Chloe smelled her own sweat, and even stinking with fear it was more pleasant an odor than the ones around her. She bit back a squeal when she felt the hairy leg of a draft animal.

Wood, the sledge. The high edge with hammered lions' heads, then the border inlaid with mother-of-pearl, she could feel the swoops and curves beneath her fingertips, the carnelian and lapis, with gold in between, not yet cold in this place.

Will it ever get cool? she wondered. Here, so far beneath the sun, in Iraq, could it get cool? Maybe the bodies wouldn't rot so fast—

She squinted her eyes shut: The deceased, all around her, soon would be teeming with new life. *Get me out of here,* she thought, and stumbled around the edge of the wooden transport, then stubbed her toe on something clay.

Chloe bit back a swear word and thought a split-second curse on whatever idiot had set a jar in the walkway.

Of course, they hadn't expected any of the corpses to get up and walk.

The chest should be just there. She'd gone over the placement again and again. She inched forward. Nothing. Slipped one toe along the mat. Nothing. A whimper escaped her and Chloe clapped her hand over her mouth.

She was going to die in here. Another body among the many, with no legacy, nothing to show she'd ever walked this earth. Tears streaked her cheeks. She was trapped in a tomb.

Chapter Six

*H*e could just kill them all; there were only six. Six more deaths on a conscience that had lost track of the lives it had ended. Snuff six humans, then drop down into the ditch, dig through the dirt in the shaft, then scramble over the sledges in the doorway and the corpses lined across the room and find Chloe.

Cheftu's skin crawled when he remembered moving her body into position. Closing her staring eyes. How badly he'd wanted to check her pulse, look for any sign to prove she lived. Because she had looked dead, pale and tinted blue from the combination of drugs in her body. He had to believe the cup had worked—he'd wanted to check it, see if it felt heavy, but he hadn't dared. Cheftu just had to believe. Faith is believing what you can't see.

He wanted to spit.

What madness had they embarked upon?

"We're ready for the floor, *en*," a priest said.

Cheftu's last chance to slaughter them and run. But if he did, there would be no time wasted in tracking him down. No ship could sail far enough, fast enough. No marsh was that impenetrable, no land that distant. Cheftu didn't trust his voice, so he motioned for the bricklayers. It was quick work to dump the clay on the packed dirt, until it was even. The men slicked the clay flat, then climbed out. It would dry quickly in the heat of summer, even at night, but not fast enough for Cheftu.

"When will it be ready for the next offering?" he asked one of them.

"Did you want to install drains, for the drink offerings?"

Cheftu didn't want anything that would help sound travel. Nothing that would make it easier for the priests to go back down or would inhibit Chloe's movements. "No. The dead can receive offerings poured directly into the ground. No drains are necessary."

"Do you need aught else, *en*?"

I need to know she is breathing. "Nothing," he said. "I will pray the night through."

A new team would arrive at dawn.

Meanwhile, it was Cheftu alone with the open sky, and his wife entombed below with the dead.

~

If anyone had been alive, they would have already gotten up, Chloe reasoned. The chest had been made of heavy wood, with an inlaid front and filled with . . . grain? Clothes wouldn't weigh that much. But she'd nudged it far enough. Now she touched the ground with relief, her fingers outlined the escape. The hole to freedom.

It was bricks, the roof to the pit underneath her. The original death pit, the one Cheftu had the map for.

The air from below was definitely cooler, and the smell was musty. Much better, though there wasn't going to be much oxygen. *I'll be out of there in no time,* she thought. Carefully, she felt the edges of the opening and blessed the tomb raiders who had gotten here first and done all the work. It was big enough for a person, but no one had told her how far the fall was.

Drop and roll, she thought, and eased her way through

the space, hanging from her fingers, trying to sense the ground. She felt a piece of wood beneath her feet and set her weight on it. It held. She stood. The thieves had been extremely thoughtful.

Chloe grasped the edge of the trunk above her and pulled, feeling the effort all through her abdomen and back. The chest moved a few inches. It would cover enough.

"Another day, another tomb," she said. "And I have a voice that sounds like a pack a day." The noise was obscene in the silence. How many bodies were in here? All she had to do was cross to the king's grave, and there was a passage in the wall.

The last sacrifice had walked away, too. If Cheftu hadn't stepped into the body of Kidu and known how to read the sacred texts, if Shama hadn't liked Cheftu and shown him the tablets and the goblet, this would all be turning out very differently.

Her toe touched something dry and . . . bony. Chloe recoiled. Skeletons. "At least there is nothing living," she whispered. *Don't think about the bodies above.* She couldn't help it. Striking out from the furniture she'd landed on, she headed straight. Bones, beads, clay. Every time she touched something, she moved faster, until she tripped on the sunken edge of a depression and crashed into the wall.

"Way to go, graceful," she said as she sat up. At least it was the right place; the passage was here somewhere. All she had to do was kill a little time, break through a fake wall, then crawl out to the well.

Do these people go to heaven or hell, or is there really a purgatory? Chloe wondered. *Maybe we go to what we think there is. Any Sumerian is going to have a miserable time of it, if that's the case. I wonder why these people believe in such a gloomy afterlife. Slaves to the gods now, in the heat and caprice of the elements, and then slaves to the gods below, in the dust and darkness.*

She shivered.

Surely I know something that is light and cheerful. Chintzy. High tea with biscuits. Mom's roses. Cammy's laugh. Popsicles in the summertime on the porch in Reglim. The feel of Cheftu's skin in the darkness, that moment when he kisses me—

The chamber reverberated with sound.

Someone was moving the chest away from the hole.

⌒

"More is required," Asa said.

The *lugal* and Cheftu looked at each other. "What more is there?" the *lugal* asked. "We've given almost every mina of gold in the commonwealth, emptied the temple's stores and almost depleted the granary. Countless clients weep tonight because the women they love are gone—we don't have anything else!"

The stargazer lifted his hands. What could you do, if the gods weren't satisfied, you had to give them more. His gaze shifted to Cheftu.

"The first floor is ready for the offerings," Cheftu said. "This meeting delays me."

"They require more offerings."

"Or what?" the *lugal* asked. "We've had floods, barley rust, crops fail, starfall, and an eclipse. What more can they send?"

"You mock the gods?" Asa questioned. "We haven't sacrificed enough, that is all I can read in the stars."

"More lives?" the *lugal* asked.

"Clients," Asa said. "Representatives of the First Families."

The *lugal* sank into a chair.

"Another pit?" Cheftu asked. He must keep them from digging close to Chloe's escape route. Another pit could ruin everything.

"It needs to be carried out immediately," Asa said. "Stars continue to fall from the heavens. A new star burns in the house of the moon of the barley stalk. It burns red."

The *lugal* looked at Cheftu. "Is there any alternative?"

"To the choice of humans, or where they'll . . . go?"

"Ask stargazer Rudi if my word is in doubt," Asa said. "It was she who brought this to my attention."

"I'll go convene the council," the *lugal* said, standing up. "Prepare a chamber."

Cheftu nodded, his mind racing.

Asa spoke softly. "It is a harsh thing the gods ask, but we are here at their pleasure."

"We are their slaves," the *lugal* said.

Cheftu muttered something, but he made sure they didn't hear it. Cloak flapping, he raced back to the pit. His stomach growled with hunger, and his head felt light, but there was no time to eat, regardless of what his contentious body wanted. His scribe scurried to catch up with him. "Wake the diggers," Cheftu said. "Bring me a team of bricklayers, pull brick stock from the storehouses, get the remaining vessels from the treasury and send a phalanx of priests to meet the *lugal* at the city gate. Go!"

Acolytes with incense and food came stumbling out of the barracks, with eyes still glued shut from sleep. One let a ladder down into the shaft and Cheftu clambered down it. While he sang, they poured drink offerings, placed the incense, and made a primeval feast for the dead.

Cups and baked bread, and chunks of meat, stewed with onions. He was ravenous. They inverted a clay bowl over the offering, then climbed out. "Fill it some more," he said to them and walked through the dawn to the council meeting.

⌁

Guli paced his cell. Eight steps left, eight right. The smell of dung wafted through the window, but at least it was cool now, at dawn. Whoever thought to cut holes in perfectly good walls? he wondered. Did they not realize how miserable it made the room? Footsteps had pounded the streets, men and women moving back and forth in the night. Apparently the gods had accepted the gifts—they were no better than Viza—for the earth still stood.

He looked out at the gray. The afterlife was like this. Gray and dusty, with nothing but the smell of shit. He sat down on the floor with his legs bent and arms akimbo.

"Guli, is that you?" a voice said from the window.

"Justice?"

"Listen to me. Have you accepted your sentence?"

Guli looked at his hands.

"Was it worth it, to lose your freedom and life for the joy of killing Viza?"

"The scorpion deserved to die."

"It was not your decision to make."

Guli didn't say anything. Whether or not the justice was correct, the system had condemned him. "Did you disturb your rest to prod my conscience?" he said.

"No. I have an offer to make you. I'm coming in."

Guli heard the wooden gate open, then the clay seal on his door crack. Ningal must have caught the pieces because they didn't fall. The bar lifted, and Ningal stepped inside. Guli looked up at him.

"Your clothes are stained yet," Ningal said.

"They didn't give me a change of clothes before locking

me away," Guli said. "I am meditating on my future of being dead. What do you want? What is your offer?"

"Die a hero."

"I'm no fool like Ulu." He wanted to weep at the thought of her quenched of life to cold, uncaring gods. Yet he was blessed for having touched her that last time. For a moment, he had been her gentleman husband, and she had been his honored wife. It was enough to die with.

"You'll perish anyway," Ningal said.

"What's the benefit to me?"

Ningal looked away. "Tonight, in fact most of tomorrow, you can have any woman you want, feast to your contentment, and go to death with a smile."

"I'm going to death anyway. A good lay and a decent meal doesn't seem like much."

"Six double hours' difference. Poison instead of hanging. Entry with gold and power instead of as a criminal and dung layer."

Guli stretched out his legs. "I die at dusk, instead of dawn?"

"Yes."

"Do I die for you? Take your noble name?"

Ningal's gaze met his. "Not for me, but no less noble a name."

"Who?"

"Kalam."

Guli snorted. "He's a scorpion, no better than Viza. You should despise him. Didn't he betray your little sheepherder to Asa's Old Boys? She's gone now, isn't she?"

The older man's eyes shimmered with tears; Guli wanted to insult him, but he didn't have the heart. Ningal straightened his shoulders. "Kalam was a son in my heart long before he became . . ." The justice couldn't speak. "Humanity sometimes means living by one's own standards, even if they cease to make sense to others."

He looked at Guli, and somehow Guli knew the justice understood him. And sympathized.

"I accept your offer."

Ningal reached out his hand. "Then come, you have double hours of pleasure ahead of you. What do you want to do?"

"How do you know I won't run?" Guli asked, standing. He was larger than Ningal, in better condition. He could snap the justice's wiry neck and be through the door and into the marshes by noon. But there were no hairdressers in the marshes, no call for them.

"You're a man of honor," Ningal said.

Guli stepped through the door. "I'd really like to bathe."

~

"*En* Kidu," Nimrod said, bowing. "How does the dawn find you?"

"The gods require more," Cheftu said.

"I know, my family is among the chosen."

Cheftu looked into the face of his friend. "Who?"

"The *lugal*."

"Who will be *lugal* in his place?"

"Gilgamesh, my older brother, returns from his trading soon. He will be voted in by the council. It's doubtful he will have much competition."

"How is your mother?"

Nimrod looked at the ground. "We are but slaves of the gods, all of us, truth?"

"We are slaves," Cheftu murmured.

"I understand there will be a new pit?"

Ears were everywhere, curious eyes and suspicious minds. "We are building a chamber, even now."

"En," a priest said, running up. "The next floor is ready."

"Walk with me," Cheftu said to Nimrod.

The scribe was out of earshot, and Cheftu spoke quickly, softly. "We have to push back the schedule by a day, at least."

Nimrod nodded once.

"I trust . . . it has gone according to plan."

"Will she survive?" Nimrod asked, his breath barely carrying the words to Cheftu. The tenemos walls looked bloody in the sunrise, the palm trees like black claws reaching up from the earth.

"She's tough," Cheftu said, as they walked down the wide steps to the closed pit. The pit where Chloe huddled in utter blackness and dissipating air, alone. "She can do anything."

~

Blood filled her mouth and Chloe mentally cursed herself for biting her tongue. She swallowed the salty liquid and listened as the chest was dragged away from the hole. The cuts her teeth had made were tender; but she hadn't made a sound. At least.

Shuffling above.

Who?

Had she sensed movement, life, breath, sound, heat, anything from any body as she had passed through them? The leather sandal, had it been warm? What could she do? How long had it been? Was Nimrod, even now, tunneling toward her?

A grunt. Male? Female?

I'm really glad I don't believe in ghosts. Especially furniture-moving ghosts.

Chloe's hand tightened around her knife's handle.

The person crashed to the floor.

I have to go to the bathroom, Chloe thought.

No sound. Had he, or she, been knocked out? I can only hope.

Another thud.

Another!

Holy shit! We're all supposed to be dead! Two not-dead people, besides me? Had *anyone* actually taken the poison?

She heard the scratch of tinder and slipped flat into the depression as light flamed.

"Did you bring it?"

A man.

"Yes."

Another man.

They moved quickly, made a huge racket. Robbers! They were stripping the tomb. Quickly. Underneath the clash of precious metals against each other, Chloe heard the prayers of one man. The other was panting hard. Out of breath, or terrified?

Don't come this way, Chloe thought.

Had they heard her?

"Did you move it back?" one asked.

"I forgot."

"Get up there, imbecile. They might come back."

"They've loaded a thousand minae of dirt into the shaft. It would take days."

"If we know about this route, then someone else does."

Grumbling, someone banged against wood. She heard the chest moved back into place.

"Which way do we go?"

"By the door, there's a passage."

The same passage she was waiting for. *Oh God, help me!*

An answer to prayer and a natural result. The light flickered out.

The shallow breather began to hyperventilate. The men raced toward her, bones flying in their wake.

Chloe used their noise to slip away from them but against

the wall. She felt bones sliding beneath her, beads and antique ribbons under her hands. She halted at the edge of something wooden.

One of the men whimpered as they banged against the wall in panic, looking for the false section. She barely breathed through her nose.

"Calm yourself," one shouted. "We'll find it."

"They're going to get us," the other said, sobbing. "They are going to find out and torture us—"

Something large, metal and heavy hit the wall and both men shouted.

Y'all are making enough noise to wake the dead, Chloe thought. *And I'm losing my mind making jokes in a room with . . . two men who probably wouldn't hesitate to add my body to the quota in this chamber.*

"There!" one said. "Air, do you feel it?"

"Praise Sin," the other said.

Scratch of tinder, and light flickered.

They didn't look back, but rattled through the tunnel, banging their treasures and snuffling like overgrown warthogs. Chloe recited every song she remembered from church camp, from college, from those few years free in the modern world. Hours passed before she peeked.

There was no light, but she did feel some air.

She slid back and screeched at the sound. She'd brushed a lyre—the soft cry was like a human's.

The strength left her body, and she huddled, arms tight around her drawn-up legs, her head on her knees. One more millimeter and she would have bumped it. Those thieves would have heard her—

Relief was an icy shower of sweat.

Chloe crawled to the space she'd heard them make. Her touch ascertained they had pierced a whitewashed wall, the covering to the tunnel that led to the well was maybe an eighth-inch thick. A breeze definitely blew through.

Should she wait for Nimrod? Or take the initiative?

One side was death and decay, the other uncertainty and peril.

Chloe chewed her lip.

~

Cheftu paced as they worked. Two more layers before they'd build the room for the rest of the sacrifices. Funeral objects—coffins, furniture, utensils, games, pets—lined the courtyard walls. Sweat had soaked the chest of his garment, and Cheftu wished he could strip down to a kilt and stand in the cool mud.

Chloe had been buried for a whole day now. The death pit was huge—she should have plenty of air. There was food by the sledge, if she needed it. He glared at the sky, waiting for the next double hour and the next offering.

"*En—*" It was Nimrod. His skin, tanned to leather and covered by a mat of hair, was ashen.

Cheftu looked around. No scribe, no followers. The priests were still filling in rubble. He walked to the man.

"We have a problem."

"Serious?"

"Follow me."

Cheftu looked around, but they weren't watching him. He followed Nimrod out the back entrance of the temple compound into one of the storehouses, recently emptied into the pit. Two men were tied to the rafters by their wrists.

Gagged.

Bloody.

A bag of loot—funeral loot—lay at their feet.

Nimrod spoke to Cheftu with his back to them. "My guards found these thieves leaving the well."

Cheftu felt his body turn to ice. "The same—?"

Nimrod nodded once.

"What have they said?"

"Not much. One weeps most of the time, the other throws up poison yet."

Cheftu looked at them, dark faces with overgrown eyebrows, close-cut beards and woolly heads. They could be anyone. "Did they play at being guards?"

"I don't think so. They aren't very tall."

"Are these Puabi's funeral items?"

Nimrod glanced over his shoulder, then back. "If it were so, I wouldn't worry. These objects are from the tomb below."

"They know everything, then," Cheftu said.

Nimrod nodded slowly.

Cheftu looked at the ground. "Do we know who they are?"

"I can't get much out of them."

Cheftu noted the black eye of one, the bloody nose of the other. One's gaze was wide, petrified, in shock. The other's was knowing, derisive. "Let me look at their hands."

Nimrod spun around and gestured for his guards to release the prisoners. The terrified one began to whimper, the other one's expression grew more solemn.

Cheftu turned each hand over, checking the cuticles, the calluses, the palms, and the heels. "Restrain them again," he said. Nimrod gestured, and his men retied and suspended the thieves. Cheftu walked to the doorway and stared out. The sky was a heartless blue, the shadows of the palms black on the ground. His thousands of gold-beaded braids were soaked with sweat. Absently, his fingers ran over the impressions of the seals around his waist.

"What do you want me to do?"

Cheftu turned and peered into Nimrod's face, his eyes. He looked at the men who stood on tiptoe and watched him with terror. Cheftu wasn't worthy to make these choices, but by any standard, these men would be killed. France, Egypt, Aztlan, Jerusalem—no society looked kindly on grave robbers.

He spoke softly. "When you retrieve Chloe, return the loot."

"What about the men?"

Cheftu inhaled deeply, then spoke. "Take them to the marshes," he said. "But first—cut out their tongues."

Nimrod turned on his heel and motioned his men. It sickened Cheftu to watch; he was a healer, not a despot, but he had no choice. If Nimrod had to enact Cheftu's decision, then Cheftu would witness it.

The two men's cries rang in Cheftu's ears; neither was brave, then they were quickly bundled off by Nimrod's efficient mountain guards. Nimrod joined Cheftu as they returned to the pit. "Why look at their hands?" he asked.

Cheftu felt the blaze of sun on his back and shoulders, it beat down and centered in the golden diadem around his head. The priests were waiting for him, lounging on the ground.

"If they could write, they would have calluses. If they could write, they would have had to die." Cutting their tongues took away their only method of communication.

"You are merciful," Nimrod said. "If I were *lugal*, I would make you a justice."

"I'm not worthy," Cheftu said and joined the priests for the next series of offerings.

～

At twilight they started to gather, the families of Ur, the landed gentry, the leading merchants, the master craftsmen. Silent, so as not to invite the gods' greater wrath, they bid farewell to the representative who would give himself in sacrifice for each family.

Unlike those who had gone into the pit, these people were buried as individuals, named, with their belongings and coffins. And if the one who was named was not the one who entered the quickly constructed chamber, his neighbor wasn't going to betray him.

A sacrifice was a sacrifice. The gods just wanted people dead, bearing the identification of those specific families. The quays were crowded with merchant ships turned passenger vessels, heading for long journeys on the evening's tide. The road beside the Euphrates was jammed with onagers and their owners, faces carefully hidden from the sun and from recognition, on their way to extended family, or distant fields, or noted Tablet Houses in other commonwealths.

The people of Ur were accepting of fate, but they also knew the gods had an eye for a bargain and weren't above bartering, "merchandise" exchanges, or half-price sales. Destiny was designed for negotiation.

Guli's stomach was tight as the kettledrum. He'd eaten too much, spent the day in the bath with perfumes and oils, a blonde, and a brunette, then dealt with distributing his hair-dressing tools. He looked at his hands, saddened that he would never feel the weight of glossy locks across his palms again.

The intricate twists he could make with his index finger, while holding the other twists in place, would not be a skill he'd use in Kur. His cuticles were still stained from the last job on Ulu—making her golden to be Puabi. The smell of blood was washed away, though. His clothes were new—he even wore the bordered and fringed cloak of an Old Boy and carried a death mask hammered into an exact reproduction of a gentleman's hairstyle, every braid picked out in detail.

Kalam was on a boat tonight, headed for Dilmun. He would trade for spices and jewels, then return in a few months. The danger would have passed by then, no one but the priests would know about the substitution, and, if necessary, they were easy to bribe.

Gilgamesh, son of Shem, had returned to Ur, and been voted in as *lugal* during a special meeting of joint houses. He now stood at the head of his family. The basket hat looked strange on his shaved skull, and he wore no beard, but he stood with dignity, the seals and cylinders of his new position hanging from his beaded belt. The former *lugal*, Shem, in contrast, looked all of his years.

Shem's was the First Family. They had landed here after the Deluge, and the brothers had fought and been sent to separate corners of the world to ensure peace. Ziusudra, it was whispered, had had enough of their bickering on the boat. Rumor was that Ziusudra's first project of planting vineyards was because he wanted to be drunk and forget his annoying offspring.

Kham had been cursed to the west desert and beyond, Japhet had set sail across the great northern sea and now Shem, the *lugal* of Ur, the protector of the brown-haired humans, the ruler of the black-haired humans, stepped into line as a sacrifice.

Guli didn't know numbers well, but Shem had lived almost as long as the kings of Before. The healing properties of the water were gone now, though. Boy grew to man quickly, had his children, and was bent with age in less time than a boy used to grow to a man. A lasting curse of the Deluge.

Guli wondered if they were averting something as great as the Deluge by this sacrifice, as he glanced at the sky. It was orange and rose and striped with gold. The temple courtyard filled with flickering lamps.

He had just seen his final sunset.

En Kidu looked as golden as the *ensi* had, though his hair and beard were naturally fair, Guli guessed. Even his eyes were golden.

The *en's* expression was strained, and the lines around his eyes and mouth were pronounced in the twilight. The drums began and he looked down, his lips moving in prayer. Someone's wife screamed, then her cries were muffled. The priests wheeled forward a sledge holding the great copper pot.

Ningal's hand trembled as he patted Guli's arm. "For you," he said, and handed Guli a parcel.

Guli unwrapped it and rubbed his fingers over the carving. "My seal."

"It bears your name," Ningal said. "Guli, blessed of Inana. You go to die for Mes-Kalam-Dug, but the gods will not forget you, good Guli." He handed him a cup.

The old man's eyes were shiny; Guli didn't know what to say. They embraced stiffly, Guli was afraid he'd break Ningal's ribs. Then he let go and stepped into the line, holding his cup and seal. It was mostly men, representatives of their lineages, many of them aged, volunteering in order to spare their young. The handsome young priests blessed them as they walked by.

Guli counted fifty volunteers who had already disappeared down the narrow shaft, into the chamber, another sixty to go. At the landing before the tunnel led down, the priests held the pot. "Dip in, dear client," they said in unison.

Holding the edges of the cup, Guli dipped, getting it full, for he was a large man. A last glance at the temple, the stages illumined with lamps, the blue chamber to heaven shining in the night.

Would that even one god watched and cared. Even one. Guli stepped down in time to the beat of the drum.

～

It was dark out, and Chloe hadn't exactly made a decision. Should the thieves come back—she couldn't imagine why they would—but she'd been surprised by their presences altogether, so her suppositions couldn't be trusted—if she was in the well, they would find her.

Dead Chloe.

Having just dodged poison, the itching and cramping and vomiting effects of surviving it, and crawling over bones and bodies to get there, she wasn't going to die by being stupid in the end.

Provided *that* was the stupid choice.

Neither was she going to stay in the room with the skeletons beside her and the rotting corpses above. She didn't have a masochistic bone in her body.

The tunnel leading to the dry well didn't run straight. At the end, it curved. Probably a ladder or rope there. She could see that far, so she had some warning if people came down the well, into the tunnel.

Consequently, she'd wedged herself in the mouth between the tunnel and the pit. The burial pit was an arm's length away, easy to fall into and hide, but she got the benefit of fresh breezes, and the psychological boon of not being with the dead.

Something must have gone wrong with the plan, though. Nimrod and Cheftu should have been there double hours ago. It was dark again. Drums were beating, faintly, but beating, again.

All of this had been to assure that the eclipse would be only that, and just like after twilight, the sun would return.

That had been the reason for the whole exercise. What could have possibly gone wrong? Eclipses eclipsed, then it was over. What signs could they have seen that made the drums beat?

Maybe it's a continuation of the burial process, she thought. Nothing is wrong, it's just taking longer for them to get away than they thought originally.

She didn't have water; there had been no place to hide a flask in her funeral clothes. Nor did she have food. *Don't even think about candy bars,* she reprimanded herself. *Halva,* she thought. *The ancient candy bar.*

You don't have that either, so think about . . . bugs.

The fried roaches in the bazaar, the seasoned worms they sold like calamari, ant soup, grasshopper pie—okay, she was losing her appetite. She flicked a spider off her arm and stared down the tunnel.

"Hurry up and wait," she muttered. "It's becoming my motto."

Chapter Seven

Cheftu moved his lips by rote, letting the training he hadn't done and the memories he didn't have take control. The clients stepped so cheerfully, so pridefully to their death. For them, it was honor. Life was a task of serving the fickle, anthropomorphic gods, and some bets were won and others lost.

In his soul, Cheftu was an ancient man. He understood the confusion and desperation and resignation that could come with crop failure, flood, eclipses, and unexplained events in the heavens. There was a very good chance that after today, the seasons would return to their paces, the sky would stay in its appointed place, and life would return to normal. It was not his place to decide for these ancients; they were the merchants of their lives.

Aside from his soul, he had a nineteenth-century-educated mind that had been expanded by his sometimes caustic and usually skeptical twentieth-century wife.

It screamed at the insanity of this performance.

The heavens were gas and fire, as unaware of the Black-Haired Ones as the Black-Haired Ones were of viruses—so Chloe had taught him. Farming ran in cycles—some years were good and some were bad. Whole regions were wiped out by bad luck and bad weather, she said, and told him about a part of the United States colonies that had become a

Dust Bowl and brought on a Great Depression. Her family had had a farm and made it their duty to feed those who passed through their gates. But thousands had lost everything.

It was the way of the world. Cycles.

One of the things Cheftu had hated most in European travelers was how they compared everything to home. The English in Cairo who complained that the tea wasn't properly brewed; or the Frenchmen who were irritated when the right silk wasn't available for a hat. Even as a youth, Cheftu had wanted to shout at those people to go home.

Egypt wasn't about brewed tea, it was about thrice-boiled tea, made of mint and served sticky sweet, or tiny cups of coffee whose bottom half resembled damp soot. Egypt wasn't a land of silks, but of the finest, sheerest cotton and lightest linen. The only hat should not be one of Parisian design, but a turban or a fez.

Cheftu couldn't change the way he thought now. The streets of Ur were filthy, but these were the people who first conceived of writing. They slaughtered animals in the lane, and one had to step over bloody streams, but they ruled democratically and taxed men proportionately. Their eyebrows were unkempt, but through accounting and complex mathematics, they knew to the kernel how much surplus barley they stored and how many people it would feed.

If volunteer sacrifice was the means of their religion, it could be they knew more than he did. And this sacrifice would certainly help the rest of population, regarding supplies of food and water.

So Cheftu continued to move his mouth, as he watched old men, young men, goldsmiths and weavers, dyers and wheelwrights, move into the earth. Death came to all humans. Perhaps it was better to choose when, than to have it chosen for one. It was definitely better to die for a reason than just to die because it was part of the cycle.

The *lugal's* gaze met his, and Cheftu inclined his head, to show his respect. Heart heavy, he followed the leader into the chamber. Men leaned against the walls, packed the room tightly, surrounded by the outward trappings of their positions.

Shem turned to him. "I can do this," he said. "You are among the living, my friend. Go, comfort our families and tell them we do this for respect of the commonwealth, the health and affection of our lines, and in obedience to our gods."

They embraced, and Cheftu climbed up the stairs, out into the torchlit wildness of living.

～

Chloe dozed, absently brushing away the creatures that explored her arms and legs. It was downright cool, and she pulled her woolen dress and cloak closer to her body, twisting them in an attempt to discourage curious multipeds. The drums were soft, especially compared to her stomach, which was loud, talkative and irritated. The words of "To His Coy Mistress" floated through her head, and Chloe reflexively cursed her English teacher. But the frights of the night before had faded—perhaps from such frequent viewing in her imagination.

"Sss—"

The noise jolted her awake; she couldn't tell where it was coming from. Surely not the death pit?

"Sss—"

"Sss—" she hissed back. And hoped she was hissing to the right person.

"Chloe—" It was Nimrod, whose pronunciation of her name always sounded exotic, though he'd told her in Sumerian it meant little clods of dirt. "Don't move."

"Yesss—"

"There is a problem. It will be later."

Later? How much more later? "Yesss—"

"Good girl," he said. "I leave food here. Be careful, quiet, and return to the pit when you have gotten it. It's the safest place to hide you. I'll come for you there."

The sound of a soft impact.

The tunnel was long, maybe a block and half. Food was at the end, though. *I wonder if this is how rats reason,* she thought, slinking her way through the dust, the spiderwebs and the dirt. She seized the bag, chanced a glance up, saw starlit sky, and returned down the tunnel. Back to death, back to decay.

At least now she had lunch.

Fried quail, barley bread, and pea paste, followed with a jar of date wine. From Ningal's treasured hoard, no doubt.

She put the jar down and sat, thinking. She wrapped the uneaten food and turned so that she was on her knees. She tried folding her hands, then clasping them, and settled for lacing her fingers in her lap.

"I owe You an apology," she whispered in her first prayer that wasn't accusatory. "I've bitched and moaned constantly about my body, this place, why and where, and why again. You gave me friends here, people who looked after me, who keep on looking after me.

"Ningal, who decided to protect me and bankroll me. Nimrod, who didn't think I was crazy when I realized that me and the marsh girl were in the same body. That we're the same person. And Cheftu, God You brought Cheftu to me. As the *en,* he's the only one who could have decided to save my life. I guess if I say it's like You already knew, it's a little redundant."

She reached up and tucked some hair behind her ear. "And thanks for the body. I really like the way I look now, and I'm more comfortable in my skin than I ever have been. I always thought I was too pale. Can't accuse me of that now." She chuckled. "I am one hot babe. Guess I shouldn't speak that way to You, but what's the point of pretense? I was so unhappy in Jerusalem, and I didn't realize it until I got here.

"I don't know how I got here, I need to ask Cheftu, but thank You. If there is some other place or time we're supposed to be in, You're going to have to make it really obvious, because I don't want to leave. And, oh God, You picked an awesome body for Cheftu. I know he's a little wigged-out about everything, but . . . I guess You know."

She glanced up at the bricklaid vault roof. "You'd think I'd learn by now, but I don't. This isn't a challenge or anything, but, God, I'm not going to doubt again. You've saved my bacon every time. And it's always better than I dreamed anything could be, when I just let You . . . do what You do best."

She played with the beads of her belt. "I guess that's it, I just wanted to apologize, formally. It's hard to believe You do care, with the whole world to look after. All time and space. You know me though, You know me well." Chloe wiped the tear that had gathered at the edge of her eye. "Thanks, God. I really mean it. I'm sorry for being such a brat so much of the time. I'm going to be better. I don't promise, because You *do* know me, but I'm going to be better."

Her legs were falling asleep, so she said amen, twisted around again to be comfortable, thought for a minute, then opened her lunch. Now she could enjoy eating.

⌣

"Drink," the *lugal*, Shem, said.

Guli looked at his cup, then put it to his lips. In one swallow it was gone, the bitter taste masked by dates and honey, cardamom and cinnamon. A lutenist played, no one spoke.

His lips went numb, then his fingers. His chest rose and fell faster as the sensation of no sensation crept from his feet to his groin, up his arms and neck. There was no name on his lips, no love he mourned. He pitied those who had joy they were turning their backs on here. There was no joy in Kur.

Noises filtered through the daze growing in his mind. His neck was stiff now—not painful, just final. Lamps glowed in all parts of the room, and Guli could see the bodies lying close together, filling the chamber. Coffins stacked against the wall, riches beyond his imagination heaped in the center.

He blinked; the feeling was a little like falling asleep after drinking too much beer. Disconnected awareness. It seemed that mist rose from the dirt, shapes that were long and translucent.

A tugging at his head—not the body—but at his awareness. He let go and was squished through a narrow opening, then popped out and soared—weightless. Free.

All around him, perceptions poured in.

He couldn't taste, or smell, or see, but he knew everything. Every man in the pit; every concern of those above. All was laid before him, explained and known and understandable. Joy bubbled inside him. If only the others realized! Could he tell them? Just a moment with Ningal.

No, resounded through him. *It's not for you to do.*

Below him, he saw the death chamber. Wax and dirt shapes, freed of their users, melting back into the comfort of the soil. The gold would last, but its meaning was less than the dirt. The body of Guli was stiff, but his eyes were blankly peaceful.

If only Guli had known, Guli thought.

Other mists swirled around him, their joy contagious. With laughter and excitement they passed through the arched brick roof and up into the night. Dirt and wax stood on feet in the courtyard, hundreds and thousands of them, lined up, burdened, worried, shallow, and wonderful.

Tears poured from Guli. He hadn't wept when he was dirt and wax, but when he saw them he couldn't stop. How incredible, how intricate, how ignorant they were. Their frets and fears were written on them like envelopes. That is what they are, he thought. Envelopes, inscribed with the contents, protective of the true document and once broken, impossible to reuse.

Dirt and wax, wrapped around joy and breath.

He could see from horizon to horizon, around the globe of the world. The world was round as a fruit, filled with a million souls. They lived in places and ways Guli had never even imagined. It was a storehouse of envelopes, unaware that they were, and unaware that they were exactly like each other, except for each one's dream.

He rose above the Plain of Shinar. It stretched out, the twin rivers twisting and winding through the land. Already he could see the channels the heedless waters had abandoned and he realized the Euphrates wouldn't run forever beneath the western wall of the commonwealth of Ur. Fish jumped in the south sea, and Dilmun's orchards shone beneath the clear, full moon.

Ziusudra, who would never be free of his envelope, and who thought that was a blessing, looked up. Age had been arrested in him, but it had happened too late, and he was bent with years and crippled by disillusion.

Kalam, on board a ship a day's sail from the port of Ur, looked back fearfully. His fingers were white around the wooden prow, and his eyes were wide, peering through the night, anticipating the *lugal's* soldiers or the priests of the temple approaching and demanding that he take his place in the pit.

Thank you, Guli said to him. *You blessed me, and you*

didn't know it, didn't intend it. But that doesn't make the action any less a blessing.

Kalam shivered and pulled his cloak around him. He eyed the air, and Guli whisked away on the breeze.

Leave the envelopes to their own.

His joy floated him like foam on the sea, to land on the distant shores of a new, higher world. But he knew the face he held dearest, he would not see. Ulu, fearful and wounded, but free to start her life again, was headed north. She was alive.

But someday, she too would know this joy.

～

It took eight priests four double hours to arrange the bodies, give each an individual funeral for his name, cover him with dirt, carry in the remaining bribes, pour the libation offering, set the table for the funeral feast, and climb out of the pit.

Cheftu ached, he reeked of death and dirt, his stomach was cramped from hunger and his desire for Chloe. To touch her was a craving that he feared would drive him insane. He didn't see Nimrod anywhere in the courtyard; consequently, he didn't know where Chloe was.

"En," a priest said. "You need to, uh, bathe and change before the final set of offerings. The people will return with their farewell wishes, then we'll fill in the rest of the shaft."

"Of course," Cheftu said.

"A bath is drawn for you."

"Who?"

"Shama serves you now. As you requested."

Cheftu muttered thanks and headed toward the labyrinth of offices and quarters. When he didn't think about where he was going, he didn't get lost. His door opened at his touch, and he stepped inside.

A woman's leg moved in the other room, as she filled his bath.

"I specifically requested Shama," he said, irritation edging his voice. "No women."

"Okay," she said, stepping into view. "But I thought I'd try to change your mind."

He seized her, and she held him as they both shook. "Chloe, my beloved. Oh my Chloe," he murmured against her black hair.

"Never let me go," she whispered. "Don't ever take your arms from around me again."

"I can't." he said. "I won't. My beloved wife, oh Chloe."

~

The house was his. As soon as the coppersmiths got new copper, he could order a bathtub. He had money now, position as Asa's eyes, power over the old stargazer to do whatever he wanted. Ezzi was set for life.

He'd fired Ulu's servants and sold her slaves. It was quiet, and dark. Her perfume lingered in the air; he had the strange sensation she might walk in and disturb his blessed peace. She couldn't. She was dead, buried beneath a shaft of dirt as deep as the stages of the temple were high.

The stars looked far away, removed from man's touch. The showers they had sent seemed to have passed. The gods had been sufficiently bribed. Ezzi sat at the table, hungry. Then he realized he had to get his own food.

He lit a torch and walked back into the kitchens. Everything was bare—no bread in the basket, no stew on the fire. The stores of peas and onions were empty, the narrow flaxen twists of spices open and stacked.

"That is just as well," he said to the lonely darkness. "I can just go to the tavern. Get a warm dinner, and refreshing beer. Chat with the clients from my street as civilized men do." He walked back to the courtyard and let himself out.

There were no shouts tonight, no laughter, no mirth. It was as dark and silent as waiting in front of the temple had been. No matter, humans would be clustered at the tavern. Ezzi's steps were quick and loud against the packed-dirt road, and he turned the corner.

No torches burned without. No lamps glowed from within. He tried the door, but it was bolted. The tavern wasn't open. "She always was a lazy old ale-wife," he muttered. Her competition, whose brew was superior anyway, was just across the canal. He'd go there and be better off for it. "Maybe I will just go there from now on," he said to himself. "A whole new start."

Ulu hadn't worked there. That would be good—they would recognize him as Ezzi stargazer, instead of the whore Ulu's useless whelp. He wouldn't have to listen to them talk to him about her, how much fun she was, how much they missed her. He'd be an independent man, an impressive one. He halted in the street and pondered if he should return home and put on his fresher Old Boy cloak.

It was late; he was too hungry.

Doors were shut tonight; birds cooed in the trees, and occasionally a wild dog howled. He heard no people. Ezzi was alone.

He walked across the bridge, toward the other tavern.

The torches by the door were lit, the warm welcome glow bid him come in and eat. The ale-wife looked up. "What is your pleasure?" she asked. Her teeth were split and black, her hair as thin as cobwebs spread over her head. Huge hoop earrings dangled from stretched earlobes, and her eyes were swollen nearly shut.

"Beer," he said.

"That's a surprise, boy. What kind of beer?"

"What do you have?"

"Sweet barley beer, tart barley beer, spiced barley beer, dark barley beer," she ticked off on her fingers. "Fresh green beer, corked beer, New Year beer, harvest beer—"

"Do you have a breakfast beer?" he asked.

"Sure do."

"I'll take that."

"I don't serve breakfast until after dawn."

"The day starts at twilight," he told her.

"It does, Old Boy, but you don't fast until you go to sleep, and you don't go to sleep until the night, so you aren't breaking your fast until the dawn. So I don't serve breakfast beer until after dawn."

Ezzi glanced around. A whore ministered to a man in the far corner. Some sailors played dice at a table, foreigners from the look of them. The other seats were empty, the floor was sticky, and the tables weren't balanced. "Sweet beer," he said.

"Honey sweet? Date sweet? Date honey sweet? Malt sweet? Fresh mash sweet?"

"Uh, date sweet," he said, then remembered he really preferred honey sweet. But she was gone already.

She brought back the jar and started to crack the seal. "How are you paying?"

Ezzi froze. He'd always had beer, food, anything he wanted at the tavern.

Because his mother worked there.

He made a production of reaching for his seals and purse, then slapped the bar. "By the gods! I can't believe it. I spent all day with the great stargazer Asa—I'm his colleague—I came home and changed for the ceremony outside the temple . . . and I must have left my purse on my other belt. I'm so sorry," he said reaching for the jar. "I'll pay you on the morrow."

She pulled the jar out of reach. "Not so fast, Old Boy. You pay now, or you don't drink."

"I don't have my purse, I told you. I'll send my slave with double fees tomorrow. I'm good for it. I live on Crooked Way." He spoke the truth.

Her gaze raked him. "What do you do, to live on Crooked Way? Stay with your family?"

He drew himself up. "Certainly not! I am a stargazer, as I said."

"You're the one who advises the *lugal* and *ensi*?"

Ezzi smiled. Now he was getting the recognition he deserved. "I am indeed."

"You were the one who discovered the new star, who predicted the moon would fight the sun?"

"You are a very knowledgeable woman," he said, smiling at his most charming.

She simpered back, finished pulling the seal off the throat of the jar and pried off the wax top. He could smell it; sweet beer to warm his body and fill his belly. Who needed food when you had beer?

She handed it to him, and he took it, staring at her. "My good woman," he said, "I need a drinking tube." She might follow the news of the day, but she was hopeless about running a tavern. "And if you could wipe off one of those tables, I would appreciate it."

"Hand me the jar, and I'll slip it right in," she said.

Ezzi handed it back, and she put it on the floor beside her. Then she wiggled and writhed, crouched and he heard the sound of liquid on liquid. "Ahh," she said, then handed it back to him. The mouth was wet—

"You pissed in my beer! What kind of whore are you?"

She knocked the jar with her hand and sent the mixture across the bar and into Ezzi's face, onto his cloak; bathed him in it. "My son died yesterday because some fool saw a sign in the stars! Get out, and never come back!"

Ezzi stared.

"He killed your brother," she said to the two sailors. They looked at Ezzi and rose to their feet.

He turned and ran. The door banged behind him, then he heard it bang twice more. Terror pushed him on, across the bridge. He heard their feet against the wood, but they were losing the chase.

Ezzi threw himself in the shadows by a house, panting. Fire raced through his chest, and his face felt aflame. He couldn't catch his breath. He peered around the corner. No one was coming.

The assistant stargazer limped home to his dark, empty mansion and climbed the stairs. The sheets had been removed from his bed for laundering, and had not been replaced. A beetle crawled across the palm-frond mattress, black and glistening in the moonlight.

He ripped off his Old Boy cloak and beat the beetle to death, then threw it all, urine-soaked wool and squashed bug, across the room before collapsing on the bed.

No one called up to ask if he was all right.

No one knocked to see if he needed food or drink.

No one was there.

Ezzi buried his head under his arms. It was better this way.

No one to interfere.

∼

Cheftu's stomach growled, and Chloe tightened her arms around him. They didn't want to let go of each other. A knock at the door.

"Who?" Cheftu called.

"Sir, the courtyard is beginning to fill with clients who are paying their final respects."

"Are you supposed to be there?" Chloe whispered in his ear.

He nodded. "I'll be out after my bath," he called.

"A half double hour, sir," the priest said.

"Yes," Cheftu said. "Thank you."

"I poured some water for you, it's probably cool by now," she said.

Cheftu walked forward, her lightly veiled body clasped to his. He stepped into the tub and sank down, soaking them both. "Hold your breath," he said, and pulled them below.

They came up, Chloe smoothing her hair back, Cheftu wiping the water from his eyes. She looked at him, up close. His face was the same as always, knife-blade nose, square jaw, intelligent forehead and heavy brow. His eyes were deep-set and thickly lashed. But in different coloring—on a different physique—he looked completely different. She was really glad she'd gambled on a feeling.

"You look like you've been gilded," she whispered. "Your skin and beard match your eyes now. You're all golden." Droplets hung from the thousand braids of his hair and shimmered on the diadem he wore. She reached a finger out to trace his cheekbone, his lips.

"Oh, Chloe," he murmured, and kissed her. No hesitation, no exploration, just flat-out claiming what was his.

"Make love to me," she said as his mouth moved from hers, down her chin and neck.

He stopped.

"What?"

Cheftu sighed and looked at her. "My duty is to get out there, cleaned up, and complete this business. I—"

She placed a finger on his lips. "I understand. Do you need someone to wash your back?" Her grin was impish.

His gaze kindled. "Help me by getting *out* of my bath and finding me some food."

She stood up, dripping wet, her wisp of a dress totally transparent.

"When I get back, we'll discuss how you got in here," he said.

"And where you got these clothes," she said, plucking at her gown as she stepped onto the floor. "Women's."

Cheftu's ears reddened.

She laughed. "You're blushing!"

He pulled his cloak off and slapped it on the drying rack, keeping himself immersed. "I am not."

"You're fair-skinned," she said. "You're tan, but you're really pale."

"I'm a Berber," he said. "This body is, anyway. Berbers were originally from the mountains, big fair-skinned people with blond or red hair. Before they settled in Africa."

"I can't believe it, you're always dark. Now you are a white boy."

He glanced into the tub. "You have no idea."

She stood on tiptoe but Cheftu pulled her down for another kiss, openmouthed, deep, and penetrating. Chloe was gasping when he pulled back. "Food," he said.

His cheeks were extremely pink, beneath the bronze of his skin. "I'm going," she said.

Chloe was seated on a chair when Cheftu came out of the lavatory, freshly dressed and clothed. He had time for one kiss and three pieces of bread, before a priest summoned him from the hallway. "Don't leave," he whispered to her. "I'll be back. Get some sleep."

He closed the door behind him, and Chloe was alone in the apartment. No details revealed Cheftu lived there. It was ornate, every piece of furniture inlaid and gold-leafed, fussy, with all the blankets edged in fringe, the pillows beaded with lapis and carnelian, statues and bottles on every available surface, and colorful. If it wasn't red, it was blue or yellow. The walls were cone-mosaicked in red and blue and yellow, a giant zigzag pattern in one room, and herringbone in the bedroom. Cheftu's bed was draped in tissue-thin wool, and piled with pillows. Not to mention that his bed was three times the width of the ordinary ones she'd seen.

After all, Chloe reminded herself, *he's the high priest of fertility.*

On the inlaid table beside the bed, she saw the only signs of the Cheftu she knew: a stack of tablets and a handful of cylinder seals made from lapis and agate, delicate things that were art in and of themselves. She glanced at the tablets; they would make no sense to her since they were written in the priestly code.

She sat down on the bed. She should take a bath—she could now, she was home free. But it didn't feel real, it didn't seem like the death pit and burial chamber had existed. Chloe stripped down and crawled into the bathtub. The water was lukewarm and probably dirty, but cleaner than she was, at any rate.

Her hair was still somewhat of a mystery. It wasn't strictly Caucasian hair, and she didn't know how to treat it. She wet it, combed it down, and made sure it was free of cobwebs and spiders. Then she scrubbed away gold paint for at least an hour. Finally, she took Cheftu's razor to every part of her body she could reach. Nicked in a half dozen places, Chloe climbed out of the tub and tried not to bleed on anything white.

When she'd scabbed over enough, she walked nude into the bedroom and pulled back the covers. The sheets smelled of sunshine and had been hammered to velvety softness. With a groan, Chloe cradled a pillow and fell asleep.

∼

Ningal threw his cup into the room, to land with a chink on top of the others—clay and copper and gold and silver: inlaid and molded and fired and glazed—there were thousands upon thousands, the final tribute of the clients in the commonwealth of Ur. *En* Kidu stood at the mouth of the mass grave and watched the clients pass, throw their cups, and climb the three steps from the landing.

Sunlight didn't reveal what was inside, and incense burned to cover up the smell of dead and festering flesh. Heat scored the pavement around the temple, and the people were a sweaty stinking mass though the sun had been up only two double hours.

The populace waited to see if Asa would say the curse had been averted. Ningal had done all he could for those he cared for; thank the gods it seemed to have gone well. Kalam had lived, Chloe had been spared, and justice had been served.

All that remained now was to get on with the business of living. How he missed his wife, the warmth of a house where bread was baked with love, beer brewed with understanding. He didn't think of her often; there was no point for she was so many years gone. Perhaps he should take a journey, go visit his children and grandchildren and great-grandchildren. A voyage to see them all should take the rest of his life.

He looked at the temple. Was everything from now on just waiting to die?

En Kidu stood like a bronzed statue of the god. Chloe's fate had been sealed and witnessed. She didn't need Ningal, and her young man had the soul of an ancient one with its attendant wisdom. Ningal couldn't fathom the story Nimrod had told: the two, Chloe and Kidu, brought from another time and place to inhabit these bodies. Yet Ningal felt it was true. Like stories from Before, it rang with authenticity.

What was Ningal's life for, then?

"Ningal, Justice," a voice said.

He turned and greeted the new *lugal*. Gilgamesh was a fine figure of a man, even though he was clean-cheeked. The look of another commonwealth, no doubt. "How are you, my boy?"

"We just laid our cups," he said. "Mother is at the house."

"How is she?"

Gilgamesh had eyes as black as pitch, hard to read. He had been a hard taxman, a relentless leader, and ambitious for territory and water. Ningal wondered if the years had tempered him at all. "Bereft, sir."

"True, true."

"She would probably enjoy seeing some old friends," he said.

Ningal looked at him. "Are you inviting me to visit your mother?"

"She is a young woman," he said. "Vital. Used to managing a household and looking after children."

Ningal patted his shoulder. "Then invite another man, for I am old, sir." He shook his head. "Old."

"Of all the justices, my father thought you were the most honorable. You had the greatest understanding of humanity, he said." Gilgamesh's strong hand shook Ningal's. "Think about the visit. You would be welcome at any time."

"Thank you," Ningal said and walked out of the compound, down toward his street. *Old,* he thought. *If I'd been asked, I would have died, too.* What was left, really? Each day to wake up and see what more of his body had failed, until the dawn when he wouldn't be able to move enough to see, then the next when his sight would have failed him also? He turned on to Crooked Way. Sunlight poured down, drawing lines of shadow on the walls and doubling the length of palm trees on the street.

He wondered why he occupied his huge house. A family should live there, with children and grandchildren running around the courtyard and wondrous smells rising from the hearth. Not an old man sipping wine under the only tree in the yard. "I'll sell it," he decided. "Better yet, give it to someone. A young justice or scribe who is in the family way."

Ningal stopped talking to himself. Not only was it a dotty, aged habit, but he heard another voice.

"Help," it whispered. "Please, help me, somebody."

Ningal turned his head to hear better. A whimper. He sniffed the air and smelled blood. This far from the butcher's, he shouldn't smell blood. Someone was hurt. He threw open the door of his courtyard and shouted for the slaves. "Look around," he ordered them. "Someone is crying for help."

Four sets of eyes and ears located the victim quickly. The blood seeping beneath the door was the key. An Old Boy was in his courtyard, bleeding profusely. The slaves all pushed and opened the door, sending his body rolling. There were no people inside, and the place smelled of stale smoke and old urine. Ningal stanched the Old Boy's blood flow with the edge of his cloak, then the four slaves shouldered the man and took him down to Ningal's house.

"Fetch the *asu* and *asipu*," he told his new scribe. "See if there is any sign of who did this. Borrow the *lugal's* guards if you must, but find out."

Ningal washed the man's face and chest. He'd been stabbed four times, but luckily no organs had been struck.

"Don't let me die," the Old Boy muttered. "She'll be waiting for me, and I can't face her. Don't let me die."

Ningal paused, then added willow bark to the water and continued his ministrations. The gods worked in mischievous ways. He beckoned a slave. "Go to the *lugal's* house and ask for Shem's widow. Tell her that the Justice Ningal needs a woman's touch for a young cousin who has been wounded. Most especially, she needs to have a strong barley brew for the boy, because he won't be able to eat solid food for many weeks."

The slave dashed off, and Ningal proceeded to spread an herbal salve on the chest wound and clip it together with ants' jaws. Ezzi was quiet now. He would recover from the chest wounds, for he was young and strong. Nothing, however, could be done about his gouged-out eyes.

The stargazer would gaze no more.

Chapter Eight

*T*he covers blew off her, then she felt the heat of a large, naked male body. Cheftu's smell enveloped her. Chloe buried her head against his chest, and he wrapped his arms around her. She was yet asleep, lost in the delight of sensations when something began to dawn on her. She stretched out her toes, and felt Cheftu's ankles. She opened her eyes, and was right at the crook of his neck and shoulder. "Hey!" she said, pushing him up. "You're tall!"

He braced himself on his elbows and looked down—really down—at her. "I noticed that, too, though it took me a while. At first I thought all the ceilings were low."

She ran her hands over his body, heavily muscled and perfectly proportioned. And much, much larger. "We used to be the same height," she said.

"I grew."

"No kidding."

He kissed the top of her head, just to prove his point. Another thought dawned on Chloe. "Are you uh . . . ?"

"Touch me," he said, the humor gone from his voice.

Heat rushed through Chloe and she pulled his mouth down to hers, while her hands explored the breadth of his shoulders, the V of his back, ran over abs that felt as hard and rippled as a six-pack, and down. "By Sin," she said.

Cheftu groaned, then held her face as he kissed her

deeper. With one move, he plunged inside her and Chloe climaxed, there and then. He chuckled. "Not so fast, *chérie*," he said, then sat back, held her face in his hands, and worked her into a frothing frenzy. He kissed her throat and squeezed her breasts. For Chloe it never ended, each summit only leading to a higher high. His body was slippery, impossible to hold on to, and his every breath made her gasp more.

"Now," he said, pulling her hips closer as she felt him pulsate inside her.

They fell back on the bed, their breathing the only sound in the world.

"Wow," Chloe said after a minute. "Wow."

Cheftu rolled off her, still deep inside. His arm lay across her chest, heavy, and marked with tan lines from bracelets and bands. "I will second that," he said.

"I don't want to fall asleep," she said, blinking away sleep. "We've been apart so long, how—"

Cheftu leaned over her, his face close enough to smell the cinnamon of his breath. The ends of his braids were rough and tickled her bare breasts. "How did you get here?"

"Nimrod got me, like he said."

"He is a good man. How did you come to be in my rooms, though?"

"Anyone who has cleavage can get into the great *en* Kidu's chambers," she said.

"I told them not to admit any women," he said.

"Think about it: Shama," she said and leaned forward to kiss his arm. "I returned the cup to him. Are you sorry to see me?"

"No, no, have you lost your reason? I may not let you up for hours. Days. Months. You may have escaped one kind of death to meet another."

"Starving to death?"

"Are you hungry?"

"Ravenous, but I don't want you to go anywhere."

"There is no need," he said, then reached down for the blanket and covered her to her chin. "Scribe!" he bellowed.

"Are you crazy? What if he discovers me? Who all knows about the substitution?"

A priest stepped to the door. "Bring me food," Cheftu said. "Enough for six."

"Meat, sir? Beer? Bread? Salad?"

"Everything. And wine."

"Of course, sir," he said, and scampered out.

"Who knows who is still alive?" Cheftu asked, putting his arm around her shoulders. "You, me, Nimrod, Rudi, Asa, Ezzi, and, of course, Puabi. And Shama."

"Who knows that I escaped?"

"You, me, and Nimrod. Ningal."

"And Shama."

Cheftu nodded.

"So we just hide here, enjoying room service with a smile?" Chloe said.

"Should enjoy it while it lasts," Cheftu said, moving on top of her, rotating his hips gently. "It's going to last a long time, *chérie*."

"Is . . . this . . . you . . . or . . . Kidu?" she asked in gulps as the pleasure built.

"Do you care?" he said.

"N-n-no," she said. "I—" Conversation became pointless, useless, extraneous, as Cheftu played her body as though he were blind and she were a lyre. He loomed over her, sheltering her, tasting of salt, moving like a piston, adjusting to her every reaction. It seemed they were in a dance, connected at the root and shifting their bodies around that connection. Chloe knew nothing except the blood that sang through her, the reality of slick hard muscle and speechless need.

Again they collapsed in a heap, and this time Cheftu lay

beside her quietly. A breeze from an oven door flowed through the room.

Cheftu's stomach made its presence known.

"Where's that waiter?" Chloe muttered, spread like a starfish across the bed. "Man, it's hot here."

"He left the food outside," Cheftu said. "It was hours ago."

"Am I going to be able to walk?" she wondered out loud.

"If so, I mustn't be doing my job right," he said, swinging his feet to the floor. "Excuse me."

When she woke up again, he was setting a tray on the end of the bed. They'd ripped the sheets from the four corners and tossed pillows to every part of the room. "I ache in places I didn't know I had to ache," she said, sitting up and reaching for a cup.

Cheftu peeled the seal away and opened the jar of wine. Its sweetness perfumed the air. He leaned over and kissed her. "Do you complain, *chérie?*"

"Mmm . . . as you said before, are you mad? I was just going to kill you if you've known that stuff all along."

He sipped his wine and raised an eyebrow. "Wouldn't you like to know?"

"Actually, I don't care where or when you learned it, just don't forget it."

"I won't." The flippancy faded from his eyes, and they reached for each other again, winding like vines together, holding tight. Chloe listened to his heart beat against hers. Perfection.

"It was far worse than standing before a firing squad to have to move your lifeless body," Cheftu whispered. "No food or water, left in the dark."

She shivered. "It was pretty hideous, but the reaction to the drug kept me busy for a while."

"You are so brave, so courageous, my love."

"Not by choice," she said. "And I never, ever want to be in the dark again."

His embrace tightened. "We will sleep with a fire burning every night for the rest of our lives."

She chuckled. "Darkness here is misnamed. There's ambient light. There, it was just nothing. No reflections, not a clue visually. It was like being wrapped in black felt. Muzzy-headed pitch."

"I couldn't have done it."

She remembered the countless visions of worms and rot, maggots and decay, and shivered again. "I wouldn't have thought I could. It doesn't seem like I did. It's so unreal."

"It was real for me," he said. "Leaving you there, hoping you didn't get so sick from the drug that you couldn't function, or that you wouldn't trip and fall, bleed to death on your way out. Then we found some robbers—"

"You caught them?"

"Nimrod did. Did they hurt you?"

"They were so scared by the time they were leaving that had I raised my head, they probably would have thought I was a ghost or demon. At the time, well, I was petrified. How did they survive?"

"Nimrod thinks they were in the chest, drugged to sleep silently. Then they woke up, moved the things, crawled down, raided the tomb, and slipped out."

"How did they know about it?"

Cheftu sighed. "I don't know."

"Did you ask them?"

"They didn't say." His tone was curt, and Chloe let it go. She closed her eyes and reveled in the weight of his body— some of it, anyway—on hers. "Are you hungry?" he asked.

"Yes, but I don't want to let you go."

They fell asleep, and only woke when the drums sounded outside. Cheftu sat up, instantly alert.

"What does it mean?" Chloe asked.

Cheftu was up, half-dressed. "I don't know. I must find out. Eat, I'll be back."

He was out the door again, and she was half-sitting up. The tray sat on the corner and she reached for a plate. Sliced mystery meat, bread, onions, and pea paste. She fell on her dinner with a passion.

~

Nimrod looked at the map, then at Gilgamesh. "Well then, how are the fields around Fara?"

Gilgamesh shook his head. "They've been there since Before; in truth Ziusudra was there. The barley grew to half-size this season. The dirt is frosted with salt."

Nimrod's finger crossed the channel that connected the Euphrates to the Tigris. He was still looking in the Plain of Shinar. "Nippur? Are they open to settlers?"

"Brother, I've told you. Every commonwealth is facing the same problem, from Kish to Eridu. The water dries the fields. The fields aren't producing."

"If there were fewer people, you think that would solve the problem?"

"Less work for the land. Then we could rotate crops and let fields lie fallow? It would help."

Nimrod stared out at the slash of shadow on the wall. "Is the frost another curse from Before?"

"The dying fields? I don't know. Not a stated one, not according to Ziusudra."

Nimrod looked at the map again. "What about farther north, farther from the sea?"

"We have cousins in Agade, almost to the headwaters."

"What of this land in between?"

"It's desert."

"So was this, before irrigation."

"This was marsh, first," Gilgamesh corrected him. "It always had water. Easier to drain water already there, than to coax water into a new place."

Nimrod sighed. "Maybe we should take just artisans and trade for food, avoid the problem completely."

"No fields?"

"No commercial growing. People, individual humans, could have their homesteads if they wanted, but nothing like Ur."

"What happens to your people when the droughts hit? They will, they always do every few years."

Nimrod was silent. "What always happens. People die. People survive." He snorted. "It's in the hands of the gods."

"Truth, surely. How many were you thinking to take?"

Nimrod sat back. "A hundred to start, then add another few hundred in the next season."

"You always wanted to be a *lugal*, didn't you?"

It was a baited question: Gilgamesh, the oldest son of Shem, had been *lugal* in Ur. His rule had been so oppressive that the council had begged Puabi to intercede. She had gone to the mountains with Nimrod to find Gilgamesh a companion to take his mind and energy off whipping the residents of Ur into his idea of efficiency. Nimrod had considered capturing a wildcat, but Puabi had seen Kidu and desired him. After Nimrod had trapped Kidu, and Puabi had used sex to tame the man, they had brought him as a gift to Gilgamesh.

The ploy hadn't worked. So the council had pleaded with Shem to become *lugal* once more. Gilgamesh had left in a rage and gone to rule another commonwealth. Nimrod had seen the conflicts between his father and brother, and decided in his heart what was fair and just. Nimrod must walk carefully around Gilgamesh, however; he needed him at the moment.

"Not here," Nimrod said. "Someplace to start new. I'd

build the staged temple first, to establish the infrastructure that would support a council and community. Provide clothes and grain, order and law."

"Are you ready for the responsibility? Your life is no longer yours, if you become *lugal*."

Nimrod ignored his older brother. "It's probably wild up there yet," he said, pointing to a blank space on the map, just below where the rivers flowed parallel. "The people need a good hunter to keep them safe. Not to mention a defense against raiders."

Gilgamesh looked at the spot Nimrod pointed to. "The people will need a defense against Pazuzu and his demons there. You've pointed to Bab-ili, the gate of the gods."

Nimrod withdrew his finger. "Those tales are nonsense."

"They are from Before; indeed, those are the spirits who haunt the place."

"Have you been there?" Nimrod asked.

Gilgamesh shook his head. "I am brave, but not foolhardy. Monsters inhabit the remains. It is one of the gates to the underworld."

"It's by water," Nimrod said. "Both rivers."

"It's full of ruins from—"

"The fields are probably good."

"You are going to risk your people there?"

Nimrod shook his head. "There is no reason to, I was merely curious."

Gilgamesh sighed with relief. "Were you thinking on leaving soon?"

Nimrod stood. "Yes, now."

"Now?"

"We'd need to get there in time to dry some bricks for housing, plant fields with the winter crops."

"Who is we? Whom are you taking?"

"My family, a few of my men, not many people. But we need to leave immediately."

Gilgamesh nodded. "Before Ur gets back to normal, just make your absence part of the loss of . . . the sacrifices the gods required."

"We need to be there by the cool season."

"What do you want from me?"

"Grain."

Gilgamesh hesitated. "I am not the one who makes that decision."

"In a time of war or persecution, you can make all kinds of decisions. Make that one for me. Give me the grain to start with."

"It will come with a cost," Gilgamesh said at last.

"I expected as much. What?"

"Taxes, brother. I'm going to ask for a percentage of your taxes to see Ur through."

Nimrod glared at his brother. "What percentage?"

"Twenty, not much."

"Five."

"Eighteen."

"Seven."

"Sixteen."

Nimrod groaned. "Ten, my last offer."

"You forget, brother, you are asking from me. Not the other way around."

"You forget also, brother, that ultimately I will be taking hundreds of mouths you would have to feed, away."

"Fourteen."

"Ten."

"Fourteen."

"Ten, I tell you! They will have to pay five to the temple, five to me . . . my people are taxed by 20 percent already!"

"I wouldn't tell them that as you are rallying them," Gilgamesh said, standing up. "Best to wait until they are there, engrossed in your building project, or finished with it, before you tell them about the 20 percent."

"I'm taking my soldiers," Nimrod said. "You won't have a guard any longer. Eleven."

"I'll find some sailors," Gilgamesh said. "Mercenaries are truer because you know exactly what their loyalty costs." He reached out and clapped Nimrod's shoulder. "We don't know each other at all, do we? Twelve it is. For the sake of our father."

"When do I get the grain?"

Gilgamesh sighed. "I'll have it delivered to your house, by dawn tomorrow."

"Twelve," Nimrod said. "Thank you."

"Twelve," Gilgamesh said. "Because you're my brother."

~

"What exactly did the Crone of Ninhursag mean by 'God's Mercy'? Chloe mumbled, mostly asleep. Cheftu cradled her body with his. Neither of them had an ounce of energy left to raise a finger; most of Ur felt the same way, for no sounds issued from the streets. Exhaustion had overtaken the people. That, and sorrow.

Sorrow was the antithesis of Chloe's feelings. Though exhaustion counted. They had both eaten like kings, then burned off every calorie and more. The time with Cheftu blurred together like some delicious erotic dream. Conversation had been limited: hot, but concise.

"Who is she?" he muttered.

"You wouldn't believe me if I told you," Chloe said. "But . . . how did I get here?"

Cheftu snored.

She prodded him with her elbow. She must be tired; that

was the first time she'd touched his stomach and not been drowned in pure, animal lust. "How did I come to be here?"

"Do you remember anything?" he asked. His voice sounded far more awake than she felt. "About Jerusalem?"

"A little. Did I hit my head?"

His hand moved over her scalp, found the ridge of the healing cut. "You did."

"The marsh girl must have, too. That's when we ... merged. I guess."

"Hmmm ..." Cheftu said.

"What do you remember? Why are we here? How did we get here? Why were you so late, or have you been here the whole time? Did I forget—"

"I'd forgotten how you chattered once your belly was full and your tensions were eased," he said.

She waited a minute. "Are you going to answer my question?"

Cheftu kissed the top of her head. He didn't say anything.

"Are you going to tell me?"

He was quiet so long that she almost fell asleep. "There was a fire," he said. "It happened on the spring equinox, which coincided with a lunar eclipse. You were dying. I—" He pressed his lips to her temple. "I begged God to take you anywhere so that you could live, be happy, be fulfilled. You weren't, in Jerusalem. Not happy or fulfilled."

Chloe was very still, listening.

"I waited, I don't know, for hours, listening to you breathe. Then, finally, you slipped away. All I could do was hope."

"How did you get here?"

His chuckle wasn't all that amused. "That was rather a trick. You appeared to have vanished. Witnesses saw me enter the house and not return. No bodies were found. I lived in the catacombs, got what I could for food, prayed a lot. And waited.

The more I thought about it, the more I became convinced that the astrology of our birth dates was involved with the eclipse."

"Was it?"

"I don't know. I haunted the place until there was a blood moon in late spring. I pleaded with God."

She turned then and wrapped herself around him. "You saved my life," she said. "You . . ."

"Ssshh, chérie. You are my beloved. There is no meaning for me without you."

"To them, in Jerusalem, we both just vanished?"

He nodded. "To them, we did."

She was falling asleep again, this time for real. "I want to stay here," she said. "I like this place."

"We're leaving the commonwealth," he said. "We have to. You are quite publicly dead."

She nodded. "But I want to stay with these people, the people who think like this. They're the true originals, Cheftu. The Greeks, the Egyptians, the Renaissance, no one created anything that these people didn't think of first. Probably not even nuclear fission."

"Nook clear what?" he said.

"Nothing, it's just . . . I want to be here. These minds could put us on the moon in the thirteenth century. There's no need for Dark Ages."

He patted her head. "Remind me, I want you to tell me about space someday. What happens with the fire and gas during an eclipse."

"Someday," she murmured as she fell to sleep.

Then she woke up, sharp and alert. "Cheftu, how are we going to get you out of here?"

He sighed. "I have to become quite publicly dead, too."

"Your hair is the most important thing," Chloe said, as they plotted later. "It's beautiful and so identifiable."

Shama nodded. Then he ran into another room. When he came back it was with a wig.

"A wig," Cheftu said. "Agreed. My hair won't be enough to convince them, however."

Shama patted his chest, coughed, then spoke in a voice as raspy as a camel's. "Leave to me. I will do it. Tonight, you go to the temple and be seen. A sign of disfavor will be shown to you. Tomorrow, you will be dead. I myself will attend the body, struck down by the gods. Those viewing will see a healthy man, with hair and beard, already consumed with maggots."

"Tomorrow? Is that enough time?" Chloe asked. She reached out and touched Cheftu's long, golden braids.

Shama nodded.

"I cannot believe you are worried for my hair, *chérie*," Cheftu said.

"You're just so damn sexy," she muttered. "Pure selfishness."

Shama went to his bag and withdrew a long, wicked, metal blade. "Scalp," he said.

"The scalp!"

"No blood." He smiled.

"What about the temple tonight?" Chloe asked him.

Shama smiled and pointed to Chloe, then he waved the wig. "I think I've been nominated to build your wig," she said to Cheftu.

Shama nodded.

She smiled. "Show me how."

The priesthood gathered in the courtyard, a few stragglers from the populace stood outside the tenemos walls.

Rudi and Asa, tall in their star-struck robes, watched from the roof of the stepped temple. A silent lamb was led to the *en*. He placed a hand on its head and bent over it to pray. Lamplight flickered over the gold that covered him from the diadem on his head, to the thousands of beads that tipped his long, braided hair and were woven into his beard, down the sweating strength of his chest to his sword belt, with empty scabbard.

He looked powerful.

While petting the ewe with one hand, he slit its throat with the other. Blood shone on his gold, and the sheep sagged to the ground. "Why does he read the omens?" Rudi asked Asa, as the youngest, least qualified of the augury priests stepped forward. He crouched beside the animal, then slit it from throat to tail. He reached in and removed the liver.

The priestesses sang.

The priest mopped the blood off the liver and moved to stand by a burning lamp. He stared at the organ, then glanced over to his mentor, who stood in the shadows.

Rudi held her breath; the boy's face was white.

"One more," the priest whispered in words that echoed through the courtyard like a shout. "The gods will choose a final sacrifice."

~

Chloe and Cheftu were in the marketplace, bartering for goods the next morning, when the cry rang out: "The *en* is dead! *En* Kidu is dead!"

Like everyone else, they exclaimed in shock and horror. The best place to hide, Chloe had suggested, was in full view. They joined the throng that raced to the tenemos walls.

So they stood—Cheftu shaven-faced and bare-scalped, with dyed eyebrows and lashes, and Chloe, painted fair, a cloak drawn over shoulder and bracelets around her bicep, like a Harrapan woman. Carefully, she balanced their belongings on her head—a useful ancient talent. Cheftu's arm was strong around her waist, though he slumped in order to blend in better.

From within the temple, the cacophony of weeping and wailing washed out to the clients of Ur.

"They must be killing a ewe," one of the nearby Sumerians said. "They'll want to read its liver."

"Who needs to read the liver? The gods weren't pleased with him, so they took him," another said.

"I bet Puabi missed him, so she had the gods call him," a woman said to the men. "What wasn't there to be pleased about?"

"Indeed," Chloe whispered beneath her breath. Cheftu squeezed her waist.

"His job was to keep the populace—"

"The *en* is dead," a priest announced. "The gods sought another sacrifice and have taken his life, willingly, I'm sure. The *en* was a vessel for their powers, and in his death he bows to their wills again."

"You're going to be a saint," Chloe whispered.

Cheftu's look was designed to shut her up. But she didn't see any need for fear; they'd obviously bought the story, completely.

They were home free.

～

"I don't believe you," Gilgamesh said. "The *en*, who was perfectly healthy, and you tell me, already with a female, didn't awaken this morning?"

The acolyte, who had stumbled on the corpse, nodded.

"When did you last see him?"

"With everyone else, sir. At twilight."

"Who else attends him?"

"Shama, sir."

"Puabi's old chamber keeper?"

The acolyte nodded.

"Why wasn't he put to death with her?" Gilgamesh asked.

The acolyte shook his head. "I know not, sir. Perhaps he was a gift to the *en* from the *ensi* Puabi, upon her death."

Gilgamesh turned to Rudi. "The *en* is dead?"

"The gods proclaimed they needed a final sacrifice," she repeated. "We are their servants, sir."

The new *lugal* muttered, "As though I could forget," beneath his breath, and turned to the *en's* chamber door. "Open it," he told the acolyte.

"Shama . . . he, he prepares the body," the acolyte said. "I daren't disturb him."

Gilgamesh set his own hand on the door and pushed it open. Rudi felt ill at the smell—a body well on its way to dissolution.

Gilgamesh covered his nose and mouth, and stepped inside.

Flies swarmed.

Shama was hunched on the ground, his back black with flies, rocking to and fro and moaning. The stench grew stronger as they moved toward the *en's* rooms.

Gilgamesh gently raised the old man to his feet, and had two soldiers escort him from the room.

They looked into the *en's* bedchamber.

The former lover, the toast and envy of Ur, was laid in his robes on a stretcher, ready to be taken to his eternal resting spot. His golden braids were carefully tied into a knot, and the diadem that denoted his authority was seated on his brow. His eyes, once vivid with light, were murky. Rudi didn't look closely at the swelling and squirming of his once-perfect body.

Gilgamesh stared. "It's not possible," he said. "Kidu cannot also be dead."

"The gods took their final sacrifice," Rudi said.

Gilgamesh dragged her closer. "Death is a horror to see," he said. "I should avoid it at all costs."

Rudi tried to look everywhere except the *en's* body. Gilgamesh shook his head as he looked at the wild man. "His corpse is rotting quickly," Gilgamesh said. "Was he this corrupt?"

A worm crawled out of the *en's* nose.

Rudi ran from the room.

She heard the doors close behind her, and Gilgamesh's words: "Prepare his tomb immediately. We'll bury him in a double hour."

～

Ningal listened to Gilgamesh's tale, while the few remaining members of the council shook their heads. Now it would be safe for family members to return, for commerce to begin again, for Ur to rebuild.

Ningal wondered if Chloe and Kidu fled the city already. If they were embracing as they walked along the river's edge, dizzy with relief to be together, to be free? For not a moment had the justice believed the word of the *en's* death. Of course, Kidu had to create that illusion so that he could leave with Chloe. It was the only way for the two of them to be together. Though what the *en* would do for a livelihood, Ningal couldn't guess.

Had she thought of him at all? Why should she? He was an old man who had loved her as best he could. He had to believe, though he hadn't seen, that she had survived the nepenthe, escaped from the death pit, and abandoned Ur.

The real Puabi would return soon. She would select another *en*. The world would continue its forward motion, but Ningal wondered if he would ever feel real excitement and joy again.

"Justice," a woman said, and touched his elbow. "How fares the boy this day?"

He turned to the beautiful, tired face of Shem's widow. Ningal smiled at the light in her eyes. "Ezzi asked for you," he said. "To thank you."

Part Five

THE
JOURNEY

I can't believe we have to walk when there is a perfectly good river, right there," Chloe said. "I was a lady too long. My feet are killing me." She looked up at her flock. "Hey you, back over here!"

Cheftu didn't even glance at her. "That river goes one direction. South. Do you know where we're headed?"

"North," she said crossly, glaring at the recalcitrant Dadi sheep. He always led the flock astray. And they'd only been walking for two days. "I'm getting in the mood for mutton," she said to him. He ignored her words, but rejoined the group.

"The current is too strong to try and fight," Cheftu said.

Chloe paused and watched a *guf* filled with onagers and parcels, piloted by two men, go sailing by. "It looks like a Six Flags ride," she said. They swirled and bobbed on the racing current.

"Do you want to rest?" Cheftu said, halting a few steps away.

She looked behind them at the twisting and haphazard column that followed. "No, we can walk on." The sheep moseyed along, and Chloe herded them. Another skill she had picked up along the way.

The sun was blistering hot, at least 110 degrees in the shade of the palms, but Chloe knew Cheftu wanted to get as much distance between them and the temple as he could before nightfall. It was a precaution, should Gilgamesh or the newly instated Puabi decide to act on any suspicions they might have about the *en's* sudden, mysterious death. Chloe swatted away flies, mosquitoes, and gnats. Trees and water made the heat that much more unendurable—by adding 80 percent humidity.

Even the sheep looked bedraggled.

They trudged on. Cropped fields, interlaced with canals, ditches, and channels carpeted both sides of the river. Palm trees and orchards filled in the narrow islands, the only spaces where emmer, cucumbers, onions, lentils, peas, and barley weren't planted. Even then, on the outskirts of the fields, the soil looked like it was frosted.

Salt.

In modern-day Iraq the Persian Gulf was at least a hundred miles farther south, and she could see the reason why.

Silt. The mouths of the rivers silted up over the centuries, the millennia, putting more and more land on the edge of the gulf. The salinity of the water was cumulative, driving the people farther and farther north in order to find decent soil. "Do we know where we're going?" she asked Cheftu.

He shook his head, and Chloe saw the streaks of sweat running down his back. Fuzz glinted golden on his head already, and Chloe wondered how long it would take for those long braids to grow back. Years probably, if Cheftu's hair grew like hers did—like hers used to.

She'd blamed his hair, his body, for the way she felt: drugged with desire. An exotic and new covering on the soul she loved so much and knew so well, was her excuse. There had to be some reason she couldn't keep her hands off him.

He seemed to feel the same way about her.

It will be a miracle if we make it to wherever Nimrod leads, Chloe thought. Neither Chloe or Cheftu had had even a double hour of sleep since they'd found each other. Cravings ran just too high actually to sleep beside each other. *Is this how a junkie feels?* she asked herself as she swatted a sheep on the rump, encouraging it back into the group. It was insane, but when she touched Cheftu—she had to have him inside her. Usually the sooner the better.

And it *got* better, every time.

I have to stop thinking this way or we won't make it any farther today.

Another *guf* zipped by, the wind blowing the cloth around the sailors' heads. They looked cool, exhilarated. Chloe put one foot in front of the other and felt the sweat drip off the end of her nose.

Ahead, Nimrod walked with his family; his two wives, his brother Roo, who'd been Chloe's classmate, and a mass of sheep, goats, and cattle. Chloe was down to three sheep now. When she'd been listed as being among the "chosen," someone had taken four of her sheep. Mimi, the goat, she couldn't give away. As though he knew she was thinking of him, he turned wicked yellow eyes her way, his jaw moving furiously.

She was still dressed; Cheftu was, too. Who knew what the goat was eating.

"Hya! Hya!" she called, and hustled her livestock forward.

Ahead of her, Cheftu walked in a very short skirt and bare chest.

Oh yeah, it was hot. . . .

Larsa

"From the north to the south, from east to west. Everywhere, there is the taxman."

By dusk, they'd reached the outskirts of a town and a broken dike.

"I've never seen a place so flat," Cheftu said. Because of the flatness, any depth of water made the entire world look flooded, with the exception of the walled commonwealth of Larsa, which rose on the northeastern horizon, built up on generations of clay remains.

Chloe wondered if when she'd woken up in the plain of Shinar, this had been the depth of the water around her—four inches. Except she'd known there were houses and people and animals beneath the water, so it had to have been deeper. Still, this image was chillingly familiar. Flood. "I don't see any animals going two by two," she joked.

Nimrod walked back to them. "It's not that deep. Step carefully. The walls of Larsa protected that commonwealth from the waters, and we can be in the city tonight."

They slogged through the water, which was only calf deep. The sagging heads of barley poked through the surface occasionally, and palm trees, appearing stunted, grew from the blue water. Mosquitoes formed a mist on its face, and Chloe wrapped her head in her top to keep her nostrils and ears from becoming plugged with the incessant buzzing.

The walls of Larsa were wearing away; the brick had only been sun-baked, so sitting in water was starting to dissolve the clay. At the gate, a series of men, dressed in skirts similar to those in Ur, and black-haired or shaved bald, awaited them.

"Greetings," they said to Nimrod. "Where do you journey from?"

"The great commonwealth of Ur," he answered.

"How many are in your party?"

"Male humans?"

"No, everyone."

It took some counting, but with the addition of children and women, they arrived at 63 humans and 109 animals.

One scribe started figuring that, while the first man told them of the sleeping arrangements available. "As you saw, our fields are in dire shape. Most of the freedmen and slaves who live out there had to take refuge within the city walls."

"Is there room for us?" Nimrod asked.

"After a fashion," the man said, then accepted the numbers from the other scribe. "Each of you will owe a 45 percent night-stay tax—"

"That's—!"

"And an additional fee, paid to each of the homes in which you stay, plus payment for food for you and your families, overnight rental space for your animals, the temple tax so the god Ningirsu allows you to stay, and, of course, payment to me and my accountant here for our services."

It was dark now. The moon and stars reflected on the waters that formed a moat around Larsa.

"Forty-five percent of what?" Cheftu asked the man; Nimrod looked like he could strangle him.

"All your estimated wealth. Travelers from Ur, you must be quite well-to-do," he said with a wink and smile.

Cheftu drew himself up. "Then let me be the first to inform you that all the citizens of Ur beggared themselves in order to barter with Sin, who interceded with the sun god, not to destroy us. None of us have anything of value anymore."

"Well," the man said, "that is unfortunate. Either you pay the tax, or you keep walking."

"Where?" Nimrod asked.

"Out of our territory, which is another half day's journey, most of it through water right now. I'll send escorts with you."

"Who will no doubt, need to be paid?"

"Welcome to Larsa," the man said. "Choose quickly, we close the gate in a few minutes."

Nimrod and Cheftu looked at each other. "Would they take sheep in payment?" Chloe asked. "A goat?"

"I wonder if the people inside the walls are taxed like this," Nimrod said. "They should rise up and kill these men!"

"What is our decision?" Cheftu asked.

Water. Possible malaria. Confusion, exhaustion . . . "What if the next commonwealth does the same thing?" Chloe said. "Then what will we do?"

"If they take 45 percent here and now," Nimrod said, "then the next time, 45 percent is considerably less."

"I have an idea," Chloe said. "Barter for us to pay when we leave, and let us stay here a few days. And make sure I get to stay in a place with a big kitchen."

Nimrod nodded as a light dawned in his eyes. "Is Nirg going to want to help you?"

"Oh yeah, I think so."

~

Chloe got to sleep at dawn, and woke a double hour later, feeling refreshed. Cheftu was gone, and she stretched in the not terribly big or comfortable bed. At least they weren't walking today. She'd just opened her eyes when something fell on the bed.

Chloe squealed and sat up.

The snake writhed in the sheets. She screeched and jumped off the bed. The snake, equally alarmed and rudely awakened, slithered off to a corner of the room.

Cheftu threw the door open. "Chloe?"

She stood stark naked in the center of the chamber and stared at the ceiling suspiciously.

"Good day," he said, blocking her from outside view.

"I wonder. A snake just fell on my head."

"Are you hurt?"

She shook her head. "But I'm awake, that's for sure."

"You wanted to know when market day was? Today, it just began."

She scrambled into her dried-out dress and paused to kiss him before she ran out to the makeshift souq stalls. Their whole plan depended on two things: her good cooking and the residents of Larsa's imagination.

Either that, or the Urians would be short a few animals and lose a few months to slavery.

Nirg, Nimrod's silent Aryan wife, walked beside her. "We need sage," Chloe said, "coriander, marjoram, bay leaf, and pepper." Ur's marketplace had had everything—she only hoped Larsa's did.

Compared to the metropolis on the gulf, Larsa was quiet. The market was almost empty of sellers, and the buyers didn't seem to be buying. After she found the perfect cuts of meat, she learned why.

Chloe was wrapping the parcel of venison to tuck next to her pork slab, when a man approached her. He coughed delicately. "Yes?" she said.

"That would be another two minae," he said.

She looked at the butcher.

He raised his hands. "Taxman," he said.

"The whole cut was only four," she said to the taxman. "A 50 percent tax on the meat?"

"Venison and pork? Yes."

"If I got mutton?"

"Fifty percent also."

"Pigeon?"

"Fifty percent."

"A fig?"

"Fifty percent."

"What if I don't have the percentage—I just spent all I had on the meat?"

"Then, I fear, I will have to intercede with the butcher to return half the meat so you can pay your taxes."

Chloe weighed out another two minae and got rid of the taxman. "Would you like a receipt?" he asked, gesturing to his scribe who scribbled furiously on a lump of clay.

"Can I deduct it?" she said.

"From what?"

"No, no receipt." Chloe walked farther down the stalls, and paid more attention. Every shopper paid the vendor, then paid the taxman. Every vendor had a taxman. Nirg related the same thing on her purchases—50 percent tax.

"I'm finished," Chloe said. It was hot already, and she needed to prepare the meat before it turned. "Let's go."

At the archway leading into the market, they were stopped. "Did you enjoy your shopping, ladies?" a man asked.

"No," Chloe said.

"That's too bad," he said. "The two of you, purchasing—" he calculated what they spent, "owe—" he named his price.

"For what? We bought our stuff and we paid our tax! This is unbelievable!"

Nirg laid a calming hand on Chloe's arm. "Why do we pay you?" she asked the man.

"A shopping tax. It goes to maintaining the courtyard, keeping the awnings in good shape, watering the palms that provide ease from the sun."

Chloe looked over her shoulder. The market consisted of patched and pitched awnings that leaned against the walls and three palm trees planted in the center of the plaza. A lump of clay, formerly a staged temple that had lost its facing bricks and experienced too many seasons of water, huddled to the side of the market. Three other people shopped, cautiously.

"You're going to kill the economy," she said. "If people

can't shop, then they won't, which will put your vendors out of business here. Everyone will start going someplace else to get what they need."

"They do," he said. "We just tax them when they return."

Chloe exchanged glances with Nirg; she didn't have anything else that could be considered "cash." "This has been a terrible day," she said to the taxman. "It started when a snake fell on my head. Now my meat is going to go bad, and I will have wasted all my time and money. If you want to tax me, you can follow me home." She walked away. Nirg followed. The man shouted at them, but didn't pursue.

They reached the gates of the estate where half of the group was staying, without meeting any more taxmen.

After washing their hands, Chloe and Nirg tore into the meat. Nirg, an expert with a metal blade, started chopping— Chloe added the spices.

"Where did you learn to do this?" Nirg asked. "It is not a food of the Black-Haired Ones."

"No, it's not," Chloe said.

"Then again, you are a foreigner, like me."

Nirg's hair was the color of a Florida beach, and her eyes were azure blue. Next to Nimrod she looked like an Olympic swimmer, with broad shoulders and a muscular body.

"Yes, I am," Chloe said. She remembered a little of the marsh girl's life. Enough to know that her mom was a black woman—a Khamite—and her dad was fair. "Did you grow up in the mountains?" she asked Nirg.

"Yes, with the people of Kidu's tribe. We ate food like this, but we put it back in the intestines and smoked it. For hunting."

Anything that went back into the intestines was gross, Chloe thought. *How could you ever get it clean enough . . . don't go there.* "It makes it easy to eat," she said. "Bite-sized."

Nirg's strong fingers mixed in the herbs. Then Chloe added the cheese—not the cheese she'd known—preshredded cheddar—but the only slightly hard cheese she could find. Then flour and a little bit of leavening, some milk and salt.

Together they mashed it into a mass, then divided it into greasy little balls. Chloe watched the fire and when she thought it approximated 375 degrees, they put the trays in and closed the door to the oven.

Nirg excused herself, and the heat of the day wore on. *August,* Chloe thought. *It's August and I'm slaving over a hot stove outdoors.* "I'm certifiable," she muttered to herself, and went to sit under the lone palm. The garbage pile was opposite her, so she pinched her nose and closed her eyes.

She jolted awake and checked on her concoction. They were still baking, not quite ready yet. Chloe wiped the sweat off her forehead, then squelched a yelp when she was yanked into the shade.

"Now," he said as he lifted her up and leaned her against the tree. Chloe gasped as Cheftu entered her. She locked her ankles behind him and held on to her tree above her head. "Silence," he whispered. She clenched the bark of the tree and gritted her teeth as ecstasy unfolded within her. Her head was spinning, her eyes were shut, her hands became claws as she fought to be quiet. Cheftu's mouth was on her neck, her breasts, sucking the air from her lungs. Then he held her tight, his lips on hers, and she opened her eyes to see his, unfocused and glazed as he trembled inside her. She put her arms around his neck and whispered in his ear. "I love you."

His only reaction was a hiccup, then his grip loosened. "Your food is going to burn." he said.

"My balls!" she cried, and pushed him away. Tugging her skirt into place, she raced to the oven and opened it. They were just about perfect, brown and sizzling.

"What's that smell?" the man of the house said, as he

closed the door behind him. Chloe just smiled. Her plan was going to work.

∽

The taxman looked at her. "You are paying your 45 percent by giving me a recipe for food?"

"No," Chloe said. "I'm paying my 45 percent by franchising my recipe to my hosts until the payment you claim we, from Ur, owe, is completed. Then they will pay me for the use of the recipe."

"What is the recipe?" he asked.

"That," Chloe said, pointing to her creation, the cooled brown balls nestled in a bowl. "Taste it."

"I don't think this is going to be acceptable," he said. "We need our high taxes to afford to buy what our fields can't grow."

"If you will allow my hosts to buy their supplies at a discounted tax, then they will be able to make more money, which means you will get more tax in the long run, instead of mina-ing them to death right now. Which means you can buy more, when the crops are bad."

"They're always bad," he muttered. "What is it?" he asked as he held one of them up. "What do I call it?"

"Just bite it. It won't kill you."

He sniffed it. "I've never smelled such a thing."

"No, I doubt you have."

"What's in it?"

"Fresh food that's good and good for you." Not exactly a lie.

He looked over her shoulder at the assembly who waited: those from Ur; their hosts; and a few ubiquitous tax collectors.

He bit. He groaned. He fanned his mouth.

Chloe pushed a jar of beer toward him.

"By Ningirsu! That must be what the court of heaven dines on! That—is there more?"

"My hosts," Chloe said, beckoning for them to step forward, "need a third partner. If you wanted to underwrite them in this business venture, then they would be able to feed you this recipe."

"If I don't?"

"Then the people of Ur are willing to offer you ten sheep, fourteen woolen cloaks, and a new hoe," Nimrod said. "That will be our payment, in total."

The taxman looked back at Chloe. "How do I know that what you give them will be the same as what I've eaten? You might keep the . . . what did you call it, recipe? For yourself."

"No, and I'll tell you why. Every major metropolis in the land of the Black-Haired Ones is going to sell these. A different person in each town will make them. The trick is, you'll know it's my recipe because of this." She picked up a stylus and motioned for the ever-present scribe to hand over his tablet.

"A snake fell on her bed this dawn," one of the hosts offered to the taxman while Chloe drew. "It's a good omen. How can you ignore such a clear sign from the gods?"

With a hand trained in advertising, expert at copying and aware of how confusing this was going to be to any Sumerologist, Chloe drew two connected curves. "Everyone who sells these balls will show this sign for authenticity. Imagine it in yellow on a red background."

"Golden arches?" he said, looking at the image.

She looked up at the taxman. "Trust me, you want to be part of this. It's going to make history."

Uruk

"Pay heed to the word of your mother, as though it were the word of a god."

"Nothing, *lugal*," the aide said.

Asshur paced, enjoying the flow of energy and heat through his legs and back. The early sun was warm already; the afternoon would be sweltering. He didn't look at the drying canals; they just irritated him and made him worry more. "Tell me what happened, exactly."

The aide referred to his tablet. "Your surveyors followed the path of the rivers—"

"Yes?"

"Until it reached the mountains—"

"Just as Ziusudra said—"

"Yes, *lugal,* and the tablets in the library referred to the same location."

Asshur turned and looked at the man. "And? Tell me. What did they find?"

"Nothing, *lugal.*"

"The stories are wrong? Those from Before told falsehoods?"

"No, *lugal.* The sources are missing."

"We have the rivers, yet."

"The glaciers are gone, *lugal.* You can drink the water, cold."

"The stories say you can't drink the water unless it is warmed, without great pain."

The aide nodded. "Which is why Lud concluded that there is nothing there."

Asshur turned away, until he could control his expressions again. It was part of the job of *lugal* to remain stalwart and unflinching, so as to give the people strength. Maybe Lud was too old; maybe Asshur should have sent someone else. "Did anyone go farther up into the mountains, to see if the glaciers, the water, was there?"

The aide jostled through his tablets. "I believe, oh here it is."

Asshur held his breath, waiting for the man's words.

"They went into the snow, *lugal*. The very ice is changed."

"There must be other sources! The rivers can't both come from one small location! Where is Lud?"

The aide watched him with an impassive expression. "Lud left two surveyors behind, to monitor the waterfalls."

Asshur bowed his head. Of course Lud would; he, more than anyone, knew what the loss of that water would do to future generations. The list was long. Already Asshur saw young women strutting around, full with child. So many of them. He looked out the doorway again, onto the city, forcing the fear to melt away. Impassive and strong, that was his image. But this was too important; on this one topic, his logic and reasoning fled, and all he felt was panic and worry.

Panic and worry were the two things he should avoid, for they brought age and illness. "What about the attempts at re-creating it?"

"Ima works her way down the list. The last addition of copper to the experiment served no purpose."

Asshur inhaled deeply and flexed his chest and arms. More weights, he must push his body more, eat less, sleep less, and get back to his potter's wheel to soothe his soul. "Very well. Thank you, Ukik."

"I'll bring the next update when Ima finishes it."

Asshur felt hope bloom in his chest as he looked over his shoulder. "When will that be?"

"Tonight, a double hour before midnight. That is her estimate."

Asshur's gaze rested on the courthouse, where the finest men and women he knew waited, administering justice, building a worthy city and culture . . . to leave it to children raising children on top of children. "What is next?" he asked.

"Your schedule? You start with negotiations. Then you have a meeting with the engineers to discuss alternatives to the canal issue."

Asshur nodded.

"Later you have a council meeting, which will take up the remainder of the afternoon."

"Very well, I'll see you in chambers."

The aide bowed, a sign of deference that Asshur felt was unnecessary, but much better than obeisance, a choice of other communities. And there might come a day when Asshur needed all of the respect, real or feigned, that he could raise. So he would let people bow. *Oh gods,* he thought as he stared at the city. The door closed behind Ukik, the draft moved the bottom of Asshur's beard, and tickled his navel.

"*Lugal,* your breakfast," Harta, who had just taken him to husband, called. He stepped inside, momentarily chilled away from the sun, and sat at the table. She had prepared, according to his family's traditions, a small meal. Asshur never ate more than fit in his palm, and that he ate with careful bites, pondering: the way the seed had fallen to ground; the time it took to take root and grow; the season it had weathered the heat and rising river; the hands that had harvested it and prepared it for his table.

Today, as he promised himself, he ate even less.

When he finished his food, he drank his water. Not water like his forebears had had, but ordinary river water, purified through heating. He drank until he felt full, then washed his face, his tongue, and donned the clothing a citizen, every citizen of the city, wore.

His only concession to being the leader was his horned hat, just one horn on either side of the white-wool cone that covered his shaved head, for he was only a mortal. The gods' similar hats had several horns. Harta moved slower than he was used to seeing, and she looked worn, tired. "How was Dor?" Last night had been her evening with her second husband. Asshur was her third.

Harta was fertile, so she was married to several men. Asshur hoped the next seed that took root would be his, but who could know. One woman for many men was a safe way to establish an economy—and hinder population growth. "He was well," she said, kissing Asshur's neck as she cleaned away the dishes. "I'm off to the shop."

She went into his room and came back with a linked necklace, heavy gold with inserts of green stones. "For you," she said, handing it to him. "For today, your meeting. It's good luck."

Asshur didn't speak; he was too touched. He lifted his hair so she could fasten the necklace. She kissed him again, and he held her there. "I missed you this dawn," he said, immediately regretting the weakness. They hadn't been married long; still, he hated to complain. "Thank you for the gift."

She pulled back, her smile was wan but some of the tension was gone from her shoulders and neck. "Just another reason to keep a granddaughter of Tubal-Cain around." He stiffened, and she withdrew. They made no promises for twilight, and Asshur felt that lack as the door closed behind her.

~

"I don't remember sausage balls in Jerusalem," Cheftu said. Rather, he complained. They were on the road again, if the narrow pathway that ran beside the brackish river could be dignified by the term "road." The sheep ran in front of them, the immigrants from Ur stretched out behind them. The sun glared from above, and Chloe wished she had caterpillar eyebrows. "Why don't I remember them?" Cheftu said.

"We never ate them," she said. "It was hard to buy pork and venison, you may recall. Lamb isn't fatty enough."

"Are they a food from your past?" he asked.

"Definitely. For hunting trips or football games, which amount to almost the same thing. They travel well, they're filling and easy to make. My brother, who never picked up a gun, and my father, who adored guns, and both men, who disliked each other, would endure the pretense of quail season just to eat Mimi's sausage balls." She didn't think she could explain Thanksgiving Day and its attendant American traditions—including the food.

"It's extraordinary that you can make something from that world, in this world. I never thought you were that much of a cook."

"Cheftu!" she said, halting.

He glanced back at her. "Ah! Forgive me, I didn't mean it that way."

"Did you starve?"

"Well—"

"Okay, after it took me the first six months in Jerusalem to learn how to make bread, did you starve?"

"I am here," he said.

Noncommittal rat, she thought with a smile. "In my time, sausage balls had three ingredients: sausage, cheddar cheese and Bisquick."

"Bees-queeck?"

"A shortcut for busy women who still wanted to make biscuits. I don't know. I just know it was the hardest thing to figure out in ancient times, what was IN Bisquick. That's where learning how to bake really *great* bread—ahem—"

"Excellent," Cheftu said on cue.

"—bread helped me out."

"And in your country, are those golden arches for the ownership?"

Chloe laughed. "Someday that trademark is going to be everywhere." She looked at Cheftu's furrowed brow. "We'll talk about trademarks some other time too." And whether or not the trademark being "everywhere" was a good thing or a bad thing. McDonald's as the true ambassador of American culture could be interpreted in many ways.

"Good," he said. "Tell me about space? I know what you said before, about the moon, the gases and fire, but tell me more."

Their hosts had told them to rub basil, which grew in the fields, on their exposed skin, and the bugs wouldn't bother them. With basil-scented bodies, the annoyance factor of their journey was down. Still, it was unspeakably hot, even walking in the shadow of the palms.

"Space?" she repeated, and walked along. What else did she know about space?

What was that Stanley Kubrick movie . . . *2001*?

Relating that should kill an afternoon.

"Have I ever told you what a computer is?"

Asshur picked at the fruit in front of him. "Do we have any alternatives? Make a list."

"We could buy grain and vegetables from other markets, places where they have excess," his merchantman cousin suggested.

"Great concept, but no one has excess. Ur, the richest of us all, is almost starving."

"They'll survive, they always do."

"Do we have any other sources for water other than the rivers?" Asshur asked.

"Is that a different list?" the scribe asked him.

The *lugal* nodded.

"If we could remove salt from the water, we would control our destinies," the stargazer said.

"Does anyone know that secret?" Asshur asked.

"No, if they did they would need only to sell it to every commonwealth," another merchantman said. "They would be established for generations with the profit."

Asshur picked the seeds of the fruit. "Perhaps that is a solution the Tablet Houses could pursue?"

"My liege—"

"Don't call me that. I hate it when you say that," Asshur said to Nia—his former wife. They shared a daughter.

She dropped her almond-eyed gaze, the same one his little girl had. "Very well. We're seeing problems in the Tablet Houses."

Asshur looked up, then glanced at the other representatives of Tablet Houses. They all nodded. "The students aren't interested in education much past the age of twenty-five," Nia said.

"I had a student the other day who was wedded at thirty," someone offered.

"What of her poor husband?" one of the farmers asked.

"He was twenty-five."

"Already she'd received her cycle?" another questioned.

"As the Fathers said, our days will soon be only 120 years," the vintner reminded them.

The whole group, every one of whom was over that age, sat silent.

"They are grown too soon. From twenty to eighty, to have children? Eighty is barely old enough to birth two children. Their life spans are going to be a ninth of what our fathers knew."

"We are doomed," someone else contributed.

"It was foretold," Lud said.

Asshur picked at the flesh of his fruit and concentrated on calming himself. "The Tablet Houses are not a possibility, then?"

"I fear not, *lugal*," one of the priests said.

Any hope of calm fled. They had to find the water, they had to stop the raging growth of the people, their speedy reproduction, their waste.

Every day the problems of Uruk, the most ancient city of the Shemti, just grew.

And more were conceived.

~

"Uruk," Cheftu said, staring out the window at the city. "Something pricks my memory, but I can't get to it."

Chloe slipped beside him, draped his arm over her shoulder. Uruk was about a hundred miles outside of Ur—they were sister cities. Gilgamesh had been *lugal* there before being recalled to replace his father as *lugal* in Ur. Consequently, Nimrod and his coterie were being treated like royalty. Chloe and Cheftu were staying in the palace, a more colorful and dazzling building Chloe hadn't seen in ancient Iraq.

"Uruk," she said. "I don't know, it doesn't sound familiar to me. Do you know when we are, what year it is now?"

He shook his head and sighed. "No, I don't. Before these Black-Haired Ones had interaction with Egypt—if Egypt exists yet. Someday, this will be Babylonia, but how many millennia until then, I don't know."

"Everyone talks about the Deluge—are they talking about Noah?"

"No, a man named Ziusudra, and his story has multiple gods and immortality in it. Noah, he just gets drunk and is humiliated by his sons," Cheftu said. "Not the same story. The names aren't even close."

He continued to speak. "So many things Kidu knows, that I don't. It's as though there wasn't enough space in my mind for all the knowledge, so I lost a lot of it to make room for his."

"You don't remember the Bible?"

"Not details. The capacity I had for remembering anything I ever saw in writing is gone."

"Changing bodies made you lose your photographic memory," she said. "That's . . . odd, I guess."

He hugged her to his side. The staged temple of Uruk was directly opposite them. Thus far they hadn't seen a taxman. "Dinner is purported to be an occasion tonight," he said. "Do you want to bathe?"

She slipped an arm around his waist. "Alone? Or will I have company?"

"*Chérie*, when you touch me, I am a madman," he growled. "We need to discuss something, however."

She knew what was coming. She nodded, and they walked to two chairs, then sat down, facing each other. Cheftu leaned forward and took her hand in both of his. "It's late summer, early autumn."

"Yes."

"December, 23 December approaches."

"It happens every year."

He gave her a look for her levity. Chloe forced her face into mock-seriousness. "What are you trying to say?"

"I . . . my," Cheftu stopped, and shook his head. "I do not think this is because of the creature whose body I have, but it is undeniable." He looked at her. "All I want to do is make love with you. I want to take you in every way, to bend you to my desires—"

Chloe could barely think, she was so aroused by his words.

"—make you swell with my child. Our child," he amended.

Silence. Not awkward, but steaming.

"Such a thing, I know we both realize, was not possible before. You, me, the combination, the time, it was not our destiny to be parents, yes?"

"Truth," she said. A word from Ur that was so useful. "That is true."

"We are now, both of us, in new husks, and before we—"

She looked at him. Despite the movie matinee façade, he was still her careful, honorable, precise, emotional and God-fearing spouse. "If I get pregnant, then we'll be stuck here, and you want to know if that is all right with me. If not . . . you're going to get us bunk beds?" she said.

"I understood most of that," he answered in his heavily accented English. "But . . . what is bunk beds? You lose me in your native tongue."

And I always speak it when I'm nervous, she thought. *Even after seven years of living anywhere but the U.S.* "I want to tell you that it doesn't matter—"

"I don't want you to feel trapped here. Do you remember Jerusalem?"

Chloe felt a pang and remembered standing alone at the well, hearing whispers about how God hadn't blessed her, but had made her barren. She recalled how friend after friend had become pregnant while her stomach had stayed flat. The rest-lessness Chloe had felt as she wandered the streets of the bur-geoning city, alone. A woman's life shouldn't be judged by whether or not she's a parent, she'd argued.

But it didn't stop the whispers . . . what has she done for God to curse her? Will good Cheftu take another wife? Let's not invite her, she doesn't understand what we're talking about . . . God has rejected her.

And month after month she would wait so hopefully, count off the days—and have her dreams dashed again. Family was denied her; her family in twentieth-century reality, and a new family with Cheftu.

"What about Jerusalem?" she asked. Her memories were vivid, but it was like revisiting a movie. It seemed unreal and a step removed. "Why didn't I like it? Why wasn't I happy there?"

Cheftu's grip on her hands changed, he rubbed his big thumbs over her knuckles.

"Every day, you saw women losing position. You saw violence growing. You told me that the people were turning more inward and less outward. We were watching the beginning of nationalism, *chérie*. There is no room for compassion toward others when a country is feeding itself the theory it is the best, the select, the only."

He didn't realize the ache her heart had known; and there had been no substitute for having a family in that society. A woman was named after her children, "The mother of Rebecca, or the mother of Shaul." There wasn't room for a career woman. And as a visual artist in a city that prided itself on no images, there wasn't much work. David had dismissed his female soldiers, for he needed more little Israelites.

"How do we know it won't happen here?" Chloe said, suddenly filled with fear. "That we won't make the decision to stay, anchor ourselves so we can't leave, then . . . the same thing? You're supposed to get more conservative as you age. I think I'm getting more liberal."

He lifted her hand to his lips. "Your heart is growing, my love. You see the world beyond yourself. Many people never do." He kissed her fingers, and the heat of his mouth, the softness of his tongue, brought their initial topic to bear.

I'm shaking I want him so bad, she thought. *And I want him for him, not for any other reason, not for anything that might result from it other than being with him.* "Now that we discussed this," Chloe said in a rush, "the truth is, I don't care. If it happens, it does, if it doesn't—just get your clothes off and—"

And he did.

~

Ima looked over at him, without actually moving her eyes. Asshur was never completely prepared to be in her presence. Since childhood, his beautiful cousin had unnerved him. That she had no need for men, or for children, confused him. Most of the women he'd known, cousins and sisters included, held their breath waiting for those things, once past their training. Ima, never.

Always, she was in the scroll room. Reading tablets in the library. She had the blood, the disposition of their ancestors. Age hadn't touched her, or infirmity. Her mind was wiser, sharper than it had been, and her body—

Asshur could immerse himself in Harta's athletic, energetic body, but Ima's was the form in his dreams. She stood as tall as most men, without the curves of most women; nor did she shave her head for wigs. Instead, her black hair fell like water over her shoulders and down her back. The edges of her eyes were creased from squinting into the sun for so many decades, but her eyes themselves were dark and thickly lashed. Her mouth was wide, but thin-lipped, her face sharp at the chin and nose. Thin eyebrows, hopelessly out of fashion, rose in points so that she always looked surprised.

"How are you, Asshur?" she asked. She was surrounded

by tablets, the same way a wrecked sledge scattered its contents around the site of impact. Cross-legged in her chair, with a bronze drinking tube close enough to lean into, she reminded him of a feline. Creases between her brows—lines of determination, according to the seer who analyzed faces—had drawn themselves on her face since last Asshur had seen her. "Or is the fact that you are *lugal* indication enough?"

He laughed and wondered if he should step inside her chamber as a cousin or request her to treat him like a ruler.

"Are you too important to sit for some beer?" she asked, and he saw a glimmer of humor in her eyes.

"Never," he said as he walked in. Ima called for beer to her assistant and offered him another chair. "How is the research?"

"You see Ukik. He tells you my results before I'm even certain of them," she said. "What more do you want to know?"

Asshur wove his fingers together in his lap. "Is there anything to lend hope?"

The assistant brought a jar of beer and gave Asshur a drinking tube. The beverage was cool, refreshing, but Asshur remembered that he shouldn't be consuming it. Any relaxation of his standards could lead to demise. He sat back and watched Ima drink down half the jar. The concentration on her face, the effort he saw, was discomfiting. Asshur shifted in his chair.

Thankfully, Ima leaned back and wiped her mouth with the back of her hand. "I had hoped Lud would bring the answer."

Asshur waited.

"In my studies, I can't find anything yet to produce the same effect. Combinations that make the water cloudy, as it is supposed to be, assure that it can still be drunk cold. What makes it agitate, again, as eyewitnesses claim, doesn't make it milky. It is an association of several elements, and each one must be tried alone, then when we find that—"

"You'll add the other element, the other thing."

She nodded. "Regarding other things, have you pursued the legend?"

Asshur sat back. "It's an old mothers' tale," he said. "Just like the nonsense that the underworld can be reached from a cave in the center of town."

Ima's eyes narrowed. "My grandmother was a wise woman, she wouldn't have told untruths."

He shook his head. "I cannot believe, it doesn't stand to reason, that the First Father knew that the world would be destroyed once by flood, once by fire. So he commanded the stories to be inscribed on two standards. One was brick, the other stone, so at least one would survive."

"Maybe he knew the water would change?"

"So he wrote the location of the source? Or perhaps the formula for creating it?" Asshur reached forward as though to pat Ima's arm, but didn't. "You are a woman of science. The First Father lived in a cave, his son was a murderer, what could he know of writing, or mapmaking, or even the concept of time? He was an ignorant ancient."

"We are any better?" Ima asked. *"Dust we began and to dust we return, the white dust for our bones and veins, the green for our pale skins, the black for our bowels and red, for the life of us, the blood."*

Asshur could recite it with her, an oft-told saying, practiced in the Tablet House until one could write it like the Tablet Father. "We are made of the same thing as the First Father, but we have journeyed so far beyond him," he reasoned.

Ima turned away from him. "Perhaps the seers know something."

"They are too young, none of them born before the Deluge."

"Have you thought to seek out Ziusudra?"

"He wouldn't speak to his own sons about this, why should he converse with me? I'm just the son of a son."

She reached over and touched his arm. Even through his despair, Asshur felt his body leap. "You are elected to get us through this time, not to save us. To guide us, Asshur. You don't have to know all of the answers. You're merely a shepherd."

He wanted to touch her hand, but he mustn't. Her choice had been to live apart from men, to live in the world of research and information and not dilute that with the responsibilities of a home or family. He had accepted Harta. "Do you ever regret it?" he asked.

She withdrew her hand. "I must prepare for tomorrow's classes. Because, while to you I am a thinker and a cousin, to twenty-five boys, I am Nergal come to winnow through them."

He laughed as he rose, eager to leave. "I remember that drawing you did of our Tablet Father, with the scythe of Nergal."

"I have been repaid that insult," she said with a chuckle. "Time and over, I have been the object of that drawing."

"How nice to tell them they aren't original," he said, as they stood on the threshold. "Good lessons," he wished her.

"I'll let you know when I have anything," she said. "I'll send Ukik."

"You don't have to wake him," Asshur said.

Her gaze was cool. "He's here now."

"Ukik?"

She nodded. And said nothing else.

Asshur mumbled something and fled. He needed to think about his guests, not about aged cousins who lived with their young aides.

~

They were seated in the temple, so that the patron goddess of the city, Inana, could participate in the feast. It was two temples, actually, placed at right angles. Between them was a courtyard with a wall of bright mosaic cones in black, white, and red zigzag. One side of the courtyard led to a terrace lined with massive columns adorned with shell and mother-of-pearl rosettes.

Low tables, lush flowers, sheepskin-covered pillows and metal drinking tubes completed the feeling of complete luxury. Chloe and Cheftu reclined next to each other—another place where men and women ate together, Chloe thought. In the Middle East. When did this practice go out? It was way gone by the time David of Jerusalem had shown up. Who was responsible for that step backward?

Lyras played softly in the background. Asshur was the new *lugal* here, the man responsible for the feast, Gilgamesh's successor. Fish of every description were served, complete with eyes. The marsh girl's knowledge told Chloe it was a sign of respect to show the eyes of the catch. Then the guest would know how fresh the fish was.

Chloe's fish's eyes confirmed he'd been caught an hour before he'd landed on her plate, no more. *Now if I could just cover him up,* she thought. Bread, stacked, formed a ziggurat in the center of the table. Vegetables stewed with spices, broiled with oil, and layered with cheese and baked were presented on colored plates. "Hard to believe that in Ur they're hungry," she whispered to Cheftu.

"Not terribly hungry," he said. "If the city's population decreased enough, everyone would be fine. Maybe enough people fled."

"Okay, then hungry in Larsa."

"When you've left them the wonders of sausage balls?"

"Don't be sarcastic."

"Me, *chérie?*" he said, as he drew her hand up his thigh.

"Cheftu!"

"I'm a lunatic where you're concerned. I warned you."

"Drink your beer."

"It'll just make it worse, later," he said.

"Good," she said, and gave him a wicked smile.

He threw back his head and laughed.

At the end of the meal, Nimrod's responsibility was to bestow gifts on Asshur. Those from Ur had pooled their resources that afternoon. In the mix, Asshur was going to receive an expectant sheep and a goat. Dadi and Mimi were going to be parents. It was really rather twisted.

But, finally, Chloe was ridding herself of the goat.

Nirg was handing over an ivory comb, Nimrod was giving up a lion's skin cloak, Cheftu donated three gold necklaces, and the various other women, guards, and children were casting something of value into the community pot.

Asshur expressed delight at his gift and promised a percentage—once the taxmen had done the math—would go to Inana. "Though," he said, "we could arrange a little . . . competition now. Wager with these gifts you've given me."

Nimrod didn't look at Cheftu, but Chloe could sense he wanted Cheftu's input. They communicated without speech, most of the time. How that happened, she didn't know, but it seemed to go with the extra shot of testosterone Cheftu exhibited these days. And the long history the two men shared.

Nimrod was still smiling. "What type of competition?"

"A sacred wrestling match. A bowl."

Chloe paused, her cup halfway to her mouth. Surely not: Was this the first bowl? The Palm Bowl? The Mosaic Bowl? The Inana Bowl?

Nimrod sipped his beer. "Who would be the opponents?"

"A champion of your people against a champion of mine."

"Thus we would win back our host gifts or you would keep them? That hardly seems a wager," Nimrod said.

"Agreed. Instead, you could win back your host gifts or . . . we get to keep three of your people as slaves."

Quiet, disturbed only by the rustling of the wind in the fronds above them.

"How long would the slavery last?" Nimrod asked.

Cheftu hadn't appeared to be less interested in the amount of food he was consuming, but Chloe knew he was watching everyone and noting every expression. She had a sickening feeling who the "champion" might be.

"The slavery? Oh, nothing serious, a few months. Until the end of the season perhaps."

"Anyone in mind?" Nimrod said, gesturing to the men and women who were his.

"She would be a lovely addition," he said, pointing to one of the guard's girlfriends. "Maybe that man there, he seems to be light on his feet. And her—"

Cheftu froze.

Chloe stared into the dark eyes of the man with the crown.

Nimrod laughed. "I am afraid we have no agreement," he said. "Keep your gifts, with my blessing." He made as though to rise; Asshur didn't move.

Tension settled more thickly on the table. Cheftu had set aside yet another *poisson* skeleton and had washed his fingers in the scented water beside him. He watched Asshur like a very large, barely tamed cat. Chloe swallowed silently. *Let's get out of here,* she thought. *I don't like these games. And we don't want the goat back.*

"Let me sweeten the offer," Asshur said to Nimrod. "If you win, you get all you gifted to me returned, plus 200 percent more. Paid in seed and grain."

Bull's-eye, Chloe thought. Seed and grain were really the only things they needed. Ur hadn't had much to spare, obviously, and no other city was selling grain and seed. Asshur must truly want new slaves, she thought. *They needed that grain.* But did Asshur get it from his fields? They hadn't looked very healthy.

Nimrod shook his head. "Impossible."

"Who is your champion?" Cheftu asked Asshur.

Asshur stared at him. "I am."

The man had biceps like ham hocks and thighs the size of . . . Chloe drew a blank. Big, big and brawny. He wasn't as tall as Cheftu, but he had to outweigh him. "Don't do it," she muttered to Cheftu.

"Are you the champion for *lugal* Nimrod?" Asshur asked Cheftu.

"I am," Cheftu said resolutely.

Chloe sent a pleading glance to Nimrod, but he ignored her.

"Do we have a deal?" Asshur asked, and looked at Chloe. Deliberately. Up and down. I'm the ante, she thought.

Nimrod and Cheftu spoke simultaneously. "We do."

～

There wasn't time to prepare, to talk, to discuss, to plan. The bowl began then and there. A priest, the "bowl master," ran up on the portico and drew a circle on the pavement. Cheftu and Asshur stripped down to loincloths.

Asshur was enormous, especially for this day and age. But he wasn't young. Chloe couldn't begin to guess how many years he had. She had gotten as close to him as she wanted to. Cheftu had retreated into another world, a mental world of competition. He rose from the table, took his place, and never once looked at her.

This must be the Kidu part, Chloe thought. *He would never risk me otherwise. He's out of his ancient mind.* Asshur leered at her, and Nirg stepped closer to her side, protective.

"The rules are as follows," the bowl master said to the two men. "You mustn't step out of the circle.

"You will compete for as long as you both can stand."

Cheftu's gaze flickered over Asshur's body, but Asshur refused to give Cheftu the same respect.

"You must have both hands on the opponent at all times."

Cheftu's face was inscrutable.

"No one must be killed."

That was good.

The bowl master brought out the jars. "To win, you must break your opponent's jar, and yours must remain unbroken."

The citizens of Uruk cheered. Asshur knelt, and the jar was placed on his head, atop the crown, and tied around his chin. Cheftu's jar made him at least six-foot-six, but Chloe could tell the strain his body was enduring already. The veins of his neck bulged as Cheftu tried to move.

The bowl master slowly drew Asshur and Cheftu into the circle.

"May Inana decide," he said, and placed Cheftu's hands on Asshur's arms and Asshur's hands on Cheftu's arms. "Begin when the music starts."

The two men were a head's width apart. Cheftu had only the advantage of height, which was no advantage because that meant his jar was proportionally taller and that much more unstable. The flutist began and Asshur pushed at Cheftu. He recovered his balance quickly and pressed against Asshur. The singers started, a soft melody, accented with chimes.

Like a boxing match set to Enya, Chloe thought.

Both bodies glowed with sweat, and Asshur seemed to be waiting. Cheftu held on, his muscles shifting and swelling beneath his sweaty skin. Cheftu's grip looked like it was getting harder, and he'd slipped his leg between Asshur's feet, as he tried to trip him. Asshur slammed his head, consequently his jar, against Cheftu's. The crowd roared above the gentle music, and the high notes of the singers.

"What did you say?" Asshur said to Cheftu, panting from the effort.

Probably something in French or Egyptian or English, Chloe thought. Her own hands ached from clenching her folded arms.

Cheftu pushed him, hard. "Nothing." Sweat from his face fell onto Asshur's arms, and the *lugal* slid his hands up to Cheftu's clavicle. The only way Chloe could see for someone to win was to snap the breastbone of your opponent, then as he fell, kick his jar. Or to kick high and catch it at a moment he was unaware.

Cheftu's attention and exertion were unflagging. His breath was heavy, his body wet, but he was unmoved.

The clapping of the crowd spurred Asshur on. He pushed at Cheftu, forced him backward.

Cheftu gave way, and Asshur fell forward almost two steps, unsteady with the jar on his head. Cheftu struck out with his jar at Asshur's, but the latter turned his head. The glancing blow left both men stunned. For a moment they clung to each other, not in combat, but in an effort to stay upright.

They pressed each other, and the singers' voices rose into the silence. The crowd no longer cheered; they watched with fear.

～

Neither man was winning.

Or losing.

"Do you thirst?" Asshur asked Cheftu. "We can agree to drink."

"I do," the blonde grunted.

"Drink!" Asshur called. The crowd cheered. The priest brought them a jug, much like the ones tied to their heads, with two drinking tubes.

"You both have to agree to relax," the bowl master said to them. "Agree not to take advantage of the other while you rest."

Chloe chewed her lip and watched. They kept their hands on each other, but eagerly slurped down the cooling beer until the jug was empty and the priest took it away.

"On the count of three, you resume," the bowl master said. The music began, the crowd cheered, and the game recommenced. Cheftu was slower to respond, and Asshur moved him back a step. The crowd roared, and began to chant his name: Asshur, Asshur, Asshur.

Cheftu didn't move after that. It was like his feet had grown into palm trunks that fastened him to the ground. Periodically, he and Asshur tried to bash each other's jars. However, they were so closely linked that any indication of movement gave the opponent time to evade it.

They struggled on as the moon sailed across the sky.

⌒

The blackness of night had broken and Cheftu couldn't move. His hands, even these big strong Kidu hands, were aching vises around Asshur's arms. His legs were frozen in place. In truth, the two men were hugging each other fiercely. They hadn't spoken in hours.

What happened if no one won?

Cheftu heard scratching on the pavement. "Inana leaves our world for the other in just moments," the bowl master said. "The circle is narrowed. Whoever pushes his opponent out of the circle by sunup wins."

The crowd cheered, though somewhat less enthusiastically than before. He didn't know how close he was to the edge of the circle, so Cheftu shoved forward. Asshur met his strength and pushed back. Cheftu's toes clenched into the pavement as the cool of the night faded from his back and shoulders.

Asshur bellowed, and the pressure on Cheftu's arms doubled. He shouted, too, tightened his grip, and smashed his head against Asshur's jar. The sounds of shattering clay, shouting people, and ringing in his head coalesced into blackness.

~

"We're going to see the gateway to the underworld, Kur," Chloe said. "But I bet you don't want to go."

Cheftu opened an eye; she sat on the bed's end with a nimbus of light behind her.

"Head hurts, huh?" she asked.

"Yes."

"I'm glad you won," she said.

He closed his eyes. *"Moi aussi."*

"What possessed you—?"

"Kidu," he spat and rolled over. "Kidu was a champion in the mountains before Puabi seduced him into the city."

"So when you heard the challenge—"

"I lost my rational mind," he said from the pillows.

"You were very sexy," she said, running her finger down his back. "Sweaty and angry and wild."

He wanted to sleep, to forget this lunacy, but her touch was as undeniable as any of the other desires he had, and he had to sate. "When do you go to the underworld?" he asked. Her hands were on his shoulders, kneading those muscles around his neck. He felt the heat of her skin and smelled the fragrance of her femininity. Cheftu groaned. *"Chérie—"* He turned onto his back, ready to plead for time or—he saw her face. "I will never be able to resist you," he said.

She smiled. "You just lie back and relax. I'll do all the work."

≻

"Your mate is sleeping?" Asshur asked, when he met Chloe in the hallway of the palace. No guards, no aides, no scribes followed him.

The lasciviousness in his eyes was missing also.

"He is," Chloe said evenly. Standing closer to the man, she had to marvel at how he'd almost beaten Cheftu last night. Asshur was not a young man. Not by a long shot—but he was still built like a WWF contender.

Would it be a social gaffe to ask his age? Chloe wondered. Probably more of an offense than they could afford. "Did you want to see him?"

"He's a mountain man, I am told?"

"Uh, yes," Chloe said. That would be the French side of the Alps. Though perhaps Cheftu remembered more of Kidu's life than she did of the marsh girl's. "May I ask why?"

Asshur hesitated. "I would like to speak with him. The others are waiting, for the trip to the gate of the underworld."

"Is it really the gate of the underworld?" she asked him.

He rolled his eyes. "Old mothers' stories, to frighten children. They claim that anyone who goes down there can be struck dead or be given life everlasting. Tales for little ones."

"Come with me." Chloe said. "I'll wake Ch—Kidu."

≻

"Wake up," she said, and kissed him.

"Chérie, even I—"

"Don't be so vain. Asshur is here. He wants to talk to you about the mountains."

Cheftu's eyes opened. "Here?"

"In the next room. That's why I'm whispering."

Cheftu sat up, then looked down to see he wasn't dressed.

"I'll tell him you'll be there in a minute," Chloe said as she slipped back into the receiving room.

Asshur and Chloe stood in uncomfortable silence, while she waited for him to speak. That much she'd learned in seven years in ancient times. Kings spoke first. Period. Asshur was impossible to read, lost in his own world. Chloe found herself studying his face, his hands. He wasn't attractive, but he was . . . intriguing. For the first time in years, she itched for a pad and pencil to get him on paper.

"You are Khamite?" he asked, finally.

"Part," she said.

"The other part?"

"Marsh dweller."

He nodded. His head was shaved, so Chloe didn't know if he was black-haired, brown, or fair. His skin was evenly tan, his eyebrows medium dark, and his eyes curiously flat, emotionally guarded and garden-variety brown.

Cheftu opened the door, and Asshur greeted him. With relief, Chloe noticed. They spoke about the weather, exchanged news of the towns, and then refreshments arrived. Chloe hadn't asked for any, but maybe the *lugal* had. It was sweet and minty tea, minus the leaves—the only connection to the modern Middle East Chloe had known.

"You may speak before her," Cheftu finally said. "What is on your mind?"

"You are a son of Jepheti?" Asshur asked.

"Great-grandson," Cheftu said. "Jepheti lives still. He moved across the green sea to the islands there."

"Your people, do they age?"

Cheftu raised a brow in question.

Asshur leaned forward. "Did Jepheti ever mention standards? Carved? Set into the earth?"

We aren't discussing behavior, Chloe guessed. *Standards, as in notices? Like the ones standing outside Ningal's court?*

Cheftu shook his head, in thought. "No. But Jepheti was conscious of what he ate, and no one was allowed to drink his water."

"You have his water!" Asshur almost came out of his seat.

Cheftu's sleepy-cat gaze narrowed. "His water was finished before I was a man." He leaned forward. "Why do you ask me these things?"

Again, Asshur looked at Chloe. "I will not speak of sacred matters before one who is cursed and ignorant."

"She is half-Jepheti," Cheftu said. "And only half-Khamite."

Chloe bit her lip to keep from reminding them she was still in the room.

Asshur rose. "I cannot." He looked at her. "It is no disrespect to you, ma'am, but only honoring the wishes of my male human forefathers. Kham was cursed. Banished. He had no part of the continuing line."

Chloe glanced up at Cheftu; he wanted her to go. He wanted to know what Asshur was talking about, and her leaving was the only way he was going to get it. In this way, they were a team.

"Well," she said, "I will go visit the gates of the underworld, then."

~

The sledges were lined up in front of the royal residence like taxis. Chloe climbed in and told the driver where she was supposed to go. Uruk was a beautiful, colorful city, more subdued than Ur and Larsa, but maybe that was because, on the whole, the population was older. Not many children ran in the streets, and Chloe saw a lot of sledges—exactly like taxis—taking people back and forth between the municipal buildings and temples.

"What are those?" she asked the driver. Before each of the doorways were huge stones, planted in the ground, and intricately inscribed.

"Judgment standards," he said. "That's the judicial complex. Each judge commemorates his best decisions by writing them on stone. That way, you know what to expect. Some are harder on civil cases than criminal, some specialize in contract law, or land negotiations. You save time and costs if you know to whom to appeal."

She wanted to ask if they had plea bargaining, but couldn't translate the concept. The sledge stopped beside a public park. "The gate to the underworld is right down those steps," he said, pointing to a hole in the ground. "Did you bring an offering?"

Chloe was stuck; she hadn't.

"If not, these are the finest watchers," he said, pulling back a blanket on the seat beside him to reveal crude figures with enormous eyes. It was hard to tell which was male and which was female. Chloe exchanged a few beads from her belt for a purportedly female "watcher" and dismounted.

At least it wasn't Rolexes, she thought. Though in Saudi Arabia, it was usually Cartier knockoffs that the taxi drivers sold.

No one else seemed to be around. There weren't guards or priests, nothing and no one. *I just go in, I guess,* she thought, and took the steps downward.

～

"Tell me of this water of your forefathers," Asshur said. The look in his eyes was lustful, more so than when he'd looked at Chloe the night before. Cheftu sensed all the travelers from Ur had been manipulated, but to what purpose?

"Where did he get it? When did he begin to drink it? What age was he when he fathered his first child? When did—"

Cheftu held up his hand. "I don't know the answers," he said. "I am sorry, but I cannot help you." It was true; Kidu's memories were hazy at best. Not thought processes so much as emotions and reactions. Hence Cheftu's inability to control them very well. Though he had dodged a number of green-eyed women. "What do you seek?" he asked Asshur.

"My years are counted in centuries," Asshur said.

Centuries, plural?

"I do not deceive you. I was the last child born Before the Deluge."

Cheftu blinked, the Deluge that was now accorded the status of legend?

"Lives were long for humans and their kin. Men matured slowly, having fewer children much later, learning gradually, but more, for they had many years to do so. The First Father was 930 when he died, and he didn't have his first son before 130 years."

The numbers were familiar to Cheftu the scholar; the story was familiar to Kidu the mountain man.

"Where do you think the knowledge of the Black-Haired Ones springs from? No one family could learn about animals, land, metals, medicine, and writing in a single generation—unless such a generation were hundreds of years old. Ziusudra's children were, are, that generation. You said my uncle Jepheti is well-aged, yet still he travels."

Cheftu had told Chloe Ziusudra wasn't Noah, but he was beginning to doubt himself. If only the names of Noah's children, three sons, would come to Cheftu's mind. "What do you want? What do you seek?"

"Holy water," Asshur said, standing slowly. "Water that confirms life, sustains it."

The fountain of youth. The phrase flew through Cheftu's

mind, but it wasn't attached to anything else. "How do you know what it is?"

"I've seen it, I've heard about it. It's a very special water," he said. "It has these properties . . ."

The caverns were damp, deep, deep beneath the earth. In a land that was hugely oil deposits and mosquito breeding grounds, Chloe was astounded to find this space. No wonder the old mothers had thought it was the gate to the underworld. "It's certainly clammy enough," she muttered to herself.

The walls were illustrated with sloppy depictions of pregnant women and wild, horned animals. "Oh my gosh," Chloe breathed in astounded English. "These are cavemen paintings!" She'd been to caves in Spain and France where the hunters and gatherers of previous millennia had written their stories in pictures on the walls of the places they lived. Iraq had had cave dwellers? She touched the drawings, almost to check if they were dry; the colors were still so vivid, the illustrations kinetic. Were they old, even now?

After all, she was barely IN historical time the best she could figure. If Cheftu didn't recognize anything, then either little green men were responsible for civilization, or there was another explanation.

These days, Chloe didn't bet on either option being the answer.

She walked on.

Torches had blackened the walls and ceilings throughout the cave, and she wondered for a moment how long ago that had been, when man first figured out fire. "Not that I want to find out firsthand or anything," she said out loud, just in case Someone was listening.

On the floor in the next room, she found the watchers. Hundreds, maybe thousands of the big-eyed statues and plaques, paintings and dolls, faced forward, staring through an archway.

"Ohmigod," Chloe muttered as she picked her way through the field of votives. "This is it, Cheftu, the gateway out."

She walked up to the archway—a natural one, misshapen, and plain, and looked around. Of course, there wouldn't be a blue light or anything—it was the wrong time of the year. But . . . "There are no symbols," she said to herself. As she looked into the room beyond it, she heard the trickle of a stream, water hitting a pool. Faint, but distinct.

She was thirsty. Cool, fresh water would taste great after the months of warm, marshy Euphrates water. *That's why they made beer here,* she reasoned. *Anything to disguise the flavor of the water.*

The stream ran down the wall from some higher, hidden source, then fell into a small pool. Enough to splash her face and fill her stomach. "That's weird," she said, as she watched it flow. "Maybe it's not water?"

～

Cheftu had heard the *lugal* out, but he still doubted the man's veracity. But what motivation could there be for such a patently false story? He dropped his gaze.

"You doubt me?"

"You tell me that somewhere there is a stream where the water is too cold to drink, it foams as it falls, and it can't be taken away in containers or skins, but must be consumed at the source."

"We think there is some connection between the snows of the mountains and the water," Asshur said. "It's sacred water, and the sources for it are dried up. Were there any ponds or pools, maybe grottos beneath the earth, that you remember in the mountains?"

"Jepheti would go on long walks, sometimes for days, up in the snow," Cheftu said, using Kidu's patchy memory. "That is all I know. Why is it so important?"

Asshur looked at Cheftu, and for the first time Cheftu believed him, or at least believed Asshur believed what he said. "Our people are aging too quickly, multiplying too fast. We're running out of water, of grain, of occupations. We had to create a police force to keep the poor from killing each other over a cup of water."

"You think if everyone had this water, it would make things better?"

"Most assuredly. Four children for a household, in the course of sixty years, instead of the reverse. But the water must be consumed from birth, for it slows the process from the start, not somewhere in the middle. Time is running out."

"What happens if you don't find it?"

Asshur clasped his hands tightly. "We'll devour each other like rats. We'll forsake our humanity. For all our learning and heritage, we are but animals."

Cheftu looked away from the intensity of the man as he pondered Asshur's words. "What about the standards you mentioned?"

~

The water smelled fine to Chloe, but she couldn't see any reason it should be so foamy. It wasn't falling a great distance, and it wasn't churned in any way. "Did someone put soap in it?" she wondered. A finger test proved it was bitter, freezing cold; the deep chill that feels hot at first, then frigid. "I'd have a headache in a second from drinking that." The kind of head pain you get from slushy margaritas or biting ice cream. It looked like that souped-up water you poured on cuts to keep from infection. What was that called?

Having paid her respects, left her watcher, seen no one and realized the archway was not hers and Cheftu's pathway out, Chloe started back to the entrance. She tried to, anyway, but the cavern chambers were circuitous, the rooms all looked the same. When she'd stumbled into the watchers' area for the third time, she felt a twinge of panic.

Follow the art.

Gazelles on one wall led to a pregnant woman portrait in the next room. From there, she went up a slight flight of stairs to another room with a family on the wall. Three women and one man, four children and an old person—at least to guess from the markings. By that measure, though, what would future generations make of Picasso? "There's a reason he wasn't painting on the walls," she said.

A three-pronged fork in the hallway. Torches still burned; she wasn't scared, this was a peaceful, comfortable place. But odd. "Alice and her rabbit holes," Chloe muttered. Talking to herself was kooky, but the sound of her voice in this space made it a little less . . . intense.

She took the center hall, which went straight. "This isn't the way," she thought as she passed by several smaller rooms. The hallways opened into a conference-sized room. Off to the side she saw a tiny space with two standing stones.

Actually, one was brick and one was stone. They were carved, just like the judgment stones in the complex of the city. The brick one looked like it had spent some time underwater—the writing was faded, and it was considerably shorter than the stony one.

They must be very old, she thought. The pictograms were recognizable as pictures, instead of the series of markings she was learning at the Tablet House. She took a step closer, then felt a chill.

Was someone watching her? She turned quickly, but didn't see anyone. Still the eerie feeling stayed, grew. *I want out of here,* Chloe thought, as she retraced her way to the fork in the hall. She took the right-hand branch, up and up and up . . . and blinked in the waiting sunshine.

The creepy feeling still hadn't gone away, so she race-walked back to the palace. When she finally stepped into the building she was sweaty and breathing heavily . . . and feeling quite ridiculous.

It seemed like she had been down there for years, yet it was only minutes.

And it wasn't the gate to Kur.

∽

"What did he say?" she asked Cheftu later that night when they were falling asleep, the breeze from the river blowing across them. "Why did he need such privacy?"

"He's an old man, following fairy stories," Cheftu said. "He's afraid to acknowledge that death comes for him."

"Why would he talk to you about aging? I mean, by any account you are young."

Cheftu sighed, and his fingers played in her hair. "Because my, Kidu's *grand-père,* lived for hundreds of years. Asshur thinks there is a fountain of youth, a magical elixir that will slow the maturation process and help people live longer, have children later. It's all about too many people."

"I have a two-word solution: birth control."

Cheftu shrugged. "He knows this thing. But making his people do it when they are young, it—"

"So his talk was boring, and his being rude to me served no purpose?"

Cheftu kissed her. "None whatsoever. Forgive me for allowing him to treat you that way. How was your journey?"

"Strange. Eerie. Like being in the womb of the earth."

"Did the others feel that way?"

Chloe opened her eyes. Thought. "You know, I didn't see anyone else. I wandered for a while, but I never actually saw another person."

Cheftu must have heard something in her voice. "Are you well, *chérie?*"

She chuckled. "I think I understand why that place has a reputation for being the gate to hell, or purgatory, or wherever. There was definitely a strange feeling, like something invisible was watching." She shivered, and he pulled her closer.

"You are safe now. I shouldn't have let you go alone."

"Don't be silly, I just let my imagination run away with me."

Cheftu turned onto his side, his arm tight around her waist, his breath on her neck. "I love you, *chérie.*"

"I love you, too. Good night."

"Sweet dreams."

Chloe lay awake, her memory replaying the cavern. The millions of staring plaster eyes, the water that came from nowhere and wasn't drinkable, the old standards, the misshapen paintings, the echo and chill of the place. She didn't believe that Kur was a physical place that could be reached from the surface of the planet, but she certainly understood why the marsh girl and everyone else around here did. That cavern was freaky.

Marshes

"The poor man is the silent man in Sumer."

"We'll be in the marshes for the next stretch of the journey," Nimrod said. "In *mashufs*. Women will travel in the middle of the group, men surrounding them. Watch the surface for crocodiles and snakes. Pay attention to the movements of birds and test the depth of any water you step into before you step."

Chloe knew the reason for his precautions—marsh dweller was synonymous with outlaw. And if they didn't get you, then nature would.

The other women, most of whom had been city dwellers all along, looked terrified. Chloe couldn't explain it, but it seemed as though part of her was being packed up and another part was being assembled. To her, it seemed her vision grew sharper, her right arm stronger, her movements more sinuous to blend in with the grasses, the reeds, and the river. The marsh girl's instincts lived inside her body, the girl's knowledge of the plants, the animals, and their behaviors was information in her brain. She was the marsh girl.

And the marsh girl was her.

The marsh waters were low this late in the season, so the *mashufs*—really, very skinny canoes—were lightly loaded, so they moved easily. Chloe didn't remember many details about the marsh girl's life, but the images were consistent. Images and feelings were all she really had.

A heron poised for flight, with twilight behind him, confirmation that sun would return on the morrow. Though, Chloe thought, in this place if the sun skipped a day or two, people would just be relieved for a break in the heat.

Not funny to joke about, when she considered how they reacted to an eclipse.

Someone was buried under the name Puabi, or as it could be read, Shub-ab.

Chloe pushed her *mashuf* through the long grass and shallow water, watching the birds, the fish, the crocodiles, and other amphibians whose names she'd never known in any lifetime. It was a peaceful, if not a quiet place.

In the distance she saw the huts of the marsh dwellers. Formed of reeds that were arched together and tied, they looked a lot like greenhouses in the modern U.S. Or petite aircraft hangars. The sides were decorated in woven patterns, and each family's was different. *I wonder what the marsh girl's had been,* Chloe thought. *I wonder if I picked up some reeds and started weaving if I would discover that I have that knowledge.*

Water buffalo wandered in the water. Mothers, with babies tied to their breasts, washed their clothes in the water and watched the string of *mashufs* glide past.

How many more miles of this? Chloe wondered. And she pushed off again.

Twilight filtered down on the village; Chloe could only see it on the palm that slanted over their reed house. Cheftu twined his arms around her waist as they sat in the doorway. "You've been quiet."

"In separate boats, there wasn't much to say."

"Did your marsh girl come from there, that territory we sailed through?"

"No," Chloe said, and rested her hands on his forearms. "From some village between Uruk and Ur. West and north, I think."

The palm tree's bark looked stained with gold, then salmon, and plum, then, finally, night fell. "I always thought twilight was the end of the day," she said.

"To us it is."

"Is that because our thoughts were based on thinking in a straight line? If this is A, then B has to happen?"

He kissed her forehead. "I never analyzed it."

"Neither did I, until it dawned on me how safe it is to have twilight be a beginning instead of the conclusion."

"Cute pun," Cheftu said, and kissed her cheek.

"Unintentional, but thanks." She wasn't looking outside anymore, but inside. Her mind, she seemed more aware of its mechanics than ever before. How did she shift seamlessly from being the marsh girl to being her modern self? What mechanism slipped from dealing with politics and religion to knowing which birds were good raw and which weren't? Small things, like knowing what plants were poisonous, how to climb a palm tree, how to read the seasons.

Things, that for all her well-trained body, modern information and technical skills, she would have died without knowing. How did all the mental cogs and wheels work?

"Are you ready to dine?" Cheftu asked.

"Do you like this life?" she asked. "Living as a well-to-do vagabond who is feted and celebrated wherever he goes?"

"In my country, it is the way the wealthy and titled always lived," he said. "The people were only concerned with pleasing themselves."

"Does it bother you to be indolent?"

He laughed, and she turned to watch him. His face was so beautiful, and now he was gilded from head to toe. "I grew accustomed to being rich and lazy quickly."

They exchanged a quick kiss, then hurried out to join the others for dinner.

~

"Hydrogen peroxide!"

Cheftu looked at her as though she'd blasphemed.

"That's what that stuff was, I can't believe it's taken this long for me to remember."

"What are you babbling about?"

The heat and the endless marching had worn both their tempers thin. They were headed north again; the river ran south, so they were back on their feet. Long days of walking, for Nimrod feared they'd miss being able to dry bricks before the rainy season hit in their new, unnamed, location.

Chloe couldn't remember what rain was. Cool and wet? Not possible. "In the cavern, the gate to the underworld. Somewhere inside, there was a fountain of hydrogen peroxide."

Cheftu turned on her, his eyes wild. "It foamed?"

She nodded.

"Bitterly cold?"

She nodded.

He started laughing, gasping for air, holding his belly, slapping his thighs—she pushed him into the river. He came up, still laughing. He climbed up the bank with the occasional giggle. Chloe stood, her hands on her hips, fighting a grin.

"Next you will tell me you saw two pillars, one of brick and one of stone."

"No, I won't tell you that." Though it was true.

He laughed again. Finally, she sat down. Obviously they weren't walking for a while. The sheep gnawed on the grass and watched Cheftu with big brown eyes.

Then he stopped. Abruptly. "If that is truth," he said, "then the other must be truth."

"The other is?"

"Ningal of Ur is three hundred years old."

Chloe walked away.

∼

"Repeating that it is not possible does not change the fact that it might be possible," Cheftu said as they walked along. "We've heard tales from almost everyone about longevity in numbers that seem—"

"Like lies?" Chloe said.

"But there is consistency. I find it difficult to ignore."

Chloe swatted a sheep into line and frowned at the ground. "Ningal? You met him, Cheftu. Three hundred years old? It's not possible!"

"I believe," he said over his shoulder, "you once called me Horatio and told me there was more in heaven and on earth than I could conceive?"

"I hate it when you quote me," she muttered. "Especially when I've misquoted Shakespeare."

"Why should it being true bother you so much, *chérie?*"

That thought occupied her for at least an hour.

They stopped for lunch, pitched a tent to nap under, ate in silence, then nodded off. When Cheftu woke up, Chloe was staring at the river, frowning. "I don't know which way is up anymore," she said.

He pointed to the sky.

She didn't laugh.

"Do you need to have this answer?" he asked.

They packed the tent, gathered the sheep, and walked on. The river channel they were following led east, toward the mountains, though they were going to stop far before then.

Twilight fell, and they pitched their tent again. Somewhere behind them, the other Urians spread out with flocks and children, set their fires, and fried their fish. Cheftu cooked, Chloe was intent. She thought all through the meal she scarcely touched, then looked up at the sky until he took her hand and led her to the tent.

With soft kisses and touches, he made love to her. Silent, gentle, easing her to sleep. He was soundly asleep when she spoke.

"I do."

"Do what?" he said, groggy.

"I do have to know which way is up, I do have to know what I believe. This new information, these stories, how everyone is convinced people lived longer before the Deluge, that everyone on earth is from the same family—" She sighed. "I don't know what to make of it."

"Why can't you let it be, and be apart from it?"

"I'm an American. I believe in instant gratification and having all my questions answered."

He was still pondering this when she spoke again.

"That's an exaggeration, but it's sort of true. I come from a world where our need for concrete answers is so consuming that we've developed an entire system to prove to ourselves that the way we feel is how the ancients felt. We're not alone, we tell ourselves. We've been here before."

"A system?"

"Archaeology. You're responsible," she said. "At least Napoleon is."

"From what you tell me of history, Napoleon is responsible for much," Cheftu said disparagingly. "What satisfaction do you require, *chérie*? What answers will help you know again, which way is up?"

"How can you not know? How can it not eat away at you. I don't understand."

Cheftu sighed, sat up, and drew her to him. "We are similar, we know, but very different in some ways. I think, maybe, this is our upbringing. You fight, always."

"I do not."

He chuckled. "You do. Oppressors, institutions, ideologies, difficulties. You need to strive against something. I . . . I guess I accept."

"Fatalism," she hissed. "I've resisted that my whole life. *Inshallah*. God wills it. Why does God get blamed when we're too damn lazy to defend ourselves or pursue what is honorable?"

"For one person to feel like you do is good, he inspires the rest and something can get done. But for every man to feel this way is chaos, *chérie*. Eventually, one must learn that there are opponents too big to fight. One will just wound oneself, dashing against the rocks."

"That reasoning is why France had an aristocracy for so long," she snapped.

"It is," he said. "That is why Egypt was so amazing a place to me. A man could make anything of himself, regardless of where in the hierarchy he was born."

"This place reminds me of the States," she said. "Do people, humans, always make the same mistakes? Will we never learn?"

"What lesson do you want us to learn, Chloe? What is the thing eating you inside?"

"Which way is up," she said, then turned into his chest. His fingers played in her hair as she cried, sobbed, and railed against her unnamed tormentor. Cheftu held her and wondered.

He looked out at the night sky; for him, that was proof enough of everything. The heavens revealed a benevolent Seigneur, an intricate, unfathomable plan, and a mind, artistic and otherwise, that reveled in beauty, organization, justice, and mercy. All of the best in male and female humans, granted by a Creator who was both male and female divinity, who was in fact, whole.

Cheftu was startled and soothed at the thought. *Have I become a pagan,* he thought, *living in these places and these times? Or have I finally turned to see what is there, instead of seeing only what I was told to see?*

Chloe slept finally. He cradled her head and blessed *le bon Dieu* until he saw dawn streak the sky with orange, bronze, and blossom red, melting away the navy. He looked at the sleeping woman in his arms and knew a moment of perfection. In this moment, Cheftu was complete: contented with his god, his world, and his wife.

Shapir

"He who possesses much silver may be happy; he who possesses much barley may be happy; but he who has nothing at all may sleep."

"It is grim, isn't it," Nimrod said to them.

"He's the reaper of the dead," Nirg said. "Even in the mountains we know that."

Shapir, a harbor city on the Tigris, was dedicated lock, stock, and *mashuf,* to Nergal, the god of the dead.

Their first indication had been the boundary stones, portraying Nergal, complete with scythe and hood, as a warning that invaders would die an eternal death. It was a small city, and Chloe could see why. Despite its great access to the rivers—from Shapir one took a boat straight to Kish, for here was where the rivers connected—it was a creepy place.

"It smells like hell," she muttered.

"Sulfur," Cheftu said. "Bitumen, too."

"Are we staying here?"

"We have no choice if we want to get to Kish," Nimrod said. "The plains north of Kish are the only available ones in Shinar." This small band had struck out from the others, moving faster along the way, to prepare for the other fifty-something people.

"So if we're running away from home, we have to stop here," Chloe finished the thought out loud.

Twilight was falling; it would be best to be inside the gates, regardless of who was painted on them, than outside this close to the desert, mountains, and all their dangers.

Chloe kept reminding herself of that, as they drew closer and closer to the city. The walls were painted red, so it looked as though they were soaked in blood.

"You're just in time for the lunar festival!" the already-intoxicated gatekeeper cried. "Nergal's date of death is tonight!"

"You celebrate his death?"

"He's the god of the dead, it wouldn't make any sense to celebrate his birth, would it?" The gatekeeper laughed. "Beer and bread are free tonight, as are the temple prostitutes." He winked at them. "Sleep anywhere, the residents will!" Off he went, laughing and staggering.

Nirg, whose only concern was food, made an announcement. "This place is evil. Look, it sticks to your skin." She held up her bare foot, blotched with black. "This happened as I was walking on the road."

Nimrod put his arm around her. Lea stepped to his other side. "I agree, there is something wrong with this city," she said.

Cheftu was reading the wall, a frown between his brows—where Chloe had tweezed an actual demarcation line. "Nergal rules the black lake. What is that?" he asked.

Chloe sniffed the air; she didn't grow up in Saudi for nothing. "Black gold." That's what Nirg had stepped into. Texas tea.

They stared at her—with her strange knowledge of refining, processing, and the almighty price at the pump, they didn't know any of those details—but at moments like this they knew she was different. "Oil," she said. "It's everywhere around here."

The streets were filled with half-naked, wholly drunk citizens. The music seemed a little off-key, the people a little odd, the food suspicious, and the conversations confusing. Nevertheless, they found a park to sleep in, some nourishment that was recognizable as bread and fruit, and opened sealed beer jars.

Dancing, laughing, congressing. "This is a serious orgy," Chloe said to Cheftu. "I think I'm kind of repulsed."

He looked at her with surprise.

"No, I don't care what they do . . . I just feel . . . unclean. Like I need a bath or something. The intentions are wrong. Weird stuff is going on here. I know it."

Nirg and Lea huddled together. Nirg had eaten nothing, she just watched, with the torches of the residents flickering in her eyes.

"You are correct," Cheftu whispered in her ear. "This is the celebration when Nergal kidnaps his daughter and takes her to the underworld as . . . his bride."

"I thought it was his death day?"

"It is, *chérie. L'automne* is upon the land. Nergal seems to die—"

"And his daughter is the rebirth of spring."

"Yes. Expectant of his offspring, by the time she returns."

"We're celebrating incest?"

"More than that: rape, kidnapping—"

"Don't tell me any more."

"Sleep if you can," he said. "I will watch over us tonight. We'll be well."

~

"Join us!" the loud shout woke Chloe. She opened her eyes and saw a group of men, blind drunk, talking to Nimrod and Cheftu. "It's uncivil not to celebrate."

She blinked and realized the men were naked, and looking for companions. Cheftu blocked her almost completely, they couldn't see behind his broad back.

"Leave them alone!" a man shouted back. "They're tourists, not residents!"

"They're here," one of the naked men said—he was spotted with tar, like a Holstein or Dalmatian. "They want it, why else would they be sitting in the park."

"They're my guests," the man said, then turned to Cheftu. "Brother, I am so sorry to keep you waiting. Please, please, come in."

The naked men were undecided, but eventually convinced as the man—a total stranger—kissed everyone in the group from Ur, acted like a long-lost relative, and got them inside his house. He bolted the door. "They won't forget you're here," he said. "Now, at least, you will have more of a chance."

"Thank you," Nimrod said. "We are from Ur and—"

"If you aren't a native of Shapir, you can't hope to understand us," the man said. "As soon as the sky is bright, we'll get you down to the wharf and on a ship. Kish?" he said.

Banging on the door. "Send those men out!"

"They're here, and we want them!"

Nimrod and Cheftu comprehended it—the demand—at the same time.

"Send them out, or we'll break down your door!"

"He's big enough, he could do it with his rod!"

The comments became cruder and cruder. Their rescuer motioned for help, and the five adults barricaded the door on both sides—in case the hinges were popped or the dead bolt lifted.

Chloe looked at the roof. If those guys wanted in, they could just scale the walls and drop into the courtyard.

The mob outside was growing. "What else do you suggest?" Nimrod asked the man.

It was a long time before dawn; the crowd was getting rowdier, rougher. "It is the policy," their host said. "Law is on their side."

"What law?" Cheftu asked.

The man groaned. "It was a mistake to settle here, but they needed instructors and Kish had no need for attorneys so I moved. The laws are . . . perverse."

"What law?" Chloe asked. "How is it perverse?"

"Hospitality," Nirg answered. "The laws of hospitality usually require that a guest be protected even more than the family members themselves. But in the city of the dead, in the world of Nergal, the laws of hospitality favor the crowd. If you have a guest, it is your honor to share him with the populace."

"How do you know that?" the host asked her.

"I am named Nirg, for Nergal. After I was born, my mother died. My father hated me."

Chloe grabbed Cheftu's hand. "Do you smell burning?"

"They're setting the front door afire!" Lea called.

"Do you have anything to barter with?" Cheftu asked the man. "Or should we—"

"Absolutely not," Chloe said. "Get those ladders over there. We'll go over the roof to the next house, and so on and so on, until we reach the harbor." She looked at the man. "Is that possible? Are there houses the whole distance?"

He nodded. "I must stay though, this is my home. The fires are common, the sign of disapproval from Nergal."

"They will destroy you," Cheftu said. "They are no longer responsible men; they are beasts who roam the night in a pack."

He shrugged. "It's my destiny. Some must die so there is space for the rest to live."

"Don't be stupid," Chloe said. "Come with us."

～

They were three houses down from their host's, who had chosen to stay and face the mob: those men he knew in the council, at the temple, and in the administration. They were all lawyers together. And as he said, his legal greed had brought him here. Chloe and crew had thanked him, then taken the ladders and left the sheep.

Cheftu had blood on his hands; Chloe was pretty sure why, though she wasn't going to ask. To leave them alive would have been cruelty to animals, she was sure. She laid the ladder between two more houses and scampered across. Cheftu was always the last, being the heaviest, with Nirg his close second.

How horrible to be named after such a god, Chloe thought.

She was in the middle of the ladder when the populace set off the fireworks. They had fireworks? Wasn't that China? Chloe turned to look, astonished

The host's house was on fire. As she watched, the spark that had begun at his door vanished for a second, then the middle of the street exploded in flames. A moment of darkness, then a flare in another part of the street. The park; the door opposite their host's. A courtyard.

The fires the host mentioned. Not set fires, natural fires.

"Ohmigosh," Chloe whispered. "Oil fire!" she shouted to Cheftu. "Oil!"

~

There was no longer time for a ladder. Chloe ran and jumped at the next house. Beneath her, behind her, the streets became an inferno. The roar of flames nipped at her heels. Her nose was clogged with the smells of burning fire, burned hair, and baked brick. She prayed she was heading in the correct direction. Lea and Nimrod followed her, she turned every few steps to check they were there, and to confirm a blond giant brought up the rear.

The houses were getting smaller, just one story now, with flimsy rush roofs. The streets were lethal, so they had to stay on the buildings. All the pools of tar, all the sticky remains of bitumen or drops of oil on the road, caught, flared, and moved in zips. Fire jumped to fire jumped to fire, unextinguished.

What had happened?

She looked back; they were still behind her.

She could see the harbor through the smoke; and boats, many setting sail in the middle of this insanity. Day-Glo orange and neon red and screaming yellow reflected off the river, off the whitewashed buildings, and within the slick pools of fuel in the lanes.

It would never go out, Chloe thought. This fire was going to burn until the fuel was gone. CNN and the oil fires in Kuwait would be a campfire compared to this. *If we thought the crops were bad before . . .*

She jumped to the ground, sprang up, and dashed across the pier to a boat. Any boat. Nimrod ran behind her, hacking at lines with his knife. Rats raced screeching into the water; Lea beat them off the ship's prow. Cheftu kicked the boat away from the dock while Nirg grappled with the anchor. Everyone grabbed an oar and heaved, pushing the vessel toward the mouth of the harbor, beyond the boats filled with people who watched, slack-jawed. Once outside the arms of the breakwater, Cheftu called a halt.

Shapir was a pyre.

"The gods are destroying them," Nirg said. "Even in the water."

A flicker of flame caught on the surface of the river, follow the stain of oil to a boat that caught fire. They saw another fire follow the track of the oil to a different boat.

"None shall escape," Nirg said.

"Row!" Cheftu called.

Kish

"If you take the field of an enemy, the enemy will come and take your field."

The aide saluted, but the *lugal* paid him no mind. "Fire came from the heavens?" he said.

"Yes, sir, *lugal* sir!"

"Destroyed everyone?"

"No survivors reported, sir!"

"I guess we don't have to concern ourselves with that enemy," he said. "The men will be disappointed."

"Yes they will, sir, *lugal* sir!"

"Our courts will certainly be freer without their multiples of attorneys descending upon us every time a dike bursts."

"Freer courts, sir, *lugal* sir!"

"Who was next on our battle plan to attack?"

"I'm at a loss, sir, *lugal* sir!"

"Yes," the *lugal* said, glancing at the aide, who stood so straight and tall in his flocked skirt and newly shaven head. The *lugal* had a whole city full of new recruits. He'd raised taxes and the awareness of the enemy who was, according to him, poised to invade. Now what?

"Damned inconvenient," he muttered. Fires came from the heavens on Shapir, as well they should. He just wished the gods had warned him. Now he was going to have to change his plan. Shapir had been such a convenient, local enemy. The next closest city was Nippur—bad choice for invasion, or Agade. It was too small to be worthy of his army. And he'd have to trek past Bab-ili's haunted environs to get there. Not a desirable situation, not desirable at all. "Go find my sergeant," he told the waiting aide. Perhaps the man would have a suggestion.

∼

Five horrified people stared at each other while the boat they were on bobbed in the water. Black smoke stained the sky. Chloe knew they would see that smoke and its consequences for years to come. Years.

"It happened so fast," Lea said.

"Thank the gods the others took the slow route through the fields," Nimrod said. "If Roo—" He shook his head. "Thank the gods."

"How many humans lived there?" Chloe asked in a soft, slow voice.

"It was small." Nimrod said. "Five thousand, no more."

"Five thousand humans," she said.

Nirg put her arm around Chloe. "We need more salt, do not worry."

"Salt?"

Cheftu leaned forward and took her hand. "The mountain people, where Nirg and I come from, believe that evil souls don't enter an afterlife. They are so bad that the gods can use only the divine part of them. The salt in their bodies. Salt is the only good found in a bad person."

"There will be piles of salt," Nirg said. "I challenge that by our children's time, it will not be called the Plain of Sipur, but rather the Plain of Salt."

Salt. Fire. Brimstone.

No way.

"Five thousand souls," Chloe said. "Five thousand humans."

"Five thousand minae of salt."

∼

"Just five thousand?" the *lugal* asked the sergeant.

"It's the biggest village, unless you want to attack Nippur—"

"No, no. I guess it will do." He looked up at the sky. "Is that plume of smoke going to ruin my view all day?"

"It could be an omen," the man said.

"Go pay an exorcist to make it go away. When do you think the troops will be ready to fight?" the *lugal* asked.

The sergeant seemed less than enthusiastic. "First, we need to inform the town that they are in arrears. What did they do?" he asked.

"They were the suppliers of Shapir," the *lugal* said. He was pleased with how authentic a reason it sounded. "Though Shapir has been obliterated by the gods, the evil they promoted against the people of Kish must yet be stopped."

"They are villagers," the sergeant said. "I don't know that they have carts, even."

"That is bad," the *lugal* said. "We must rectify that."

The sergeant stared at the man. "I don't understand, sir."

"We'll supply them with weapons and machinery. Great for our economy. Then when they are ready, we'll have a war. Our soldiers can even train theirs. The commonwealth can come watch us beat them. It will be splendid. Maybe we should make it a feast day. How long do you think it would take to outfit them?"

"I have not been a citizen of Kish long," the sergeant said. "However, I find this reprehensible behavior. Have you been in battle, sir?"

"Of course not! We've always gotten what we wanted through negotiation and bartering."

"Then why go to war?"

"The glory of it, my boy. The glory."

Twilight wasn't heartening. Their first night in Kish was going to be horrifyingly memorable. No sooner had they rented rooms in the local tavern, than they had heard the proclamation demanding the populace's attendance.

"I've never been to a public execution," Chloe said.

"It's not to be missed," Cheftu replied. His tone was bathed in irony.

"Firestorm in one city, a traitor executed in the next. I'm not so sure Nimrod's plan of heading north was so good. Maybe we should have headed south," Chloe said. "Dilmun, maybe."

Cheftu was shaving, contorting his face to get every little hair, so he didn't reply.

"Dilmun," Chloe repeated. "It's just a straight journey south on the river—"

Kettledrums jolted them both.

Her husband cursed as blood ran down his hand.

An omen.

Cheftu's blood. Blood on Cheftu. An omen.

"*Chérie,* are you well?" he asked.

Chloe nodded, then turned away. An omen.

After he spotted the blood and changed cloaks, Cheftu was ready. Outside, Lea, Nirg, and Nimrod sat in a row, waiting. The five of them joined the rest of the visitors and residents in the main square.

"My God, it looks like home," Cheftu said in French.

The square was missing Madame Defarge, but it had everything else.

Gallows.

Cart with prisoner.

Clergy.

Aristocracy.

Commoners.

The latter were clustered around the gallows, the former

examining a clay replica sheep's liver, and the aristocracy were all military, watching as they stood at attention, helmets beneath their arms.

"For the acts of treason against the commonwealth," the scribe cried out, "Sergeant Olal of Akkad will be executed by severing his neck with a blade."

"I may puke," she whispered to Cheftu.

"No," he said.

"I can't help it."

"You can and you will," he said. "If this people believes in public executions, then that means the attitude is neighbor against neighbor."

"We're just passing through."

"What better disguise for spies? No one can suspect you are anything less than supportive, *chérie*." He looked at her. "You are tough, my warrior. Better to appear bloodthirsty than condemning of the rulers."

"Just let me find my crochet hook," she snapped.

"Knitting needles."

Chloe faced forward and stared blankly. She looked through the scene before her. No analysis; no scrutiny of the various elements on the gallows. Gaze straight ahead and see nothing. Still, the sounds were awful. The sun had clouded over from the oil-fire smoke, which sent the residents of Kish inside as soon as the traitor was declared dead.

In a grim line, the five returned to their tavern. Outside, a young man in uniform waited. "Are you the survivors of the Shapir fire, sir?"

Nimrod said they were.

"The male humans are requested to come with me, sir."

"Where?" Cheftu asked.

"To see the *lugal*, sir."

Chloe squeezed his hand; she'd throw up while he was gone.

"Mighty hunter, eh?" the *lugal* said to Nimrod. "Quite a reputation there, boy."

Nimrod was pleasant, but that was all. Like Cheftu, he was deeply suspicious of this place.

"Traveling for pleasure?" the *lugal* asked him, glanced at Cheftu, then turned back to Nimrod.

"We're moving north," he said.

"North? Agade?"

"No, no, on the Tigris."

"We have lands that reach quite far," the *lugal* said. "I wouldn't want your humans, your villagers, to get caught up in any property disputes, especially being new to the neighborhood."

"We'll be much farther north," Nimrod assured him.

"That spy who infiltrated my army was from the north. Did you know him? Either of you?"

"No," Nimrod said. Cheftu shook his head.

"Got your families with you?"

"Our wives," Nimrod said. "The rest are going to meet us."

"Good thing they weren't in Shapir when you set that place afire, isn't it."

Cheftu tensed.

"I believe your impression is incorrect," Nimrod said, choosing his words with care. "The fire fell from heaven."

"Don't lie to me, boy. Fire hasn't ever fallen from heaven, and even if it was a city of attorneys, firefall didn't start last night." He peered into Nimrod's face. "I think you are some sort of reconnaissance team, masquerading as Urians, come to check the defenses at Kish."

"Why?" Cheftu asked.

"You're a mountain man; I don't need to give you any excuses. Everyone knows how your humans are wild, animalistic, greedy. You want Kish. What other reason do you need." He smiled. "That's all the citizens of Kish will need to hear. We thought we had the enemy dead to rights, but the ruler of the enemy returned, and now our fight is even more vital."

"What do you want?" Nimrod asked.

"Simple enough. You're a mountain man and a hunter. I want you to train some troops in the marshes." He turned to Cheftu and smiled. "And I want him to lead my men against yours."

"For what purpose?"

"War, gentlemen. Competition breeds invention, invention requires experimentation, and that needs a field study. War is good for business."

Cheftu touched his naked chin. "What have your annual floods been like?"

"We lost every grain of the winter crop and most of the summer."

"You have to start a war to make the economy boom again?"

The *lugal* looked Cheftu dead in the face. "I have to eliminate half my population so I can feed the others."

~

"Are you okay?" Chloe asked.

Cheftu nodded, but didn't stop doing his stomach crunches. He was alternating them with straight-leg scissors. This exercise routine had come to Cheftu through her, from the U.S. Air Force. They'd done it together on cold nights in Jerusalem, and on those spring days when they could get time alone, they'd done it in the fields.

"Are you sure?" she said. "You haven't been yourself since you met with the *lugal*." Cheftu halved his speed, sweat flying off his muscled body—before her eyes, his abs were pumping up. "You haven't said a word, hardly, for three days now." He paused, then turned over to do push-ups. Watching his body in motion was usually the only aphrodisiac Chloe ever needed, but Cheftu was exercising as though it was an exorcism. Nimrod hadn't spoken either. "If you think you and Nimrod are being clever and keeping something from us, you're wrong," she said.

Cheftu stopped, holding his body above the brick floor, triceps bulging. "I don't think I'm being clever," he said.

"Is this Kidu or you?"

"I don't know. Is this nagging from the marsh girl or you?"

Chloe felt stung; she could react to his words, or she could figure out why her husband, who was so careful, precise, and understanding, would deliberately be rude. Whatever had happened, he'd sworn he wouldn't tell. "You promised, didn't you."

Cheftu released himself and lay on the floor, nose to the ground. He didn't say or do anything, just breathed heavily and sweated.

"You even promised not to talk about the promise," she guessed.

He said nothing; he wouldn't.

"You are an honorable, wonderful man." She spoke in English—he listened harder when she spoke in English. "I love you with my whole heart."

He looked up. His eyes revealed a tortured man. "Oh honey," she whispered, and opened her arms. Cheftu crawled over and embraced her, his head against her breast, his hands in fists. "Anything . . ." she whispered.

"Don't," he said. "You don't know what demon you deal with."

They were still sitting, Chloe rubbing his shoulders, when there was a knock on the door. "Kidu, sir!" the man called. "The *lugal,* sir, requests to speak with you, sir!"

Cheftu pulled away from her and opened the door. "Tell him . . . Sergeant Kidu reports at once."

"Yes, sir, I'll report it, sir!"

He closed the door, his back to her.

"I'm so blind," Chloe said. "The training—you've put yourself through a three-day boot camp, based on the exercises I showed you. You . . . this is the deal with the demon?"

"Whisper!" he hissed. "There is no security here, *chérie,* no one to trust. Remember that."

"I have you."

"I've become the enemy," he said, and stormed to the door.

She chased after him, grabbed his arm, and whispered. "Cheftu, have you ever been a soldier?"

"No."

"Then it's a good thing you sleep with one."

He turned to her. "You don't want to get involved in this, Chloe. It is not your concern."

"Don't insult me and don't be dramatic. Tell me what you need."

"I'm supposed to lead men into battle. Heavy casualties are expected."

"When?"

"After I set my seal on the contract with the devil," he said.

"Let's leave tonight," she said in a rush, the image of Cheftu stained with blood still clear in her mind. "Right now. Before you sign, before this gets out of control."

"We're nowhere close to where Nimrod wants us to be. We lost everything in Shapir."

"We'll lose our freedom, too, if we don't leave. Leave now."

Cheftu turned and looked at her. "Just walk away?"

"We have each other, we can work—anything. Let's just go!" Chloe was away, packing a few things in a small bag that wouldn't draw notice: water bottle, some sausage balls, knife—

"Oh-kay," he said, and knocked on their common wall. Nirg grunted acknowledgment. Seconds later, Nimrod stepped in the back window. Chloe hoped the spies weren't watching the courtyard also. She knew they were at the front door.

"What are we close to?" Cheftu asked.

Nimrod shook his head. "Nothing."

Cheftu stared at him. Nimrod thought for a while, then spoke slowly. "A haunted place."

"Would we be pursued?"

Nimrod twisted his eyebrows. Then he shook his head. "Not to Bab-ili."

Part Six

THE TOWER

The euphoria of getting away had faded—it had faded some twelve hours earlier when Chloe realized she was the one who had persuaded everyone to just up and leave.

She was responsible. *I'm not usually impulsive,* she thought. The images that had terrified her so were faded; now she just felt silly. It had taken all afternoon to communicate the "bailing" message to the rest of the Ur group, those who had gone through the fields and not experienced the fire. There had been no argument that Chloe knew of— so in twos and threes—they had sneaked away while the rest of the city closed its eyes in the afternoon. Like ants fleeing a stomped hill, the group had scattered in dozens of different directions in an effort to confuse any search party. Chloe and Cheftu had gone north. Alone, together, on foot.

Now they were more than a solid day of walking, away. Twilight had flashed in Technicolor on the horizon, and brought with it relieving cool. Cheftu had taken her hand, and they'd exchanged a smile, the first communication since dawn. *My country for a wheeled conveyance,* Chloe thought.

North. They headed north, just off the river in case the Kishite *lugal* sent soldiers poling after them.

Chloe yawned, then glanced up. It had become night—it came shockingly fast here—and everything was dark now. Except the eastern horizon.

She tugged Cheftu's arm. "Haunted?"

He looked at her, then looked to the east. And stopped, his face turning pale. "What is that?"

"We're going to hope it's not aliens," she said. "It looks like an airport. It takes a lot of light to glow like that."

Then she looked at her husband; he'd never seen an airport, or the power of electricity light up a city and turn the night sky pinky purple. Believing it was haunted was an easier angle for him. "It's not ghosts, though. They don't need light, now do they?"

She wouldn't want to say he was scared, but his steps were slightly less aggressive than they had been for the past day. If Cheftu, who was a few rungs higher on the experience chain, felt this way, how would Nimrod and his family react?

I don't believe in little green men from Mars, she said to herself, as they drew closer. Why would they come to earth anyway? But she didn't have any explanations for what she saw. "Is that a . . . spaceship?" she asked when they had a better view.

It rose from the plain in graduated stages, tall and skinny, pointed toward the sky, mounted on a platform. All around the enormous object people scurried back and forth. Noise, light, confusion—her heart tripped, and for a second Chloe wondered at the wisdom of approaching.

"That's the tallest stepped pyramid I've ever seen," Cheftu said in wonder. "How did they get it so high?"

His words gave her a newer, less bizarre, lens through which to look at the scene. Of course—a platform on top of a platform. The stages. The "spaceship" part was a taller, thinner pyramid than she'd ever seen—more like a proto-skyscraper in appearance. A short one. "How did they build that?" she asked.

"Look at that manpower," he said, as they drew closer.

A tent city stretched out from the platform, a strange sea

of undulating goatskins, punctuated with a thousand dung fires. Huge plates of copper were angled opposite enormous bonfires to cast an almost-day-bright reflection on the workers of the temple. The hovering smoke clouds were ruddy from the light.

Agog describes Cheftu's expression, Chloe thought. Then she remembered—he'd never even seen the Eiffel Tower—it was built eighty years after he left France. They'd seen huge, impressive buildings before, gold-covered or emblazoned with jewels, majestic in their sprawl and simplicity, but never tall.

The building was *tall*.

They reached the outskirts of the tent city. No one stopped them, or even seemed to notice them as they walked through. Again, Chloe was struck by her understanding every word everyone said. Gossip, arguments, children's bribes, jokes. "It's the beginning of the day here?" she asked Cheftu. Despite the lack of sun, these people were all acting like it was morning. Washing, dressing, eating, and setting off for the structure.

Smells of scalded milk and urine mixed with the sweet aroma of the palm groves and the fetid smell of the river. A group of women were doing laundry in the water. A small group of boys gathered fallen straw among the grasses. Oxen and onagers, goats and sheep; every ten steps or so, there was a miniature barnyard.

Garbage piled up everywhere. Beside tents, behind them. Blood stained the dirt, offal, human and animal, provided a minefield for walking. Chloe saw the flicker of rats' tails and the scurrying insects as they fought to stay alive in this chronologically confused world.

Cheftu's expression had become almost a sneer as he fought against the smells, which grew worse and worse. Chloe gave up and covered her mouth with a cloth. They'd passed through the tents, now people were just camped under the sky—no shelter at all. "They sleep under the sun?" she asked Cheftu.

"They obviously have no leadership," he said with disgust. "This place is infested."

They were at the foot of the building. And they were wrong. A group of men organized the mass of workers into sections, and each had a different assignment: carrying bricks to the structure; carrying them up the dirt road that ran parallel to the structure; slicking the just-laid bricks with bitumen; hauling bitumen. And a dozen tasks in between.

The foreman saw Cheftu and assigned him brick duty immediately. "We just arrived," Cheftu said. "Who is in charge?"

"Of the Esagila?"

"Is that what this is?"

"Sure is. Next time a flood comes, we'll all be able to hide on the structure and the gods won't be able to wipe us out. Floodwaters will never get that high. Are you ready to work?"

"I'd like to, uh, settle in, speak to someone about what you are doing here."

"We're building a mountain to hide on, that's what we're doing here. Are you interested in being a day person or a night person?"

"What do you mean?" Chloe asked.

He sighed and barked a few orders at a ragtag group of men and boys who were hauling bitumen. "Do you know how to work ovens?" he asked Chloe.

"Uh, yes."

"Good, one more for the ovens," he said, and made a crude mark on his clay. It wasn't filled with writing, just the most basic scrawls for counting.

"What did you mean?" Chloe asked again.

"You came in from the south?"

They nodded.

"Keep going, around the base of the Esagila. You'll come to the other camps."

"There's more?" Chloe asked.

The man went back to his job. Chloe and Cheftu meandered away.

"Don't forget to tell them at the ovens!" the foreman shouted.

They walked around the western side of the structure and found the brickmakers. A portion of the river had been hewn out, and a mud pit put in. What looked like miles of bricks were drying, laid out as far as the eye could see. Even in the dark, men and women trudged straw into the mud, and others slung the mud into forms, then hauled those forms out to dry.

"The rains start soon," Cheftu said. "They have to work while they can."

"I've never known a Middle Eastern culture that was nocturnal," Chloe said. "The Bedouin travel at night, but only sometimes and . . . my God, there are a lot of people here." They had to step carefully to avoid the rats, the sewage, the garbage, and a few dozing people. The reflection of the copper plates wasn't as strong here, but still daylight-powered.

They walked on.

In one moment, they were in false twilight, the next was pure nightfall.

The Esagila cast a shadow over the sleeping side, and except for the glow in the sky, you would never guess the hubbub on the other side. Tents, another sea. A few flickering fires, whinnies and snorts, but all in all, a sleeping town. They couldn't see much, but they could smell it.

"What are these people eating?" she asked. "There are so many of them."

"The eastern side must be fields," Cheftu said. "Those ovens he mentioned, they must be to feed these people." Here, they could tell morning, natural morning, was approaching.

Chloe's second—ninth?—wind had worn off. She was dead on her feet. "It stinks."

"Truth," Cheftu said vehemently. "Shall we keep walking around and see if it smells better on the other side?"

"They don't have garbage pits? Latrines?" In the military, designation of those two locations was priority one in the job of setting up camp. "There's no organization."

"Not in the community," Cheftu said. Keeping close to the base, they walked on.

By the time the sun had risen, they were on the eastern side. More tents. More of a brick factory. And the ovens— were not for food—but for bricks. They walked along a path, lined with baked bricks, painted and waiting to be set. "Facing bricks?" Chloe said, pointing to the colors that corresponded to all the stepped temples she'd seen. She couldn't see the top, so she didn't know how many levels the Esagila had, but she could see from the ground, they'd only made bricks for four levels, thus far.

"What are these people eating?" Cheftu asked.

By tacit agreement they walked through this side of the tent city until they were out of range of smell and sound. The Esagila was revealed by the dawn's light, piercing the pastel dawn. "That's just amazing," Chloe said. "There's some organizing going on, somewhere."

"They're not dead," a voice said, sotto voce. "They aren't buggy."

"They aren't working," another voice said. "If you don't work, you die."

Chloe opened her eyes, just a crack. Two children stood looking at her and Cheftu. One had a bucket, the other had a basket. They couldn't be six years old.

She moved.

They screamed and ran off, dropping their bucket and basket in the process.

"They'll be back," Cheftu said as he stretched and yawned.

They came back, with adult reinforcements. The men's questions weren't rude, but they were brusque. Who were they? Why were they there? What skills could they lend? Cheftu was designated as a workman and Chloe got oven duty.

"What about food, shelter?" Cheftu asked.

"You use what you have," the men said. "Glean from the palms, the fields, or someone will sell you food, I'm sure."

"We—" Chloe started, but Cheftu put a hand on her arm.

"Does it matter where we pitch our tent?"

"Wherever you can stand the smell of the shit," one of them said. "Your shift starts in two double hours. You work for twelve, so get settled before then."

After they left, Chloe and Cheftu pondered what to do. The plan had been to meet Nimrod, and everyone else, here, at Bab-ili. Neither of them wanted to stay, but it didn't look like they could stay and not work, and if they left, they would never find Nimrod. They could backtrack, and risk running into the *lugal's* soldiers.

"A few days of work won't kill us," Chloe said. "It can't be that bad, or this many people wouldn't be here."

Fourteen hours later, she wanted to rip her tongue out from those words. As she trudged through the tent camp to the perch they'd shared, she saw why people just slept out in the shadow of the Esagila and let life take place around them.

She was exhausted. Every muscle, every joint, every tendon. The ovens handled thousands upon thousands of bricks a day. These were the facing bricks. In her dreams, Chloe worked up to being a painter and getting to sit most of the day. Otherwise, her job was kneeling to pick up as many bricks as she could carry—about eight, at five pounds apiece—then walking them to the painter, kneeling to unload them, stacking them for ease to the painter, then kneeling to pick up dry ones and carrying them to the wheelbarrow that would take them to the side where they needed to be. Then back to the ovens.

Chloe had always been thin, fit, she'd kept up her regimen from the military in the years she'd lived in Jerusalem, but this was something new. And on a mostly empty stomach. A friendly coworker had told her about some date palms. Dates, Chloe thought. That's why the camp smells so bad, everyone's stomach is sick from green dates. And it was true . . . everywhere, piles. Flies, rats, bugs—she was glad her shift had been in daylight so she could at least pick her steps carefully. This was the most repulsive environment she'd ever lived in.

On her stumbling path home she'd seen two or three fights break out over space, about water and fires. Spectators stood and cheered as the opponents' words turned to violence. When both were unconscious, the fight was over.

We're living like rats, Chloe thought as she left the tent city and collapsed on the spot—she thought—where Cheftu had been. Cool fell a while later—nighttime. Cheftu showed up with some raw grain and . . . dates. Not green, but only slightly. "We've never had this conversation before, but I'm going to dig a hole and—" she started.

"We don't need to have this conversation now," Cheftu said. "I'll dig the hole. You sleep."

When she woke up with a stomachache and diarrhea, he pointed her toward the hole. Water, at least, was plentiful.

After three days, Chloe had reached tolerance level. Her diarrhea had turned into something else and she feared dehydration. On the fourth morning, she didn't get up.

"I think you have dysentery," Cheftu said. "We have to get you out of here."

"Where?"

"I don't know," he said. "At least in Kish, you would have food and shelter. *Chérie,* I am so sorry to have put us in this position, I—"

She put a finger to his lips. Her hand felt almost too heavy to lift. Dysentery was serious, even in the twentieth century. "It was my suggestion."

"God did not bring us here to die in this stupid stinking hole," he said. "Building some fool's dream of escaping the gods' punishment! We'll head north, I don't care if we find Nimrod or not. I'm not going to let you . . . get sicker."

She was falling asleep, or passing out. They felt the same. She heard Cheftu say he'd be back; he was going to find someone in authority.

Her dreams were horrible: roaches crawling on each other, fighting for room. Rats turning on each other because of hunger. Chloe woke, it was dark, Cheftu was still gone. She crawled to her hole. Cheftu found her there. "We're saved," he said. "I found the designers of everything! We can live with them and be above all of this."

Sounds lovely, she thought.

"They have work for us, not slave labor, but skilled tasks. Chloe—*chérie,* is that blood?"

She nodded.

Chloe woke up in a different world.

Inside the Esagila.

There wasn't sunlight, but there were sesame-oil torches burning and a fresh bed of palm fronds. Her clothes, filthy beyond belief, were gone, replaced with a new woolen skirt. Cheftu had bread for her, beer.

She was too weak to lift her head.

"It's an apartment building," she said in amazement when he told her where they were. "The haves stay inside, the have-nots, out?"

"It is completely different here," he said. His voice was less sure than she recalled.

"It's certainly luxurious. What's troubling you?"

He smiled and patted her clasped hands. "Nothing, now that you are well."

"Where did the food come from?"

He didn't meet her eyes. "Bartering."

"With what? Because of my wisdom, we don't have anything."

He grunted. "I have to leave, to work."

"What are you doing?"

He kissed her cheek and left.

Leaving Chloe puzzled, but too relieved to pursue it.

She was up and around in a few days. Considerably thinner—and most of what she'd lost was muscle off of the marsh girl's lean body. There was no way to see what was going on; claustrophobia clawed at her. She begged Cheftu to take her out, or with him to work.

They climbed twenty flights of stairs from their rooms, to reach the opening to the outdoors. Chloe fought vertigo. She could see all of Bab-ili, and much of the plain, from here. Wind threatened to carry them both away, so Cheftu held her around the waist as they looked around.

"This can't be Iraq," she said. "Look at it."

Green, blue river, and green. At the edges of the green, she saw a swath of silver before the desert began. Mostly, green. "Turn around," he said.

"Oh no."

It became so clear, instantly. How Iraq became the barren wasteland. A whole forest of palms had been cut, the light wood was perfect for making molds for brick, for the infrastructure of buildings, for firewood, for looms, for arrows. The bark could be shoes, or flooring, or roofing, or stripped into fiber for ropes, or soles, or thread. On the outskirts of the northern and eastern tent cities, was another. A logging city.

Palm trunks looked like toothpicks from her position, but Chloe could see where the soil was eroding without them to anchor it. "What's the silver?" she asked.

"Salt."

Fortunately, the wind had blown the oil cloud away from them, though Chloe knew it would come back—in just a few weeks, after it had wreaked destruction on the rest of the world.

Thousands of people worked on the building, lived in their tents and beneath the sun. They scurried and stumbled. Chloe wanted to cry. "We can't stay here, Cheftu. There isn't enough space for everyone. Even when they finish this, it's not going to accommodate all these people."

"It's not designed to," he said. His tone was grim. "You don't want to know, *chérie*. Trust me."

"Why are we here? Where can we go?"

"I have to work for a while," he said. "It is part of my agreement."

"What are you doing?"

"Do not worry," he said. "It will be fine."

His tone wasn't convincing.

"Good morning, Cheftu," his overseer greeted him.

"Is it worse today?" he asked.

"Another fifteen outbreaks."

Cheftu knew the only people who "mattered" were those who could afford to buy a location under some palm-tree awning. Those who couldn't just died, uncounted. Worse, their bodies were dumped in the one direction Cheftu had steered Chloe away from looking. The stench of the mass graveyard blew away from the Esagila, but Cheftu had smelled it.

He followed the *asu* out the door and into the stinking heat. So many things he chose not to observe—he was focused on eyes.

Whatever illness had taken hold of the wealthy grew only in their children, and it bloomed like sunflowers in their eyes. The patient became temperamental, listless, unable to eat, unable to release poisons from his systems, dropped weight, then went into a coma. Cheftu was ancient enough to let those coma patients die. They couldn't take nourishment; they wasted away. Thus far, the disease seemed unstoppable. But it wasn't spreading quickly, and it didn't seem to be contagious.

It hadn't seemed to be contagious.

To make things easier for the families of the sick, when an individual began to show signs of the illness he or she was delivered to one part of the camp. The makeshift hospital was more primitive than anything a Pharaoh would have allowed on a campaign.

These people had invented writing, Cheftu reminded himself. It took centuries more for them to discover sanitation. And even then, in most European cities, they forgot those basic tenets for generations. *I must not judge. Assist. That's all.*

Pay off his debts—so Chloe could have comfort, they both could have food—and find a place to go.

Cheftu examined his fifteen new patients. Their median age was older than the first batch. He watched as a mother spoon-fed her daughter milk. The daughter was almost of marrying age, yet could no longer speak, just stare with sunflower eyes. A huge copper pot kept the milk warm, so all of the patients could be fed by their families. Cheftu shuddered to think what it must cost them to have access to it. Mercenaries controlled the Esagila.

Two patients passed on quietly during the afternoon.

Cheftu walked home through the masses, and wondered why they slaved, for what purpose. The building was growing, the speed of construction was staggering. If they'd built the pyramids this quickly, every town would have had one. Sunflower eyes, all in different stages of progression, stared back at him from tents and lean-tos, from prone positions and from sitting.

He climbed the inner stairway to the room he shared with Chloe, and Cheftu felt the ache of disillusionment. Where was God?

He handed her bread, some beer, and sat down with a sigh.

"I met the neighbors," she said after kissing him hello. "A nice couple. Samu and Ela."

"What do they do?"

"Ela is a weaver and Samu is something in construction. Ela will introduce me to the head brick painter when I'm feeling better. It's strange, but they don't have any children either."

Cheftu grunted and finished his beer. His hair was growing back, a good couple of inches already. It was shaggy, and with the way he carried himself when he walked in, the overall picture was of a whipped bear. Chloe leaned forward and kissed him.

He kissed back, but he was distracted.

She slipped over to his lap, and kissed him again, rubbing the muscles of his shoulders, opening herself to him body and soul. He gave what he could, but whatever troubled him still did. She pulled him onto their rush bed and held him. "Talk to me."

"It's deception," he said.

She stroked his temple and listened.

"The people think the gods are sending another Deluge. Every one of them, as best I can figure, has an imprinted memory of the great flood. They know their families lost their possessions, their lives."

He sighed. "The people who designed the Esagila, they did it to outwit the gods. That is the claim."

"What is the deception?" she asked when he didn't go on.

"No flood is coming. It's just a means for the poor and downtrodden to build a mansion for the wealthy and powerful. They sell food the poor have to buy. Any comfort is gotten through indentured servanthood. It will never end."

"The company store," Chloe said. Then she sang him the song: "Sixteen Tons."

"So it's a practice that doesn't end?"

She'd never heard him sound so worn-out. "What are you doing, to pay them back for all of this."

"Being a doctor."

Chloe squeezed her eyes shut. Cheftu had forsaken medicine. For years he'd worked as other things—mostly in management. Though in David's court, it was the position of counselor. "I'm sorry."

"I am also."

It seemed too pat to tell him she loved him. So she

showed him again, with her body, her mouth, her words, her cries, her tears.

And they slept.

The first time Chloe thought something might be odd about Samu and Ela, was at dinner. While Cheftu had been out working, breaking his heart, Chloe had been developing her franchise idea with the help of Ela, another female. An accountant. Part of Ela's plan was to have various wealthy people over for dinner and introduce them to the sausage balls.

Ela, as Chloe's business partner, was underwriting the dinners; i.e., she was finding meat. Chloe didn't ask. She just hoped, if it was rat, it didn't carry rabies.

Twenty people came—the family, extended, and one or two of their cousins. The cousins worked in the sun and lived in the tent cities. They thought they were dining with the gods.

They began to eat, and someone spoke to Chloe—in Aztlantu, a version of Greek she knew. Reflexively, she answered. Then everyone began speaking in Aztlantu, on cue.

When Cheftu asked her how it had gone, she wasn't sure if the language shift was her imagination or reality. But it couldn't be reality. Could it? Just because she hadn't heard any other languages didn't mean they weren't out there.

But . . . ? So she didn't say anything—knowing his wife might be losing her mind wasn't going to help Cheftu. *Just my imagination, running away with me,* Chloe reasoned. *Again.*

She knew that every death from the sunflower-eye illness wearied Cheftu even more. He'd lost his appetite, he didn't initiate sex, and he wasn't sleeping. Worse, he'd ceased to pray.

Chloe had started to.

Ela had been true to her word, and Chloe had begun painting bricks, a late-afternoon to early-morning shift. She listened to the people around her for twelve hours a day. The Esagila was going to save them. That was the only topic. Their children would live. As Chloe painted brick after brick demon-chasing blue, she pondered that. People would do anything for their children.

The violence got worse.

One day a woman came to work, missing a hand. Some other woman had stolen bread from her children, and they had gotten into a fight. The other woman was dead. After that, Chloe didn't look at the faces of the women she worked with—*we're rats,* she thought. *Rats who are burying themselves under sewage and garbage and stripping the land of everything it has.*

Cheftu stopped coming home, except every few days. He was haggard and short-tempered. Chloe cursed herself for this whole plan. She'd dragged them there. She'd been responsible. She'd gotten sick and sold him into slavery. She was torturing his soul.

She'd just fallen into bed, the moon was past its zenith, when Cheftu returned. He didn't kiss her or inquire about her day. He sat on the edge of the bed, his shoulders hunched, his hands clenched together.

"*Chérie,* I think I have the sunflower-eye illness."

She bounded out of bed and held a torch in front of his eyes. They looked the same, but how could she tell? The copper color the patients' eyes turned was the color Cheftu's eyes already were. "Why? What can I do? What—"

"I can't remember anything."

"What do you mean?"

"The languages in my mind, I learned so many as a boy."

"Eighteen, if I remember you correctly."

"Such arrogance. I thought they would help me—no mat-

er. That is the past, or the future. At any rate, I don't remember them."

She put her arms around him. "You're tired, you work too
hard, you—"

"*Chérie,* I have completely forgotten Latin and Chinese.
Not a word remains in my mind."

"You knew Chinese?"

"Mandarin, Szechuan, and four lesser-known dialects,
yes." He sighed. "It's this madness. You'll wake up, and I'll
be staring at the wall and drooling, like my patients." His
tone was bitter.

"Get some sleep," she said.

"I cannot—"

"I'll go tell them you are too ill to come to work."

He didn't argue. He passed out almost immediately.

Chloe got up, washed her face, and started up the stairs to
the roof, then changed her mind and took the staircase down
to the ground. It was dawn by the time she got there. Cheftu
had told her once before where he worked.

She asked a child for directions and sucked in her breath
when she saw his eyes. Sunflower eyes, this must be the beginning. An icy chill passed through her. His pupil was
black. Surrounding it, like petals of a flower, were copper-
colored plates that had started to obscure the brown of his
eyes. She followed his directions, and stared into the gazes
of everyone she saw.

By the time she'd reached the sorry excuse for an infirmary, she wanted to scream. Every other child had the be-
ginnings in his eyes. A lot of adults, too. She worked for a
while in Cheftu's place, feeding those who could swallow,
milk from the copper pot. She quit when she reached the
bottom of the pot; it was corroded and black—almost gone.
Milk, with rotted copper fibers swirling in it, was all that
was left.

She strained what she could, fed the man, and almost ran home.

They couldn't stay another day. If only she'd known! If only—

Chloe stopped in her tracks. Someone was speaking Arabic. To someone who was speaking Latin. She didn't know it, but she could figure it out. Their conversation was punctuated with misunderstandings. One man was asking for more bricks. The other man thought he was being told to make more bricks. He was not a brickmaker, he was a bitumen pourer, he protested.

I'm losing my mind. This is it. Completely gone. She rubbed her temples and walked on. She heard a crash and turned to see the Arabic speaker storm away, swearing to take his family and leave these idiots to build Esagila. Only in Arabic, it came out: the stairway to heaven.

Bab-ili. Gate of the gods. Stairway to heaven. Babel. Babylon.

Carefully, afraid of her head falling off because of this revelation, Chloe looked up. Images from art appreciation class slipped through her mind. A thousand artists had painted the Tower of Babel. Escher had made it impossibly tall and narrow. Doré had made it look like an ice-cream cone, upended. And Brueghel had left it abandoned and crumbling on a lush plain, the guts of it spilling out.

But no one had portrayed it accurately. No one in the future had trusted the ancients to be as clever or more clever, as creative or more creative, as ingenious or more ingenious than they themselves were.

For the first time, Chloe realized what had struck her as so strange about this place, but she'd never really identified what that strangeness was: *I always understood everything here.*

Not because I knew the languages.

Because everyone spoke one *language.*

To her side, someone cursed in German. She wasn't fluent, but she knew how to swear. The person he was speaking to answered in Sanskrit. Sanskrit!

The sun was blinding. She should get some sleep, but she had never felt less tired. She turned down one pathway and saw a family packing up. They were speaking in some Asian tongue, a tonal language punctuated with sharp vowel sounds. Their neighbors seemed bewildered and talked about how they'd started babbling.

Babble.

The tent city was breaking up. People were screaming at each other in tongues she didn't know. They left their garbage and their waste and cursed the ones who'd been their friends. And they left.

Chloe raced to her work, to see the same thing in action. Bricks were thrown, punches exchanged, hair pulled. And people left.

The forty bricks she should have painted in one day ended up being ten. Even those weren't delivered to the wall, because the wheelbarrow man and the woman who brought the bricks couldn't agree where they should go. A jangle of sounds.

When she reached the top of Esagila, she noticed it hadn't grown taller today.

Chloe ran back to their room.

"We're in Babylon," she shouted. "That's why we're here!"

"We've known that," Cheftu groused. "We've known that all along."

"Cheftu, listen to me. The languages you can't remember. Did you ever use them here?"

"Why would I do that? We speak Sumerian."

She patted his thigh. "Think about it. Latin, Chinese, did

you ever have a conversation with anyone in those languages. Here."

He sat up, groggy and grouchy. "I don't think so."

"But you're not positive?"

"Why would I do such a thing?"

"I don't know, but Cheftu, I don't remember a word of Greek."

"Wonderful. I've poisoned you, too. Your eyes will be sun—"

"Silence yourself!"

She had his attention now.

"Every dinner I've had with Ela and Samu, we've . . well, we've spoken a different language."

"You're more ill than I am," he said, reaching for her pulse.

Chloe ducked back. "It always seemed so far-fetched that I figured, yes, I was losing my mind, because no one ever reacted. Conversation just flowed, the way it always does with multilingual people. One word, change language, slipping into another. But Cheftu, every language I've spoken with them, is gone."

"From your mind?"

She nodded.

"That's impossible."

"What?"

"It is impossible for a language to be stolen from a mind, or even a mouth. It takes years to learn, to—" He crossed his arms and closed his eyes. "I'm going back to sleep now."

Chloe glared at his closed eyes, then got up and paced the eight-by-eleven room.

"We time-traveled. That's impossible," she said.

"We saw water turn to blood. We saw firstborn-only die. We've seen a sea part. We've met immortals. We've watched a civilization vanish in a day and a night. We've

een lightning harnessed. We've watched people we've
nown from history live and breathe.

"Cheftu, for God's sake! We live in other peoples' bod-
es! Our lives are built around impossibilities."

He didn't move.

She was pretty sure he was playing possum.

"Try this on for size, Mr. Impossible. The Tower of Babel
s a co-op, and baby, you're living in it."

When she went up to the top at sunrise, Chloe saw that a
hird of the tents were gone. A third of the people had left.
ome of them so recently, she could see them still walking
orth or south, east or west, or any of the eight compass
oints in between. They'd stopped felling the trees. They'd
topped draining the river. They'd stopped building. Mostly,
hey argued. Their voices floated up to her, and she wished
he had a list of the languages Cheftu spoke so she could
now which ones were out there.

But she knew one thing: which way was up.

"Latin," he said in her ear, then slipped his arms around
er waist.

"Do you remember it?"

She felt him shake his head. "No, I just know enough to
dentify it. That voice is speaking another Chinese." He
ested his forehead against her neck. "Forgive—"

"No," she said and turned to him. "Nothing is wrong. No
orgiveness required. That," she said, as they listened to the
ising racket, "do you remember that?"

"Aztlantu. A precursor to Greek." His arms tightened
round her. "I thought I'd lost my mind. I would have these
lights of fancy in which I would conduct conversations in

these languages. I knew it must be impossible. I must be going crazy."

"What's that?" she asked, inclining her ear.

"Sanskrit. One of the firstborn from the original Indo-European tongue. English is related to the Teutonic languages, German, Dutch, Scandinavian tongues. Latin, you know—"

"Yes. Yields French, Spanish, Italian, Portuguese."

"Also Greek, Russian, and Baltic-states tongues."

Above them, thunder rumbled.

"Arabic and Hebrew are related."

"As are Chinese, Burmese, the Asian languages."

"The season of rains begins," Cheftu said.

"There were only three in the beginning. The roots," Chloe said. "And they become, grow into, three hundred languages."

Thunder drew closer; they saw a flash of lightning.

"God gave us minds like his." Cheftu smiled in wonder. It started to rain. "Endless possibilities."

"Since one of those possibilities is being struck by lightning, I suggest we go downstairs," Chloe said. "But one more question—was there any specific person around, in those conversations?"

"No, no." He shook his head.

Chloe started down the stairs. *There was for me,* she thought. *Who was Ela, really? Or should I be asking what was Ela?*

～

It rained for two days. Cold, winter rain that soaked through wool and made the entire camp smell like a sheep farm. The sick had been left, so Chloe worked at Cheftu's side as they watched the patients grow more and more ill.

They hadn't gone back to the tower; there had been too

much to do. Wind followed the rain, and Chloe spent half her time tying down skins and rushes, trying to keep the patients dry. Finally, both wind and rain abated, and Chloe and Cheftu slept.

Chloe was pouring the remnants of milk into the copper pot before the children awoke, when Cheftu attacked her. "No! Put it down!" he shouted.

She dropped the pot and pulled away from him, the corroded copper spoon still in her hand. "You really have lost it! You made me spill the milk!"

"It's poison, Chloe."

His eyes were bright, his shoulders back, he looked like a different person. "The copper, it's what's killing them."

Chloe looked around at the few awake patients who all stared at her with the same copper-tinted gaze. Sunflower eyes, copper plates on top of brown irises, extra copper in the body. Copper—she looked at the ladle, at the pot. The milk had pooled on the ground, and tiny fibers of copper stood up from it.

"Copper," he said. "I'm such a fool! I've seen this before."

She was confused, and looked it.

"As a boy, when I was in Egypt, as Jean-François, my brother and I . . . ah, the details don't matter. We were walking with a French physician. A woman begged him to make her child well. He looked into the eyes of the child, and refused to help."

"That bastard!"

"No, he was wise actually. He knew the child wouldn't live, the copper was too much in its system. If he took the case on, and the child died, the Egyptians would just have an excuse to retaliate. We would be child murderers on top of tomb robbers. The child's eyes, they were the same as these people's."

"So we don't feed them any more copper-poisoned food, but, what do we do to make them well?"

Cheftu scratched his head, pushed hair out of his eyes. "Water, to flush it out. I don't know what else. Something must bind with the copper to remove it from the body, but I don't know what."

~

Lightning struck the Esagila.

The unfinished top caught fire and fell to the ground, landing in one of the bonfires in the middle of the night.

Then and there, the remaining people scattered.

Chloe supposed there were a hundred or less who were hanging on, maybe who still understood each other. The patients, whose systems they were trying to wash out by feeding them copious amounts of water, were improving. Or dying.

Winter had arrived. Cold, wet. Frost on the ground.

I'm standing in the shadow of the Tower of Babel.

Cheftu, just rinsed, stepped out of the protection of the infirmary tent. "They're all sleeping." He'd buried a few more the previous night, but the sorrow of it wasn't attached to him anymore. He whistled as he went about his rounds, he smiled and joked with the healing patients. Though he proclaimed he hated medicine, Chloe had to admit she hadn't seen him as satisfied and eager to go about his day, in years. What he hated, she realized, was being inefficient and ineffective in medicine. He loved to make people well.

"You saved sixty people's lives," she said.

"You saved mine."

They joined hands and walked to the edge of the Esagila, where bricks were left in the rain, wheelbarrows frozen in their tracks, garbage everywhere. The flies were fewer, the rats, too. Operating during mostly daylight hours prevented Chloe from seeing too many insects.

The top of Esagila had been burned black, and they didn't know how much structural damage had been done. Neither had taken time away from the copper patients to climb up.

"It was all for this," Chloe said. "Your knowledge of languages, my knowledge of languages. Everything. Circles and cycles. Wheels within wheels."

Cheftu stared at the building. "Do you think we saw the fathers of the nations here?"

"Yes." She chewed her lip. "We read it so wrong, in my time."

"The Tower of Babel?"

She nodded. "We ridiculed the idea of God's jealousy and fear that the people would actually make it to heaven. When you realize that heaven isn't a location, that it's nothing but space up there, that statement seems pretty silly. We need a cleanup crew around here." She kicked dust at an emboldened rat. He ran away. "We started it here, the tradition of not learning. We never do."

Cheftu looked at her. "I'm sure I agree, but to what are you referring?"

"Abusing the planet. Look at this. Piles of . . . yuck. Just left. Garbage. People on top of people."

"God told the people, after Ziusudra, to spread out and multiply."

"Instead they multiplied and clumped together. And worked on ruining the land."

"Now, they will be divided but alive."

"You were the tool," she said.

Cheftu looked at her.

"All those languages, all that time, the memory, the experience, disseminated here."

"Ah, circles you said."

"Though, I'm a little confused how just speaking them made us forget them. How the words were stolen that way."

"Egyptians thought words were items, tangible presences."

"The Sumerians—us—words are power, here. Writing them is controlling them."

"Speaking them releases their power to the air," Cheftu said. "At least, that is my guess."

"Somehow when we released those words, they were imprinted on the minds of other people? I'd say that's impossible, but—"

Cheftu laughed, and said something in French. He looked at her, as though expecting agreement, then spoke in Sumerian. "You don't remember French?"

She shook her head. "One of those dinners with Ela."

"I must confess, I no longer know English."

He raised his head, and Chloe heard a fight taking place in some other language. He looked at her. "Some of your work. Those are Frenchmen leaving now."

The other part of the fighting group—a stout, black-bearded man, came barreling toward them. "Imbeciles!" he shouted. "No sense of how to structure a city!"

Sumerian, he spoke.

Chloe and Cheftu grinned at each other. God, however He was called, had made up the list of citizens for this place and designated them clearly.

"We need latrines so we aren't defecating in the street like animals, we need some organization of children and someone to plant the fields. Those palms are going to rot, left in the rain. Waste, such waste."

"I couldn't agree with you more," Chloe said.

He beamed. "What a delight! Someone who doesn't babble!"

Not anymore.

~

Nimrod arrived three months later. Enki, the black-bearded man, had organized the cleanup. Most of the copper patients were on their feet, doing small tasks. A garbage dump had been designated, and the Esagila had been partially dismantled for building materials.

It took less than a week for Nimrod to be elected *lugal.*

By spring, the new Babylon's numbers had swelled to almost three hundred. Houses, laid out on carefully straight streets and wide boulevards, were spacious and tiled in beautiful colors. Bricks were waterproofed through firing.

Wells had been dug in the center of the few squares. Nirg set up a window through which she sold Chloe's sausage balls and other, easy-to-eat items. Chloe had fallen in love with palms and spent the winter transplanting those that had been half–dug up, to places within the city. Irrigation ditches were next.

Cheftu came for her one afternoon from his position at Nimrod's side as a city planner and part-time justice, who mostly oversaw the writing of contracts.

"I'm busy," she said, her hands covered in mud, after giving him a kiss.

"Come with me."

She excused herself and followed him. They strolled through the palm groves south, hand in hand, to where they'd first seen the strange glow in the sky over Babylon.

"This is for you," he said after they sat down.

Chloe looked at him, then unwrapped the small parcel. A cylinder of ivory fell out, intricately carved. She looked at the writing on the side, the drawing of a woman and a child writing.

"Nimrod wants you to open a school, a Tablet House."

Yes!

It sang through her veins, a profound sense of *fit*. This, yes, what she was made for. This dream, this moment. Children, not born of her body, but of her heart. She examined the carving through a prism of unshed tears. The why of her future was answered. The why of here and now was answered. The why of everything, from her first step into ancient Egypt to her most recent step into this palm grove, was answered.

My whole life has led up to this moment. I'm home.

"He even turned the logograms ninety degrees," Chloe said through a throat clogged with tears.

"He did. He said it was your school, you should hire teachers who instruct what you felt comfortable with. Teach to males, females. This cylinder seal, it's for you." Cheftu looked at her with golden eyes, the fringe of his blond hair framing them. "Women are going to be equals here, in politics, religion, socially. You're a client, Chloe."

She clutched the seal that would be her legacy in one hand, and, with the other, Chloe reached for Cheftu.

Author's Note

If it appears to any trained student of early Mesopotamian history that I took the elements of Sumerian culture, threw them in a blender, then spread them on these pages, he or she would be correct.

These people, even more than my beloved Egyptians, fascinate me. However, definitive answers about who and where and when and why are few and far between. So while I don't know the answers per se, many things in this, Chloe and Cheftu's final adventure, are based in fact.

The death pits; substitution theory; exorcism with a goat; all the artifacts mentioned, the clothing worn; the school, even the translation of alumni to "Old Boys"; Ur was the first place to have a restaurant; Enkidu and Gilgamesh are characters in one of the most well-known myths from ancient times; there is record of one female Tablet Father, and an ancient school for girls in Ur; mourning the loss of extreme old age and appreciating the concept of "humanity" are common threads in both Sumerian mythology and Genesis; Shem, Kham (Ham) and Japheth (Jepheti) were the three sons of Noah (Ziusudra); Roo (Reu) is Abram's (Abraham's) great-great-grandfather; Lud is another Biblical relative; Nimrod is credited with founding Babylon; Asshur with Ninevah and Calneh; the cycle of eclipses was certainly not known or predictable to these people; the standards, mostly famously the Code of Hammurabi, are now thought by scholars to be examples of judgments that had been meted out rather than absolute laws; writing, in about this time period, did change direction and angle; a dictionary, or as Ningal puts it: "list of lists."

A million books aided me in this search. Books that I could not have written this without are: *The First Great Civilizations* by Jacquetta Hawkes—a brilliant survey of all things Sumerian. *The Birth of Writing,* by Time-Life; *Cultural Atlas of Mesopotamia and the Ancient Near East* by Michael Roaf; *The Genesis Hypothesis* by Douglas B. Scarborough, my source for how to live to be three hundred; *Return to Sodom and Gomorrah* by Charles Pellegrino—one of my all-time favorite reads; *The Alphabet versus the Goddess* by Leonard Shlain. I wasn't able to use the information outright, but it provided me with motivation and understanding within my characters. A mind-bending book, *Totality,* by Mark Littman and Ken Wilcox, who shared just how many eclipses, and what kinds I could realistically have, in a celestial action-packed year.

Two authors stand head and shoulders above the other writers in this arena—one, Sir Leonard Wooley, whose excavations yielded the wealth of information we have on Sumer and whose descriptions helped me reconstruct the Great Death Pit and the King's Tomb and Puabi's (Shub-ab's) Tomb. It's all there—the hole beneath the chest, used by tomb robbers to strip the tomb beneath hers, the extra crown set beside the corpse of Puabi, the seventy-plus souls who willingly took poison and lay down to die. And most importantly, the absolute lack of explanation for such a sacrifice. I read dozens of his books, even old *National Geographic* articles, in order to prepare for this project.

The other author synonymous with Sumer is Samuel Noah Kramer, who brought the wonder and amazement of how creative and ingenious and downright "modern" these ancient Sumerians were, to me. The first math, the first writing, the first astrology, the first astronomy, the first irrigation, the first hybrid crops, the first arch, the first vault, the first dome, the first musical instruments, the first accounting, the first democracy, the first divorce, the first city planning, the first recorded myths, the first megaliths, the first baked bricks, the first skyscrapers, the first centralized government, the first commonwealths, the first laws, the first judicial system, the first record keepers, the first beer makers, the first goldsmiths, the first mosaicists, the first use of architectural entasis, the first loans on credit, the first banks, the first fast food, the first restaurant, the first advertising, the first calendar, the first minute and hour, the first zodiac. At one point I was going to have Chloe keep track of all of these "firsts," but the book would have run a thousand pages. Much better for her to experience them.

What struck me most about these people is how easily they paralleled the *fin de siècle* world in which I wrote this book. More specifically, how like the residents of the United States Sumerians were. As in my own world, they paid little attention to the destruction they were creating for their future, they were excited by the newest thing, they wanted results immediately, they trusted little beyond money and occupation, and they searched for reasons in a world where science and faith appeared to be on a collision course. Through it all, they sought after and believed in the elusive concept of "humanity."

Legend says that when God struck down the Tower of Babel, he banished the people rather than killing them. Not because they were any less sinful than the generations that had perished in the Deluge, but because the nature of their sins had changed. Before, man had turned on man, civil war. At the Tower, man had joined with man and pitted himself against God. To paraphrase, God thought man had at least improved, and if this particular skirmish was avoided, there was hope man would actually mature.

The Sumerians had hope. They believed twilight would promise a new day.

What better world for Chloe and Cheftu to walk into?

Acknowledgments

This journey would have been impossible without:

Hanne, who first mentioned Sumer and Gilgamesh to me, who shared her home, her library, and her extensive knowledge of ancient and modern things, and Sydney, who always encourages me; Drue my coach, and Renee, my compatriot, who independently give me a shot of confidence and curiosity to savor each week; Daniel, who believes, who supports better living through caffeine, and is my best promoter; Danny boy, who cheers and prods; George and Peter, who edit and analyze, who ponder my theories and challenge my logic—while never doubting my ability; George, who also gave me rust, and Peter, who also gave me a map and copper toxicosis; Michka, whose conversation inspires me to look within; Melanie, whose enthusiasm buoys me; Mathias, whose introduction to Magic Hat Brewery made writing about beer a simple, joyful task; Issie and Connie, whom I love and miss; Sally, Barbara, and the SMU crowd who root me on and give me a place to teach; my students, who challenge me to be a better writer every day; Barbara, who makes me respect my business; Walter and Steve, who are in the trenches with me, who share their stories and make me laugh; Tom and Dad, who ask questions and make me ask questions, who take me to lunch weekly and pray for me daily; Kati and Brent, who are far away, but in my heart; my agent David, and Seth; my editors on this project—Susan, who guided Chloe and Cheftu; Jessica, who gave me time; and ultimately, Jackie, who completed this with me. To you all, a thousand thanks.

And strangely enough, to Chloe and Cheftu, who have been my most constant and dear companions these last years, who are as real and alive to me as anyone I know, and who now fade into the dust of history. Through them I kept alive my grandparents, my Texas heritage, my military brat upbringing, and my passion for the ancient world. How I will miss the excuse for research, for taking the journey, for dreaming this big. How much I have loved it. Thank you, dear reader, for loving it—and them—too.

TGG.
Suzanne Frank
June 17, 2001

Discussion Questions

What is the known progression of civilizations and which culture has had the most effect on Western civ?

Many cultures have a Noah-like myth. How do you explain that?

Chloe considers herself a professional time traveler. What skills did she use to survive in this time period and what skills might have helped her more?

Chloe chooses to go to school. What other options did she have?

When Chloe and Cheftu realized they could get the sought-after water of vitality, should they have gone back for it? Told Asshur its location? Given it to all the sick children? What would you have done?

At the end of the story, it seems Chloe and Cheftu are going to stay in Sumer. If you were to give them another adventure, where would they go, what would they do and why?

Ezzi and Ulu had unsaid expectations of each other. How could their relationship have been improved, and this disaster averted, if they had talked to each other?

How do Chloe and Cheftu's relationships with the Divine differ from one another? And how do those two relationships change in the course of the story?

What would be the concerns of a world without prejudice? Where would conflict come from, if not from the differences of color and/or creed?

Each of the "journey" stories starts with a Sumerian proverb or saying. What would be the proverb or saying that would define your place in time, history and location?

Chloe and Cheftu continue to struggle through the issue of childlessness. How does Chloe come to terms with that? What other choices did she have in that time and place? (Remember the story of Isaac and Ishmael.)

What is the most important lesson Chloe learns in the course of this story? Is that a lesson you have had to learn in your own life?

The parallels between ancient Sumer and modern-day America are astounding to Chloe. What similarities did you see? Which were positive and which were negative?